THE SLIGHTEST GREEN

THE SLIGHTEST GREEN

A Novel

Sahar Mustafah

Interlink Books
An imprint of Interlink Publishing Group, Inc.
Northampton, Massachusetts

First published in 2025 by

Interlink Books
An imprint of Interlink Publishing Group, Inc.
46 Crosby Street, Northampton, MA 01060
www.interlinkbooks.com

Cover design by Aya Moybadeen; author photo by Lamise Shawahin

Library of Congress Cataloging-in-Publication data:
ISBN 978-1-62371-583-0

Printed and bound in the United States of America

For Mariam and Aida, and every Palestinian carrying home wherever they may be.

And for the people of Gaza, who've taught us what it means to be human.

نحن دائما معكم

To be Palestinian is to write the ever-present past.

I started this book in 2018, never imagining I would bear witness to a genocide of Palestinians on such a horrific scale, and which has been brutally expedited by manufactured consent. The ethnic cleansing of Palestinians, we must affirm, has been an ongoing colonial-settler project since the Nakba. It has not slowed, nor been disrupted by the international community. We are all complicit.

Does a story mitigate tragedy, or absolve me or anyone who engages it? No. But I hope entering this story is one doorway, no matter how narrow, to liberation.

Free Palestine.

"We inherit memory, the way we inherit the color of our eyes and skin."
—Ibtisam Azem, *The Book of Disappearance*

"We believed that freedom was possible, despite all its demands, and that our sacrifices might not be enough. We didn't stop believing for a single day. We would have died, had we stopped believing."
—Nasser Abu Srour, *The Tale of a Wall*

BAYT AL-HAWA: SEPTEMBER 2007

CHAPTER I

Sundus checks for spiders. Under a fig tree, she crouches on her haunches, inspecting crates of golden and red grapes. She lifts each newly shorn cluster, delicately probing sprigs of succulent orbs.

Outside her orchard, a black Mercedes pulls up, its tires crunching gravel. Sundus turns her head and her jaw instantly tightens. Soon the man approaches, this snake in a blue suit, white shirt unbuttoned, slithering onto her land. His head is swaddled in a keffiyeh, held in place by an elegant headband. Abdul Waheed pretends to be one of them, fingering his prayer beads, thumb sliding over each one between his fingers. "May the Lord smite him," she mutters under her breath.

"Salaam, ya Hajja!" he calls out, waving at her.

Abdul Waheed descends the stone steps and heads toward Sundus. She pretends to ignore him, though her heart beats faster. She's preparing for the trickle of villagers clutching their coins in exchange for a kilo or two of her grapes.

It was a decent harvest, alhamdullilah, enough to cover the labor of the migrants from the south who help her each season.

She hoists herself up and removes an old-fashioned scale from a burlap sack and sets it on a small wooden plank. Its base is solid iron, its trays hang from brass chains and are wide enough for two bunches at a time. Her late husband Jalal had acquired the scale and its black, one-kilo measuring discs from a retired vendor at the souk, a seller of oranges. *Now you are a legitimate business,* her husband's smile had congratulated her.

Atop a weathered rug, she settles down on a low wooden stool. Uninvited, Abdul Waheed does the same, pulling another stool close to her. He leans forward on his elbows, as if he's about to explain something important to her. His strong cologne bristles her nostrils. Sundus has never trusted a man who pampers himself. Around his neck is a gold necklace—another shameless indulgence. Abdul Waheed's smooth, pale face glistens in the bright morning light. It's one that has been sheltered from the sun. He extracts a linen handkerchief from his jacket pocket and dabs his neck.

"How is Hafez?" he asks, feigning concern, as if he hasn't stolen the deed to her land, hasn't forged her husband's signature. His lower teeth are crowded, like a cluster of grave markers.

Her hands curl into fists at the sound of her son's name on the tongue of this crook. His headdress—meticulously arranged—is a tactic to ingratiate himself as he swindles villagers. He pretends to be a legitimate soomsar—a broker who's already sold over twenty dunum of land in Bayt al-Hawa, convincing their owners to sell for less before mustawtaneen swoop down and steal it. *Look how close the settlers are getting to you*, he wheedles them, pointing to the western hill.

It started as a military post—or so the sign declared in Hebrew and Arabic, warning the inhabitants of Bayt al-Hawa to stay away. Ten years ago, the hill opposite Sundus's house had a scattering of stone-brick houses with orange-tiled roofs like hers, where laundry flapped in the air during the warm months. Gradually, the houses disappeared, the original owners gone. The military post has swollen into a compound of settlers. A barbed-wire border separates them, but not stern enough to ward off children who play nearby until a man in civilian clothes, a machine gun strapped to his back, shouts at them in Hebrew to get away or he'll shoot. He spits at them and curses their mothers for the day they were born.

Now, here is Abdul Waheed in his headdress, who'd already swooped down on her land, desecrating her late husband's name with the worst untruth: Jalal had sold all of it. Abdul Waheed had sauntered onto her terrace last fall, clutching a document with the golden seal of a bribed notary. "It is all legitimate, Khalti," he'd assured her with hollow remorse and a sad smile, as if it were out of his hands.

Neither Jalal nor Sundus had ever heard of Abdul Waheed. No one in the village knows where he's come from, who his people are. Some whisper he's one of the mustawtaneen, stealing dunum of Bayt al-Hawa and reselling to the settlers. Others say he is more than a land-thief. That he is something much worse.

"May Allah keep evil far from us," Sundus mutters under her breath.

Abdul Waheed nods, accepting this as a response to his question about her son's condition. Hafez is dying and it's only a matter of days now. Precisely what the snake is counting on. But what he hadn't anticipated was the arrival of an American-born daughter, the rightful heir to this land. It is a flaw in his deceitful plot. Someone has suddenly materialized who could challenge the alleged sale of her land. With Jalal gone, and soon Hafez, her granddaughter Intisar is her only hope.

As if reading her thoughts—his same thoughts—Abdul Waheed glances toward the villa.

"Has bint Hafez arrived?"

Sundus looks him straight in the face, clenching her fists against her thighs. Anger simmers in her chest before it turns to frigid fear. She struggles to hold her flat expression, hopes Abdul Waheed can't hear the thumping of her heart. What if the land is stolen from her after all these years? He'd given her a year to vacate her home. Only months remain as her lawyer works against the clock. But none of it will ensure victory unless her granddaughter verifies what they called *hisil irth*—the legitimate claim of a child-beneficiary. Sundus herself has no legal claims, a bitter reality she's had to swallow. Her dearest Jalal had purchased this land before he met and married her. The birth of their son had ensured its perpetuity, and their grandchildren would safeguard it for the next generation, holding fast against their oppressors and until Falasteen would be liberated.

Abdul Waheed is watching her face. "I have a reasonable offer."

"To be silenced as you rob me of my life," Sundus swiftly retorts.

"Hajja, use common sense," he cajoles, tapping two fingers to his temple. "You have no legal sway here."

He leans in and Sundus is ready to slap his face if he so much as dares touch her. He doesn't, instead letting his musbaha dangle between him and her. She wants to snatch the holy beads—another prop—from his blasphemous grip.

"I'll make you comfortable for whatever remaining years

you have, by the will of the Lord," he tells her. "And your granddaughter. A consolation for losing her father. A more generous offer could not be brokered here." He leaned back on his stool. "Surely, it's what Hafez would have wanted."

It's too much to bear—speaking as if Hafez were already dead. Sundus bolts from her stool as swiftly as her aging limbs will permit.

"Ya harami! Thief!" Sundus shouts at him. "Shame on you! Robbing your own people! Insulting my son! Get away from me! Get away from my home!"

Slowly and deliberately, Abdul Waheed rises, too.

"Hajja Um Hafez, do not be stupid," he tells her plainly. "Take this gift or you'll end up with nothing."

He disappears through the side entrance of the stone wall bordering her property. A few moments later, Sundus hears the revving of his engine as he peels away, hidden behind dark-tinted windows.

Her body quakes and she shuts her eyes for a few moments, composing herself before she returns to her son. Inside the villa, Sundus pulls a pitcher of distilled water from the refrigerator and pours a glass. She carries it down a short hallway to her son's room. She enters quietly, places the glass on a nightstand beside his bed, and sits on a high-backed chair she's pulled from the dining room. It's too formal for this bedroom, yet somber enough for the occasion of a dying man.

And Sundus has seen plenty of death. A fetus noiselessly wrenched from his mother's womb in the middle of the night on the side of a lonely road. An aging body once upright and dignified suddenly falling in the blink of an eye. And now here is Sundus, helplessly watching her adult child expire. Is this what her own mother had felt all those years ago?

She listens to her son's awful wheezing, watches his chest rise and fall with great labor. His eyes are dull when he looks up at her from his bed. The sickness has hollowed out his cheeks, turned his lips gray. She searches for her dear boy in the face of a condemned man. Where have his pink lips and his once-golden skin gone?

"Has she come?" he asks her in a raspy voice.

"Not yet, Son," Sundus says, patting his hand.

The girl—Intisar—is expected to arrive this week. Arrangements were made as quickly as possible. She'll fly into Tel Aviv and a car will bring her directly here. Sundus holds up the glass of water to his lips and her son accepts small sips before dropping his head back onto his pillow.

"If I don't—if she's too late—" he stammers.

"Pray to the Prophet!" Sundus cries, squeezing his hand.

Hafez slowly inhales, mustering enough breath to say his next words. "Tell Intisar—it is all for her. Tell her, Yamma—where she—comes from." He squeezes her hand back and lets go.

"Where do I begin?" Sundus starts to ask him, but her son's eyelids droop and she leaves him in peace, quietly shutting the door behind her.

The first time her husband Jalal brought Sundus to Bayt al-Hawa, they stood together on an empty plot, all that they'd lost behind them. A sense of promise—quiet, but firm like a mother's hand—had gripped Sundus. She hadn't yet known she was pregnant, that Hafez was a tiny miracle—smaller than a nigella seed—growing inside her. And after her first bout of nausea, leveling her beside the toilet in her parents' flat in Ramallah, she had no doubt it was a son.

Does she begin there?

For Sundus, it begins with seashells. She shuts her eyes and her childhood house appears behind her lids, her mother ambling toward the stone brick wall, her swollen belly intruding upon the space between her and their neighbor, Um Husni.

Her mother rubs her belly in wide circles as she listens to the other woman, cuffing her eyes from the sunlight. Spring warms the air, mingling with traces of the salty sea.

"Aywa, aywa," her mother murmurs, nodding her head in acquiescence to whatever Um Husni is telling her. Sundus's mother is a beautiful woman, slender and tall, her thick wavy hair gathers into a bun at the nape of her neck. She wears a house dress she can no longer belt, the color of purple thistle Sundus and her friend Amjad have plucked for their playhouse under her family's loquat tree. The two of them are busy lining it with seashells from their holidays at the shore. It is an elaborate design so far: a kitchen, a parlor for receiving guests, and a private sitting room for Sundus to enjoy her books.

"It faces east so you can have the morning sun," Amjad proudly declares, the chief architect on their project. They diligently work under the canopy of branches, protecting them from the late morning sun. Their houses are separated by the stone brick wall no higher than her waist; Um Husni is Amjad's mother. Sundus can't recall her eight-year-old life without Amjad, her childhood defined by a few significant adults and schoolmates. He netted Sim-Sim for her, a lovely rock thrush, its blue head fading into a grayish body. It watches the two of them playing, skittering to and fro inside its domed cage, speaking to them in chirrups and short whistles. Besides Sim-Sim, Amjad is her first real friend in the whole world.

They've played every day together since their schools have

been shuttered. The headmaster assured students that they would resume classes soon. But Sundus knew this was a lie because Sayida Mansoor's voice shook when she told the class they had nothing to fear. The next day, her teacher was gone and Sayida Rahman—she taught the older pupils and had a large mole on her chin—appeared for part of the day. She instructed their class to work on grammar exercises longer than Sundus could stand, so she doodled flowers on the back of her copybook. The headmaster stepped in for the second half of the day and the murmur of her schoolmates died down under his watchful eye. Now there is talk the schools will be integrated as attendance continues to drop; more of their classmates are kept home to be tutored. This makes Sundus happy: she can see Amjad all day long.

On the playground, her friend Hiba told of horrible things happening in the countryside, things the yahood did in a village called Safuriyya.

They round up all the men and shoot them first. Then they find the pregnant mothers, cut out their babies.

She's seen Jews before. On his monthly visits to the neighboring villages around Haifa to tend to his patients, her father takes Sundus along with him and they drive past a neighborhood where fair-skinned and blue-eyed folks live, mothers pushing baby prams, men in slacks and button-up shirts—just like what her father wears. Some are deeply bronze-skinned like Arabs such as Abu Musa, who delivers a crate of fresh cactus fruit to her mother every season.

And Sundus sees them at the beach at eid when they stay at a small inn off the coast of the Mediterranean Sea where she's collected shells every holiday. But Sundus never plays with the children of yahood—not that she's been forbidden, but she never broaches the invisible boundaries that are inexplicably drawn between them. Children like her and Amjad splash near the shoreline while their parents lounge on blankets, enjoying a spread of goat cheese, figs, and apricots. The older women hitch up their thobe and tuck one side of their embroidered caftans into a widely striped belt, exposing a white underdress. Sundus fills a basket of seashells she's collected on every trip. At home, she deposits them into a large clay pot her mother let her have, previously occupied by a small trellis of hot peppers.

She and Amjad busy themselves under the loquat tree. He blows sand out of a conch with delicate pink swirls before wiping it on his shirt. As they frame imaginary rooms, Sundus asks Amjad if what Hiba said was true: do they kill babies, too?

Amjad shrugs his shoulders. He picks at a scab on his elbow. Days before, he fell from his bicycle and blood seeped from a small gash the size of a coin. He looked disappointed when Sundus hadn't gasped and quickly looked away from his injury. Her father taught her that blood is natural, rich in minerals and vitamins.

"Safuriyya is far from here," Amjad assures her. "Don't be scared."

Still, fear puckers inside her like she's eaten a sour plum. Each evening, her father instructs Sundus to read aloud from *Filasteen*, one of several newspapers scattered on the floor at his feet, and he listens and smokes absentmindedly as she recites details on the latest ambushes on villages whose names she knows because she's driven to these places in her father's black Ford, sitting beside him on the tan leather seat. When she announces the death tolls, her mother interjects, smacking her hands together. *Bas! I don't want to hear anymore.*

By the boundary wall, Amjad's mother's voice is high-pitched, distracting Sundus again. "My husband says we should leave soon." Sundus cranes her neck, can see the white mandeela wrapped around the other woman's head. "Travel to the coast, then up north. God protect our son Husni."

Sundus listens, rubbing the belly of a seashell with her thumb.

Husni is Amjad's older brother, ten years older, which makes her friend an only child like Sundus. Husni has joined the Arab militia, disappearing one night and sending word to his family that he would suck out the Zionist poison infecting their country. Um Husni had wept on her mother's shoulder.

"How long do you think we'll be gone?" Sundus hears her mother ask. There is a tremble in her voice.

"No more than a few weeks, inshallah," Um Amjad reassures her mother, clasping both of her mother's hands. She is shorter than Sundus's mother, her body stoutly shaped like the bottom of a copper ibrik. "Be ready. Take only what you can carry. On foot if necessary." Their mothers exchange a few more words before parting ways back to their respective homes.

"Let's finish this," Amjad says, squatting down.

But Sundus can no longer concentrate on their playhouse. She stands up, still clutching the seashell in the palm of her hand. Beyond the countryside, she has only traveled once to Al Quds, to visit her father's old mentor, a retired professor. She cannot fathom any other place worth living that doesn't meet the sea. Her first memory is of water, rushing her toes, rising to her belly while someone holds her arms, and there's an exhilarating feeling of trusting she will be safe and the thrill of being swept away by this powerful force that envelops her from every angle.

Amjad stands again and lightly touches her shoulder. "No matter what, our families will be together—we'll be together. I'll protect you." He puffs out his chest like a rooster. When he plays with the boys, Sundus watches them from her bedroom window, child-soldiers, each claiming to be Fauzi al-Qawuqji, the leader of the Arab Liberation Army, who endured a dozen bullets and survived. Amjad owns a pocket-sized rendering of the warrior in a white headdress, a black cord securing it around his head. His profile is regal and exudes courage. The image is dog-eared and cracked down the middle, but Sundus smiles in exaggerated admiration. She is moved when Amjad withdraws it from a cedar box of treasures to show her.

From the saha of their stone house, her mother calls to her. "Sundus! Where are you, girl?"

"I have to go," she tells Amjad, dusting red dirt from her short pants.

He grabs her hand. "Remember what I said. Don't be afraid. We'll be together."

Sundus nods, pretending to believe him like she always does. Last spring when a bird had fallen from the nest of a fig tree, Amjad had assured her it would live and return to its family. The next day, she'd come back to the spot and it was gone.

I told you, Amjad had said. *It's flown back to its mother.*

Later on she discovered a small burial mound a few meters away from the fig tree.

Sundus throws Amjad a smile before dashing away to help her mother prepare for a journey whose destination is uncertain to her. She carries Sim-Sim as it frantically chirps in its cage. She stops to reassure it, petting its head through the bars.

She hops onto the saha, where magenta bougainvillea blooms

at the edges of the landing. Her mother's herb garden has begun to flower. There's a fire pit full of ashes in the center of the saha, surrounded by wooden stools. Her parents often welcome the neighbors for evening qahwa. The men smoke pipes and English cigarettes like her father. The ballads of Leila Murad soar through a pair of open windows from a record spinning on a gleaming Victrola their neighbor Abu Ziyad pulls outside on his saha, turning the volume up high. Like a lovely haze, the lyrics drape over Sundus and the other children roaming the orchard:

Sing for me always, and tell me always
Love is a song full of dreams…

Their mothers hug their elbows beneath their knit shawls as the men tap their feet, smoke curling like vines then vanishing into the night.

Inside their bayt, her mother is on her knees, spreading a linen sheet across the floor. Because of her slender body, it is hard to tell she is with child until she turns around. Sundus rushes to grab a corner and pulls it toward her feet. Her mother then gives her small rags and leftover fabric from her sewing and shows Sundus how to wrap each glass of a hand-painted tea set that had belonged to her mother's maternal grandmother. The blown glasses are from Al-Khalil, blushing pink with gold leaf.

"Why do we need these?" Sundus asks, carefully cradling the glasses.

"If yahood come this way, who knows what they'll take."

She ponders why these people will take what belongs to them. What need of them do they have? But Sundus doesn't ask her mother, whose lips form a taut, straight line—a sign she is deep in thought and planning.

Sundus gazes at the small pile of other objects her mother has already assembled. Two framed photographs of Sundus's grandparents, a carved treasure box with pearl inlay her aunt, Khalti Azeeza, had gifted her mother.

How does her mother decide what to take? Suddenly objects seem to emerge as individual entities, permanent features in the daily landscape of their home, now rushing up, demanding to be valued, to be taken. The gilded Quran that sits on a wooden display. A mantel clock with hands in the shape of peacock feathers.

"What about these?" Sundus points to the brass chargers displayed in the curio cabinet in the dining room. Her father brought them back from Cyprus during his medical studies.

Her mother shakes her head and sighs. "They can have those." She rests a hand on her belly, her eyes roving around the room, a sad expression clouding her face, as if it will be the last time she'll see this room, their bayt.

And will they give up the books that line her father's study? Or the atlas that Sundus spends hours poring through, tracing a finger over borders and rivers, mouthing the names of countries that sound like mythical places? She races to the study and grabs a pair of copper binoculars she's peered through from the shoreline, following the journey of seagulls across the horizon until they vanish deep into the sky.

She holds out the case. "Can we take these?"

Her mother starts to protest then smiles, her eyes shining. "Of course, habibti. They might be of use on our trip."

Satisfied with the bundle, her mother instructs Sundus to pull the corners of the sheet to its center and she ties them into a knot. "Now go to your room. Fold some underwear and a few clothes. Yalla!"

"And my books?"

Her mother holds up two fingers.

Sundus scampers to her room. She scrutinizes her windowsill where her books sit. Several have been gifted to her by her father's professor friend who'd returned from Europe last summer. They are mostly in French—*Le Petit Prince* and *Le Avventure di Pinocchio*, the latter which gave Sundus nightmares when the wooden boy is hanged for his offenses. The professor also gave her a diary with a lock. *For all your secrets*, he'd winked at her. She doesn't possess any secrets so she gifted the diary to her friend Nuha who's been pining for Malik, the shortest boy in their neighborhood. Sundus is certain Nuha carries more secrets than her.

She glances around her room. Her mother did not say anything about her toys. Sundus grabs her favorite doll, a little girl with yellow bobbed hair and eyes with lids that open and close when Sundus tilts her. She goes to her wardrobe and riffles through dresses she wears on holiday and for school pageants. She pulls a forest green one from a hanger, presses the soft velvet fabric against her face. The collar and cuffs are white lace, and pearl buttons run down the back of the dress. Along with a few shirts and slacks, Sundus returns to her mother, offering her traveling attire.

"You don't need that dress! Hang it back up," her mother orders.

Sundus's shoulders slump. She is crestfallen. She has no idea where they are heading. All the adults seem to be planning to leave their homes without a clear destination—or at least not one her own parents will share with her. How long will they be gone? And how does her mother know she won't need a dress at this place once they arrive?

Her mother sets down a pair of her father's slacks and pulls Sundus close, the scent of jasmine on her skin. "It's temporary, habibti. We must only take what we need."

"What if they steal my books, my clothes?" Her lower lip trembles. The image of strangers pawing her belongings threatens tears.

Her mother's pained expression answers her question: she can't guarantee anything. Sundus starts to cry.

"My love, such things can be replaced, I promise you," her mother cajoles. "For now, we have to travel wisely."

Sniffling, Sundus returns the dress. Above her bedframe is a portrait of the sea she'd painted with watercolors. Once a month, a beautiful Armenian woman comes to her school to teach the students about art. Sundus carefully untacks the thin sheet of canvas and rolls it up before tucking it into her school satchel. She roams the bayt, every object suddenly calling to her to carry it along on an unknown journey.

A hacking cough pierces memory and the present seeps back. Sundus blots her tears with the heel of her palm and listens again at the door. The horrid cough stops and only wheezing comes again from Hafez's room. She quietly returns to the saha outside and descends the stone steps to the vineyard.

Beyond the dawali is the orchard whose trees she and her beloved Jalal had planted; she knows each one, the formations and blemishes on their limbs like the marks and scars on a child's precious body.

Her parents have gone, and Jalal after them—Allah be merciful upon their souls—and soon her son will join his father. *To God we belong and to God shall we return.*

The trees have remained for her granddaughter to inherit. Will she accept them and land on which they stand tall? Or will she turn her back on all of it?

A wind from the valley flutters the hem of her thobe. Sundus turns and, for a moment, it sounds like the rush of waves from a distant sea.

CHICAGO: SEPTEMBER 2007

CHAPTER 2

All around them, families are hauling airport caddies piled with suitcases and plastic shopping bags that threaten to topple over. Relatives huddle around their departing members, hugging and shaking hands. Intisar wonders how many have been summoned to a deathbed, how many are returning to their homelands.

"Once you're out of Tel Aviv, be sure to speak Arabic as much as possible," her stepfather Ali advises before he embraces her at the TSA point. "Don't let anyone take advantage of you. Our own people can be crooks."

"Bas!" her mother sniffles. "Enough! She'll be fine." Mama waits for Intisar to confirm this, her eyebrows, a shade darker than her auburn-dyed hair, raised in expectation. But Intisar says nothing to lessen her mother's guilt. "You have your passport?" she asks for the twentieth time, as if Intisar is six and not twenty-six. And yet she feels like a child again, abandoned for the second time.

"Listen," her stepfather says in Arabic, laying a hand on her shoulder. His voice is deep and reassuring. "You're a strong girl, Tee-Tee. Everyone's happy you're coming. Isn't that right, Nadira?" He glances at her mother. "And we've spoken to your father's friend Mu'tassem—and to your grandmother Sundus. They can't wait to see you." He kisses the top of her head. "And of course," he adds, "your father is thrilled."

Intisar sucks her tears back and nods. She turns to her mother.

"Ali's right," Mama says, pulling Intisar in for a long hug. Her scent lingers, a familiar combination of cigarette smoke and Chanel No°5. "I raised you strong. You can do this, Tee-Tee."

Intisar wants to argue this, wants to tell her mother she's not as strong as she wishes Intisar was, that she's not like the other woman at all. She wants to beg Mama to come with her, to be at her side when she sees her father again for the first time in nearly twenty years. But the words clot in her throat and instead of speaking, Intisar gives them both one final wave before entering the TSA line. By the time she's removing her shoes and jewelry, they're out of sight.

A young mother a few travelers ahead of Intisar hoists her toddler's stroller, his blanket covered in baby turtles, a small carry-on, and her oversize purse onto the conveyor belt. He's whining and tugging on her hijab as she hands him to a security agent on the other side of the body detector before going through it herself. It beeps and she tries it again. It beeps again. The people lined behind Intisar—shuffling without their belts and shoes—groan. Another security agent instructs the woman to step aside. By the time Intisar walks through the detector, the woman is claiming all of her items, including her toddler, whose face has turned an indignant red and is wet with tears. Intisar is desperate for one more cigarette before boarding, but it's too late.

On the plane, she checks her ticket twice before sliding in beside the same woman with the toddler. Intisar offers her the aisle seat though she's prone to motion sickness and deliberately reserved this seat when booking the flight. "Wallahi, it's no trouble," Intisar says.

At the sound of Intisar's Arabic, the woman looks relieved but adamantly shakes her head. She's finally gotten her son to sleep. "Alhamdullilah!" she whispers loudly. "Thank God it's a direct flight."

Asleep, the child is cherubic, serene, belying a set of demonic vocal chords he'd exhausted before takeoff.

A flight attendant, cordial and bright-eyed, briskly nods at Intisar and the other passengers, her eyes roving over each row as her co-attendants begin their preflight safety presentation. It's an uninspired choreography of extended arms and airbags, their faces frozen in a half-smile, eyes gazing above the passengers' heads.

"His brothers have never given me trouble," the woman next to her is saying. She adjusts the hem of her hijab with one hand, patting her son's small chest with the other. "They used to sleep the entire time. The humming of the plane soothed them." The woman pauses for a moment, waiting for Intisar to ask about the whereabouts of these other children. The woman goes on, "They're with their father. Teenagers. This one was a surprise." With an expression of irritated wonder, the woman looks down at the child softly snoring against her chest, a vague smile tugging her lips. She eyes Intisar's ring finger, then bluntly asks, "You're not married?"

Intisar smiles politely. "No." *Shit.* She is too exhausted to realize she's opened up an interrogation. She quickly attempts to insert the earbuds attached to her iPod, but is thwarted.

"You're so pretty, mashallah. No husband?" the woman asks again, as if Intisar couldn't possibly be telling the truth.

She shakes her head, closes her eyes, hoping the woman will get the hint.

"Neeyallak," she says conspiratorially, elbowing Intisar. "I envy you. You can still enjoy yourself." The woman looks down wistfully at her son. "I suppose you still have time."

Intisar nods, grateful the question of her singlehood is resolved. The woman doesn't ask what she does for a living. Unlike her marital status, this is an uncomplicated response. She works at Pine Woods, a senior living facility south of Chicago. She's a day-nurse, or a "wellness facilitator," as her identification badge announces. Her third-year anniversary was marked by one of those edible fruit arrangements in the shape of a floral bouquet and a buttercream-frosted cake in the Community Room of the three-story building. Like the residents of Pine Woods, her job is quiet and slow-paced. And she's more than grateful not a single patient has died during her shift. When their condition worsens, they're swiftly taken to a local hospital. The manager, a tall and slender white woman with a pixie haircut, doesn't want body bags on stretchers coming through the service elevator, let alone the lobby where residents play their games of chess or cards on leather chairs. Intisar's relieved she, too, is spared.

Isn't it depressing? Mama had declared one day, sitting with her sisters on the wooden deck. Ali paints it a walnut-brown every other spring. *I couldn't do it.*

Intisar's aunts agreed, sucking on their cigarettes, each balancing a souvenir ashtray on her thigh.

But Tee-Tee has always been gloomy, Mama had added with a chuckle. *Even as a kid.*

Intisar had hated that word—gloomy—as if she were a weather system ruining everyone's day. But it was true. She wasn't a happy child as far as her memory stretches. In photographs, she appears glum and exhausted from bouts of crying that turned into pathetic hiccups. And then came the look her mother gave her. The one that narrowed Mama's eyes and tightly pursed her lips. The one that brandished Intisar as weak, sinking her stomach with shame.

Stop that crying, her mother would hiss in her ear. *You're a big girl. Ayb!*

But they were not the tantrums of a spoiled child. Intisar's crying fits began after Baba left. Traces of him faded around their apartment. Framed photographs of her parents' wedding day. A portrait of Baba standing with two men in front of Altgeld Hall at the University of Illinois. She was nine years old and those outbursts had later converted into an adolescent sullenness, then gradually a quiet disposition she was required to shed around her patients at Pine Woods, where her job description explicitly demanded *an always cheerful personality*. At the end of her shift, her face hurt.

On the plane, Intisar tries a second time to insert her earbuds and shifts her shoulders toward the aisle, but the woman is undeterred. "What balad are you from? Who are your people?"

Intisar's mother was born in America. In Chicago, Mama owns a salon she named Shalabiya Hair Design. It's her excuse for not being able to accompany Intisar on this trip when they both know the real reason: Mama doesn't want to face her ex-husband's family.

"My father is from Bayt al-Hawa," Intisar tells the stranger beside her. She wraps her fingers around her iPod, quieting their tremble. The name of Baba's village sounds foreign on her tongue, like exotic fruit Intisar is trying for the first time, incomparable to anything she's ever tasted.

In the second grade, her class was assigned a "Where We Come From" project and everyone had to dress up according to their heritage. Intisar's mother dressed her in a child-replica of a traditional thobe, a linen dress with an intricate chest panel of cross-stitched flowers. Around her head, Mama draped a red coin-lined cap. Intisar could see something come over her father as she posed for him, holding her arms out and spinning though the dress didn't flutter and the fabric was a bit scratchy against her skin. Intisar didn't care. Baba's expression was like he'd unwrapped a gift he was expecting but still surprised him. It made her instantly forget her discomfort.

In the school gymnasium, her teacher hung a rectangular sign made from construction paper around each of their necks, on which every child had neatly printed their country of origin. The class was then assembled for a group photograph, their parents snapping away on new digital cameras and filming on portable video recorders. A white boy named Joshua standing next to Intisar had hissed in her ear, *There's no Palestine on the map.*

This was true as Intisar had squinted her eyes at a map mounted on the classroom wall. Her face flushed hot with a shame she couldn't articulate. But there is such a place, she'd wanted to scream at him. Her father—*you see him?*—he's from there! Intisar, too, had witnessed it. She had proof.

It was in the summer of 1987. A photograph shows Intisar standing beside a lamb, her expression revealing her utter disillusionment. Its fleece was gritty and stiff, a disappointing contrast to the pristine-white storybook characters she'd loved. Still, Intisar remembers being excited about having a lamb of her own, a new friend with whom she could frolic, in that new, strange place. Intisar was blithely unaware of what would come after that photograph was snapped: her lamb's decapitated head on a platter, its blackish tongue splayed between half-opened jaws, and someone saying, *For you, habibti! Welcome home!*

Intisar sometimes wonders if she'd ever been to that place, that perhaps the pictures her mother has preserved from her first marriage are made-up like the stories in those children's books, the same books Intisar's father had read to her in his stilted English. In between those Western stories, he told her funny tales of the antics of a man named Juha and his beloved donkey, ones Baba's own father had told him. That was all before Baba left and never came back.

"Bayt al-Hawa!" the woman next to her is gushing. "I think my husband's sister-in-law is from there." Her son softly snores and Intisar watches his chest rise and fall, envying his oblivion.

A reading light flashes on a few rows ahead. In ten hours she lands, arriving at a destination as foreign to her as any far corner of a globe she might have spun and lain a finger on. What can she claim of Palestine beyond a biological father? The answer is as obscure as the tidy, quilted patches of land disappearing beneath the stratosphere of the plane when it first takes off.

At Ben Gurion Airport, the woman and her toddler separate from her at customs, and Intisar feels a pang of apprehension, suddenly alone.

She finds herself in a very long line of fellow Arab passengers, women in Western clothes and tightly bound hijab, men smelling sharply of aftershave and sweat. She monitors the flow of the other rapidly moving queues of white Americans, Jews, Europeans, and Asians who travel in large tourist groups embarking on the Holy Land, lanyards with passports hanging from their necks. It's obvious she's been herded along with others like her into a special line that barely seems to progress.

When Intisar finally reaches the security booth, her passport is examined by an impassive agent then dropped in a plastic tray. She's then routed from room to room, offering the same answers to slightly altered questions—*what's your grandfather's name, when was the last time you were here*—as if the security detail is trying to trip her up and reveal she's hiding something. Each new agent regards her with cold politeness, eyes darting between her and her passport.

"What brings you here?" the third agent, a woman about Intisar's age, inquires with a thick Hebrew accent. She taps her keyboard, eyes flitting from her screen to Intisar's face then back again.

Does she tell her it's the wish of a dying father? To behold his only child after nearly two decades? "To visit my grandmother. Sundus Jaber," Intisar offers instead, sticking to the script she's been given. Her stepfather's advice echoes in her ears: *Stay calm and smile—they'll let you go eventually. Don't say more than you need to—and don't let them see you sweat. They won't mess with you as much as they do a man.*

Intisar pulls a slip of paper from her backpack and slides it across the desk. "She lives in Bayt al-Hawa."

The agent ignores it. "And your father? Hafez Jaber?" *Tap-tap-tap.*

Intisar nods, trying not to look startled though she's anticipated this question. He is an enemy of the State of Israel. A terrorist is what the news articles called him. She was a senior in high school, researching her father's crime. Her mother told her nothing and her aunts quickly sealed their lips around their cigarettes when she overheard them talking about his arrest. In the search engine on the library computer, she typed her father's name and glanced over her shoulder, afraid someone was watching. Several articles returned and she clicked each of them and read until the bell rang. She didn't dare print any of them—no one knew about her father. Most of her classmates didn't even know where Palestine was.

In her next class, her teacher's voice had droned against the troubling facts still flashing across Intisar's brain.

Military outpost.

Improvised explosive device.

No casualties.

One soldier injured. Loss of leg.

She was relieved to find out no one had died. How could her father be responsible for anyone's injury? He'd been a generous man, rarely moved to anger, always smiling down at her and Mama.

But here was the proof she'd dug up like unearthing the fossil of a creature unknown to man. Who was her father? She'd never had the chance to know. He was sentenced to life in prison until cancer released him to his family. A pretense of humanity by an Israeli court, but which had come too late. He'd been denied treatment during his detainment.

Heat spreads across Intisar's face and neck. She can smell her ripe armpits, her bra cups are damp with sweat. "My father is dying," she blurts as if the officer doesn't already know. Intisar gropes for a bit of sympathy from this stranger, but the officer holds her steely gaze, blue eyes trained on her.

Tap-tap-tap.

The phone call came in the early evening last week, after Intisar's shift. Mrs. Anderson in 311 had cardiac arrest, but was recovering. Mr. Knox in 202 sprained his ankle coming off the stairs though he'd been instructed to use the elevator. *I can still walk, goddammit,* he'd said with a scowl as Intisar wrapped his foot.

At home, they'd just sat down to her mother's zahra stew when her mother handed Intisar the cordless phone. *It's overseas,* Mama had loudly whispered, cupping the receiver. *He's asking for you.*

She braced herself for her father's voice. But it was another stranger on the other end.

Intisar? Is this Intisar? His accent was thick. *I am your father's friend, Mu'tassem. Your father is not well, my dear. You must come home.*

Intisar had difficulty registering this information. *Who is this?* she asked dumbly, pushing her chair back.

Mu'tassem, habibti. Your father's friend, the man repeated patiently. *Your Baba. He is dying. You must come home.*

She glanced at her mother, who was pinching her lips the way she always did when she was worried, forming a fish mouth. Her stepfather Ali lay down his fork across his plate and stood up, his eyebrows raised in question.

Intisar, the man on the other end of the line implored, saying her name as if he'd known Intisar her whole life. *Your father. He is waiting for you.*

Stunned, she handed the phone to Ali. He left the kitchen and spoke in muffled Arabic to the man. Intisar glanced at the clock on the wall—it was two o'clock in the morning over there. She'd become adept at quick calculation. The first month Baba was gone, Intisar had wanted to call him every night before she fell asleep. To say goodnight. She missed the sinking of his weight on her mattress, the creaking of the springs when he cuddled her.

It's the middle of the night, her mother had scolded. *I told you, Tee-Tee, it's a seven-hour time difference.*

But Mama was wrong. It was actually eight hours between Intisar and Baba. She spent much of her time at school staring at the classroom clock, calculating the hour, wondering what he was doing, hoping he was thinking of her.

Intisar gripped the edge of the table and stared at her plate of rice and cauliflower stew, frozen by a stranger's jarring dispatch from a continent away.

Tap-tap-tap. "How long will you be staying?" the agent is asking her.

"Ten days."

"With Sundus Jaber?" the agent asks again. "In Bayt al-Hawa?"

Intisar nods. What if she's sent back? She is the daughter of a state terrorist. For a moment, her chest swells: secretly, she'd be glad to go home, endure another ten hours aboard a plane. She clenches her eyes shut and breathes deeply. She can go back to her quiet life, to the residents of Pine Woods, to dinners with Mama and her stepfather. She can sew up this tear in the curtain of her past and move on.

Except she really hasn't moved on. She's been frozen like the snow globes her mother collects from their vacations, encasing a tranquil scene—a farmhouse or castle or a mountain range. Until you shake it up and the scene is transformed, everything obscured by delicate snow.

Mama never talks about her father. On her eleventh birthday, Intisar dressed up as Belle from *Beauty and the Beast.* Her mother had styled her hair because the wig had been too scratchy and didn't match her olive complexion. Secretly, Intisar had always hated how close her birthday was to Halloween, how even more alienated she felt from herself in disguise. That day, Intisar cried after blowing out the candles, her teary vision blurring the characters from the Teenage Mutant Ninja Turtles who surrounded the kitchen table, her cousins eagerly waiting for their slice of cake.

Intisar's mother had quickly ushered her away, leaving her grandmother and aunts to cut and serve the cake. It was the third birthday her father had missed. Mama left her for a few minutes alone in her room then returned with a brown leather album and propped it on Intisar's bed.

He's in there, her mother had said before closing the door behind her.

In most of the 35mm photographs, Intisar's father is seated and she's in his lap, following his pointed finger at the camera. Family members blur out of focus, partial heads and bodies creeping in the corners. In a candid shot someone took outdoors, Baba is standing and he's cradling her in the crook of his arm, the other gesturing toward someone in the distance. Intisar appears weightless in his powerful grip though she was a chunky toddler. Her face is turned upwards toward him. Trees shadow them, sunlight dappling their leaves. But it wasn't the home she knew, the apartment building they'd lived in since her birth. Before Mama remarried and they moved to the suburbs with Ali.

It was that other place where he was now, his other home. The one he called *al bilad. The country.* Intisar peeled back the plastic sheath and carefully plucked the photograph from the sticky page and tucked it into a book by Carl Sagan called *Cosmos,* which Baba had left behind. After everyone left, her cousins calling out their goodbyes to her from the hallway, Intisar emerged from her room. Solemnly, she'd returned the album to Mama as if planning to never see it again. Her mother took it and said nothing. Would she suspect that a single photograph was missing?

She hadn't looked at it in years. Until Mu'tassem's phone call that night. She pulled it from a drawer in her dresser, tucked beneath pairs of socks, after years of waiting for him. She saw how they had the same eyes, she and Baba, a resemblance that still startles strangers Intisar meets who knew him. His face is square, a sharp and strong jawline. She has her mother's oval shape, framed by brown straight hair, the type Mama claims is a hairdresser's dream. *Arabiyat would kill for your hair.*

And now the photograph is tucked inside her overnight bag, where she'd stored deodorant and hand lotion. She wonders now how much the features in the photograph have changed, how age and disease have stripped her father's dark hair to gray, slackened his face. Does he still have a mustache, the one Intisar can still feel prickling against her child-cheek?

The agent finally stamps her passport and hands it back. "Enjoy your stay in Israel."

The sun has long set when Intisar is released and permitted to gather her luggage. She moves quickly toward the exit of the terminal in a cold sweat, trying not to run. What if the hired driver left, believing she's been prohibited from entering the country and was sent back to the States? She flips open her cell phone and it powers on, but there is no signal. She shakes her head, feeling foolish.

You'll get a special temporary chip when you arrive, her stepfather Ali had advised her. *They have a landline, too.*

Intisar takes a deep breath. She passes Arab men with slicked-back hair and tight shirts carrying handmade cardboard signs, English and Arabic scribbled across them. She frantically searches for her name before a middle-aged man approaches with an expansive smile.

"Intisar?" He holds up his hands in anticipation.

"Yes. That's me," she says in English, exhaling in relief for the first time since landing. She quickly switches to Arabic. "I thought you might have left. They took so long. I—thank you for waiting."

"I've been doing this for years," he says, reaching for her suitcase. "I am Emad." He presses a hand deferentially over his heart then points to the exit doors.

The warm evening air instantly absorbs the cold of the air-conditioned airport like a vacuum. Her mother put herself in charge of Intisar's traveling attire, buying loose linen blouses and a few long skirts. *Don't worry—they're all medium,* she assured her. *You can leave whatever you don't want there with relatives. They'll be thrilled to own anything with American labels.*

Intisar slips out of her zip-up hoodie and climbs into the back seat of the cab, which smells of cigarettes and coconuts. She's dying to smoke, but remembers her mother's warning about public behavior and women. Intisar doesn't think someone like Emad would mind, but she refrains from pulling her pack from her pocket. The driver makes small talk as he whisks past other cars and minibuses loading passengers, his eyes darting between the road and her through his rearview mirror.

They stop at Qalandia checkpoint. The new separation wall

sprawls high and wide and is interminable. Fresh graffiti is scrawled across it, cutting across the dismal gray with renditions of Yasser Arafat and Marwan Barghouti, whose cuffed hands are raised in a victory sign. The murals are eerily illuminated under the massive security lights. "Jesus," she gasps. In Chicago, she marched across Michigan Avenue, traffic at a standstill as hundreds of others protested the apartheid wall. Her cousins had called her up, persuading her to participate after inundating her with stories of families literally divided on either side of the wall, mothers speaking to daughters through holes they'd smashed through the concrete. But none of them has ever been to Palestine. None of them has seen this ugly concrete barrier up close.

Emad brakes as a soldier waves him to stop. He ducks and peers inside the cab then examines Emad's permit. A new kind of dread jabs Intisar's chest. Slung over his shoulder is an automatic rifle and he shifts it when he stoops to further scrutinize her in the back seat. What had she heard about the Israeli Defense Force? They'd trained Chicago police officers?

The soldier's helmet appears too large for his head, like a kid pretending in a game of war. This soldier—no older than a college freshman—is ready for combat. Intisar smiles stupidly at him, her cheeks searing. *There's no Palestine* echoes in her ears.

"Iklab," Emad says once they are finally waved through. "Dogs. I bet you've never seen anything like this in America, right?" His eyes crinkle in amusement as he glances in the rear-view mirror. He lights a cigarette, holds it outside his window between intermittent puffs.

Intisar can't resist any longer. She holds up her pack of Marlboro Lights and Emad waves his consent with a chuckle. He passes his lighter to her over his headrest. She flicks it and holds the blue flame until the tip of her cigarette catches. She takes a long drag and feels instantly nauseous. But she doesn't care and she continues to suck the filter, a light-headedness soon easing the tension in her muscles. Her mother hated that Intisar smoked, despite being a heavy smoker herself.

Your husband won't like the premature wrinkles he sees, Mama had warned. This imaginary husband has been hovering over Intisar for years. *Don't you want to get married?* her mother demands when another cousin gets engaged.

I'm waiting for the right one, Intisar replies.

There is no right one, Mama counters. *It's the one who shows up and stays.*

Intisar is mostly silent the rest of the way except to answer Emad's direct questions about her family back in what he calls *amreekya*. She stares out the window of the cab, the swell and dip of hills the only thing she can make out for certain. The darkness is disorienting—she can't tell which direction they're heading, where the borders of her father's village emerge, where one road ends and another the begins. A concert of night critters penetrates the still of the black sky.

The car begins to wind up a hill. Intisar stares wearily out her window. In the distance, she can make out a cluster of buildings, some stretching higher than others.

"The mokhayam," Emad tells her, catching her eyes. "Refugees of 1967."

An encampment. Like the ones Intisar had seen in televised raids, young men cuffed in zip ties, some blindfolded. All taken away in army jeeps.

They finally pull up to a villa overlooking a valley, mostly dark except for the lighted homes scattered below. A man appears in the double doorway of the entrance and quickly approaches the carport where Emad has parked.

"Ahlan! Ahlan!" he calls, waving vigorously at Intisar. "Welcome!" The voice she recognizes from the long-distance call belongs to this older man, tall and reed-like, his hair receding across his crown, the sides speckled and closely shaven. He is her father's friend Mu'tassem. "I am sorry I was not there to receive you at the airport, my dear. I do not have a permit," he apologizes.

Intisar extends her right hand and he grips it lightly with his left in an awkward handshake. "Forgive me," he apologizes again, holding up his right hand. It's missing a thumb and two fingers.

Intisar quickly diverts her attention back to his face and smiles as if she's unperturbed by an appendage that resembles small tree stumps and a few craggly branches. "I'm happy to meet you." She turns to Emad, who sets down her luggage. "Thank you very much, Ammi."

"Inshallah khair," the driver tells her, his hand over his heart again.

She turns back to Mu'tassem and a closer look in his warm brown eyes tells Intisar she's too late.

Her father is already gone.

GAHANA PRISON: JULY 1990

CHAPTER 3

Men were shouting in the distance. Hafez didn't lift his head toward this noise. His eyes, half-opened slits, were fixed on the scuffed floor until they closed altogether. He could only take in so much light after being plunged in absolute darkness for—what month was this? What year?

He'd stopped keeping track after the first week when he could barely lift his arm to grab a plastic spoon and drag it along the concrete floor. He marked time as tiny matchsticks. After the third day in the black box, he'd discovered that day and night no longer existed. They kept him in perpetual darkness and he felt time moving forward like a river, obliterating his past. The only sensation was pain and his tormentors descended upon him at any moment. When he wasn't screaming—into a putrid rag stuffed into his mouth, or inside his skull—he'd still wonder about the time. And when they unbolted the steel door and it swung open to the outside, only artificial light poured inside the space from panels of fluorescent lighting. And before terror made him scuttle to a corner in the darkness, he wondered what particular hour of day it was.

Now he was hearing voices. Men hooting in Arabic. He caught their words like pollen drifting on the wind and a vague sense of hope rose in his throat. A warm and sweet taste on his tongue. But instinct made him swallow it back down, the darkness licking at his heels.

"Come on, ya zalama! You've got it!" It was a young man's voice. Hafez's teeth tingled and his tongue grew heavy. If he were returned to the general population, he had a chance.

As he was dragged along, his rubber slipper disengaged from his left foot and the guard following behind the two who held him by each arm, stopped to retrieve it. He didn't return it to Hafez's foot, using it instead to slam against cell bars, quieting each group of prisoners as they passed.

The guards finally halted and Hafez looked up for the first time. Five men gaped at him from an open steel door, silent and alert. The guard following Hafez, still holding his slipper, barked at the prisoners and someone quickly lowered the volume on a radio perched on a window ledge. The noise he'd heard was because of a football game. The men had been cheering. A crackling radio broadcast cut through the other human voices. Hafez squinted up at blocks of thick glass, a sliver of natural light, the noise of the men muffled around him.

It was a window.

Something expanded in Hafez's chest and he swallowed hard.

The guards uncuffed his hands and shoved him into the cell, his slipper finally returned after it was thrust at his head. He flinched, but didn't touch the spot, conditioned to keep his arms at his side. The steel door was bolted behind him and he flinched again.

In the middle of the floor, he attempted to pull himself upright. He could feel the curious eyes on him and was suddenly aware of his own body and the space it took up. His battered limbs hid beneath a uniform that was too large for him. But it was also clean after a mandated shower and absent of all the other odors the darkness had cultivated. Feces, urine, vomit, and blood. He cinched the waist of his pants to hold them up, glad for something to grip now that he was free of the two guards. He was afraid to touch his face, his scraggly beard. He looked down at his free hand, at what had once been his fingernails, now small ugly stubs. Still he could see his hand and that could only mean he was really here.

"Ahlan! Ahlan!" someone called out. "Welcome! Welcome!" The tone was childlike and out of place. Hafez's eyes darted in the direction of a lanky man sitting on the edge of his cot. His long legs were pulled up to his chest. "Welcome! Welcome!" he parroted again.

"Over there," someone else said, pointing to a bare gray mattress on the top bunk.

Shame rushed down Hafez's neck—how would he manage to get up there? He gave an imperceptible nod and shuffled toward his new cot. For months, only a dirty blanket had separated him from the cold floor. He regarded the short ladder before climbing, the scrutiny of the other men like an extra load he'd have to carry up there on his shoulders. Hafez lifted one foot at a time, clenching his jaw. The simple exercise exposed every new and dormant pain in his muscles. Once he reached the mattress, he curled into a ball, his back to the others.

A few moments of silence passed until the volume of the radio was raised again, the men eager to return to the match.

"Ahlan, ahlan!" the parrot-voice called out again. "Welcome! Welcome!"

The next time he was ordered to move, Hafez forced his legs, one after another, over the side of his cot, and turned his body to climb down the ladder. When he heard the commands of a guard through a steel-barred square opening in the door, his stomach turned cold and he braced himself as best as he could. They were ordered to file out of the cell—where to, he was not sure. But he felt a strange sense of safety, marching between two of his cellmates, shielded from danger, until a guard slid behind him and kicked the back of his legs hard with his boot. Hafez's lower body collapsed and he careened into the man in front of him. He was helped up and the line continued down the concrete walkway until he was shoved again. Once more, the line fell out of formation before quickly assembling again like a child's tedious game.

"Leave him alone already," someone hissed at the guards. But they only laughed and shoved harder.

They finally arrived at a mess hall. At a long table, Hafez didn't eat. His nerves were frayed so thin he was afraid to open his mouth. He lay his head on folded arms. A guard marched over, his boots thudding the floor and he pulled Hafez's head up so forcefully he thought his neck would snap.

"Eat!" the guard commanded.

Talk of the match between West Germany and Argentina suddenly halted. Hafez was aware of dozens of spoons and forks suspended over plastic trays around him. An eerie silence fell over the hall.

"Eat!" the guard commanded again. The voice belonged to the one who had shoved him in line. Another guard clambered over and each one towered over Hafez. His heart beat wildly in his ears. They muttered insults in Hebrew, a word he knew: *achbaroch*. Rat.

Hafez was unable to open his mouth, even to protest. On a tray before him, the smell of the greenish slop ladled in a bowl made Hafez want to vomit. The first guard held his head back while the other used Hafez's spoon to scoop up portions of the mush and smear it across his face. More laughter, hollow and thin, as the rest of the inmates silently watched the spectacle. When the guards became bored, one of them flicked the spoon at his face, then marched away.

"Fuck their mothers' cunts," someone seated close to Hafez muttered.

"Loolad iklab," another agreed. "Sons of bitches."

Back in his cell, someone handed Hafez a towel. It smelled moldy but he used it to wipe the green soup from his face and beard.

"There you are!" This cheerful voice belonged to an older man with a bald head covered by a white skullcap. "We can see your face again," he chuckled.

"There you are!" the parrot-voice repeated.

"Bas, ya Sadeeq!" the older man admonished. His tone was gentle, but firm. "Come pray with us, Brother."

Hafez looked up from his towel. The invitation was intended for him.

The white-capped man cupped his shoulder. "I am Abu Jadallah," he said, his other hand over his heart. "Allah has not abandoned you, my son. You are here—" The old man patted the air. "You are alive. Only He can restore your faith, but you must turn to Him to get His blessings."

He'd stopped searching for God in the darkness. Could he still recite al-Fatiha?

> *Bismillahi rahman iraheem*
> *In the Name of Allah—the Most Compassionate, Most Merciful.*
> *All praise is for Allah—Lord of all worlds,*
> *the Most Compassionate, Most Merciful…*

The verse came back more quickly than he'd guessed. But Hafez slowly shook his head at Abu Jadallah, who waited with expectant eyebrows. Someone younger snickered. All five of the men stood in the center of the cell, huddled together across the concrete floor now covered with several straw mats. They faced Hafez, who had already climbed up to his cot—the effort was growing less laborious—and he lay on his side, studying each man for the first time.

Hands cupped to his ears, Abu Jadallah led them in prayer. "Allahu Akbar, Allahu Akbar…"

It was the noon prayer. Hafez glanced up at the window. Time was beginning to reassemble like the shards of a broken plate.

Next to Abu Jadallah was the tall, lanky one. His lips moved in supplication like a child trying hard not to recite the verses out loud with his parrot-voice. He kept his eyes clenched shut. This had to be Sadeeq. His head was shaved and a long, pale scar cut through the black stubble of hair, like a path cleared through a forest. It started behind one ear and snaked up the side of his face to the middle of his forehead.

Hafez rubbed his own closely shaven head. They'd neglected his beard, which had turned wiry. He didn't want to see his reflection and the record of violence his jailers had committed so exquisitely upon him. He reached for his nose, a faint bump on the bridge. They'd broken it twice, thrown him a dirty towel to catch the blood. Perhaps it was better to have a stranger looking back at him in the mirror, for Hafez Jaber had turned into a ghost.

He gazed down on the men again. Beside Sadeeq was a shorter, middle-aged man who kept his head bowed the whole time. The remaining two prostrating in the line were shabab; one young man appeared to be older than the other one though they were close in height.

When they turned their heads from side to side, offering the final salutation, they scattered to their assigned cots. The older men sat on the edge, their bodies leaning forward to keep from hitting the roof of the top bunks. To Hafez, they looked like they were waiting for someone or something. Two bunk beds were positioned on each wall. The fourth wall was bare except for the window. The small transistor radio sat on its narrow ledge. He found himself desperate to claw up that wall and press his face against the glass and the natural light.

"Itfadal." The older of the shabab held up a pack of cigarettes to Hafez. One was already poking out for him to take.

Hafez lifted himself to a sitting position, his back against the wall. He propped up one leg to form a triangle, steadying his core, relieving the throbbing in his back. He peered down at the young man's offering, hesitated then carefully pulled the cigarette from the lip of the pack. He leaned forward to catch the flame of a lighter.

He inhaled and the result was a harsh flush of smoke singeing his throat. Hafez hacked while the young man laughed.

"Take it easy, man! It's been awhile, yes?"

Just then, a memory surged through his brain. He was eleven years old, playing with his best friend, Mu'tassem. The migrant workers had come to harvest the grapes. No one was watching when Hafez first held a cigarette to his lips, his grasp awkward as his friend lit it. A toothless worker had shown them how to roll the tobacco, and they'd stowed it near the dilapidated well on the other side of his family's border wall. Hafez swallowed and doubled over as smoke invaded his lungs. Nothing had ever tasted so nasty.

Before the memory morphed into something else from his past, Hafez quickly snuffed it out like the cigarette shakily pinched between his lips.

"Ahlan wa sahlan." The young man gave Hafez a two-finger salute with his own cigarette. "I am Nasser." He pointed across the cell. "That's my father. And that's my brother Nijmy."

Hafez wasn't certain he'd heard correctly. He'd been repeatedly struck on the side of his head by the butt of a guard's rifle, which had muddled the voices of his interrogators in his left ear.

Abu Nasser grinned at him. "Alhamdullilah for my sons," he declared. Hafez would later discover that Abu Nasser was captured when his operation to hijack a tourist bus in 1981 was foiled. He'd already served nine years when both of his sons were arrested in raids during the Intifada. Nasser was twenty-three years old, his brother Nijmy twenty-one.

I am happy and I am sad, Abu Nasser would later tell Hafez concerning this perverse reunion. Combined, they had already served twelve years.

Nijmy only nodded in Hafez's direction as he reached for the radio. Upon closer scrutiny, their fraternal resemblance became obvious. They shared the same intensely black eyebrows—their father's graying and scragglier—and boxy torsos. The younger one lacked the brighter disposition of his brother, a permanent scowl etched across his face.

"Welcome, my brother," Abu Jadallah, the white-capped man joined in.

"Welcome, my brother," Sadeeq repeated from the toilet, his elbows propped on his knees. A series of wet, gassy noises erupted. The odor that rose up and drifted toward Hafez didn't bother him. He'd slept in his own shit for a year. "Welcome, my brother," the parrot-voice called out again.

"Do not mind Sadeeq," Abu Jadallah told Hafez. "He's had too many visits to the Zinzana."

Hafez nodded, dread piercing his chest. They'd aptly named that dark place the Dungeon. How much blood and flesh had Sadeeq left behind, mingling with new blood and new flesh?

Nasser handed him a rusty can, half-full of cigarette butts. "Tell us your name, Brother."

Hafez tapped his ashes inside and took another drag. This time it seeped directly into his lungs, producing a welcome light-headedness. His name? As the young man asked for it, Hafez was struck with how long it had been since he'd actually uttered it. The first team of interrogators had said his name often, as if they were his friends.

Yalla, ya Hafez. Tell us who your comrades are and things will be better for you.

What would your mother think, ya Hafez, if we brought her here to see your ass get fucked?

Then they stopped calling him by his name. He was *sharmoot* and *faggot*, the insults punctuated by a blow to his kidneys or a sharp jab between his shoulder blades.

He tapped his ashes into the can again as he collected the two simple syllables on his tongue. "Hafez," he finally offered the men.

"Hafez?" Abu Nasser stood. "Hafez Jaber?"

"It's you, man!" his son Nasser cried. "You were a part of that mission!"

For the first time, the younger one called Nijmy appeared interested and lowered the volume of a music station, static-laced songs momentarily muted. "Which mission?"

"The operation that took the soldier's leg," Nasser said, studying Hafez incredulously. "That was you, yes?"

Hafez nodded. The details of that attack made the hair on his neck stand. Would his jailers now storm the cell and drag him back to the Zinzana?

"Only a leg?" Nijmy sneered, turning the volume up again. "A drop in the ocean, ya zalama."

"Mashallah!" Abu Nasser praised. "You're a hero, son."

Nasser joined his father. "Excellent, man!"

Abu Jadallah regarded him sadly. "Ah, yes. We heard all about you. You came all the way back from America to fight?"

The question sank deep into Hafez's chest. The old man's tone was not impressed. And it plunged Hafez into another kind of darkness: he would never see his daughter again. His body had been wrecked so badly that the thought of Intisar had mercifully been extinguished, like the artificial light of the black box before the door clanked shut on him.

Now that his body had been returned to him, Hafez was gaining a new consciousness—at least for the present. There was always a worse punishment, he realized, as Abu Jadallah waited for him to respond. Worse than the Zinzana, as these men called it. The irrevocable separation from his daughter. Had she, too, been plunged in her own kind of darkness without him?

Trembling, Hafez dropped the half-smoked cigarette to the concrete floor, crushing it beneath his slipper. He climbed back up to his cot and sobbed while the men below listened.

BAYT AL-HAWA: SEPTEMBER 2007

CHAPTER 4

Behind the girl's tears are her son's eyes. May God have mercy on his soul. It's been six days since the faithful bathed and shrouded him in white. It was a Friday—a most auspicious day to be buried. Janazzat il jum'aa bequeaths more blessings upon the soul than any other day of passing. Sundus takes solace in this for her son—her only child. She watched the men carry him out of her bayt to the masjid, where they prayed over him while the women wept at home.

How can one deliver news of their parent's death over a long-distance call? The last time Sundus heard her granddaughter's voice, let alone seen her, was on an obligatory holiday greeting a year ago.

How are you, ya sitti?

Alhamdullilah, Sitti, Intisar had dutifully responded, her words practiced, as if someone was coaching her in the background. *How are you?*

Alhamdullilah, ya sitti. The next few minutes were spent on superficial inquiry: *How is your mother? Your aunts and grandmother? Has your work been good?* The phone call lasted no more than five minutes, over with a grateful click on the other end of the line.

During those early years, she remembers her son's voice reaching her across the continents, echoing promise and joy from America. Only later would she and Jalal discover the intense homesickness he'd concealed beneath the layers of stories and news. Sundus had tried to imagine the physical space in which he spoke to her. Was he near a window? What were the noises muffled in the background? A barking dog? A car speeding by?

When it was her turn, Sundus shared the news of Bayt al-Hawa: who was married; who had another child, a first son. She kept it light and cheery. After that, Hafez spent several awkward moments coaxing his young daughter to say hello.

Yalla, ya Tee-Tee! It is your grandmother Sundus. She miss you.

She had understood this last bit in English. And it was true—she had missed the girl. Or at least the idea of her. After all, Intisar was an extension of her son, of her own flesh. It was an essential kind of love. No matter how far apart.

And now her granddaughter enters the villa too late, a small and fragile-looking creature beneath a bulky shoulder bag, moving carefully as if the ceiling might collapse on top of her. She is unsure where to turn—or to whom. Pity stirs in Sundus's breast. How peculiar it must be to enter the house of strangers who are at once your closest living kin. And in a time of great sadness, unsure upon whose bosom you could lay your grief.

Sundus steps forward, quickly enfolds the girl to her body, their embrace stiff and courteous. Intisar is a woman now, taller and firmer. "Alhamdullilah asaalama," Sundus tells her. "Welcome home, my beloved." Sundus searches her granddaughter's face. *Do you remember me? This house?* she wants to say, but rolls the words back on her tongue. Her mind's eye fills with the image of a timid child all those years ago, cowering between her parents, clutching their hands.

Yamma, we're coming for a visit, Hafez had announced during a phone call in the spring of 1987. His volume was lower than usual, as if confiding a secret. And Sundus wondered if her son's wife was privy to his extravagant plan to fly his family in early June and stay for three weeks. How much convincing had it taken?

It's decided, yamma? Sundus had stammered, her chest ballooning with hope.

It's decided, he returned, his voice more determined. *I want Intisar to meet you and Yabba. To know Falasteen.*

Sundus could hardly control herself. Her son was coming home after seven years away. Her mind raced. The villa would need to be cleaned from top to bottom. She'd enlist Um Mu'tassem to help her. Her son's old room would need sprucing up. New bedding and a mattress for the little one. They'd arrive in time for apricots and her granddaughter could eat them straight from the trees in the orchard. Jalal would butcher a lamb to celebrate their son's homecoming. *Inshallah khair,* she prayed. *May the Lord grant them safe passage home.*

Emad, a newlywed man, was hired to chauffeur Hafez and his family from the airport. He was among a few taxi drivers in Bayt al-Hawa with a permit to enter Tel Aviv. Sundus awaited their arrival at the villa along with Jalal, who filled a corner of the liwan with toys for his granddaughter. In the days leading up to his son's return, Jalal was anxious and bothersome like a child.

What if he changes his mind? he'd said to Sundus, worrying his prayer beads.

He won't, Sundus said firmly, though apprehension had also taken root in her heart.

Inshallah khair, her mother added. She'd been living with them since her father's death. She'd already planned the first series of meals her grandson would enjoy. Her excellent lamb-stuffed dumplings in a rich yogurt sauce, and rolled malfoof, and tripe and intestines, which she and Sundus would meticulously clean as soon as they were delivered from the butcher, their blessed neighbor Abu Mu'tassem. And fatayer. Five dozen savory pies baked at the makhbaz including sumac-spiced spinach, Hafez's favorite.

When they finally arrived, it was a new version of Hafez who climbed out of that taxi cab. He was older, certainly, but there was something else her son seemed to radiate. He'd become amarkani. His clothes, rumpled and slept in, were those of a foreigner. He gestured to everyone with clean fingernails, and his earlobes gleamed like the inside of scrubbed seashells. Even his hair appeared softer, and Sundus ran her fingers through it, biting her lower lip as the tears came.

Jalal fawned over Hafez—*Mashallah! America agrees with him!* he said to the neighbors who'd come to celebrate their son's homecoming. Mu'tassem, his dearest friend, kissed Hafez multiple times on each cheek before pulling him in for a long embrace. Sundus's mother allowed Hafez to get on one knee and repeatedly kiss the back of her hand until she grabbed her grandson's face and planted her papery lips on his forehead. *Welcome home, my love.*

His wife, Nadira, stepped forward to be received, her daughter on her hip. Her thick auburn hair—an unnatural color, Sundus suspected—was parted down the middle and feathered past her ears. Her eyelids were heavily powdered in blue, her lashes thick like spider legs. Her face was splotchy-tan, a bright pink painted on her lips. Nadira had a brusque manner that immediately signaled to anyone that she was only a visitor to this country.

Sundus had been against the marriage, but she'd held her tongue. Deep in her heart, a single wish had burrowed: Hafez would marry bint halal from Bayt al-Hawa—a decent girl from a respectable family. On a long-distance phone call, Hafez had jabbered on and on about Nadira and all of her virtues until Sundus passed the receiver to Jalal, who squeezed her hand, silencing her discontent.

He has chosen her, her husband said after hanging up. *It is in God's hands. May He bless and keep them.*

Hafez had wanted his parents to attend his wedding, had tried to convince them to come to America—all expenses paid. A gift from his in-laws, who'd arrange their voyage. But Sundus had insisted they couldn't leave her mother alone.

Ahlan wa sahlan, Sundus smiled, drawing her daughter-in-law in close for a hug, the child between them.

This must be Intisar, she said, patting the girl's small, bleary-eyed face. Her granddaughter squirmed away. She was presented to them in a ridiculous dress, ruffles up to her chin, standing rigidly in patent leather shoes. She tugged at the scratchy lace bodice, refused to go to anyone, recoiling from any kiss or embrace. Her face flushed hot: how rudely she'd been yanked from the only life she knew in the States! Deposited in a country whose language she could not properly speak. Sundus felt a twinge of sympathy, for she knew what it was like to be wrenched from the only place you ever knew.

The little girl whined in a low voice to her mother, *I want to go home.*

Over the following days, Nadira made Intisar politely shake hands with every villager who gathered to welcome her son home. As if to show off their impeccable Western manners. By the time the little girl circled back to Sundus, tears were streaming down her flushed face.

Sundus had pulled her gently to her bosom. *Bas, habibti!* she whispered in her granddaughter's ear. *No more of that, my love.* She held her chin in her hand. *This is your home.* Sundus had missed her birth, her first words and steps, and now she vowed to make up as much time as possible before they flew back to that other country like migratory birds.

The little girl had blinked up at her, eyebrows glowering before greeting the next relative. She had only come closer on the day Jalal brought home half a dozen chicks Abu Fahmy, a bird-keeper from the encampment, had raised. Their tiny bodies trembled beneath their pale yellow fur. Intisar had held one in her palm, caressed its velvety head. Every morning, she clasped Sundus's hand, and they walked to the chicken coop where she'd arranged a special cubicle for the babies, away from the resident hens, which immediately registered the intruders and cackled their displeasure.

Can I bring one back when we leave? her granddaughter had asked.

No, Sundus had instinctively responded. *This is their home.*

When it was time to return to America, Intisar had been generous with her embrace, the kind of giddy hug you offer when you know you are finally leaving a place you didn't love. The only traces of her granddaughter were the clothes her daughter-in-law had casually draped on their temporary bed. *For the needy of the mokhayam,* Nadira had smiled. *Intisar won't miss them.*

And now here she is, grown into a lovely woman. When one steps back and regards the whole of her face—clouded by anguish and fatigue—you see both of her parents, each vying for dominance, yet somehow harmonious.

"Ya Sitti! What can we do?" her cousin Majida bemoans, inserting herself between Sundus and her granddaughter. She clasps both of Intisar's hands. "May Allah have mercy on his soul."

Intisar nods, wipes her tears on a tissue Majida has offered her.

"This is my cousin Majida," Sundus says.

"Habibti! Ahlan!" Majida coos, kissing Intisar on both cheeks. "Welcome, my dear. We wish it were better times that we meet. But—subhan Allah—your father would have been overjoyed to see you in this house. A hundred welcomes!" She touches Intisar's face and turns to Sundus. "Mashallah she has her father's eyes, does she not?"

"I thought so, too!" Mu'tassem chimes in, grinning, setting down her luggage on the marble floor. "As soon as I saw her."

Sundus blinks away her tears. How much each one of them yearns to be close to Hafez again!

"Come and eat," Sundus says briskly, sorrow threatening to implode inside her. "Yalla. Majida has prepared a pot of her delicious mahshi." Her cousin has spent the morning stuffing zucchini she'd fetched from the souk yesterday. Dearest Majida. She'd insisted on staying with Sundus after the burial, to keep Sundus company at least for a month. When their families fled in '48, Majida's family had crossed the river and resettled in Amman.

This morning, Sundus had sat opposite Majida at the kitchen table, her fingers curled around the aluminum coring tool, ready to pierce the stem of the vegetable, but they suddenly grew numb. It seems the only task she is able to accomplish is under the fig tree in her small vineyard, harvesting the grapes and selling them to the locals. Indoors, she is clumsy and has already broken two glasses and a bowl.

The four of them sit at the dining room table, reserved for special occasions. Like that very first time the imam of Bayt al-Hawa had come to bless their home and feast with them. Or the week Hafez had successfully completed tawjeehi, and his matriculation scores were published in a newspaper in Ramallah. Jalal had roasted a lamb and invited the neighbors to celebrate. Later, he'd hidden his disappointment when Hafez chose to study architecture, and not finance so he could one day take over Jalal's furniture business. His son wanted to design buildings—not tables and chairs. And unlike his father, Hafez would choose to leave Falasteen.

Sundus eats and eats, not realizing how ravenous she is. She has barely been able to put bread to mouth since Hafez passed three days ago. Now the mahshi fills the hollow of her stomach, the tomato sauce temporarily coating her sorrow. She couldn't bear the leftover mensaf, what folks served in times of birth and death. Chewing the zucchini, Sundus thinks she may never again crave that yogurt and lamb stew.

Across the kitchen table, her granddaughter takes a small bite of her mahshi and chews slowly while the others have devoured their second and third zucchini. Sundus studies Intisar. The child has temporarily lifted her attention away from grief, like a wind in the valley carrying away a leaf. The girl is a curiosity. All the softness of a child's face is gone, replaced by angles and lines, dark strands of hair tucked behind her ears. Intisar says little, nodding and keeping her eyes lowered on her plate as Majida and Mu'tassem, between hearty bites, remember Hafez for her.

"He was the best shot," his dear friend boasts. "No one could handle a slingshot like your father." He snaps his good fingers and chuckles. "And cards. Though I suspect he let me win a hand or two to keep me in the game." Mu'tassem's eyes shine.

"Your father loved my hareesa," Majida chimes in. "Not to disparage your grandmother's baking—mashallah—but he had a standing order with me every summer I visited from Amman."

To herself, Sundus remembers how much her dear son craved the crispy layer of maklooba rice at the bottom of the pot, the nearly burnt chunks of potato and cauliflower sticking to the surface. Or how he waited until she was settled at the table, once she had made sure everything was provided for him and his father. And she wants to plant these moments in the garden of memory blooming at the table. But grief swells again in her throat, stifling words.

Tonight, she leaves it to Majida and Mu'tassem to remember the small things for her prodigal granddaughter so Intisar can begin to stitch together the man who was first a son, then a husband and father. A dear friend to Mu'tassem, who sits with them now, his face is full of wonder at the young woman at their table. Perhaps, when the girl is ready, Sundus will unspool more thread for the tapestry, each color revealing the complexity of her son, the hard decisions and sacrifices he made, which meant living without his daughter, putting his country first. Choices Sundus couldn't entirely understand.

Regarding each of them with red-rimmed eyes, Intisar

struggles to smile. Shock and exhaustion etched on her face. Her plate is largely untouched. When Sundus catches Majida's eye, she silently tips her head toward the hallway.

Her cousin nods. "Intisar, habibti, let me show you to your room," Majida says, pushing her chair back from the table. "You must be tired, poor girl."

Shoulders slumped, their guest bids them goodnight and disappears down the hallway.

Mu'tassem smiles wistfully, wiping his mouth with his paper napkin. "Allah yarhamo."

"Allah yarhamo," Sundus echoes. "May the Lord have mercy on his soul."

Mu'tassem reaches across the table and pats her hand. "Don't worry, Hajja. She'll do right by you. After all, she is the daughter of Hafez."

But has his spirit infused hers? Sundus wants to know. The girl might possess his physical features, but what about his love for Falasteen? Does it pump through her heart? Will she come to accept the most powerful token of his sacrifice, this land—al ard? Will she claim and battle for it? And if she turns her back on it? Where does it leave Sundus? She can't fight the case alone. If her granddaughter agrees to sign hisil irth—confirming she is indeed next of kin—they'll have solid ground to stand on. Perhaps an even greater chance of overturning Abdul Waheed's claims.

Her heart clanks in her chest. Though he'd legally purchased the land before they were married, Jalal was denied legal residency after the invasion of '67. And in the absence of their son Hafez, that thief pounced. Sundus purses her lips. What a bitter irony. And now, what rightfully belongs to her family depends entirely on a young woman who is no less a stranger than any other American citizen who might have sat down at her table.

After her cousin Majida wraps a plate for Mu'tassem, he bids them goodnight and promises to return if they need anything. "May Allah bestow his greatest blessings on you, my son," Sundus says before latching the steel door behind him.

She helps her cousin clear the table. The girl has only managed half a mahshi. Sundus scrapes the rest into the garbage bin.

"Maskeena!" Majida cries as she lights a kettle of water. "Poor girl! What a shock this must be for her."

They take their glasses of tea to the barranda and Sundus lowers herself onto the aging glider—her favorite gift from Hafez twenty years ago. Jalal had oiled the bolts as soon as it creaked. Sundus has not minded the noise. It's become a part of the natural soundscape of the hill upon which the villa sits. Crickets fill the silence of the night, along with the rushing wind that gave this village its name: House of Wind. She peers down at the cemetery below, nestled in the valley, the grave markers like restless ghosts. Hafez is among them, where her dearest Jalal and her parents lie. From the opposite western hill, the lights of the settlement watchtower blink at her and Majida as they sip their tea.

Her cousin sits on a cushioned dais Jalal built in his workshop. She gives Sundus a sidelong glance. "Her time here is short. When will you tell her?" her cousin quietly asks.

"Let her settle in," Sundus responds, gliding back and forth, avoiding the other woman's gaze. But Majida is right. Sundus's eyes trace the silhouette of the settlement, houses full of mustawtaneen who are at once her neighbors and trespassers in Bayt al-Hawa. The notary's golden seal flashes across her mind, then Abdul Waheed's snide face: *You'll end up with nothing.*

There is only so much time left to reveal that Intisar is the next steward of this villa and the land that cradles it—whether she likes it or not.

Will it be enough to replace a father?

BAYT AL-HAWA: SEPTEMBER 2007

CHAPTER 5

The trilling of a telephone wakes her the next day. Intisar lifts her head from the pillow, rubs her tear-crusted eyes. Her throat is dry. She reaches for a water bottle on the nightstand, unscrews the cap, and gulps down half of it.

The woman named Majida pokes her head inside the door. "Your mother's on the phone, habibti," she tells Intisar. She points to a pair of rubber slippers. Intisar slides out of bed and follows her down a hallway. The woman is bareheaded, her hair dyed with that homemade henna Teta Rehab uses back home. Mama calls it *a cheap concoction*.

Sunlight filters through arched windows. Is it still morning? How long has she been asleep? Near the bottom of the staircase sits a telephone on a wooden console, a cushioned chair beside it. It's a rather old-fashioned one, a black rotary phone she's only seen in old TV sitcoms. Intisar settles down on the chair and cups the round speaker. "Thank you," she says to the woman beaming at her.

"Come and eat when you've finished," Majida loud-whispers to her.

"Hello? Intisar?" Her mother's voice is an ocean away.

"He's dead," she blurts.

"I know," Mama says. Intisar imagines her mother pinching her lips between her fingers.

She can hear a faucet running, then Mama opening and shutting kitchen drawers. Or is she at the salon, preparing for her clients? Intisar spent her days off from school there, carefully unloading new products and dusting shelves. She loved sorting the tubes of dye that came in numbered boxes with fancy names: *7-43 Medium Blonde/Red Gold, 3-68 Dark Brown/Violet Pearl.*

Before her clients arrived, Mama would sing Arabic ballads, her silky voice filling the salon like warm honey. Later on, Intisar would listen to her mother's clients gossip about marriage and divorce—their own and those of the other women in their community. Sometimes they complained about their sons or daughters, at once blaming themselves for spoiling their children while absolving themselves of the sense of entitlement young people possessed. Intisar wanted to be a good daughter, but it was hard to exude the brightness she'd always felt around her father. Baba had been its source, like the sun for the earth. His leaving cast a permanent shadow over her life; a glumness turned the corners of her mouth downwards. She could never light up a room the way her mother did whenever she entered a space.

Intisar would overhear the clients asking Mama, *What's wrong with her?*

Tee-Tee's shy, was her typical response. *I don't know how—she didn't get it from me.* And the women would laugh again at her mother's clever barb.

"How are you?" Mama is asking now, in that high-octave pitch that pretended everything was fine.

Despite the distance she's felt between them, it's strange to be this far apart from her mother.

"What do you think?" Intisar shoots back, then quickly lowers her voice. "I wish you were here." She wraps the cord around her finger, hating herself for admitting this.

"You'll be fine. Majida sounds nice," Mama offers. "I remember her from that summer we visited." She doesn't ask about Sitti Sundus.

You're lucky she's overseas, Intisar had once heard Mama telling a client who was complaining about marriage meddling. *A long-distance mother-in-law is the best mother-in-law.* And the women had laughed.

Had Sitti Sundus liked Intisar's mother? Or had she wanted someone else for her only son?

When she thought Intisar wasn't paying attention, Mama had called Baba a *Green Card.* As in, *I'd never thought I'd marry a Green Card.* Then over her clients' cackling, *My sisters wanted to have him deported. But I loved him.* This last part had sobered the laughter of the women.

"You won't be there for very long," her mother is saying. "You'll pay your respects and come home."

The sound of rubber slippers slapping against the marble tiles distracts Intisar. It's Sitti Sundus, nodding at her as she passes.

"I have to go," Intisar says into the receiver.

"Drink only bottled water," her mother tells her. "I love you, Tee-Tee."

Intisar hangs up without responding, then feels guilty. She's all alone here. How she wishes Mama could help her navigate this place, untangle her from her confused sadness! But her mother had closed this chapter in her life a long time ago, demonstrating it was easier to excise a husband than a father.

The rift in their marriage began after they returned from their first trip to Palestine. Intisar was an oblivious child. In the apartment, she listened more closely from her bedroom, sitting cross-legged on the carpet, her Barbie dolls strewn around her, her parents' bickering growing sharper and louder:

I won't ever live there, Hafez, her mother had argued. *You promised me.*

She will never know who she is, Baba countered.

She's my daughter, Mama snapped. *An American citizen, like me. What kind of a future would she have there?*

Once the yelling stopped, her father knocked softly on her door though she was expected to keep it open no matter what. He stood in the threshold, his eyes soft and dejected. He smiled sadly at her.

I want to go with you, Intisar had instantly declared, springing from the carpeted floor, her doll tumbling from her lap. She threw her arms around his waist and held on. Wherever Baba was, she would be happy there, too.

Intisar stares at the black telephone, gliding her palms along the wooden arms of the chair. Had Baba sat on this same chair when he'd spoken to her?

The first year he was gone he'd called her once a month. Baba asked her questions about the fourth grade and made her laugh with their old stories of Juha. He'd start a line: *Someone asked Juha, "Why are you so happy and smiling, although you have not found your donkey yet?"* And Intisar would fill in the rest: *And Juha said, "I am happy and smiling because if I had been riding on my donkey I, myself, would have been lost."*

But she could hear something strange in his voice, as if he were about to cry.

Baba's final phone call had been short. His sentences were raspy, as if he'd exhausted all of his words. He'd just been released from prison.

I thank God to hear you, my love. It was a stranger's voice, not the one she remembered from two decades before. It was a voice so absurdly incongruous with everything in Intisar's twenty-six-year-old life. And then silence.

Baba? She'd gripped the cordless phone, her knuckles turning white.

It's me, my darling.

Then her grandmother's voice came on, telling her that her father was too weak to talk any longer, and then the line was disconnected.

She swallows a lump in her throat and heads back to her room. She passes a large clock mounted on a wall, its hands in the shape of peacock feathers telling her it's after two in the afternoon. There's a room, the only one with a closed door. Intisar glances down the hallway. Pots and pans clank in the kitchen. She quietly turns the knob. She's been put in the guest room—there are no personal effects indicating a previous tenant except for a sewing machine in one corner.

But this room is lived in. This room is her father's.

On one wall are pencil sketches of iconic buildings: the Eiffel Tower, the Hagia Sophia, a cathedral whose name she can't summon. She goes to a wooden desk and sits on its matching chair, the legs creaking under her weight. She flips through a sketchbook of her father's work—images of a less steady, less certain hand. On his bed, a beige quilted blanket is neatly spread, two pillows resting against the headboard. There's a 5-x-8 framed photograph of Intisar—at her pageant, the one where that white boy had denied the existence of Palestine. Her stomach flutters as she studies it. Her mother had dabbed her cheeks with a bit of blush, her lips with a shade of pink. Her brown eyes joyfully twinkle at the camera—now a rare expression for Intisar, it seemed.

In the corner of the room, she spots the suitcase he'd brought from America and her throat dries up. She goes to it and lifts it, but it's empty. She looks around the room. Had that photograph been the lone possession of Intisar he'd packed? Had he actually believed he'd return to her and Mama?

Majida calls to her and Intisar noiselessly closes Baba's door behind her.

Back in her room, she finds Sitti Sundus stowing her clothes inside a large cherry-lacquered wardrobe. Intisar's cheeks flush at the old woman folding her cotton panties and padded bras. She eyes her pack of Marlboros sitting on the nightstand next to her flip-phone, a lighter positioned on top. Her grandmother had emptied the pockets of her hoodie and hung it up. Draped over a cushioned chair by a window is a black tunic. Intisar holds it up and runs her thumb over a delicate pattern cross-stitched in red and green across the bodice. She hasn't brought anything black to wear in honor of the mourning period. She'd naively believed there would be time. Time for what? To forgive? To share twenty years of her life Baba had missed, packing them together like an overstuffed suitcase? She blinks back tears, not quite sure it's grief churning in her stomach. It's some kind of loss, a feeling that something's been taken from her though she'd been warned. And now here she is, in the country her father had chosen over her.

Sitti Sundus holds up the picture of Baba that Intisar had brought along. She'd taken it out of her overnight bag. "He is happy," the old woman says in English. "Alhamdullilah." She jerks her chin toward the window, its aluminum blue-painted shutters open, flooding the room in crisp sunlight. "This is our orchard."

So that's where the photograph was taken. Intisar peers outside the window. To the south is a small vineyard forming a canopy over a swath of land.

Her grandmother joins her. She smells of lemons and parsley. Her gray hair is parted down the middle and braided in a single plait that reaches past her stooping shoulders. How old is Sitti Sundus?

She points to the east on the other side of a border wall. "Your father fell into that birr," her grandmother says.

Intisar peers in the distance until she spots the decrepit well. It's partially collapsed, with a pile of reddish-brown bricks on one side of it.

"If it wasn't for Mu'tassem, he might have died," Sitti Sundus adds soberly, as if she's scratched an old wound. She glances sidelong at Intisar. "Did he tell you about that?"

Intisar tries to retrieve this story, sifting through the multitude of compartments in which she's preserved Baba like the album her mother had kept. *He's in there,* Mama had said. Perhaps now Intisar might discover more of him in this place, but nothing comes back about the well.

She blinks back tears and shakes her head, turning away from the window. "I'll get dressed."

"Breakfast is ready for you," the old woman tells her.

After Intisar washes up in a small and tidy adjoining bathroom—her facial soap, deodorant stick, toothbrush, and tube of paste are neatly assembled on the ledge of the sink. For her migraines, a travel-size bottle of Excedrin, which she usually takes around her period, but they can strike at any time. That jarring phone call from Mu'tassim had triggered the most recent one and she woke up the next morning, nearly blinded from the pain. In the mirror, she tugs the skin away from her puffy and tired eyes then splashes cold water on her face. She pulls on a pair of jeans and slides the black tunic over her head and torso. It's a loose, comfortable fit. Her cigarettes are on the nightstand, along with the duty-free carton she bought at the airport, which her grandmother had also unpacked. She snatches up her cigarettes and slides the picture in her back pocket.

The villa looks different in the daylight, a bright glow cast onto everything. Last night is a blur. Today objects come into sharp relief. Antique chandeliers hang from low ceilings in the formal salon. Gold-gilded frames of the Quran are mounted on walls. A gleaming wooden shelf stands in a corner and Intisar examines the spines of dozens of books, her finger gliding over their Arabic titles. She is surprised by one she can make out—a translation of Shakespeare's sonnets.

In the kitchen, her grandmother sips tea at a square wooden table covered by a vinyl tablecloth. Cabinets are painted white with round wooden knobs. On an ochre laminate counter, jars full of pickled turnips and pressed olives are neatly lined alongside a pair of ceramic storage containers—Intisar guesses sugar and flour. Back home, in their newly renovated kitchen, her stepfather Ali detests clutter—this space would be claustrophobic for him. A large mixer and food processor take up a corner of the counter next to a yellow refrigerator. Her grandmother's kitchen is tidy, yet sorely outdated. A toaster oven sits on a console, a basket of root vegetables on its bottom shelf. There's a bowl of golden grapes on the table.

"Salaam a'lakyum," Intisar says respectfully. She remembers her mother's advice: *They have different customs than us. They think we're all spoiled Americans.* Intisar can't picture her mother in this villa, can only imagine her harsh critique, the jokes she'd likely told her sisters after their trip that summer in 1987.

The old woman's gaze settles on the tunic. "It fits," she nods, satisfied.

Intisar pinches the hem of the tunic. "Thank you. It's very pretty."

Sitti Sundus hoists herself up from the table. "You must be hungry. You didn't eat very much last night."

Her grandmother sets a plate of savory pies before her. Intisar takes one stuffed with spinach and sumac. It's delicious—more delicious than the ones her own mother bakes from tubes of Pillsbury instant biscuits. "Bless your hands," Intisar says respectfully. Her Arabic is sound enough to hold a conversation, thanks to her maternal grandmother Teta Rehab. She insisted Mama and her aunts speak only Arabic in her house and demanded the same of her grandchildren, but Intisar's cousins were not forced to attend Sunday school like her. That had been Baba's doing, and it was one of the few things Mama continued to honor after he left.

At Iqbal Mosque outside of Chicago, Miss Sawsan stood at the front of a small classroom, a ruler in her hand, pointing to words on a whiteboard:

صباح /sa-bah/morning
ليل /layl/night
قط/kut/cat

Mama drove her every Sunday morning until Intisar turned fourteen, before academic and extracurricular commitments squeezed out any extra time. She needed the weekend to study and work on projects and attend volleyball away games. Then came the SATs, college applications, and tuition. Mama had set aside the money her father had committed for a dowry: ten thousand dollars—a large sum in 1976. After Baba was arrested and their American marriage was annulled, her grandfather Jalal, a prosperous furniture-dealer according to Baba, had wired eight thousand dollars for the mutakhir—the amount each party had agreed upon if the husband was responsible for the dissolution of the marriage—and an additional two thousand dollars. It was Mama who'd asked for the divorce, coerced by the uncertain circumstances of her husband's detainment.

I never touched a cent of it, her mother boasted to her clients as she rinsed dye from their hair with a faucet hose. *It's all for Tee-Tee.*

And this was true. It was her stepfather Ali who'd helped Mama open the salon.

When the first scholarship award letter came in the mail, her mother fastened it to the refrigerator door. *I'm good at doing hair,* she'd told Intisar. *We were never encouraged to continue to college. But you. You're smart like your father. He*—and then she'd stopped. And Intisar wished the rest of the sentence would come tumbling out, dispensing other interesting and delightful details about Baba like candy into her lap. She knew he'd come to America to build something, to be an architect. His student visa was issued for three years. By his second term, he'd abandoned the University of Illinois in Urbana and came to Chicago where he met her mother. He hadn't built anything. Still he loved architecture, and on his

Sundays off from the gas station where he worked long shifts, he took them on tours of the city, teaching Intisar about its architecture. She loved Marina Towers, two identical structures that looked like gigantic corn cobs. Baba wasn't impressed with the height of skyscrapers like the Sears Tower. With great patience and passion, he talked to Intisar about depth and dimension, aesthetics she was too young to grasp. But she was mesmerized.

It is about how a building make you feel, her father had told her, squatting down beside her on Michigan Avenue and pointing to the white edifice of the Wrigley Building, which overlooked the Chicago River. All Intisar knew about the landmark was what her teacher had told the class on a field trip to the Tribune Tower. It was owned by a chewing gum magnate.

Mama walked behind them and wondered, mostly to herself, how much the building was worth now. Intisar sensed her boredom, but Baba seemed immune. She was the center of his attention when the three of them trekked across the city. Perhaps Mama had heard it all before.

"How is your mother?" Sitti Sundus is asking her.

"She sends her regards," Intisar lies.

There's a flicker of skepticism in her grandmother's smile. "Inshallah her family is well. Your grandmother Rehab and I were schoolmates a long time ago. We weren't close friends. I remember she was first in our class reciting Quran." The old woman jerks her chin at the spread. "Eat up. Before folks arrive."

"Who's coming?" Intisar asks between bites. She's already eying a cheese pie on the plate. There's open-faced bread doused in crushed zaatar and olive oil, and spicy ground beef mixed with minced onions, green peppers, and tomatoes. And freshly cut cucumbers and salted cheese dotted with nigella seeds. For the moment, all Intisar wants to do is eat.

"The neighbors. The women of Bayt al-Hawa. They want to pay their respects," Sitti Sundus sighs, as if she's already exhausted. "And to see the daughter of Hafez."

Intisar sets the spinach pie down on her plate. "To see me?" Heat creeps into her cheeks.

"Do not fret," her grandmother assures her. "They don't bite."

Majida, the old woman's cousin, ambles into the kitchen and stoops at Intisar's side. She holds her face in her hands. "Look at that those eyes of Hafez, mashallah!"

Intisar isn't accustomed to this new appraisal of her face—how her features once belonged to her father. Her mother's side would challenge such claims.

Majida asks, "How's the ikras?" And before Intisar can answer, her grandmother interjects, "Delicious. The meat pies are oversalted, but the dough is airy." Intisar realizes it's not her opinion being solicited. The two women speak over her.

"I warned Um Salih the last time," says Majida, shaking her head.

"It's her new hired hands," Sitti Sundus says. "Fil zaman they were not so heavy on the spices."

Fil zaman. In the old days. A familiar and nostalgic assertion that times were better. Just like the way Baba used to start his childhood stories. *When I was growing up in the old country...*

Outside, the azzan halts their debate. The women's lips move in silent supplication. Intisar watches their faces, eyes closed in deference. She heard the call for prayer last night, moments before she fell asleep. It's hard not to feel like she's stepped into another universe, hearing the man's melancholic voice. She's heard recordings of the Holy Quran, played in a loop at funerals or in her mother's kitchen when she prepared their Ramadan meals, but never alive like this. Everything she's known in the States is a like diluted replica of this country.

"Have you kept wudu?" her grandmother asks Majida.

"Alhamdullilah." They both turn to Intisar.

"I—" she stammers. "Please, don't wait on me."

Intisar watches the retreating backs of the old women, both slightly stooped but strong-footed. She finishes another savory pie and takes her plate and glass of water to the sink. She washes and dries them, sopping up excess water on the edge of the counter. She searches for her sneakers and remembers she'd removed them at the front entrance. Back in the kitchen, she unlatches a turquoise-painted door and steps onto a large patio where hemp-rope stools are assembled.

She breathes deeply. The air, too, is different here—*fresh* is the word that comes to mind. And more than that. It carries the scent of flowers and fruit. The sun shines in a cloudless sky. Intisar pulls out her pack of cigarettes and lights one, throwing furtive glances back at the villa.

If you're gonna smoke, her mother had warned, pointing her cigarette at Intisar, *don't be so public about it. I bet your father won't approve*. Her cousins smoke hookah—the latest trend in their community. And her aunts keep portable ones in their cars. Teta Rehab constantly admonishes them, *There is something salacious about a woman smoking argheelah*. Intisar had tried it a couple of times, but the flavored tobacco gave her headaches.

At the edge of the patio are urns of flowers Intisar doesn't recognize. They are in no particular order, like an informal assembly. She crouches down in front of one that appears to be dying, its tiny leaves scraggly and dry.

Spearmint stalks shoot up from one side of the patio, their sweetly cool fragrance infusing the heat. Sweat beads her forehead. Ahead is an orchard and Intisar walks toward it, descending a few stone steps to where the property appears to drop a level. Grapevines form a wire canopy, a temporary shade. Beneath a large tree, a worn woven mat is spread on the ground. A few empty crates sit beside it. She strolls past, sucking on her cigarette and flicking ashes onto the rocky field. A wind rushes through the trees. She stops and studies one tree, raising her fingers to touch a leafy branch. What kind of fruit did it bear? Had she just missed it?

She drops her cigarette to the rocky ground and crushes it with the tip of her sneaker. She closes her eyes. The rustle of leaves becomes louder. She tries to remember standing in this orchard with Baba. But nothing returns. She pulls the picture from her back pocket and holds it up. Where had it been snapped? She changes direction, facing the villa, but the picture doesn't seem to fit into the greater frame of the orchard.

She imagines her father as a child—*fil zaman*—scampering between the trees. How long before he began dreaming of America?

"Intisar! Ya, Intisar!" A stranger's voice cuts through her reverie.

Intisar quickly slides the picture back into her pocket and cups her eyes in the direction of the voice.

"Here you are!" A woman appears, younger than Intisar, with gorgeous curly hair and hazel eyes. She kisses both of her cheeks and gives Intisar a tight hug. "I'm Lubna! Mu'tassem is my father." She points at the villa. "We live on the other side, across the street." A spattering of freckles stretches across the bridge of her nose. Her smile is contagious, white teeth gleaming at Intisar. Around her neck is a digital camera and a brown leather bag is strapped to her back. She clasps both of Intisar's hands and squeezes them.

Intisar tries to conceal her surprise. "Lubna. It's nice to meet you."

"We're honored to have you here," Lubna gushes, still clasping Intisar's hands. Then her volume drops: "Allah yarhamo, your father. We all loved him." Sincerity shines in her eyes. "He and my father were like this." She crosses her middle finger over her pointer finger and holds them up. "Very, very close." She pulls Intisar in for another embrace. "How very sad for you!" Lubna blurts in English, and it's at once dramatic and endearing. "My family love him too much." She pulls out a pack of cigarettes from her backpack and offers it. Intisar holds up her own pack and they both laugh. And it feels good when her stomach unclenches.

She offers Lubna her lighter. "So you knew my father?"

The young woman nods and her curls bounce in a dark wave. "Before he go to prison." She exhales smoke through her nostrils. "I was very young, but I remember him. He is like brother to my father."

For a moment, Intisar is tempted to slide the picture out again and ask this stranger if she can help orient her in this orchard. Instead she says, "I need to get ready for the guests."

Lubna takes a few more quick puffs before snuffing out her cigarette. She pops a stick of spearmint gum in her mouth. "The house is already starting to fill." She walks beside Intisar, clutching her camera with one hand as they head back to the villa. "I know it is very hard for you," she continues in English.

"I am your friend." She squeezes Intisar's arm as they cross the field. "A new friend," she adds with her expansive smile.

My only friend in this place, Intisar thinks, tears welling in her eyes.

Among a dozen women in the formal salon, Intisar sits between two who chatter merrily over her and intermittently pat her thigh and smile as if remembering she is there. Intisar watches Majida and Lubna serve a series of drinks, beginning with a sugary orange juice. Then black coffee arrives, then honey-colored tea. Platters of golden grapes and wrinkled palm dates—the latter a familiar staple of mourning to Intisar—are set on a large oval coffee table. It is a strange kind of gathering, both a welcoming reception and azza for the deceased.

Intisar hates being the center of attention, yet each attempt she makes to help with the serving is thwarted by cries of protest and the clucking of tongues.

"Laa, laa, laa!" Majida scolds. "By God, you'll not lift a finger, ya Intisar! You're our guest."

And though it's meant in kindness, Intisar's chest tightens. In her father's house, she is like every other woman passing through to pay her respects, then gone.

She studies the walls of the salon, full of black-and-white framed portraits. In one, her grandfather Jalal and her father stand in the orchard where she just met Lubna. In another, her grandmother Sundus is a young woman in a shift dress that hangs above her knees. She stands behind an older couple—Intisar's great-grandparents? On an adjacent wall, she is startled to find a wedding portrait of her parents, her mother in a lacy, long-sleeved dress, wearing a fashionable hat instead of a traditional veil on her head. Her father's in a white tuxedo with an emerald-green bowtie and matching cummerbund. Their wedding day in Chicago. The winter of 1980.

Next to her parents' wedding portrait are photographs of Intisar: a round-faced baby with a chubby body tucked inside a pink ruffled dress. And school portraits, with her head slightly titled, torso straight, and bangs cut straight across her forehead. She smiles with missing teeth. In the last one—third grade—her hair is pulled into high ponytails fastened by yellow ribbons.

She glances around the parlor. Where's the rest of her childhood, her teenage years? None are on display. Had Mama stopped sending her grandmother those 8-x-11 envelopes with the cellophane window? Intisar shudders. It's as if her childhood was put on pause, time suspended after Baba was imprisoned.

Her eyes rove across the opposite wall where several women are crammed on a long sofa, talking over each other. An enormous rendition of the Dome of the Rock hangs in a gold frame. She's seen versions of it in nearly every Muslim household, including her own. Her stepfather Ali had brought one home from a trip to Jordan. He'd spent a few days in Palestine before crossing the bridge again. Intisar hadn't gone to Jerusalem that summer of 1987. According to her mother's account, she developed a horrible case of diarrhea and Mama had refused to leave her. Her father had gone to pray without them and brought back a wooden replica of a camel for Intisar.

Above the frame of the Dome, she notices a few small holes. Were they made by bullets? She feels a pang of fear in her chest, remembering the Qalandia checkpoint, the boy-soldier and his machine gun.

"It was the night those dogs took your father, God rest his soul," the woman on her left tells her, following Intisar's gaze. She juts her chin at the wall and leans in close to Intisar. "Alhamdullilah your grandparents were unharmed."

Speechless, Intisar nods dumbly. She hadn't heard this story. The woman abruptly changes the subject and begins to launch question after question at her. Other visitors join in:

"Are you engaged?"

"Why are you not engaged?"

"A nurse, mashallah!"—and in a sidebar—"So she'll want someone educated, too, no doubt."

"What does she need a man for?" Lubna teases, gathering empty glasses onto a mirror-bottomed tray.

Her mother, a short, slender woman with hands meekly folded across her lap, chides her. "God keep evil from us, girl!"

A pregnant woman seated beside her, chuckles. "And what will we do without our men?"

"Live in peace!" Lubna says. Her camera is back around her neck and she snaps photographs of the women. Intisar automatically shields her face. Her eyes are puffy, and she hasn't applied any of the makeup her mother insisted she pack.

"Bint Hafez can have any man she wants—look at her, mashallah!" the women cluck in agreement, smiling into the Lubna's camera.

They call Intisar *Bint Hafez*. Daughter of Hafez. A designation as heavy as the tray of glasses once filled with amber-colored tea.

Across the parlor, she catches Sitti Sundus watching her. Her grandmother's expression is impenetrable. What does she think of her American-born granddaughter? They are strangers and this is a temporary stay. Just like these guests paying their respects, Intisar will fulfill her duty and leave in ten days. A pang of sadness turns to relief.

"With your permission," she says to the women on cither side of her. She rushes to the washroom, feeling her grandmother's eyes penetrating her back.

In the gilded mirror, she searches her face for her father. A new wave of desolation washes over her.

Who is she if her father is no longer alive to claim her?

GAHANA PRISON: OCTOBER 1993
CHAPTER 6

The lawyer wore a gray suit with a crisp white shirt, her hair pulled into a tight, low bun. Hafez understood her look was an attempt to be taken seriously in spaces dominated by men. Since his arrival at Gahana, he had come to fathom the perpetual violence against women. This young woman—he couldn't decipher her exact age—was sharp and diligent. He saw that from the first moment she sat across from him and withdrew a yellow pad from her messenger bag, already full of copious handwritten notes. In a small room of the prison reserved for official business, Hafez studied her penmanship—tight and precise—saw how she only wrote down his initial and not his full name: ح. This made him feel like a subject, an entity—not a whole being.

Her name was May Boustany. Hafez had known someone called Elias Boustany—a Christian student he'd met at Bir Zeit University. He wanted to ask her if she knew him, but it was much too intimate for this room and it might pierce the new, hardened skin Hafez had grown to make himself impervious to the past. This prison was his eternal present.

"Are you Christian?" he asked instead.

She glanced up from her notepad, gave him a stony look. She wore no makeup, but her eyelashes were naturally thick and curled. "Will it be a problem?"

He shook his head. His face reddened. He hadn't meant to be disparaging. Elias had been an aspiring architect like himself, a fine pupil. But that didn't matter anymore. None of it mattered. He sat across from May Boustany and intended to go through the motions because some outside folks believed he should fight for basic human rights. They'd kept him in solitary confinement for one year, which in itself constituted torture, according to the Geneva Conventions. That's what this young lawyer had explained to him on a telephone call he was granted last month. She'd introduced herself as his representative, authorized by his parents. He'd begun to sweat and gripped the receiver more tightly. Would she ask him about what happened to him inside the Zinzana?

Today May Boustany didn't linger on his broken nose, or the scars on his shaven head where hair no longer grew, or the scraggly beard that had prematurely sprouted white, wiry whiskers. He kept his hands concealed under the table, his damaged fingers clenched into a single fist in his lap. She was here for a specific agenda. "One—" she pointed to the ceiling—"they cannot continue to deny you visitation by closest kin without offering legal reasons. Two—" she lifted another finger—"Commissary rights."

Hafez felt a flutter in his chest. "Can I get some paper and pencils?" He considered the more expensive items his cellmates were permitted to have. He'd been aching to sketch as stagnancy and boredom cloaked his days.

She nodded, her lips in a straight line. She licked her thumb and flicked through several lined pages. "The commissary is the easier of the two."

The flutter turned to a quivering in his chest as Hafez imagined a pencil between his finger and thumb, creating and recreating. He'd been doing this with an invisible one as he stared at the ceiling from his bunk, his vision penetrating the ugly concrete to the intersecting beams and rafters. Then he allowed his mind to roam back to the places he'd been in Chicago: the historic Water Tower and the Rookery, where stairs spiraled into infinity. And places he'd once hoped to see someday like the Eiffel Tower. Now these visions were confined to his mind like his body was confined to this prison.

"Would you like me to send a message to her?" the young lawyer was asking him.

"Who?"

"Your daughter."

"My—Intisar?" His daughter's name clamored in every chamber of his heart. He hadn't dared say it out loud in this place.

May Boustany held her pen against her notepad as if it were buttressing all of her weight. "Would you like me to convey a message to her? I was under the impression your ex-wife has made communication difficult with your parents. I can try to..."

Her words trailed off in his ears. His former life began to bead like tiny droplets of blood. The lawyer had unknowingly inflicted a cut on Hafez's new skin. His face and neck flushed hot. Intisar would be turning twelve this month. Three years he'd been absent. He pictured her on the last day he'd seen her. She'd come home from school, backpack bouncing behind her, begging to accompany him to the airport. He was taking a connecting flight from New York to Copenhagen.

Please, Baba, I want to come with you! she'd whined in his arms. His wife had stood by, arms folded across her chest.

You can say your goodbye here, Nadira instructed their daughter. She'd given Hafez a suspicious look as if he were plotting to kidnap Intisar. Deep down, she was right to be nervous. He'd have taken his little girl back with him to Bayt al-Hawa, replanting her American roots in the soil of her native people. She was Falasteeniya, like him, no matter where she was born.

"Would you like me to send her a message?" May Boustany was asking him again.

What could a single message contain? How could it possibly carry everything he wanted her to know? To tell her that he loved her wasn't adequate when he could no longer show her. Did she remember their tours of Chicago and the constellations they'd admired from the courtyard of the apartment building?

And would she ever know how terribly sorry he was that all of it had suddenly stopped? How could he explain that Falasteen was calling him back? He'd returned home if only to quiet, once and for all, the screams that gutted his dreams. To erase the blood gushing from his grandfather's neck, and the wicked red flower that had bloomed across his grandmother's dress.

He hadn't told anyone about that day—not even his wife. He'd felt complicit, a child-witness to that horrific moment that would define him in irrevocable ways. Yes—he'd survived. And what had he done with his life? He'd been greedy, snatching a future in which he could dwell in safety and freedom.

But his shame and guilt was the bedrock of his existence. He could never be truly free when others had lost so much—starting with a cherished home, the one he'd seen with his own eyes as a young man.

In the spring of 1976, he'd driven his father's car to Haifa with his best friend Mu'tassem. He was determined to glimpse the house in his mother's stories.

Because they were enrolled at Bir Zeit, they'd miraculously secured half-day visas. They'd rode along the coast, stopping to dip their feet in the sea.

When they arrived at the stone-brick house, the first thing Hafez noticed was a large bougainvillea bush on the side of a short path to the blue-door entrance. Its branches climbed to a low window, its purple leaves like the striking florid feathers of a bird. That was before the owner stepped out, shouting in Hebrew and disrupting the quiet of the neighborhood street. He'd spat in Hafez's face.

Then a bloody cleaver flashed across his mind, a vision of his friend shrieking in agony. Hafez clenched his eyes shut and tightened his balled hands in his lap. For the second time in his life, he'd been a bystander as someone else was slaughtered. He was incapable of fighting back, paralyzed by fear.

But what others couldn't see was that he, too, had sustained a wound, a secret one that throbbed inside of him. A wound that perpetually festered and stank. It oozed shame and terror and powerlessness.

Everyone had given up something. Was his life worth more than others?

He'd finally give up the only thing equal to his own life. His daughter.

"Hafez?"

He shook his head at the lawyer.

May Boustany nodded and gave him a sad smile. "If you change your mind, let me know." She tapped her pen against her notepad. "Inshallah khair," the young woman said.

Back in his cell, Sadeeq rushed to him with a pack of cards, nervously rubbing the back of his head with his free hand.

Except for Abu Jadallah, Hafez was the only one Sadeeq permitted to be close to him. They sat facing each other on prayer rugs. Hafez was teaching the man how to play hend, a game everyone knew but Sadeeq had forgotten. His battered body was like a half-empty vessel being refilled with joy. It had been weeks since they'd snatched Sadeeq from his cot in the middle of the night. Lying on his own top bunk, Hafez had stopped breathing, terrified they were coming for him. He'd broken out in a cold sweat, crossed his arms, and turned over, trying hard not to make a single sound.

When Sadeeq returned from the Zinzana and was tossed back into their cell, he'd kissed a tattered photograph of his mother someone had smuggled in for him. Like Hafez, he was permanently denied visitation.

Alhamdullilah, Yamma, I am here, do not fret over me. I am still here.

To the other cellmates, this was a degrading display for a man who was over forty years old, though Sadeeq could no longer remember the date of his birth. He tugged at the gray whiskers on his chin as he studied his photograph, his shoulders stooped like a bent spoon.

Alhamdullilah, Yamma, Sadeeq had cooed at the image, the edges of the photograph curling, a white slash across the middle like a bolt of lightning had struck it. *I am still here.* Then he commenced to crushing it in his fist, before quickly smoothing it out again, regretful tears plopping down on the photograph.

According to Abu Jadallah's account, Sadeeq had been accused and convicted of killing five yahood at a popular beach resort in Eliat. It was the summer of 1980. In Chicago, Hafez recalled watching the nightly news with Nadira, who was five months pregnant. A young, handsome anchor named Peter Jennings was reporting on *ABC World News Tonight.* An American tourist had been among the dead. Sadeeq's accomplices remained at large; some claimed they'd escaped to Lebanon or Libya—maybe Europe. Sadeeq had vaguely listened to Abu Jadallah tell the story as if it were about someone else.

Even after fifteen years, his jailers were relentless. Their bottom line: each and every Falasteeni assailant would be found. Dead or alive. And yet no conclusive evidence had been found to link Sadeeq to that day.

Hafez felt a deep pity for Sadeeq. His shrieks woke the men when he was dragged out of his cot in the middle of the night, turning to pitiful whimpers down the walkway. Still, the man would not confess.

And so the rampage of poor Sadeeq continued like any cruel sport played by ruthless men. And still he would not confess. He was like the damaged photograph he clutched. The only sounds escaping his lips were indecipherable cries of anguish before a rag was stuffed deep into his mouth. From his top bunk, Hafez clamped his hands over his ears as they dragged Sadeeq away.

On the crushed-velvet mat, Hafez shuffled the deck of cards and began dealing. Nijmy stood behind Sadeeq, closely inspecting his cards. He raised his eyebrows in approval or turned his mouth downwards at a bad draw.

"Your turn," Hafez advised Sadeeq.

Nijmy squatted down, hovering over the other man's shoulder. "Hold onto that." He flicked the corner of Sadeeq's card. Sadeeq instinctively pulled his limbs together, folding himself in.

"Leave him be," Hafez said. "He's getting it."

"Getting it, my ass," Nijmy jeered. "He'll forget in a minute."

"Bas, yabni!" Abu Nasser admonished his son. "Let him enjoy it. It's just a game." His older son, Nasser, was preparing tea from a portable hot plate. He poured the piping liquid into a chipped glass. The sons took turns in this ritual of serving their father.

Hafez discovered that the older tenants of the cell had earned privileges such as the hot plate and the transistor radio. Abu Jadallah also boasted a small, gold-embossed copy of the Quran and a short published stack of the Prophet's teachings. He arranged them inside an old cardboard box. A label in Hebrew advertising canned peaches was partially peeled off on one side.

The other men spoke as if Sadeeq was deaf or a child. Hafez was a patient teacher and Sadeeq eventually won a round.

"Only a parent can be so patient," Abu Jadallah said in a praising tone. Abu Nasser concurred.

"Queen of hearts, queen of hearts," Sadeeq revealed at one point.

"Keep it to yourself, you dummy!" Nijmy chided him.

"Queen of hearts, queen of hearts!" Sadeeq held it up triumphantly for Hafez to see.

"Azeem," he praised the man.

Nijmy shook his head. "He's hopeless." But even this was offered cheerfully, for today was visiting day and the other men were in good spirits. Nothing could dampen the mood.

When the alarm sounded—a terrible wailing horn—Abu Jadallah and Abu Nasser and his two sons quickly got to their feet, straightening their ugly brown uniform shirts. Pairs of guards appeared outside their cell and directed a single-file formation down the walkway. Hafez and Sadeeq paused their game to watch them file out. The steel-barred door clanged shut and Hafez began another round, instructing Sadeeq to return his cards to the deck.

The quiet in the cell was unsettling on these days. Hafez rose from the floor between rounds and tuned the radio on the window ledge. A transmission cut through loud and clear:

"...and twenty days since his illegal confinement. We pray for justice for our son." It was a scratchy voice, as if the man's throat had been scraped with a razor.

In the beginning, Hafez hated hearing the messages from the loved ones of incarcerated men languishing in prisons across Israel. It had filled him with an exquisite dread. The transmissions were one-sided, and several men from the other floors of the compound who'd also been denied visitation shouted gleefully if their name was mentioned. In spite of himself, Hafez listened closely as he shuffled the deck, imagining one day hearing the adolescent voice of his daughter and how much it would have changed in a few years.

Sadeeq rubbed his head. With Hafez's help, he learned how to handle his cards in a one-handed fan. He, too, seemed to be listening to the radio.

The next message came from a woman, loud and robust: *"For the prisoner Majeed Abdul-Rasool, son of Mohammad and Haleema, brother to Wajee and Sabah. Ya habibi, yamma! We remain samideen, by the will of God. One day you'll be liberated, the terrorists of the Occupation will pay. Habibi, yamma, your father is well and sends his blessings..."*

"Habibti, Yamma!" Sadeeq murmured, his large hand like a paw sliding over his skull. "I'm still here."

BAYT AL-HAWA: SEPTEMBER 2007

CHAPTER 7

She studies her granddaughter's profile, wants to reach out and touch the girl's hair, curl a dark strand around her finger. Instead, Sundus clasps the rim of an empty reed basket and steadies it on her hip. Her granddaughter does the same with another basket and follows her beneath the dawali. Intisar, having changed out of the black tunic, wears a lighter blouse with short sleeves. Their visitors are gone and Sundus can return to her grapes. Her granddaughter follows behind her as she stops to shear the stem of a bunch from a vine. It's the last of the season; most was harvested before the girl arrived. If she stays long enough, she'll have loquats and figs.

The late afternoon is bright and warm, the sky clear of clouds.

"You sell these grapes?" her granddaughter asks, breaking the silence between them. She transfers the half-full basket to her other hip.

"I do," Sundus says and thinks for a moment. "This is my thirty-fourth harvest, by the will of God." Does the length of time she's tended the land matter to her granddaughter? Will it convince her to take on the case? She promised her cousin Majida she would discuss the matter as soon as possible. In spite of the urgency, the timing isn't quite right. She searches for a spark of longing in her granddaughter's demeanor—can she feel this earth beneath them calling to her? But the child strolls as if she's on an excursion, oblivious.

Sundus sets her basket down and breaks off a cluster. She splashes it with water from a bottle she's tucked under the belt of her thobe and holds it out. "Eat."

Intisar steadies her basket under one arm and reaches for the dripping grapes. She snaps a golden bulb into her mouth with her thumb. "Wow," she says in English between chewing. "Delicious."

Sundus smiles. "Your father was almost five years old before the first grapes appeared. You know? As he grew older, he helped the migrant workers harvest each season. They taught him to roll cigarettes and your grandfather Jalal caught him by that old well, smoking and hacking." The memory releases a tautness under her skin, like one tin plate on her scale has come free of its black metal disc. An unfettered chuckle rises up from her throat.

Her granddaughter seems to absorb the story, a smile tugging at the corners of her mouth.

Sundus leads her back to the fig tree where she signals for her granddaughter to transfer the grapes to a clean towel she's laid out.

Intisar waves her hand over the field. "How long have you lived here, Sitti?" She settles beside Sundus on the rug.

"More than forty years, which is most of my life," Sundus says, sorting through the grapes and gently shaking each bunch to check for spiders or beetles. "I was born in Haifa. Came to

Bayt al-Hawa after we fled. We escaped in the middle of the night." She glances sidelong into the girl's face for a flicker of familiarity, but Intisar's expression is merely one of wonder. Her son's words echo in her ears: *Tell her where she comes from.*

Sundus gazes in the distance, past the saha and through the villa. She can see her father's old black Ford in the carport. "We could barely see the road ahead." How quickly she's swept back there, seated between her pregnant mother and Um Amjad, her best friend's mother. Memory swallows her up like that night had swallowed up the distance on the road between them and their home by the sea.

"They'd sent me to bed early so they could plan," Sundus tells her granddaughter. Her parents' hushed voices come back, trailing the breeze through the branches of the fig tree they sit under.

Her father sat in his chair, folding over a page of *Filastin.* "They're attacking the eastern villages, ya Wajeeha. And this paper's two weeks old." He rolled a cigarette from a silver case he kept on the mantel. He only smoked one cigarette a day, after dinner, but this was already his third of the evening. The scent of tobacco was sweet and pungent.

Sundus sat on the floor of the liwan, a book open in her lap. She stopped munching a slice of bread spread with molasses. They'd acquired two large jars from a carob tree farmer in Ayn Hawd—payment for her father adjusting the dislocated shoulder of the farmer's son. Sundus would eat the dibis right out of the jar if her mother would let her. Their pantry was full of bartered good. Jugs of olive oil from Ijzim, tobacco from Abu Shusha, dried fish from Qisarya. And now Sundus wondered if those villages had been the ones attacked according to her father's reports. Where did the inhabitants go? What had they carried with them?

She remembered the riots at the oil refinery. Her father had been gone for days, treating the injured at the hospital. *It's a horror,* she'd overheard him telling her mother, believing she was asleep. *There was only so much I could do. God help their families.*

"Um Husni says we should sail to Akka and wait it out," her mother said, leaning against the kitchen sink, one hand propped on her pregnant belly, the other holding a dish towel.

"That's where everyone will be headed. The roads might be too crowded," her father said. "It's not the safest way for you to travel. But, don't worry, habibti, I'm making arrangements."

Sundus thought of Amjad: *I'll take care of you.* Did men and boys have no fear? Is that why they fought wars? But she wondered which required more strength, shooting a man or repairing his blasted body as her father did?

"The important thing is to be ready at a moment's notice," her father added.

"How can one ever be ready for war, ya Yousef?" her mother said, her eyes shining with tears.

The next night, Sundus lifted the veil from the bird cage and through tears said goodbye to Sim-Sim. It fluttered its wings when she inserted her finger in his cage, but the bird wouldn't come close.

Her father stood behind her, his hands resting on her shoulders.

"But you said we're coming back, Yabba," Sundus whimpered, refusing to wipe away the snot dripping from her nose, a declaration of her discontent.

"Yes, we are, but it might be too long for poor Sim-Sim," her father said.

They took the cage to the saha and she unlatched the clasps on the dome.

"Yalla, Sim-Sim," her father coaxed the bird. It roved back and forth on its wooden perch, unsure whether to cling or fly away. He inserted his finger and it finally hopped on.

"Ma asaalama!" her father said as the bird flitted away. Through teary blurred vision, Sundus watched it soar over the loquat tree until it was absorbed by the inky sky.

It was close to midnight. Her father and Abu Husni, Amjad's father, loaded the trunk of the Ford and tied the rest of their belongings to the roof. Amjad sat between the men in the front; Sundus mirrored him in the back seat between the women. She lay her head inside the crook of her mother's left arm.

A few of their neighbors—the Abdul Haleems and the Al-Najjars—had decided to wait out the conflict, refusing to leave their homes—even those with automobiles. On the road, the Ford passed a horse-drawn carriage with people clinging to their stacked belongings and each other. Sundus craned her neck to see if any of them were children.

She pressed her doll against her chest, its plastic limbs stiff and unyielding. She wanted to toss it on the floor of the car, then immediately felt sorry and held the doll in her lap, twisting the legs into a sitting position. Its lifeless eyes fluttered with every bump on the road.

"How far, Yamma?" Sundus whispered. She'd been practicing being quiet as she had been instructed. She wanted to be brave for her baby sister—she was convinced it would be a girl. Amjad was a boy and her best friend—and now there'd be another girl in their family. *A sister is a very special kind of sibling,* her mother had told Sundus. *Inshallah khair.* Her mother had two sisters, Khalti Azeeza and Khalti Kowthar. They had already fled over the bridge of the Jordan River. She might never see her cousin Majida again. She was the closest to a sister Sundus had ever had. At least until her mother gave birth.

I won't mind if she's a boy, Sundus had said, when she gently pressed her hand on the firm bump that had started to form in her mother's belly. She hoped she wasn't tempting fate. Her mother had laughed at her concession, her brown eyes twinkling down at her.

Now her mother kissed the top of Sundus's head and tucked strands of her hair behind her left ear. "Try to sleep, habibti. It's a long way."

Sundus shut her eyes, listening to the tires of the Ford crunching along the gravel roads, as it snaked up hills and down wadis. Was Amjad asleep, or only pretending like Sundus? Her mother had packed dried figs and apricots, khubuz and salted cheese, from which Sundus always secretly picked out the black nigella seeds. She'd helped her mother wrap these foods in wax paper and store them inside a wicker basket they took to the beach. The basket was positioned directly beneath Sundus's feet and she was tempted to reach for a fruit preserve when her mother's eyes fluttered closed. But she didn't wish to disturb her slumber.

The car's headlights cut a dusty ribbon across the darkness. Sundus wondered how her father could drive at night, shutting one of her own eyes and assessing how quickly her peripheral vision disappeared like flicking off a light switch. He leaned his body forward, clutching the steering wheel with both hands as Abu Husni helped navigate. Sundus could see Amjad's head tilting toward his father—a sign he was sleeping. They were following the rail line southeast to Jinin and the mountains slowly fell behind them.

Sundus's mother shifted, slipping her arm away from her and softly grunting as she massaged her belly. Hours earlier, her mother had silently wept as they gathered and loaded their belongings. Sundus marveled at such a delicate display of tears, so unlike the loud, undignified sobbing she'd displayed when her father liberated Sim-Sim. Only at the prospect that she and Amjad would be together as he'd promised did Sundus gather her composure and told herself to be brave.

It will be an adventure, ya Sundus, Amjad had said, his brown eyes gleaming. He'd been helping his mother prepare, carrying a suitcase and his school satchel. He'd emptied his copybooks and primer, replacing them with *The Adventures of Tintin* comic books Sundus had received from the professor and in turn had gifted her friend. In one of them, called *Les Cigares du Pharon*, all the Egyptian men had enormous noses and the women wore black veils with only their eyes showing, black marbles inside jarring whites. Amjad had narrated the stories despite not speaking French, which had impressed Sundus. Soon, they'd be home again, finishing their playhouse under the loquat tree.

Sundus had finally fallen asleep when a cracking *drrrrr* jolted her awake. She'd never heard gunfire before, an awful sound that pierced the night sky. Amjad woke too, rubbing his eyes and scoping his surroundings.

"Is it yahood, Yabba?" he asked, his voice quaking with something Sundus hadn't heard before in her friend. His head and shoulders were engulfed in shadow.

"Don't be afraid, yabni," Abu Husni said.

But it wasn't enough for Sundus. She needed to hear it from her own father, but he seemed to be concentrating hard on the road, never slowing.

"It came from the west," was all he said. "We must keep pushing as far as we can before daylight."

Sundus burrowed her face in her mother's arm. Her mother was strong, too, in a different way from her father. She was instinctive, determined, and ever-present. Once Sundus had fallen from a tree and hit the back of her head against a jagged rock. A gash opened and she nearly fainted when her fingers came away bloody from the wound. She'd instantly forgotten everything her father had taught her. She mustered a shriek and her mother came running. She carried Sundus to the saha, instructed her to sit up straight on a hemp-rope stool and then disappeared inside. Her mother returned with a bowl of qahwa, the aroma of cardamom rising and temporarily soothing Sundus. She watched her fill her palm with the ground coffee beans before pressing it firmly against Sundus's head, stemming the flow of blood. Her mother's hand cradled her head like a baby.

Later that day, her father had examined the wound and cleaned it with an antiseptic. *Your mother might have been a great nurse if she hadn't married me*, he boasted, winking at Sundus.

Now she felt for the spot at the back of her head concealed by strands of her dark brown hair. She reached for her mother's hand, the one that had healed her, but her mother was pushing her away. A sudden wetness touched Sundus's thigh as if a glass of water had spilled on her.

"Akh!" her mother groaned, hugging her belly. "Yousef!"

"Hatem! Wakif!" Um Husni shouted. "Stop the car, Hatem!"

Her mother's grunts sliced through Sundus's stomach. She fought back her own tears, wanting to be brave for her mother.

"Khair inshallah." Um Husni reached over her and patted her mother's forehead. "I think it's coming," she called over the seat.

Sundus's father pulled off the road and the men scrambled from the car. Sundus crawled over Um Husni, giving her mother space to recline across the back seat. Um Husni cradled her mother's head in her lap. *La howla walla koowat ill billah.* But the supplication did nothing to tamp down Sundus's fear.

"Is the baby coming?" Amjad asked her, for the first time looking to her for an answer to a matter that he did not understand.

Sundus vehemently shook her head. "She needs more time to grow," she said, trying hard to sound confident. "It's too early. My father said we'd meet the baby in June." Two months away.

Her mother's whimpers grew into yelps of pain, piercing the quiet of the land. Sundus looked around, straining her eyes against a hill in the distance. A small acacia bush scratched her leg. For a moment, she worried about scorpions. A boy at school had died from a poisonous bite before her father could reach him. It had been lurking in a laundry basket his mother had told him to carry inside. Amjad had taught Sundus how to suck out the poison in case no one was around. He'd demonstrated on his forearm, pinching a small patch of skin then bringing it to his lips. Now she stood perfectly still, careful not to disturb her surroundings until she could climb back into the Ford.

"Stay right here," Abu Husni commanded them.

Sundus could not see much; all she could hear were voices and her mother's yelps of pain. Without thinking, she grabbed

Amjad's hand and he laced his fingers through hers. They remained hushed.

"It's coming," her father announced in a strained voice. It was the same tone Sundus had heard when she'd accompanied him in the countryside, like the time a villager's foot had turned gangrenous and her father's jaw tightened. *It will need to be amputated.* His words never faltered, wrapped in a harsh reality of few to no choices at all. The villager's tearful wife had taken Sundus away but she could still hear the screams. "Listen to me, Wajeeha. You must bear down," her father was now instructing her mother.

"No, Yousef!" her mother screamed. "It's too early!"

"Listen to the doctor," Um Husni coaxed.

Sundus shuddered as she caught flashes of her father's perspiring forehead. Then something appeared in his hands, a chord dangling from it. It was the size of a baby rabbit. But there was no tiny, indignant cry.

"Allah yarhamo," Um Husni said, tears streaming down her cheeks. "Let me have him. He's gone to our Lord, ya Wajeeha."

Her mother's wailing momentarily drowned out a round of gunfire in the distance. Abu Husni darted in front of the Ford. Something glinted in his hand. He was on his knees and Sundus watched him digging with a small pocketknife. Amjad ran to his father's side, grabbed a jagged rock, and helped Abu Husni.

Sundus remained frozen in place, paralyzed by her mother's wailing. Her brain could not grasp what was happening around her and she felt herself slipping away, like being tossed on a wave of the sea. It left her cold and scared.

"Wajeeha, let him go," her father was saying, his voice breaking.

Let who go? Sundus wondered as her heart pounded in her ears. The baby? Had she arrived? But it was too soon.

Um Husni climbed out of the car and went around to where her father was ducked inside the passenger seat, his arm extended. Finally, her mother relinquished the tiny, slimy figure into her father's hands, and he quickly wrapped it inside her shawl. He walked slowly to where Amjad and his father were working and stood over them, the fringes of the shawl fluttering in the night breeze.

Sundus couldn't unroot her feet until the moment her father passed the bundle to Abu Husni, who recited Quran as he gently laid it in the fresh hole. Then she ran to him and threw her arms around his waist. Her father was tall and lean. He lifted Sundus up and she whispered in his ear, not wanting to look at the hole and what was buried in it.

"Is that our baby?"

But it was too soon. The creature her father held had not been perfectly formed, the slick chord like the intestine of a small lamb she'd once seen butchered in the countryside on eid.

Her father trembled against her and her cheeks became wet with his tears. She gripped his shoulders, terrified.

"*We belong to Allah and to Him shall we return,*" Abu Husni recited while her father wept.

Another round of gunfire pierced the night and her father put her down. "We must carry on. Before day breaks." He wiped his face with his handkerchief.

They returned to the car. Um Husni was wiping down her mother's thighs with water from a canteen. She used strips from the white sheet they'd used to protect their belongings. The inside of the car had a sickly smell of iron and sweat. Sundus caught sight of something from between her mother's legs, purplish-red and wet like a creature from the sea. It was a flattened clump that Um Husni quickly gathered up and wrapped inside of a soiled sheet before throwing it as far as she could across the desolate land.

"Leave me here with him. In the name of God, leave me here." Her mother's voice was cracked and hollow.

Her father kissed her mother's forehead and ordered everyone into the car. Sundus was relegated to a window seat as Um Husni patted a wet cloth against her mother's flushed face. Her hair was damp, as though her mother had just washed it and was getting ready to set it in those prickly curlers like she did every Thursday night. She cried into Um Husni's bosom as the other woman gently tucked strands away from her mother's face.

Her father sat in the passenger seat. Abu Husni had insisted on driving for a few hours. Amjad's head bobbed in the center.

"My son is dead. They killed my son," Sundus heard her father say, in a voice that was dazed and not his own. "My son is dead."

The chilling words rang and rang in Sundus's ears.

"Hajja!" someone is calling from the saha. A pair of young girls skip down the stone steps.

Sundus wipes her hand over her face as if the memory is like sweat. She turns to her granddaughter with eyebrows furrowed—the same rapt expression her dear Hafez had possessed.

"My God," Intisar breathes.

The young girls approach them. "Three kilos of red, Hajja," the shorter one says.

"Mama said green." The taller one nudges her sister, though she appears to be the subservient one. They are from the mokhayam. Their feet are dusty, their jeans tinged yellow from lack of washing.

"Which is it then?" Sundus demands, flicking a nylon bag open.

"Red," the shorter one says decisively.

Both girls admire her granddaughter, smiling eagerly at her. "Have you come from America?" the shorter one asks.

As if just noticing them, Intisar shifts on the rug, tucks a strand of hair behind her ear, and nods.

"Why have you come here?" the taller one asks.

Her granddaughter is silent, looking down at her folded hands in her lap.

Sundus fishes into the chest panel of her thobe and extracts a drawstring bag full of shekels. She exchanges their paper bill with a few coins. "Here you are. Go straight home and don't talk to strangers."

"I'm not afraid of anyone," the shorter one asserts before they run off.

May the Lord protect them, Sundus prays.

Another customer descends the stone steps. It is Um Farris. "Welcome home." The woman smiles at Intisar, revealing a gold incisor. "Say hello," she says, nudging her child, who's been charged with holding a mesh bag.

"Salaam," the little boy offers begrudgingly, his eyes fixed on the newcomer seated beside Sundus.

"Mashallah, bint Hafez is lovely!" the woman gushes. "Allah yarhamo your father," she quickly adds.

Sundus adjusts the scale again and lays three bunches on one side. The little boy hands her a mesh bag and Sundus drops them inside. "Allah be with you," she bids them.

"I—I never heard that story," her granddaughter stammers, not looking at Sundus.

"There's much you probably don't know, ya sitti," Sundus says, her words laced with sympathy and bitterness. "And only what you've been told. Your father thought he had more time. He loved this place." Sorrow prickles her heart like the thorny stem of a rosebush after its fragrant blossom has withered. *Yalla! Tell her now,* a voice urges her. *Tell her this land is now hers.* It is the perfect moment, and yet the words still won't come. How can her granddaughter simply earn it by default, without all of its attendant history, its pain and joy, its loss and triumphs? Sundus's pridefulness swells hot like the sun above them. Not once did Intisar ever come to spend time with them. Her father may have been locked away, but Sundus and Jalal were still here. Sundus's mother, too, had waited. And now it seems too late. She turns away, hides her tears in the sleeve of her thobe.

"You never went back?" Intisar is asking, though it sounds more like a demand, an accusation. "I mean to that place where the baby—"

"No." Sundus's lips wrap firmly around the word, its definitiveness. "How could we? It was too dangerous."

"And what about your bayt in Haifa?"

Sundus hears the desperation in her granddaughter's voice, recognizing the immediate need to separate oneself from tragedy. To be less complicit in hearing such a story.

The azzan sounds. Sundus replaces the scale in the burlap sack and covers the remaining grapes in a crate. "Your father drove there with Mu'tassem. In 1975, they were young men. We hadn't any idea of their plan to return to the bayt of my parents—Hafez's grandparents."

"And what happened?" her granddaughter asks in a quivering voice.

"It was very bad." Sundus recalls Hafez's expression—stark-white. His best friend's hand bleeding through the shirt Hafez had been wearing that day. A failed tourniquet. The surgeon at the hospital in Ramallah could not save his severed fingers. Those cursed thieves. The ones who'd stolen their bayt in Haifa had attacked him with a cleaver. Mu'tassem had challenged the irate man, shouting at him that the house was not his.

"That's how he lost his fingers?" Intisar's eyes are wide like a child.

She instinctively pats her granddaughter's hand. "He could have been killed, habibti. But your father could never forgive himself for that day."

She watches as her granddaughter absorbs the weight of what she's just heard, the details slumping her shoulders, as if Sundus has just handed her a heavy bundle to carry.

BAYT AL-HAWA: 2007

CHAPTER 8

Lubna hands Intisar a helmet and she tucks her hair inside it. The young woman—her new friend—prattles on about the tour she's planned. Today, she's offered to take Intisar around Bayt al-Hawa, but all Intisar can see ahead of them on the street leading away from her grandmother's villa is a dead baby on the side of the road. She couldn't get rid of it last night, the image lurking behind her lids each time she shuts her eyes.

Lubna points down and says something Intisar can't hear over the motor. A wind whistles past her head as they curve down into the valley. The sun bakes her back and arms beneath her peasant shirt.

Had she heard the story before and simply forgotten? No. How could an awful story like that not have taken root in her brain, sprouting like a weed over the course of her life? Baba must have kept it from her—she was too young to know such a thing. Instead, he'd filled her imagination with stories of his blissful childhood and silly folktales.

Once, he'd explained how Palestinians had lost their land after World War II. His history was nothing like the ones in her school textbooks, with their illustrations of bold US soldiers freeing countries from tyranny. Even the Native Americans whose lands were stolen could claim heroes like Geronimo and Sitting Bull. But she hadn't heard about any legends from her ancestral country. Palestinians were called terrorists on the news and by the school bullies—never were they called resistance fighters or revolutionaries or heroes.

On the walls of the Markaz, the Arab community center in Chicago where Baba first spotted Mama, Intisar had stared at posters of a smiling Yasser Arafat and a more pensive Leila Khaled. Both were holding up two fingers in victory or peace—depending how you looked at it. But even their images hadn't evoked a sense of pride in young Intisar, only an inexplicable fear of a menacing force, one which even the machine gun strapped across that woman's slender body could never vanquish.

It had started with *a bad Englishman*, as Baba had told her, conjuring in Intisar's mind the character of Ebenezer Scrooge from an illustrated version her teacher read before their winter break. But her father was pointing to the pages of another book called *The Palestinians*, full of black-and-white photographs of men, women, and children huddled on a dusty road, some in horse-drawn carts, most on foot. It had been written by two white men.

And they never went back? a wide-eyed Intisar had asked, her chest filling with a dread she was too young to articulate.

Baba had shaken his head. *They dreamed of their homes. Many held onto their door keys,* he'd told Intisar, his voice solemn in a way she didn't hear when he read her other books. *And this is why one day we'll go back*, he'd added.

Intisar had looked up at him, surprised. He, too, seemed startled by this promise, as if it had been lurking near the surface of his lips and just then he was sure enough to utter it.

Later on, she'd asked her mother about this and Mama had snapped at her. *We're not going anywhere. Your Baba didn't mean it.*

And then more bickering. Her father insisting how important it was for Intisar to know her roots, to spend time with her people.

Her people are right here, her mother had countered.

She remembers that single suitcase Baba had packed for himself. It sat at the end of the hallway for a week, taunting Intisar. If she could only hide it, he'd stay longer. When no one was looking, she tried to lift it. But it was too heavy for her.

It's one thing to visit, Hafez, but I'll never live there, her mother had said, arms folded across her chest. *That was never a possibility.* To Intisar, it had sounded like a contract her father was trying to break.

Had Baba ever told Mama about the dead baby—a boy who, if he survived, would be Sitti Sundus's brother—Intisar's great-uncle? Was that the reason her grandmother had remained an only child, and Baba her only child, as Intisar was his?

Her father's version of Palestine had grown into a vaguely familiar one Intisar could weave into all the other ones she and her American-born cousins had heard their whole lives. But never had she encountered a story like her grandmother's. A woman burying her unborn on the side of a road she'd never travel again.

As the wind rushes her face, Intisar clenches her eyes shut and a small mound appears: a fresh grave. *The size of a rabbit,* Sitti Sundus had said.

Lubna slows and brakes at the entrance of a cemetery. She climbs off the worn leather seat and shakes her curls free from the helmet.

Intisar sits frozen on the leather seat. "What are we doing here?" she asks, knowing the answer.

Lubna gives her a compassionate smile. "I thought you might want to give du'aa to your father, Allah yarhamo," she says, hooking her thumbs under the straps of her backpack.

Intisar's heart catches in her throat. "I—I thought women here were forbidden from entering the cemetery." It's a foolish thing to say, but can it be her excuse now?

Seeing his grave will make it real. Intisar was spared his cancer and a funeral and a final glimpse at his dead body, his head wrapped in a white shroud, one piece fastened firmly to hold up his jaw. That's how Jiddo Riyad—her mother's father—looked. Mama and her sisters had begged to see their father once more before his casket was carried out of the funeral home. Intisar had crept closer to the wailing women and caught a glimpse of her grandfather's diaphanous face.

Lubna smiles and holds out her hand. "It is okay," she tells Intisar in English, taking her helmet. "You pray for him. For your father." She gestures toward the tombstones. "Every du'aa for the dead counts in their favor." Lubna catches her hand and helps Intisar off the bike. "Yalla. Do not be afraid."

They walk through the entrance and among graves arrayed like a spontaneous gathering. There's no order as far as Intisar can tell. In America, her grandfather and other relatives are buried at Parkhill Cemetery, inside an Islamic section that's separated from the Christian graves, its rows neatly designated by year of death.

"That's my father's sister." Lubna pauses in front of one engraved white stone, cupping her hands together, her lips moving silently. She does this again over her grandmother's grave. "How are you, Sitti?" she muses. "I've brought bint Hafez. Isn't she beautiful, mashallah?" She turns to Intisar. "We're not supposed to talk to them, but I don't care. I would be happy if someone kept me company."

They walk past more headstones, red anemones poking between them. Others have urns of flowers set beside them like the ones on Sitti Sundus's patio. Intisar notices a large plastic water jug with a spigot at the edge of the cemetery.

"And here's an old schoolmate," Lubna is saying. "He was only nineteen." A young man's likeness is etched on a raised marker. There are two more graves with the images of a boy and another young man. Lubna reads the Arabic inscriptions out loud: "The martyr Amer Abdullah Hassan…" "The martyr Othman al-Rahmy…" The other headstones reveal nothing more than their names and birthdates, lives extinguished by old age or unfortunate calamity—or maybe cancer like her father. Was he considered a martyr?

Intisar follows Lubna along a very narrow row of graves, and before Lubna points to it, she immediately recognizes her father's name: حافظ. When Intisar was learning to spell her own name in kindergarten—a challenging feat of seven letters—she'd proudly shown her father a series of five clumsy renderings on a sheet of wide-lined paper on which her white teacher had made the class practice their names.

Do you know how it is spelled in arrabi? he'd said, his eyes lighting up. This was before she'd started attending Sunday Arabic school. Beneath the English version of her name, Baba guided her pencil, his thumb and finger above hers, and they worked in the opposite direction. Right to left. It had felt odd. Only the letter "I" was recognizable, the rest of it as foreign to her as hieroglyphics. Baba asked her to try it on her own and Intisar balked. It was the same feeling as petting a stranger's dog or trying a new food she didn't want to. She shook her head.

Her father chuckled. *Here is mine,* he'd said, taking the pencil from her. And he wrote it five times, just as she'd done for Mrs. Sullivan, as if the teacher had assigned him the same task. *Arabic is a beautiful language, habibti,* he'd beamed down at her.

Intisar stands over his grave now, studying his name carved into a bright, pristine white stone—not yet weathered—until her vision blurs. The tears come hot and too quickly for the sleeve of her shirt to absorb.

"Folks say our tears torment the departed—but it is too sad," Lubna sniffles beside her. She dabs the corner of her eyes with her fingertips. They stand huddled together for a long time, silently weeping. Intisar isn't sure if Lubna is crying for Baba, or perhaps she's crying for Intisar and how pitiful she is.

"I should have come sooner," she says. The wind slashes her words.

"You are here now." Lubna wraps an arm around Intisar's shoulders.

But is it enough for either of them? Does he see her now?

"Yalla," Lubna says, pulling her hand. "I want to show you something special."

Intisar climbs back on the motorbike. She breathes deeply, then clenches her eyes shut until the next stop. Baba's really gone. And so is her secret wish to see him again. What is she doing here? She'd missed her chance. What a miserable, terrible daughter.

Before she can signal Lubna to take her back to the villa, they're whizzing along a road toward a dull cinderblock compound. It seems disjointed from Bayt al-Hawa, a dismal place. And then Intisar remembers. It must be the encampment, Intisar realizes. The mokhayam that Emad the driver had pointed out her first night.

Lubna slows down along a narrow alleyway between shanty structures crammed together. Satellite dishes are mounted from rooftops or stationed on the ground. Some buildings jut several concrete floors high—vertical expansion to overcome the crowding. Intisar gets a whiff of something putrid and traces a stream of sewage Lubna that carefully maneuvers. They pass an unattended toddler, his face splotched with dirt, a soiled diaper drooping as he toddles behind a small yelping dog. It feels to Intisar as if she has suddenly been plunged into another country.

Lubna pulls up to a building that appears to be a school. There's a blue UNRWA sign in Arabic outside the gates: مدرسة للأطفال. The Children's School. "I volunteer here every week," Lubna announces.

Inside, the walls are dilapidated, white paint curling in their corners. The linoleum floors are scuffed and chipped. Lubna leads Intisar to an office where a woman sits behind a desk. She leaps up and claps her hands.

"This is Sayida Najla," Lubna tells Intisar. "She is the mudeera—how you say—principal? Yes, principal of the school." She switches to Arabic. "Sayida Najla, this is my friend from America."

The woman pulls Intisar in and kisses both cheeks. "Ahlan! Ahlan! Welcome to our school. We need some good cheer."

Lubna nods. "I heard there was another attack."

"Amara's sister. We haven't seen either of them for a while." The principal shakes her head. "May God keep evil far from us.

As you know, banat al mokhayam are easy targets." She gives Intisar a sad smile.

Intisar is confused. What attacks?

"Poor girls," the principal is saying. "Every parent in the encampment is terrified. Khair inshallah." She gestures down a corridor. "Don't keep the kids waiting."

Intisar follows Lubna and they pass posters of cartoon-drawn children learning how to maintain clean hygiene and good citizenship. Before Intisar can find out more about the attacks, a cheerful roar goes up inside a classroom as soon as the pupils spot Lubna.

"Miss Lubna! Miss Lubna!"

"Salaam, my little ducks! I brought a friend today. All the way from America."

A few eye Intisar, assessing this stranger. Others run toward her—mostly girls—and they take turns hugging her waist, looking up at her with toothy grins. The boys eventually offer her bashful smiles.

"Okay! Let's get started," Lubna announces. She grabs a roll of butcher paper and the students file after her into the corridor. The beleaguered teacher adjusts the hem of her headscarf and looks relieved for some time to herself. She closes the door behind them.

Intisar stands off to one side, unsure what's to come. She didn't expect this as part of the tour Lubna promised. To come from a cemetery to a school teeming with young lives is jarring. She watches silently as Lubna claps her hands, halting the children's chatter. They sit upright and look attentive. Intisar is impressed, though not surprised at how easily Lubna commands the space, the way each child's face turns toward her and follows her every movement. They're like nestlings tittering around their mother.

"Remember what we talked about last week?" Lubna smiles. "Today we are going to create a mural!"

It's the students' turn to clap, and they squirm against one wall of the corridor where Lubna has lined them up. Intisar can't help but picture the separation wall, the murals painted along the dull gray concrete.

"Our mural will be whatever makes you happy," Lubna declares. She unfurls the roll of butcher paper and gives Intisar one end and a tape dispenser. She directs Intisar to pull it across the corridor. "Bas!" Lubna calls to her, holding up her hand. "Right there! Azeem!"

Intisar lays the end on the floor and secures it with a piece of tape. She watches as Lubna assigns each student a section marked by faint lines she draws with a ruler. Each child happily collapses to the floor, folding their tiny legs beneath them. The teacher reappears for a moment, handing Intisar a tub of crayons and paper cups. Intisar automatically fills each one for students to share, slipping into this unexpected role of the artist's assistant. A few scuffle over who gets to be in charge of holding the cup. Others complain they have two of the same color or missing red or orange—popular colors.

"If we don't have it—" Lubna says loudly, cupping her hand to her ear, waiting for the pupils to finish her sentence.

"We invent it!" they call back. Lubna reminds them how to blend primary colors, demonstrating on a sheet she's torn off and tapes to the wall.

Intisar strolls back and forth behind the children, stopping when one taps her leg and asks if the hands on the figure of her baby brother are just right, or if another's oranges look more like apples. Lubna does the same, snapping photographs on her camera in between questions and checks on their progress.

Over the course of half an hour, the roll of butcher paper blooms into a spontaneous landscape. It's full of stick figures kicking soccer balls and hands jutting in the air and others carrying a lapful of flowers. The children bustle on the floor, each leaning forward on the paper, staking their piece, conjuring a small bit of happiness from their daily lives.

Lubna crouches down behind one child. "Yabayay!" she gushes over his shoulder. "Look at that tree!" Its dark and light green foliage billow from a brown trunk. On its branches, two children dangle their legs and wave.

"It's a fig tree," the child explains. "The one me and my brother climb. One time, Miss, he fell and broke his hand. Our father had to take him to the hospital and I was…"

A girl tugs on Intisar's hand. "Miss, Miss! Look here!" Her name is Salma, a third-grader, and Intisar compliments her on her rendition of brown and white-furred kittens. She gestures for Intisar to squat down next to her. The girl's tone changes to a serious one. "The world will see what Israel does to us," she declares, with an expression so earnest it shames Intisar. She's a US citizen after all—*amrikeeya*.

"These are happy kittens," is all Intisar can think to say and smiles at Salma.

When time is up, a collective groan rises from the children. "Mashallah! What amazing work today, everyone! Azeem!" Lubna applauds them as they scramble to their feet. "Who will help me hang this masterpiece?"

Everyone's hand shoots into the air. "Miss Lubna! Miss Lubna! I want to help!"

Intisar gathers the crayons back into the tub and stacks the cups. Each pupil holds up the edges of their square and waits patiently for Lubna to tack it up. Then they all stand back.

Intisar's stomach flutters. From the derelict walls, blue skies with yellow suns shine down on families and friends. The children titter with pride, admiring their contributions.

Their teacher emerges from her classroom, one hand covering her mouth, eyes crinkled with emotion. "Mashallah, children! Bravo!"

A young boy taps Intisar's arm. "I'm going to marry Miss Lubna." His cleft lip gives the illusion of a misshapen nose. His expression is solemn and sincere. He blinks up at Intisar.

Before they leave, the children form a line and each one gives Lubna a high-five or a hug. A few shyly shake Intisar's hand.

"Our funding's running out," Lubna whispers in her ear. "Inshallah khair." She gives Intisar a bunch of lollipops to hand out. The teacher instructs her pupils to stow them in their desks until recess, but several have already discarded the wrappers and popped them into their mouths.

"See you next week!" Lubna waves.

"Bye-bye!" The children wave back, skipping after them.

"You are so good with them," Intisar says when they are outside and Lubna hands her a helmet. "Would you consider teaching full-time?"

Lubna sucks her teeth before climbing onto the motorbike. "I get to have fun with them. I don't care for all the other boring stuff."

Intisar slips on her helmet. "That little boy—Omar?" She slides on behind Lubna. "He told me he will marry you one day."

Lubna laughs and fastens her helmet, crushing the spiral curls around its periphery. "Omar's a sweetheart. His older brother Othman was shot and killed in a raid two years ago. That was his grave we saw earlier. Omar was six years old." She turns the ignition and the motor roars to life. "Are you hungry?" she asks loudly.

"Yes," Intisar answers. She feels a combination of joy and sadness, her energy replenished and simultaneously depleted. She gazes back at the children who crowd the windows of their classroom and wave as Lubna speeds away. The fabric of her sleeves billows. The azzan echoes from the loudspeaker of a masjid, crackling in the heat. Intisar can't spot it from the bike, can only hear its reverberation, the only sound rising above the rumble of the motorbike.

Lubna steers toward a main drag and soon they're in a bustling marketplace. Vendors wave and hold up their produce: bananas and cucumbers, and guava and prickly pears she's never seen or tasted before. They whiz along a street littered with discarded peels and plastic wrappers.

Lubna honks cheerily as annoyed drivers wave her off, arms extended from their car windows. Intisar is impressed at how easily she maneuvers through traffic, undaunted. "Donkey!" Lubna shouts at a taxi driver who's cut her off.

As they pull up to a restaurant, the spicy aroma of lamb roasting on spits wafts over the street.

"This place is thirty-three years old," Lubna boasts. "Abu Basel makes the best shawarma in Bayt al-Hawa. People come from all over to eat it."

As far as Intisar can see, the first floor is occupied solely by men except for one table with a pair of women in hijab. They survey her quickly before returning to their conversation.

A young man with slicked-back hair guides her and Lubna upstairs to a table that overlooks the village square. "Please, Sisters. Enjoy."

Lubna thanks him as a boy suddenly appears at Intisar's elbow, pouring two glasses of water and offering a plate of olives and pickled turnips. "Shukrun, habibi," Lubna smiles.

Intisar gazes down at Bayt al-Hawa. "Wow! This is incredible." She searches for her grandmother's house across a hill dotted with white-bricked villas. Cypress trees pierce the sky, yellow flowers blanket the valley.

"It's amazing, isn't it?" Lubna gushes, pleased by Intisar's reaction. "This is the best view. Except for your father's villa. Have you been on the roof yet?"

Intisar shakes her head, embarrassed as if she's failed a test.

Lubna points to a storefront down the street. "You see that brown one?"

Intisar cranes her neck. She sees a large sign above showroom windows: *Lux Furniture.*

"That's your Siddo Abu Hafez's old furniture store."

The honorific feels too intimate to Intisar. She'd only met her grandfather once, and been forced into polite conversation with him on a long-distance phone call. "You were born here?" she asks, changing the subject.

Lubna pats the air. "Here? In Bayt al-Hawa?" She shakes her head, sips her water from a straw. "When my mother was nine months pregnant, she went to visit her parents in al-Quds—Jerusalem—and got stuck there." Lubna launches into an animated tale of demonstrations and curfews and roadblocks. "My mother had no way of returning to the village. Then her water broke."

It was Lubna's great-grandmother Hala who delivered her. She'd been a nurse for the British Royal Army when Palestine was a mandate.

"She was ninety-one years old when she passed away," Lubna tells her. "That bike—" she jerks her head toward the street—"it belonged to Hala." She laughs. "Can you imagine a woman riding a motorbike in public in 1936?" Awe and pride lace her words. "They say I'm as smart as her. That I have her fearless spirit. She had passion like I have passion." She sips her water again and adds shyly, "I'm working on my first exhibit."

"Mabrook," Intisar politely offers.

The server arrives with their meal, making it difficult to continue conversing as she savors the tender and spicy shawarma, the lamb meat striated with juicy fat. Lubna had not exaggerated. The sandwich was absolutely delicious. She chomps on a side of fried potatoes, a generous serving for one person.

Lubna dips hers in a small bowl of shatta—a sauce of ground red chilies and olive oil. "You will come?"

"Where?" Intisar pats her lips with a paper napkin.

"To the exhibit? It's at the end of the month."

Intisar shakes her head. "I'll be gone by then. I'm sorry." And she means it. In an extremely short period of time, Lubna has been the most gracious friend.

"Do you not love it here?" Lubna asks earnestly.

Intisar shifts uncomfortably in her chair and looks over the guardrail. How can she answer this question without offending her sweet host? "I haven't been here long, you know," she begins sheepishly. "I don't know it—well." She almost says *at all*, but catches herself.

"It is your father's home," Lubna immediately counters. She points her plastic fork emphatically at Intisar before skewering another fried potato. "So it is *your* home."

Intisar turns the question back onto her companion. "Do *you* love it here?" She thinks of Lubna's father Mu'tassem and his mangled hand. "Despite the violence? The deaths?"

"One hundred percent," Lubna says in English, grinning. "Falasteen is a special place. Its people have—how you say? Sumood?" She clenches her fist to demonstrate then pulls a cigarette from her pack and slides it across the table. "We're still here."

"And what about these attacks on girls?" It's an awkward transition, but Intisar has been meaning to ask since they left those kids.

"There have been two since the school year started." She taps her ash in a tin tray.

"Soldiers?" Intisar asks. The intimidation at the checkpoint still lingers.

Lubna exhales through her nose. "More than likely the sulta. Those bastards are corrupt."

"The sulta?"

"Palestinian Authority." Lubna scowls. "Worse than the State. Easy to lure the younger ones away from their friends when these men look and talk like you. Or they might try to catch them on the road, walking home alone."

Intisar's neck prickles. "How awful," is all she can say.

Lubna shrugs, stubs out her cigarette, and says, "Even if it's not the sulta, the girls are too scared to tell their families who did it."

The server returns with the check. They descend the stairs to the main level and start a new argument: who will pay for lunch. But the host tells them it's been taken care of. He tips his chin at a corner of the dining hall.

A man who appears to be in his late thirties waves at them. He sits at a table with three other men who stare at Intisar and Lubna, their eyes sharp and mirthless.

"Ignore him," Lubna says quickly. "He is no good. He is—"

Before Lubna can finish her sentence, the man walks over to them, leaving his companions to stare in his wake. He's wearing a dark suit and a white headdress, a look that doesn't match the thinly braided gold chain around his neck.

He beams at Intisar. "I am Abdul Waheed," he says, holding out his hand. Unsure of whether to take it, she steals a glance at Lubna, whose mouth forms an emphatic *no*. Unperturbed, the man eventually withdraws it and instead places his hand over his heart. Except the gesture lacks the same sincerity as when it's made by the cab driver Emad or her father's friend Mu'tassem.

Lubna clutches Intisar's elbow. "Yalla. Let's go."

"One moment, please." He holds his hand up to halt their movement. "Please, Miss Intisar. You must convince your grandmother to take my offer. Or you'll end up with nothing." He pats his hands together and gives her a knowing look. "You are an American—you know this is a good deal. Your father would have been content—Allah yarhamo." He places his hand back over his heart.

Intisar's mind swims with confusion. How does he know her name? And what offer does he mean? "I don't understand." She turns to Lubna, searching her friend's face for answers. "Who is this? What is he talking about?" Lubna's eyes drop to the floor.

"Ahh! It appears you have not been informed!" Abdul Waheed sucks his teeth, the noise making Intisar cringe. He gives her a knowing smile, then leans in conspiratorially as if the entire restaurant might be listening. "Do not entertain those lying lawyers. It is all legal, I assure you. I have the finalized deed to prove it. And if you are smart, Sister, you'll finish paying your respects, accept my gift, and go back to America with something."

GAHANA PRISON: AUGUST 1996
CHAPTER 9

The two old people sitting across from him couldn't be his parents. A deep crease like a narrow ravine cut across his father's forehead. His hair had gone completely white. Wrinkles etched every corner of his mother's face, but her eyes remained bright. Both seemed to have shrunken in stature, as if their bones had disintegrated. The years he'd been locked away from them had accelerated their age.

Hafez, too, must have looked like a stranger to his parents. He'd tried to spruce up his appearance, finally permitting Abu Hatim, the prison barber, to shave his beard, eliminating the gray that had infested it. But it only worsened his gaunt face, the nose he'd inherited from his father now a crushed shadow of it. His eyes flickered between them. He worried that his parents could see everything that was done to him in the Zinzana and the deep loneliness that shrouded him in his cell.

"Habibi, yamma," his mother said, putting her hands up to the bulletproof security shield. Dozens of tiny holes had been drilled into it. The aroma of crushed za'atar wafted through, and the rush of home hit Hafez like a blow to the head.

Forgetting the condition of his nails, he held a hand up, too. A guard shouted over a loudspeaker: "Hands down! No touching!"

As if in practiced unison, prisoners and visitors on either side of the shield brought their hands down. They'd do it again and again over the course of the visit.

"How are you, my son?" Um Hafez asked.

"Alhamdullilah," he said. Never had the word disguised so much tumult raging inside him. He'd wanted desperately to see them again, and now that they were here, two broken creatures, he wished he could disappear. He'd never again be their Hafez. What was left to offer them? The only thing that he'd clung to were the pocket spiral notepads May Boustany had secured for his sketches.

The first time he flipped the cover over its tiny coiled wire, Hafez ran his finger across the first lined page. He lifted the tiny, unsharpened pencil, one without an eraser, and his finger and thumb began to violently tremble. Would he be capable of drawing again? Or had they stomped that creative impulse out of him, too? In his cell, despondency washed over him, an agonizing reminder of the new and complicated miseries that could befall a single human being.

Yet suddenly his pencil began to move across the 3-x-5 paper with a marvelously soft scratching sound that broke open his past life, sweet sorrow spilling onto the page. His finger and thumb seemed to possess a power of their own, never pausing, never hesitating until a foundation formed, then a retaining wall. Beams crossed posts and rafters rose to a vaulted ceiling. His vision blurred like the tears of an addict who'd been deprived a marvelous poison until another miraculous hit flooded his lungs. And his hand already ached with a cloying fear that this exquisite drug could be denied him again. He savored each of the notepad's fifty pages, sketching one image every day on each side of the lined paper until one hundred existing and imagined structures filled the notepad. Then he sat on his cot and flipped through the pages until he could acquire another one from the commissary.

"Are you eating?" was his mother's next natural question. "You're too thin, yamma!"

Hafez avoided mirrors, but he'd discerned the change in his body from the way he moved. Though he had lost twenty pounds, his limbs were perpetually heavy with apprehension.

"We should have brought more pies," she whispered to his father. Abu Hafez still hadn't spoken, his silence penetrating the tiny holes of the shield.

"I'm fine, Yamma." Hafez smiled at her. "How is Sitti?" And for a moment his stomach sank. Was his grandmother gone?

"Alhamdullilah," his mother nodded. "She would have come, my love, but they only allow two visitors. Next time inshallah."

The promise poked his heart. To see his grandmother would be bittersweet.

"Your father's sold the furniture store," Um Hafez added brightly, patting her husband's thigh. "He can finally get some peace now."

Hafez turned to his father. "Yabba, how are you?" The question sounded hollow—a polite inquiry you asked a stranger. But were they not strangers? Had he not deceived both of his parents, compelling them to wonder who their son actually was?

"We're alive," his father said flatly. Like Hafez, he kept his hands in his lap.

"Alhamdullilah," his mother interjected. "We can't ask the Lord for more." She smiled at Hafez, tears shining in her eyes.

"Forgive me, Yabba," Hafez said. "I did it for my country." Did it sound as weak to them as it did to him?

"And ruined our house," his father returned, his voice cracking. "You had a good life, my son. We always supported you. Even when you went your own way. And left us. Still we supported you." Abu Hafez looked around him as if he'd suddenly discovered he was lost. "How, yabni, did you arrive here?"

To his father he was a son. To his daughter, a father. He was tethered to other human beings, his actions falling on their lives like rocks breaking away from the hills, crushing unsuspecting, innocent bystanders. He'd believed if he joined the resistance, he could crush his own fear and shame. He wanted to tell his father how he'd felt his spirit fracture inside his body, all the pieces of himself scattered. He was only trying to be whole again.

Hafez avoided his father's imploring eyes and glanced to his left. A few spaces down the row of men on the bench, Abu Nasser and his sons huddled close together. Um Nasser pressed both of her hands against the shield and each son claimed one of his mother's with his own.

"No touching!" the command sounded again.

Hafez heard Um Nasser remind Nijmy to mind his older brother and father. And for Nasser to always be patient concerning his younger brother.

On Hafez's right, Abu Jadallah's wife gave reports on the grandchildren of their married daughters. Who'd started walking and talking, who could pronounce their Siddo's name when shown pictures of Abu Jadallah.

"Mashallah." The old man beamed behind the shield. "They're clever ones."

Hafez turned back to this mother. He was afraid to ask about his own daughter, whose being he kept locked away so no one could destroy her. "How are the grapes this season, yamma?" There had been four harvests since his confinement. Had every one of them been bountiful? Now was the season of almonds. He'd munch on tangy, unripened handfuls directly from the tree in the orchard. The floral taste of the fuzzy skin and tender mound filled his mouth like a bouquet.

"Alhamdullilah," his mother was saying, her eyes flickering with light. "The dawali is hardy." She glanced at a security guard standing at the door of the visitation room. "Inshallah we can bring some next fall?" The reality of another year of absence hung gloomily between them.

Hafez only nodded, delaying the next question roiling inside him. "And the girl?"

His mother nodded before speaking as if she had the correct answer ready. "We spoke to Intisar—" she turned to Abu Hafez—"what? three weeks ago?" She smiled at Hafez. "Mashallah she is a smart one. Head of her class."

Each year he'd been away from his daughter pelted Hafez's heart. And there was nothing he could do to protect himself against its excruciating pain. There was no shield between him and the absence like the one now keeping him from reaching out and touching his mother's aged hands.

Um Hafez shifted on the metal bench, stealing glances at her husband.

"What is it?"

"My son, Nadira has remarried."

These words were a different kind of pain—one he had been anticipating, but still ached no less. She was another man's wife. He gave a slight nod, dropped his eyes to his lap, and started rubbing the inside of his palm with his thumb.

He'd heard Nadira's voice before seeing her for the first time at a special gathering in Chicago. He'd driven up from the university with two other mates. Bashir Galayini, a Lebanese pre-med major, and Douglas Hossain, a third-year engineering student from Ghana. All three were attending on student visas.

In 1979, Hafez had come to America in search of hope and excitement—emotions he could never coax into being the way his mother had coaxed every tree in her orchard and every bunch of grapes from her vines, always producing something wonderfully satisfying. As soon as he set foot in Kennedy Airport, he felt free. On a connecting flight to Chicago, he'd sat beside another young man from Honduras, a fellow newcomer. They smiled and attempted, in halting English sentences, to explain all they planned to do in their new country.

At his university south of the city, there had been many obstacles, but Hafez had studied hard and dreamt about architecture. He didn't argue when a professor had advised him to tell people he was from Jordan. *You'll be more successful, son.*

The land of his birth was never named in this new country except to identify terrorists on airplanes. So he'd folded that identity away like an old shirt that no longer fit.

On weekends, Hafez took the college shuttle to Chicago and walked around on his own, studying the old and new buildings. Though he admired all of Frank Lloyd Wright's works, his favorite was the building on East Washington Street, dubbed the "People's Palace," with its lovely mosaics of glass, gold leaf, and mother-of-pearl and its glass dome, which reminded him of the Dome of the Rock back home. He felt less alone as he considered the great men who'd built the city around him.

Back on campus, he'd befriended Basheer and Douglas and they spent every Friday night together, grabbing a meal at a local diner and catching an American film to further their cultural education. One rainy Friday, Basheer coaxed them into driving to Chicago. There was a hafla at a place called the Markaz. It turned out to be a lively fundraiser for Palestinian refugees, though Hafez had noticed a group of young and middle-aged men hovering in one corner of the large room. Some were bearded, others barefaced. All had the look of rebellion in their eyes. Were they freedom fighters?

Hafez's neck turned hot. Would they mark him as a traitor, a native son who'd abandoned the resistance? But Hafez was never a fighter—he had no desire to fight. He wanted to live and design amazing buildings. Didn't every human have a purpose? He'd found his in architecture. Didn't he deserve to pursue his dream?

Women fed the guests spicy shish kebab and turmeric-dyed rice with pine nuts. There was waraq dawali, rolled grape leaves like tiny logs stacked on top of each other, which temporarily lifted the homesickness Hafez carried around. And there were bowls of diced salad and creamy yogurt, the handles of serving spoons sticking out of them.

After dinner, men collapsed some of the folding chairs to make room for a dabka. Hafez craned his neck in the direction of a man drumming the tablah, cradling his instrument with one leg propped on the seat of a folding chair and clapping his palms against the taut goatskin.

Young and old men formed a crowded circle, including a

few of those severe-looking ones. His friend Basheer had found a keffiyeh and latched hands with one of them. He jerked his head at Hafez and Douglas to join in.

"No way, man," Douglas chuckled.

And then a woman's voice burst from the center, guiding the men. "*A'la dal'ona, a'la dal'ona!*"

Hafez's heart leaped into his throat. The voice was rich and sonorous, somewhere between Um Kulthum and Fairuz. He craned his neck to behold the source of this lyrical bird.

She was a young woman with thick, wavy hair, sideswept with tortoise-shell combs. She held one hand to her forehead. Her eyebrows were thin and highly arched, her lips full and painted red. He could not determine the color of her eyes as they fluttered closed then opened again as she sang:

> *To the family who have forgotten us*
> *Oh, bird flying over the loved ones*
> *Say hello to the ones that used to care for us*
> *I won't find one like you in this entire world*

Hafez heard only her voice, the stomping of the men in the circle dissolving into the floor, the man's tablah fading into the walls. And then he saw only her face as the rest of the members blurred around her.

The dabka lasted for over ten minutes, the young woman at its core, her energy bursting like magma from a volcano, consuming her listeners. When the drummer gave a flourishing finish on his drum, everyone applauded and an old woman gave a zaghroota, her ululation answered by her womenfolk that Falasteen be liberated one day.

Hafez felt desperate. Would the night be over and he'd never learn her name? But naseeb had led him to this hafla, and before he drove back to campus with his friends, they were introduced.

Her name was Nadira. Precious one.

When he asked for her hand, Hafez told Nadira's parents that he would earn his degree in eight more months. Since his arrival, he'd accelerated his program by taking summer school courses when they were offered or an independent study if a professor was interested in mentoring him. With her parents' blessings, Nadira accepted. She, too, was enamored. She could only see his potential and none of his fears.

He'd have to make the long-distance phone call with his news.

Amrikeeya? Um Hafez had said, in a tone that gradually softened from accusing to dejected. It meant Hafez was unlikely to come home.

Yamma, she's a fine girl, he'd said defensively.

I have no doubt she is a decent bint, Um Hafez had offered. *But yamma, she might not be*—Hafez could hear her fishing for the right words—*what you want.*

All he ever felt was possibility. He'd never actually named the things he wished for. Only hoped. Finding a woman to love only confirmed how full of possibilities America was. He hadn't been searching for Nadira, and here she was. Even if this country didn't quite understand him, he was granted a liberty to thrive.

When Um Hafez passed the telephone to his father, the dowry was discussed, which Abu Hafez would wire as soon as possible. It was a respectable muhr and he was grateful his father had not balked. *Inshallah khair* was all Abu Hafez had said about this important proposal. They'd later decline tickets to attend the wedding, making excuses about his grandmother.

For Nadira's family, the marriage had only one stipulation: Nadira would never leave the country. If Hafez set his heart on returning to Falasteen, he'd go without their daughter. Hafez promptly agreed. And deep down, he was relieved.

He'd kept that promise.

"Inshallah khair," was all Hafez could say about Nadira's new life. "Have you asked her to send the girl? To spend time with you in Bayt al-Hawa." Intisar was now fourteen years old, entering that awkward stage of puberty, slowly shedding her childhood.

Um Hafez shook her head. "Her mother refuses. She already makes it difficult, yamma," his mother said. "The truth is, we barely get to speak to Intisar on the phone."

A siren wailed and families quickly shared du'aa, bowing their heads, hands pressed against the shield.

His parents slowly stood, each bracing against the other.

"Take care of yourself, my son," his mother said, wiping the tears with a handkerchief she pulled from the chest pocket of her thobe.

Hafez nodded. To his father, he blurted again, "Forgive me, Yabba." And as he said the words, he knew it would be the last time he'd see his father alive.

The siren keened again and the men fanned their fingers against the barrier one last time before they were ordered to stand in formation. A few of the newer ones sniffled as they marched back to their cells. Like them, Hafez clung to the warmth of his parents against his body for as long as he could, like the flaps of a coat against a strong wind before its evitable chill finally penetrated his bones.

BAYT AL-HAWA: SEPTEMBER 2007

CHAPTER 10

Her granddaughter's brow is furrowed in anger—the same way her dear father's had when he was upset. Sundus's breath catches for a moment. She is staggered by the new ways their resemblance emerges during the few days she's been here. And there's a touch of Jalal in the girl's profile. She's pacing back and forth on the barranda, barely able to look at Sundus.

"Pray to the Prophet," Majida says, patting the cushioned dais. "Please sit down, my daughter."

Wordlessly, Sundus coasts back and forth on the creaking glider. Its original shipping box was nearly destroyed coming through Israeli customs that summer long ago. The cardboard flaps were duct-taped after being torn open, and there was a dent in one of the crossbars that Jalal managed to fix with a mallet from his furniture store.

Why have you troubled yourself, yamma? Sundus had admonished Hafez.

You'll love this, Yamma, he'd grinned back, an arm around her shoulder, after he helped his father assemble it on the barranda.

It looked like a regular cushioned chair until Sundus settled into it and began to glide. Her son was right. She loved it. That very first visit her young granddaughter had sat beside her as Sundus fed her chunks of sabir fruit, her granddaughter curiously inspecting the discarded cactus skin. They communicated in short phrases and gestures:

Zakee?

The little girl nodded her delight.

More?

Another nod and tiny-toothed smile.

When he'd gone back to America with his family, Sundus had spent hours gazing into the valley, trying to imagine them away from her. And when Hafez had been stuck in that godforsaken prison, she wondered what he was doing. How was he sleeping? Was he eating better between visitations?

And when Jalal died, she stared at the right side where he always sat. Not even Majida dared to occupy the space, as if her dear husband might one day return to claim it.

Now Sundus glides back and forth quietly, waiting for her granddaughter to calm down. That snake—Abdul Waheed—got to her this afternoon. Majida was right: Sundus should have told her everything from the start. That son of a bitch has tainted everything.

Intisar refuses to sit. "Why didn't anybody tell me?"

Sundus says matter-of-factly, "Abdul Waheed is a crook. May God curse his mother and father." She is immediately reprimanded by her cousin.

"Hajja! For the Lord's sake!" Majida turns to cajole Intisar. "Let's discuss this calmly, my dear. Please, I'm begging you to have a seat."

Intisar finally takes a seat next to Majida, deliberately averting her eyes from Sundus.

"But why didn't anyone tell me?" her granddaughter implores. "Is that the real reason I'm here? I have a right to—"

"A right to what?" Sundus cuts in. Despite her secrecy, she doesn't deserve the girl's self-righteous anger.

Intisar looks startled, as if unprepared for her indignation to be challenged. "To know everything," she finally stammers.

"Ya salaam!" Sundus jeers, dramatically folding one hand over the other in her lap. "Are you sure you want to know?"

Majida intervenes again. "Go easy on her, ya Hajja!"

"Bint Hafez wants to know everything." Sundus stops the motion of the glider and clamps a hand on one of the armrests. "You'll need more than ten days to know everything, habibti."

"That's not fair!" the girl says.

This English word stings Sundus. "*Fair*? There is no fair!" she snaps back. "Only this." She holds up her hands. "Here. Now." Sundus shifts her weight forward and glides again, hoping the motion will calm her.

"Do you know what happened after the night my mother lost her son? Do you know how I settled here? To find some semblance of peace?"

Intisar shakes her head. Her eyes dart between Sundus and her cousin. She eventually leans back on the dais, preparing to listen. Majida pats the girl's hand.

"After we buried my infant brother," Sundus begins, "we drove east, soon parting with Amjad's family, who pushed on toward Jericho and over King Hussein Bridge. I never saw my friend or the sea again." It wrenches her heart to imagine Amjad's face.

Just like everything they'd lost, her childhood friend held a permanent, unfaltering place in Sundus's memory: Amjad was eternally a young boy, never to grow up. From what she gathered from Majida's family, he'd started his own family in an encampment in Zarqa, where thousands of Palestinian refugees had sheltered in the concrete shanties that had supplanted tents during the last two decades. They'd started in the same beautiful place, Amjad and Sundus. It was almost incomprehensible how their lives had splintered into so many different directions.

For months afterward, she'd imagined their house destroyed by the militias, leaving no trace of her childhood inside the walls, nothing of their belongings or the items her mother had instructed Sundus to leave behind. But the newspapers reported that Jewish families from Europe had moved into the coastal residences and that the newly born government had offered "abandoned" properties to freshly arrived citizens of the new State of Israel. Sundus pictured a young girl sleeping in her bedroom, feeding Sim-Sim—in her imagination, her beloved bird had returned home once a new family arrived—and the intruder wore her beloved green velvet dress that Sundus had left hanging in her closet.

From the valley, a wind dances onto the barranda, sending a shiver down Sundus's back. "My mother kept the key for our bayt in Haifa," Sundus continues. Her granddaughter's eyes are fixed on the hill across from them where the settlement stands. But she's listening. "In a jewelry box, along with a garnet ring she was wearing when we fled—a wedding gift from my maternal grandmother.

"We migrated south to Ramallah. My mother hocked most of her jewelry to help my father pay rent for a small flat we lived in.

Until he began practicing again at a hospital."

Sundus shakes her head. "My parents weren't the same people who'd raised me." Majida sucks her teeth in commiseration, but doesn't interrupt. "They never faltered in their love and attention, but there was a faraway look in their eyes. And I recognized what they were seeing because I saw it, too. Their dead baby son. My brother."

Sundus hadn't known him—had never tickled the soft flesh beneath his chin, inhaled his sweet scent, or held his tiny body against her shoulder—and yet he continued to exist, tethered to her memory like the umbilical cord that had attached him to her mother and which Um Amjad had expertly cut away on the side of a dark road as machine gun fire shattered the night.

Sometimes her mother's screams woke her up. She'd crawl out of her bed and listen at her parents' door while her father soothed her mother until her whimpers grew muffled. They never spoke of the infant, leaving Sundus at once relieved and resentful. How could they pretend as if her brother had never existed? There were no photographs of their former life in Haifa—no evidence beyond the pictures in her mind of her mother waddling across their saha to speak to Um Amjad over the stone wall. Or her mother rubbing her belly, her eyes softly closed and a faint smile dancing across her lips as an Egyptian song played on the radio.

As she grew up, Sundus understood how such memories cleaved the human heart, how they could break the spirit. No words could ever fully communicate the immensity of such loss, and if they were somehow conceived and uttered out loud, the world would come crashing down on all of them. Her parents weren't pretending nothing had happened. To be silent was a matter of survival.

Sundus often wondered if they could ever find the spot again where Abu Amjad had dug a hole. Or had the roadside grave been excavated to make way for a settlement, the baby's soft skeleton crumbled to dust?

When they'd first moved to their flat in Ramallah, she lay across her parents' bed on her stomach and examined the contents of her mother's jewelry box, inlaid with mother-of-pearl. Propped on her elbows, Sundus riffled with her pointer finger, poking at a medallion in the shape of coin and a pair of golden earrings knotted like rope. Sundus pulled out the brass key that hung from a simple chain small enough to loop around her child-wrist. She remembered the last time her father locked the door that night before they drove away in the black Ford.

While her mother hung laundry on the roof of their flat, Sundus looked out with brass binoculars, one of the few items she'd been permitted to bring. She searched for Haifa and the mountain range of her childhood that had receded so quickly behind her all those years ago. In Ramallah, the hills and valleys were speckled with anemones and thorn bushes, as if carved from a finite landscape. So unlike the boundless sea of her first life, forever eluding her touch and smell.

As Sundus grew older, a stone of apprehension settled in her stomach that was impervious to erosion. It was like the old childhood scar at the back of her head she'd unconsciously rub, a tiny, hidden bald spot. After matriculating from secondary school at the top of her class, she had two options: she could cross the river to attend university, or she could get married. Neither appealed to Sundus. The majority of her schoolmates had chosen the latter. Her parents wanted her to advance her education, but she'd secretly feared having to leave Falasteen.

You're a hundred times smarter than any shab we know, her father declared, his shoulders hunched over their small kitchen table. His body was gradually folding forward as if leaning toward an old friend.

It was as if one day she'd awakened and her parents had become old people. How much longer would she be able to keep them?

As if reading her mind, her mother gently took hold of her hands and looked deeply into her eyes. *You cannot be afraid of living your life,* she told Sundus. Gray streaked her crown and yet her mother was still so beautiful.

Sundus had started working at the hospital in Ramallah where her father had rebuilt his reputation. Sundus filed charts and answered the phone. Male patients showed up, nursing broken limbs or injuries from farm machinery. Sometimes they were accompanied by their doting mothers, who'd sit in the waiting area, smiling at Sundus. Some of them unabashedly interrogated her: *How old are you, ya binti? Are you still a student? Are you promised to another, my dear? My son is looking…*

Sundus was certain none of the young men could ever be as brilliant and strong as her father. He'd instilled in her a love of literature. As an only child, she'd spent solitary hours reading in their flat, books offering her a new kind of solace an adolescent girl could wrap herself in. Once a month, she and her father visited a bookseller near the hospital, a Druze from the Levant. Sundus devoured the poetry of Abu a-Tayab al-Muntanabbi, and later discovered Qabbani. By the time she was eighteen, she'd read William Shakespeare's *Hamlet* and *Othello*, translated from French, and other classics the bookseller procured from Egypt, Lebanon, Syria, and Iraq.

The bookseller's storefront was an inconspicuous space between a barber shop and a textile merchant. Sundus and her father spent Friday afternoons there, in dimly lit corners. In solemn ritual, her father searched the shelves, sliding his fingers across the dusty spines, and she wondered if he was hoping to come across a familiar title he'd once owned. He hadn't taken a single book when they fled, leaving them in their precise position on his shelves. Sundus still remembered the aroma of her father's study, curling up in an old armchair with the atlas, sandalwood and myrrh emanating from a silver incense burner that he claimed had come all the way from Saudi Arabia. From time to time, objects like these came back to her from their real home, their colors vivid and their angles sharp as if she were holding them in her hands.

As the years stretched between her childhood in Haifa and the present, Sundus wore some of her parents' recollections like a secondhand frock, something that didn't quite fit and had the smell of someone else:

Sundus, remember how you'd count all the first apricots in our tree? You'd cry if one had rotted?

Ya Sundus, remember the old Bedouin woman, Um Faisal, who sold us goat cheese in those gigantic drums? Sundus never admitted not remembering, for it never mattered. It had happened according to her parents, and she would relive those moments with them, immersing herself in every detail so that the memories might return and be hers again.

During her shift at the hospital, she always brought a book to read. The nurses constantly teased her. *You'll ruin your eyes, habibti. You're too pretty for glasses.* She ignored them and kept on reading during her breaks in the courtyard behind the hospital. In between chapters, she ate guava fruit and a slice of sheep-milk cheese.

One late afternoon at the end of her shift, a man came in, his eyes wild with pain and clutching his left jaw.

"For the love of God, I am going to die," he declared. "They tell me the only dentist in town is away. Ya rubbi! One dentist for a whole town and he's away. Please—I cannot bear it any longer," he panted.

Sundus tried not to smile. She'd witnessed many injuries, including a motorbike crash that had mangled one young man's leg, along with more common afflictions such as pneumonia and infectious rashes. She'd been amazed at how quickly some men were bent by pain or grew faint at the sight of blood.

"Please have a seat," Sundus instructed, but he wouldn't move, still clutching his cheek, his eyes wide with anguish. His complexion was glowing bronze, his forehead damp with sweat. White wisps streaked his temple and his wide sideburns were neatly trimmed. She placed her hand on the counter. "Take a seat and I'll—"

The man suddenly clamped his hand over hers, sending a volt of electricity through her body. It wasn't a shot of fear, but Sundus couldn't quite name it in that moment.

"Minshan Allah," he was imploring Sundus. "For the love of God, I need someone right away."

She looked down at his hand, where plumes of tiny black hairs sprouted from his knuckles. She buzzed an intercom.

A heavyset nurse appeared with a clipboard and escorted him to an examining room down the corridor. "See you tomorrow, ya Sundus," she threw over her shoulder.

The weight of his hand lingered. She wanted to catch one more glimpse of the stranger, but her shift was over.

The next morning she found his chart on top of a new

batch waiting to be filed. Without hesitation, Sundus opened it—something she never did—before filing the charts away. The men were merely patients, same as the women who were examined. And yet the one with a ridiculous toothache had stoked her curiosity. She traced her finger over his name.

Jalal Jaber. 44.

It had turned out to be an abscess in one of his molars. In barely legible handwriting, the presiding physician, Dr. Ramzi, had jotted a sparse note:

Patient consents to extraction to treat the severity of the infection

Sundus quickly closed the chart, her cheeks flushed at her invasion of privacy. Why had she wanted to know more about the stranger? She grabbed the batch of files, hugged them to her chest, and walked down the corridor to deposit them in the narrow filing closet. She tried hard to ignore the sudden, confusing pang at the thought that she would never see him again.

A week later, when she reported to the hospital for her shift, he was already seated on one of the long wooden benches, waiting like a regular patient. Heat rose in Sundus's neck and face as she pretended not to remember him.

"Have you been helped?" she asked, not looking directly at him. She set her lunch and a small booklet of poetry on top of the counter and pulled a clipboard from a bin. "What is the problem?"

"I'm fine, alhamdullilah. In fact, I'm feeling excellent, thanks to the doctor who saved me." He gave her a stunning grin.

Sundus fought her own smile. The heat of embarrassment reached the tips of her ears and she wondered if he could see the effect he was having on her. "I'm glad to hear it," Sundus managed. "What else can we do for you?"

He approached the counter, a package in his hand. He slipped it to her, his eyes fixed on her face, shiny coffee beans twinkling between his curly lashes. "A gift for the doctor." It was a cedar box of cigars, and for a moment Sundus was whisked back to her childhood, the memory of Amjad carefully retrieving the worn image of his hero Fauzi Al-Qawuqji to proudly show her.

"Which doctor assisted you?" she asked, pretending not to know.

"I've forgotten his name. I was in so much pain, you see." He was still grinning at her. There was no trace of shame or humiliation in his face.

Sundus nodded, struggling to be indifferent. "I'll let the nurse know. We'll be sure he receives it." Her fingers trembled as she took the box.

"Are you reading this?" he asked, holding up her booklet.

It was a rare, saddle-stitched compilation of the verses of Al Khansa, a seventh-century poetess purported to have been invited by the Holy Prophet to recite her works. Sundus preferred the modern poets, but there was something mystical and compelling about an ancient woman standing in the company of men, her words stirring their passion. When Sundus was feeling particularly forlorn, loneliness engulfing her, she found comfort in the poetess. She'd brought her precious copy to share with one of the young nurses, a fellow lover of literature.

"In school, we only studied the great men of verse," he said with a chuckle. He flipped through the pages. "No one rivals al-Muntanabbi."

Sundus couldn't help smiling at his challenge. "You disapprove of feminine poets? It was my father who introduced me to her." She flushed at offering this intimate information.

"Is he a professor?"

"A doctor. Here. At the hospital. Dr. Yousef Kareem."

He nodded as though this came as useful information. "I don't believe he worked on me." He returned her booklet. "Poetry saved my life."

Clacking heels echoed down the corridor followed by a pair of day-shift nurses. Sundus turned away from the man, making herself look busy as if she'd been caught in a transgression.

The nurses threw him an appraising glance. "Good morning, Sundus," they cooed. He was empirically handsome—possessing an air of a foreigner—his face weather-worn as if he'd been traveling his whole life. And she wanted to know every place he'd been.

"I'll be sure the doctor gets your present," she told him again.

"Thank you, Sayida Sundus," he said victoriously, and her name had never sounded so new and rich, two syllables spilling from his lips like the forbidden wine in her favorite poems. "I am Jalal Jaber." He boldly extended his hand and Sundus hesitated before taking it. He held it for a few seconds before she withdrew it, her fingertips passing over a rough callous in his palm.

After he left, casting one more smile over his shoulder, Sundus examined the cigars as though they might offer some clue to his identity.

"What's that?" a nurse piped up behind her.

"Nothing. I mean—they're for Dr. Ramzi. His patient dropped them off." Sundus fingered the etching on the cigar box: *Bahia Brazil Sortimento Extra Fino.*

"A nice change from complaints!" the nurse mused. "Which patient?"

But Sundus hadn't heard the question; her mind was thronged with visions of a life with a man she'd just met.

Two months later, they were engaged.

It was most difficult for her father. Jalal was not well educated, in spite of being a successful businessman. He was the proprietor of a furniture store in a village west of Ramallah called Bayt al-Hawa. He'd made more than a stable income. Sundus would not want for anything.

Are you sure he's what you desire? her father had quietly asked.

Yes, Baba, Sundus had answered firmly.

And so she'll have our blessing, ya Yousef, her mother said, closing the matter.

His proposal came with a tender gift: a collection of translated poetry by a European named Byron. But an even greater gift would be bestowed to Sundus.

One day, Jalal asked her to go for a drive with him to Bayt al-Hawa. Sundus hesitated—they were never without a chaperone, but there was something brimming in his eyes and she agreed. But there was something urgent in his request. They drove past his furniture store, veering toward a hill. The car climbed a winding road until Jalal pulled off and stopped.

"Yalla!" He grinned, hopping out. He came around to her side and held the door for her. Without anyone around to see, he took hold of Sundus's hand and led her to an empty plot of land. "All of this is ours."

"Ours?" Sundus said, breathless.

They were standing in front of two dunum—enough acres to build two modest villas. The land overlooked a deep valley below them where the melancholy winds gathered and moaned, living up to the village's name: House of Wind. Sundus could see a cemetery at the base, a gathering of white tombstones placed indiscriminately. She turned back to the stretch of empty property and gazed in the distance where neglected dawali and a small orchard of trees stood.

"I wanted to surprise you before the gossips told my secret." He squeezed her hand. "This is where we'll raise our children." Jalal spoke with an eager hope, the kind that was impervious to any misgiving, shielded from any possibility of loss or failure. In this regard, he was the opposite of her father, who'd never built another house again though her parents had acquired the means. They were like stalks of spearmint her mother had tenderly raised in an urn. She could see in her parents' faces how much they still felt like temporary visitors to Ramallah—stalks in an urn and not firmly planted in the ground.

Jalal guided Sundus along the rocky red dirt toward the craggly vines. She cupped a hand over her eyes, blocking the sun's glare. She stopped and reached for a small cluster of dawali, the leaves yellow at their edges but stems steadfastly green. She remembered the wild za'atar her mother had once planted in her herb garden in Haifa. It hadn't produced the first season. Eight-year-old Sundus had stood over the patch and declared it dead. The stems had turned brown.

But her mother had pointed out a single green one. *You see there, my love? If it possesses the slightest green, there's hope.*

And her mother was right. Before the summer was over, white flowers began to sprout from the stem.

Now her mother's words came back to her and hope billowed in her chest. "We'll bring back the grapes," Sundus told

Jalal. They would cultivate this land and it would give back to them every season.

"Whatever you desire, my love." Jalal smiled, bringing her hand to his lips.

A bicycle carrying a young man with a camera appeared behind them. Sundus recognized him as the photographer Jalal had hired for the store's monthly advertising circulars. "Look here, please," he instructed them. Sundus adjusted the sweater draped from her shoulders and Jalal pulled her closer. She smiled as they posed under the dawali. It was the last time the land would be vacant.

The morning after their small wedding reception, her parents' salon was filled with guests bringing the customary offerings. She thanked each visitor, standing and kissing the women on each cheek. Her mother had sewn her a lovely white satin purse with pearl beads. Sundus opened and closed it until it bulged with inqoot. Some guests handed her money in small, discreet envelopes, others offered her unmasked Jordanian dinars. Her parents had gifted her a lira coin, encased in a frame of spun gold.

Before the had guests arrived, her mother took Sundus aside. "Are you—did he hurt you?"

Sundus hugged her. "No, Yamma." Her mother looked different to Sundus now. She was a woman, the wife of a man, as Sundus had become. It embarrassed her, but it was such a precious thing to discover her parents' humanity. This marriage had brought her closer to her mother than she'd ever been.

At first, Sundus had been shy of her father, seeing him, too, with new eyes, until he pulled her in for a long embrace. "You'll always be my daughter," her father said. "Not a man's wife or a child's mother. Always my daughter first."

Her mother had whispered in her ear, "Inshallah you'll be as happy as your father and I have been. Through everything."

Through everything. Sundus considered all that her parents had weathered without splitting like the bough of a tree struck by lightning. All she'd known growing up was the perpetual sadness her mother and father had tucked away, like a tear-soaked handkerchief you slipped into a pocket. That's what you did—a lesson they'd unwittingly taught her about pain. Their first life had been stolen, and they'd assembled a new one that lacked the luster and ardor of the first one. And here Sundus and Jalal were beginning theirs.

In the salon, Jalal sat beside Sundus on the small sofa, chain-smoking. Traditionally, it was the husband's family that hosted this reception, but Jalal's clan was scattered or dead. Over the years, he'd encounter only a few people from his original birthplace, a village called Qira, who remembered his grandparents and great-grandparents. His mother died bearing his youngest sister, before the Catastrophe. His father and brother were captured by militiamen in their village and never heard from again. Separated from his siblings, Jalal fled east over the river. As a twenty-five-year-old orphan in Zarqa, he'd almost perished from dysentery. He'd lived with other children in an orphanage run by Quakers in a refugee encampment. It would take a very long time for him to forge a sense of value, that to be spared meant his life was worth something. He learned carpentry as an apprentice to an elder Quaker.

When he could finally leave the mokhayam, Jalal found work in a furniture warehouse, quickly impressing the owner.

Soon, he'd begun saving his wages and set off to broker his own furniture supply store in Amman. He'd earned enough money to support a family and crossed back into Falasteen and Bayt al-Hawa.

And then I found you, he told Sundus.

In her parents' flat, women congratulated her, kissing both of Sundus's cheeks. "May Allah bless you with a bounty of children."

Her face flushed with joy as Jalal whispered in her ear, "I can't wait to see you pregnant."

After a honeymoon in Jericho, Sundus went to work making their newly built villa a proper home for them. She'd bid the nurses goodbye at the hospital and they'd declared how absolutely radiant she looked, that marriage suited her. Her mother helped her arrange the brand-new furniture from Jalal's store. Jalal built her a shelf for all of her books. Before he sanded it down and painted its surface a glowing mahogany, Sundus ran her hand over its coarse grain. The entire villa smelled of polished marble and fresh paint. The windows shone like mirrors and the wooden kitchen cabinets gleamed.

Her mother crocheted lace doilies for the salon and arranged the linens in each bedroom.

"You and Baba can live with us," Sundus exclaimed. Jalal had come to love them as his own parents.

Her mother shook her head. "As long as he works at the hospital, your father will never leave Ramallah. And you need your privacy, my love. You're still getting to know your husband."

Sundus learned to prepare easy dishes: mjadara with caramelized onions, green peas and carrot stew with lamb chunks.

Before they reached the end of their first year, their villa was suffused with the aura of a married couple, of two people in love inhabiting a space.

"Soon you'll be cooking for a family," her mother said, tucking a strand of Sundus's hair behind her ear as they stood at the stove. Her mother gave simple culinary instructions and closely monitored the pine nuts that sizzled and browned in a dollop of samna butter. "Keep an eye on it or they'll burn."

Sundus and Jalal made love every night and Sundus learned to let her body go, abandoning timidity, asking Jalal for more, to not stop. They kissed for a long time, their tongues exploring each other's mouth then trailing the skin of their throats and shoulders.

Afterward in the dark, they told each other stories of their lives before the war. Jalal described his childhood in Qira, a small hamlet where he and his friends would go fishing in a nearby river. In his voice, Sundus heard the blissful vestiges of childhood. And in his long pauses, the deep yearning for it. Jalal never spoke of his years living in the mokhayam, what it was like to exist in a new, bleak world without parents and siblings, despite being an adult. He did repeat how poetry had saved his life, how it was imparted to him by a teacher who lived among Bedouins in Petra. As he longed for Falasteen, he'd carried the verses of al-Muntanabbi and Malik Shawqi, and other slimly printed reproductions of odes, carefully preserving them in a leather satchel.

"They were as precious as golden liras," he told Sundus. "I owned little else before my very first store." His story rested there like a spent traveler who desired nothing more than peaceful sleep.

Sundus, too, refrained from chronicling the roadside grave and how her mother didn't talk for months after they reached Ramallah. Like the brass key her mother had locked away in her precious box, neither Sundus nor Jalal ever brought out their pain to look at it. It hung in the silent pauses between their joyful stories, as Jalal smoked his cigarettes, the moonlight catching their ghostly rings.

Before they fell asleep, Sundus read the verses of Al Khansa until Jalal's soft snoring came.

"La howla walla koowat illah billah," her cousin Majida sighs. "Only God knows where we'll land on this earth."

The wind carries the memory away and Sundus returns to her glider. Dusk has begun to fall. She studies her granddaughter's shadowed face. "A refugee who'd lost everything had returned to his homeland. Built a new life for him and his family," she says wistfully. "That was my Jalal, may the Lord have mercy on his soul."

Majida offers her another supplication, dabbing her eyes with a handkerchief she's pulled from her sleeve. "That was the year before the second disaster. Before 1967," her cousin tells Intisar, patting her hand.

"And then Falasteeniya lost everything again," Sundus adds. Her father's fallen body flashes in her mind.

"But you kept this land," her granddaughter returns, the statement more of a question. In spite of the slowly engulfing darkness, Sundus can see a tired sadness has settled in the girl's eyes, replacing her anger.

"Alhamdullilah, we did," Sundus says. "Many had lost so much—many continue to lose sons and daughters. Their land.

No matter what, our trees, the dawali have remained. They've withstood a second occupation and uprisings. Were spared demolition." She pauses and holds her hand out as if reaching for something. "Can you understand what this means?"

But the girl is silent, her eyes roaming across the darkening valley.

"When they took your father away," Sundus continues, "I thought they'd taken everything from me. Except for this land, ya sitti. This has always been ours." The notary's golden seal on the fraudulent deed flashes across her mind, prowling behind her words.

Intisar stands, her shadow splintered by the iron railing of the barranda. "But the only thing I'd ever needed," she says quietly, "was taken from me." Her shoulders tremble and tears streak down her face. "I never wanted anything else."

"Habibti!' Majida cries, reaching for her, but Intisar disappears into the villa.

"Let her go," Sundus says.

"Ya rubbi," her cousin sighs. "What's to come?"

"That which the merciful Lord grants us," Sundus answers, hoping the creaking of the glider can muffle the knocking in her chest—the fear of losing it all again. And, for a second time, her granddaughter.

BAYT AL-HAWA: SEPTEMBER 2007

CHAPTER II

She can't sleep. The past lurks over Intisar like a ghost. She's come to this country to pay her final respects to a father she never knew, only to inherit property to which she is also a stranger. How can she be expected to fight for something that belongs to her when she is so far from belonging to it?

She steps onto the small balcony attached to her room, clutching her pack of cigarettes. The spark of the flame momentarily illuminates the brush of the hill. In the darkness, she can make out the old, dilapidated well. Her father had smoked his first cigarette there. Intisar inhales then exhales, white smoke curling and disappearing into the cool air. The lights of a watchtower blink down at her. A settlement? Her grandmother hadn't mentioned how close it was—as if it didn't exist. The houses in the compound are nearly identical, as far as she can tell. A chill runs down her spine. There is something ominous about that—not being able to tell things apart.

She shifts her gaze high above the settlement, searching the constellations. The stars hang closer here, not like the two-dimensional backdrop in Illinois. *Light pollution,* Intisar's science teacher had told them in elementary school. She remembers a field trip to the Adler Planetarium in Chicago, sinking back in her auditorium chair as the domed ceiling transformed into a spectacular universe. To be gazing into the galaxy while actually living and moving inside of it had boggled her young mind. She'd wondered if aliens were just as awestruck. Then she'd thought of her father and how he was seeing the same stars, wherever he was.

In the summertime, they'd camped out in the snug courtyard of the apartment building and identified constellations, matching them in a book Intisar had found at the public library. Then Baba would read: *"Look again at that dot. That's here. That's home. That's us. On it everyone you love, everyone you know, everyone you ever heard of, every human being who ever was, lived out their lives."* And she'd memorized it and could still recite it years after he'd left.

That's here. That's home. That's us.

From where Intisar stands on the small balcony, puffing her cigarette, she can make out Pleiades—the Seven Sisters, a milky cluster that flattens like a heart. Despite this same canopy, she feels utterly out of place. She pulls the photograph off the nightstand and the moonlight catches the faces inside the orchard, Baba gesturing to the camera and Intisar's profile, her eyes reading his lips.

The wind has settled and she listens to the crickets. The silence she's used to back home—occasionally broken by a barking dog or a car alarm—has been replaced here by a symphony of nature and other sounds she can't entirely identify. When the azzan signals the dawn prayer, she's still awake in her bed. It's a new day—her fourth one in Bayt al-Hawa. In six more, she'll be back in Emad's taxicab and then on a plane to the States. Unless she chooses to stay and fight for what is rightfully hers. At least, according to her grandmother.

Intisar can't pretend she didn't know what was coming. Of course something of her father's inheritance would be bequeathed to her. But couldn't Sitti Sundus appreciate that it didn't hold the same value as what was already taken from her? No amount of money can ever replace her life with Baba.

When she was a child, she'd invented a foolish scene in her mind. Any day now Baba would change his mind and come back and she'd forgive him because he loved her and had proven it by returning.

She remembers her mother teasing her about losing her share. *At least some of it will go to you,* she'd winked at Intisar. She wasn't mature enough to appreciate the implications of being his sole heir—the very word striking images of royalty and greed.

And now this very property is entangled with that awful, leering man—Abdul Waheed?

And if you are smart, Sister, you'll finish paying your respects, accept my gift, and go back to America with something, he'd said, making it sound so easy.

It was Baba's sacrifice—not hers. But is this how it worked? Is sacrifice another inheritance she is supposed to accept without question? *Yes,* she imagines her father saying. *And maybe you'll understand why I gave you up.*

Something else is nagging her: Is she strong enough to reclaim something so important? *You're a lover, habibti, not a fighter,* her mother had always teased. *Let's hope you meet someone just as nice someday.*

As the sun comes up, glowing orange over the hills, it illuminates the faces in the photograph in a different way than the moon had. She traces Baba's face, then her own before she retreats inside. Her grandmother and aunt have begun to stir inside the villa. There's the flush of a toilet, the rush of water from a faucet. Intisar hears footsteps down the hallway and waits for a knock at her door.

Majida pokes her head in. "Sabah al khair, my love," she says with a bright smile. "Breakfast is ready. Come eat."

Intisar can't help feeling impressed by the woman's nonchalance. As if nothing has changed. No secret revealed.

By the time she is dressed, Sitti Sundus is already settled under the fig tree, sorting her grapes. Majida sweeps water from the villa's floors and threatens Intisar if she dares lift a broom to help her. Intisar sits all alone in the kitchen, dipping chunks of bread into a small bowl of olive oil before dredging it in another bowl of crushed za'atar. There won't be any mention of the stolen land, she realizes, or fraudulent deeds this morning. She shakes her head incredulously. What about this incredible burden she's been handed? She chews her bread. To these women, she must be a spoiled brat who can't appreciate what they've been through. But what about her?

It's not the milestones she misses with Baba, although she's had to tolerate the looks of pity from her aunts and cousins at each celebration of a birthday, graduation, or new job. Intisar has to admit her mother has done her best in the end. Mama had considered her marriage to Ali a blessing, a loving replacement for Baba. *He treats Tee-Tee like his own,* she'd tell her clients at the beauty salon. *I got lucky.* It made Intisar's own happiness into a lottery—something depending entirely on chance. So even Ali had been a precarious entity, one undeserved, who might disappear like Baba.

She, too, is grateful for her stepfather, a kind, wonderful man. He made every occasion special for Intisar, and supported and guided her throughout adolescence. He was more patient and gentle than Mama. Still, it wasn't the same. Intisar craved Baba's presence in daily life, like at the kitchen table in their cramped apartment for meals. Then at bedtime, a book laid open between them. And in the front row during her school recitals, applauding and cheering his daughter. And in the courtyard, on their backs, arms folded behind their heads as they gazed up at the pitch-dark sky, the stars winking back at them.

Lubna's motorbike revs up the hill and Intisar quickly gathers a new pack of cigarettes. Though she's in no mood for more sightseeing, she's glad to avoid her grandmother for as long as possible. She moves quickly past the dawali, Sitti Sundus a blur of white headscarf and black thobe, and through the side entrance where Lubna waits.

They're bound for Nablus today: "Home of the best knafeh you will ever taste," Lubna declares. "But first we must make two stops." Lubna points to the nylon bags she's looped over her wrist. "Special deliveries."

"Let me hold that for you," Intisar offers, and Lubna hands over the bags. The aroma of sumac-spiced spinach and onions wafts from it.

As they wind down the hill, Intisar finds that she recognizes the neighboring villas and a few other signposts they rush by. A small sundries shop. A taxi depot where she spots Emad's car. Lubna honks at the villagers and they cheerily wave back. A few of the elderly men in their headdresses shake their heads at them in disapproval. Intisar marvels at Lubna's bodacious, carefree attitude. She can barely smoke in public here, let alone hop on a motorbike and cruise through the village where everyone knows her. Perhaps it's the bold spirit of Lubna's great-grandmother Hala coursing through her veins.

Some of the women call to Lubna to stop. "Bring bint Hafez to us. Have tea and hilba!" In America, Intisar is anonymous. The white neighbors know little of her beyond her nickname. They wave politely as they back out of their driveways or while mowing their lawns. She wonders how much one's loneliness disappears in a place like Bayt al-Hawa.

As the hill begins to recede behind them, Lubna heads toward the mokhayam. She slows to a stop in front of a shanty house with a corrugated roof like those of its neighbors. The village they'd left only moments ago has vanished again.

An old man comes waddling down a dirt pathway, leading with a cane. He waves at them with his free hand.

"Hajj Abu Fahmy! I've brought you fatayer," Lubna calls to him. "This is my friend from America. Intisar."

"Ahlan, my daughter!" His brown eyes twinkle at her. "Come quickly!" he exclaims, joy lifting the wrinkles of his face. "I, too, have a visitor." He points at their helmets. "You might scare the poor fellow."

Lubna looks at Intisar and shrugs. They dismount and remove their helmets and follow the old man, who's impressively quick. He shuffles one foot after the other, nearly outrunning his cane as they round the corner of the shanty.

Sprawled on the ground is a stork, a bushel of feathers beneath its pale red beak like the beard of an imam. It's almond-shaped eyes regard them pensively.

"Where has he come from, Hajj?" Lubna whispers, as if her words might disturb the creature. Intisar isn't as bold and hangs back, the bags of food still looped around her wrist.

"From the west," the old man says. "Europe. They stay for a few months, then return home. But this one is late in the season. He must have become ill and separated from his flock." He slowly crouches to the ground, bracing against his cane. "Subhan Allah," he breathes. "I'd only ever seen one when I was child. Near Tiberias." He reaches out and gently caresses the stork's head.

"Careful, ya Hajj!" Lubna says, inching closer. "We don't know what he's carrying."

"He's a handsome prince, this one," the old man croons. He turns to Intisar. "You see here? The males are larger. Their beaks are longer than the females."

Intisar slowly squats down beside Lubna. The bird shivers, feathers ruffling in a wave. Lubna reaches out to touch the bird, to reassure it and it seems to sense it, twitching its head in her direction.

"Watch out," the old man warns. "He's got an awful bite."

"Will he recover?" Intisar asks.

"Inshallah, my daughter." He hoists himself up with his cane.

Lubna pulls a camera from her backpack and squats down again, eye level with the stork. Then, to Intisar, she holds up one finger, indicating the bags full of savory pies.

Intisar nods, slips one off her wrist and holds it out. "These are for you," she says shyly to the old man.

"Your favorite," Lubna says from behind her camera, adjusting her lens.

"Bless your mother's hands!" Abu Fahmy smiles broadly, his mouth mostly hollow of teeth. "And you, bint Hafez. Flown here all the way from America. I remember when you were a child, my dear." He gestures for Intisar to follow him to a wire coop with a sloping side, home to pigeons and other birds. "Your father took care of them when he was a boy. Your father, too—" he points to Lubna—"helped me restore the coop, clean their mess."

Intisar feels that same strange flutter in her chest, like a feather from this magnificent bird. Here's another person who knew her father. She tries to imagine Baba outside the shanty, helping the old man whose face might have contained fewer wrinkles decades ago, yet his eyes no less sharp.

Lubna stows her camera and taps Intisar's arm. "We have to get going, Hajj."

"Allah be with you, ya banat!" he says, waving goodbye.

Intisar is disappointed. She wants to linger, to hear more about her father.

Lubna gently tugs her arm. "We'll come back," she smiles.

Their next stop is a short distance away. A building with gray siding—like one of those manufactured homes Intisar has seen on the Illinois interstate highway being hauled by a semitruck. Lubna carefully maneuvers around a stream of sewage and parks her motorbike. Her friend seems unaffected by the awful stench. Intisar fights the urge to pinch her nostrils.

"Medical center. For women," Lubna explains, taking the second bag from her. "For women and girls."

Beside it is a blue tarp-covered tent where uneven rows of metal folding chairs are set up, each one occupied by a woman or child. Lubna tells Intisar it's for those who'd arrived late. Some women sit on the ground, unperturbed, hands folded in their laps or embroidering on white netting. They chat among themselves, their dusty, naked toes peeking from sandals beneath their thobes. Lubna waves to them in greeting. They stare curiously at Intisar.

"My sister works here." Lubna rings a bell at the entrance of the building. After a few seconds, they're buzzed in.

Intisar half expects to see a cozy kitchen and drywalled rooms where a family sleeps. Inside is dull, unadorned. Heavy black-out drapes cover every window, cooling the interior. Any natural light spills from tinted narrow skylights or sneaks in when the door opens. Rooms are separated by hospital curtains attached to metal tracks on the ceiling. The odor of ammonia hangs in the air.

Little attempt has been made to make the space cheerful. Intisar thinks of Pine Woods and how she'd thought it was a hotel when she applied for the position. Here, the walls of the clinic are finished in a dull eggshell. A few posters hang from them, one commanding patients in Arabic to model proper hygiene so that their children, too, will exercise it. Another illustrates the human gestational period in full color, the fetus shaped like a kidney bean inside the cross-section of a woman's body. The image of the dead baby on the side of the road instantly reappears and Intisar quickly shakes it from her mind.

"Look who's here!" A slender woman with small shoulders approaches them. She's wearing a lavender hijab and a long matching skirt beneath her white medical coat. "Ahlan!" She pulls Lubna in for a kiss on each cheek. She regards Intisar with warm, honey-colored eyes as Lubna makes the introductions.

"Pleased to meet you," Intisar says, extending her hand, but the woman ignores it and pulls her in for an embrace.

"Amal is the best volunteer they have," Lubna is saying.

"How's Raya? Is she better?"

"My daughter," Amal proudly proclaims, holding up her mobile phone. Intisar politely nods at an image of a round-faced baby who transforms into a gleeful toddler with every swipe of Amal's thumb. "Alhamdullilah her fever broke," she says to Lubna. "My mother has her today."

A loud wailing erupts from behind one of the curtains. "Maskeena," Amal whispers to Intisar. "She's pregnant again."

Lubna sucks her teeth. "I don't know why they don't use anything."

"Because we can't supply contraceptives here," a voice says behind them.

Intisar turns to see a woman; she has the same hazel eyes as Lubna, her nose a sharper rendition. She wears a turban under which Intisar imagines the same gorgeous curls tucked beneath. "Nor can we provide abortions," she adds in fluent English, her eyes trained on Intisar, a fetoscope around her neck.

Lubna rolls her eyes. "I'm just saying. How does bringing another child into this world make matters better for these women?"

The other women shift on their plastic chairs; a few cast their gaze downward.

"Have faith," Amal scolds. "The Lord does not leave us unprovided."

"Perhaps you should protest at the UN," the other young woman scoffs, her eyes still on Intisar.

"My sister Elham," Lubna finally announces, rolling her eyes again. "The doctor." She extends the nylon bag as if thwarting another argument. "From our mother. Fatayer."

"Bless her hands," Amal gushes, taking the bag. "Hers are

the best—" she winks conspiratorially at Intisar—"even better than my mother's."

Intisar leans in toward Lubna's sister for the customary embrace, but Elham only extends her hand.

"Yes. Bint Hafez. The American," Elham says, her hands tucked inside the pockets of her gray scrubs. "How are you finding Falasteen so far?"

Intisar almost blurts that she's been here before, but the doctor's mocking tone stops her. "Good, good." Then she adds, "I'm a nurse," desperate to dilute Elham's obvious contempt and to reclaim some respect. And before she can stop herself, Intisar says, "I'm here for another week. If you need an extra hand, someone to—"

"We are managing fine."

Intisar forces a smile. "Oh, of course," she says lamely. Why has she offered? How insulting! Does she think making herself useful for a few days before returning to the States would make up for turning her back on everything else here? The doctor clearly sees her as nothing more than a tourist. Intisar clears her throat, tries to recover. "Is this a birthing center?"

Elham shakes her head. "Prenatal checkups. When it is time, they are sent to a hospital in Ramallah. As you can see, we are not equipped." Her last sentence drips with sarcasm.

A nurse comes over in green scrubs and a black headscarf. "Are you ready for the next one, Doktorra?"

"I'll be right there, Wafa. Thank you." She looks Intisar over one more time. "Enjoy your visit." She walks away without a backward glance.

"Don't mind her," Lubna says loud enough for her sister to hear. "She thinks she's so superior."

"I'm sure she's doing important work here." Intisar hopes

Elham hears this, but the young doctor has already disappeared behind the curtain of an examination room.

"Mashallah, your sister is a blessing," Amal says kindly. "These women would have to travel many kilometers to a clinic in Ramallah. Doktorra Elham fought for three years to get funding."

Lubna is quiet for a moment. Intisar has no idea what it's like to compete with a sibling—only a mother. "Yalla," she finally says to Intisar. "Time to go."

On their way to Nablus, Lubna pulls off at the side of the road where a woman peddles baskets. She's wearing a dusty thobe, a white scarf tied at her neck. Dark hairs have strayed and frame her tanned face. Her eyes—sharp like Abu Fahmy's and the color of palm dates—rove over Intisar.

"With your permission?" Lubna asks, holding up her camera.

"A trade," the old woman offers, bracing for a bit of haggling. "You can take my picture for a shekel."

"A good deal," Lubna smiles, fishing for a coin in her jeans pocket. "Here you are." The woman quickly burrows it inside the chest panel of her thobe.

Intisar admires a basket with a flower pattern in the center, its petals magenta, blue, and green.

The woman nudges Lubna. "Tell her I'll give her two for one price. Six shekels." She wiggles two fingers at Intisar. "Two for one. Tell her." She squats on her haunches and goes back to her weaving.

"She understands you, Khalti," Lubna chuckles, aiming her camera.

The basket weaver regards Intisar suspiciously. "Mish

amrikeeya?" She's missing her upper teeth, her mouth half-sunken.

"Yes, Khalti, but she's come home," Lubna assures her.

Intisar holds up a basket. "These are lovely mashallah."

"They're made from olive and almond trees," the woman proudly announces, speaking and weaving. "Wheat is scarce, you know."

Intisar watches her gnarled yet deft fingers until a new basket begins to take shape. She considers buying two for her mother and Teta Rehab, hoping they won't end up in a Goodwill box after spring cleaning. And then she remembers.

Don't bring anything back, Mama had told Intisar. *I don't need anything. Just pay your respects and come home.*

"We can grab one on the way back," Lubna assures her. She thanks the basket weaver. "May the Lord always keep you, Khalti."

"And may God bring you prosperity, my daughters," she returns, watching them climb back onto the motorbike. "Alhamdullah asaalama," she calls to Intisar, waving the finished basket. "Welcome home."

The next stop is not planned. Before Lubna begins to brake, Intisar can already smell pungent smoke. Ahead of them is a smoldering field, an acrid odor of gasoline saturating the air. She instinctively covers her mouth and nose. They pull up to a large group of people standing at the edge of the road. They're watching the burning embers of uprooted olive trees, most of which have already turned to ash by the time Intisar dismounts the bike.

She's watched, mesmerized, live broadcasts of forest fires

raging California—firefighters and volunteers working around the clock against dry and windy conditions that embolden the flames. It was like witnessing Mother Nature reclaim what was hers. Reminding them of her awesome power. No matter how old she gets, the same clammy fear rises in her throat at the thought of a monstrous maw of flames licking and devouring everything in its path.

But these fallen trees directly in front of her—she can smell their earthy smokiness, can see their charred bark. These trees have been deliberately destroyed and she's witnessing the final act in a lynching of trees. Shame and terror and despair roil inside in the storm of nausea within her. Despite the sun beating down, she breaks into a cold sweat as she tries to make sense of the scene in front of her. The trees that remain are like matchsticks when they catch, with clumps of red dirt still clinging to their massive roots. They'd been gouged by the hungry mouth of a bulldozer, then tossed on top of each other like firewood.

A small group of settlers, machine guns strapped over their shoulders, lean against a bulldozer, smoking cigarettes and laughing with its operator, observing their handiwork while their small children chase each other. Their curly sidelocks—tiny versions of their fathers'—bounce like soft corkscrews off their cheeks.

The other group are farmers. Men, women, and children quietly huddled, except for a horrible wailing rising from them. The harvest is only weeks away. October? November? Intisar can't remember what Baba had once told her about that amazing season when the fellahin gathered to reap the olives. It sounded more like a festive celebration than labor to a much younger Intisar.

She catches Lubna hastily wiping her own tears across the

back of her hand. She sniffles and pulls out her camera, snapping a dozen photographs. The rapid succession of the shutter is muffled by a woman's singular weeping and cursing. Two young men hold her up; her black thobe covered in dirt as if she's been praying on the ground. An elderly man wearing a gray jilbab, his white undergarments exposing his ankles and sandals, stands apart from the others. He turns and catches Intisar's gaze and waves a branch of silver-green leaves that he's salvaged from their original trunk.

"Look what they've done, my children!" he calls to her and Lubna. "May God exact His justice!"

Bile rises on her tongue. She tugs Lubna's arm. "Enough," she says. She's not sure the word has escaped her lips until her friend nods back.

"Let's go," Lubna says. She revs the motor, still not loud enough to drown out the wailing woman. Before she releases the brake, a jeep roars down the dusty road and almost hits them.

Intisar's heart lunges in her throat. Will she be arrested? She's nothing more than a bystander to the spectacle.

A soldier hops out. "We caught them!" he calls to the settlers.

In the back of the jeep are teenage boys, their wrists bound behind their backs, seated on two steel benches opposite each other. They are begging in Arabic to be freed. A smaller one among them is weeping for his mother, snot running down his nose.

"It wasn't us!" the boys cry.

"It wasn't you, you stupid dogs?" The soldier waves a bunch of slingshots in the air, snarling. "And what do you call these?" He points at the blazing scene. "You see there? No more hiding in trees."

The boys go mute at the sight of the ravaged olive grove

until the youngest cries harder, breaking the dark spell.

"For throwing rocks? They—they burned down their trees for throwing rocks?" Intisar stammers.

"For spite," Lubna says grimly.

"Spite?" Intisar repeats barely above a whisper.

"For being born Palestinian." She shakes her head. "For being alive."

As if hearing her, a second soldier—the driver—hops down and heads straight for Lubna. "Haweeya!" he demands, holding his hand out.

Lubna keeps one hand raised as she riffles through her backpack for her identification card. Intisar marvels at her calmness, the way she regards him with a mask of contempt—not fear. The soldier makes a show of inspecting it for longer than necessary. He tosses it back at her chest. Lubna stoops to retrieve it from the dusty road.

The soldier turns to Intisar. "Haweeya!" He gestures with his hand.

"Your passport," Lubna tells her.

"Ah! American!" the soldier muses, winking at Intisar.

It's hard to disguise her trembling fingers as she hands him the blue booklet.

"I love America!" he boasts. "Justin Timberlake! Michael Jordan! Britney Sp—" He's momentarily distracted by the boys they've rounded up.

"For the love of God, it wasn't us!" They are moaning again. "Please! Please!"

Intisar notices an older boy sitting nearest the opening of the jeep, likely the last one to be shoved in when they were rounded up. He is quiet and stares straight ahead, as if at some invisible spot above another boy's head, his back straight and stiff. There are no tears streaming down his face, no cries for his mother.

The first soldier notices, too, and, still gripping the slingshots, hauls the boy from the jeep. He topples to the ground and is seized by his cuffed wrists—a plastic, zip restraint—and yanked upwards. He winces, his limbs forced in an unnatural position. He's bleeding from a cut in his elbow. But he remains silent. He's wearing a striped soccer jersey, a name emblazoned in red across his back. He looks to be the eldest of the bunch. Thirteen, fourteen years old?

The farmers join the pleas for release, forgetting their livelihoods have been torched. "He's just a boy! Leave him be!"

"Maybe it was him?" the soldier taunts the others in the jeep. He kicks the boy from behind. He falls again, attempts to stand on his own this time before the soldier yanks him to his feet again. Intisar can't see his face. "Ha? What do you say? Was it this rat?"

Lubna steps forward. "Leave him alone! He's just a kid!"

"Stand back! Shut up!" the soldier guarding them yells. He's still holding Intisar's passport.

She instinctively grabs Lubna hand, fights the scream puncturing her vocal chords. She follows the movement of their machine guns, braces herself for a lightning crash of sounds, then bullets tearing through her body.

"Ha? Was it him?" the first soldier taunts again. As the boys protest their innocence, the silent one is suddenly on his stomach, his arms painfully bent behind him. There's a swift kick to his ribs and he cries out for the first time, a sharp noise that pierces Intisar's heart. "Was it you, you bastard?"

The boy goes quiet again, turns his head to one side away from the soldier. "Your mother's cunt," he sputters.

"He's talking! Azeem!" the soldier jeers in Arabic. "Say it was you." His tone turns deadly as he positions his boot inches away from the boy's face. "Say it was you and I'll let you all go."

The boy lifts his head as far as he can and tries spitting at the soldier's boot from his awkward angle. In response, the soldier kicks him in the ribs again then lays his boot on the boy's neck.

"Wallak, he's only a kid, you criminal!" Lubna shouts.

The second soldier shoves her backwards and Lubna falls to ground along with Intisar's passport, tossed in the scuffle.

"Stay down!" he commands, pointing his rifle at her.

Intisar drops to the ground, too, terror turning her bones to liquid. She puts her hands over her head, but this doesn't shield herself from the soldier's shouts, from the sobbing of the boys, the asphyxiated gasps of the silent one. When she looks up again, the boy's eyes are starting to roll backwards in his skull. Only then does the soldier lift his boot. He shouts an order at the other soldier, who drags the boy to the jeep.

Intisar can't tell if he's dead or alive before the jeep speeds away in a cloud of dust.

GAHANA PRISON: OCTOBER 1997

CHAPTER 12

Today a different siren went off, signaling a fresh arrival of men. Hafez sensed a complicated, morbid excitement running through his cellmates: would they know the new ones? Would they find someone from their clans? He wondered the same thing, for sometimes there were only a few degrees of separation among kin. After they were processed and dispatched, they were released onto each floor of the compound, into cells where a vacancy had opened either by exoneration or death. Some would age out and be released, others like Abu Jadallah and Abu Nasser would become old men here. And so would Hafez.

What none of them expected that day was a woman. Her name was Rasheeda Al-Badawi. She would be temporarily housed in Gahana until her permanent transfer to a women's prison. *Our brave sisters* was what Abu Jadallah called them. But they'd never witnessed a woman among them outside of the female guards and legal counsel.

Considered highly dangerous and pugnacious, Rasheeda was immediately thrown into the Zinzana in an effort to tame her. Hafez and the others did not see her, but as soon as she was released from the Dungeon, her voice rang through the prison compound.

"Do not lose heart, Brothers! The resistance charges on!" she shouted in a raspy voice. The men on her floor responded with catcalls and applause.

"Shut up!" the guards growled at her, but Rasheeda was undaunted. She began to chant, "With soul, with blood, we'll liberate you, ya Falasteen!" Her words were scratchy and strained as if she'd been screaming for a long time. "With soul, with blood, we'll liberate you, ya—"

From his top bunk, Hafez heard a skirmish while Nijmy stood at the steel door, craning his neck to catch a glimpse of Rasheeda through the barred window. Below Hafez, Sadeeq cowered in his corner of the bunk, clinging to his deck of cards. Ever since Hafez began playing with the dull-witted man, he and the deck had become inseparable; it was like he'd grown a new appendage.

As the noise of the guards restraining her died down, Hafez thought of his daughter. She turned seventeen this month, would be graduating high school next spring. She'd escaped another existence, one Rasheeda had not. In that other country, Intisar had choices and opportunities. She had freedom, the kind that was inalienable, inherited by virtue of birth. Not the same as what Hafez had been temporarily gifted then was demanded back. They'd revoked his American citizenship as soon as he was arrested. His haweeya meant nothing here; he had no privileges, let alone basic rights to lean on.

During her last visit, Um Hafez had mentioned a nursing degree. Intisar would make a life of helping others. A quiet pride had swelled inside of him, for in spite of him, she would have a good life. The other men boasted about their children and grandchildren, but Hafez never uttered Intisar's name. She only appeared in the pages of his sketchbook, a tiny, magnificent figure he'd conjured from Nadira's love, standing against the backdrop of other magnificent creations he summoned from memory. It was safe to imagine his Intisar in these spaces, safely tucked away from this violence, as if inhabiting other planets humans hadn't contaminated. Those sketches he kept private, showing only his earlier ones to his cellmates to mollify their persistent questions. What could he be possibly writing in that miniature notebook?

One day, Hafez tore a page out and handed it to Abu Jadallah.

Mashallah, Abu Jadallah had crooned, admiration and surprise lacing the old man's words. *It's the sakhra!* He held up a tiny replica of the Dome of the Rock for the other men to see. When he turned it over, Abu Jadallah looked confused.

It's the interior of the mosque, Hafez explained sheepishly. He'd sketched a naked dome, its longitudinal ribs. The drum supported by piers and columns. What you saw if you could peel away the gilded wood, the mosaics, and inscriptions.

The pious man turned it back to the exterior. *Look at that.*

The others quickly began making requests: Al Aqsa Mosque in Jerusalem, the sacred Ka'ba in Mecca. They cared only about the finished structure, and Hafez could hardly begrudge them. For Nijmy, he gladly sketched a football stadium, its stands full of tiny smudges depicting electrified fans. The young man accepted it with a crooked smile. Such unexpected joy was finite—like a small supply of tea or a pair of extra-thick socks for winter.

Hafez sketched and sketched, yet there were only so many places the men had been—and their imaginations stretched only so far. Their requests gradually petered out like the fading flourish of his pencil trailing the corner of a page. What they wanted more than anything was a picture of home; the image of it was branded on their minds, its wonderful aroma wafting through their nostrils, its tender flavor swirling across their tongues. Hafez could never capture such things.

"Women should be home with their children," Nijmy was saying, his expression scornful, as if Rasheeda's very presence was an affront. They'd finally stifled her, and familiar masculine noise could be distinguished on each floor again.

The other men shook their heads. "A Falasteeniya is stronger than you think," Abu Jadallah said, the Quran lying open across his lap.

"Would you want your daughter in here?" Nijmy challenged, baring his teeth. "To be spoiled, ruined?"

"Palestinian women have lost more than their virginity," Nasser retorted. "If they wish to join the resistance, they are entitled." He was sitting on his haunches near a wall, preparing the hot plate for tea.

"But it is different, my son," Abu Nasser argued. "Women are more vulnerable than men."

"I've known strong women," Hafez said.

All eyes turned to him in surprise. He rarely offered his opinion unless directly addressed, let alone partaking in lively banter that typically ended in cursing by the younger men.

His own voice surprised him, too, but he continued. "I've been raised by strong women."

"That's different," Nijmy countered. "On the frontlines of war, women have always been leveraging chips—not combatants."

"What nonsense you talk, ya zalama!" Nasser scoffed across the room. He finished pouring a glass of unsweetened shai for his father. A small sack of sugar—a gift from Um Nasser's recent visit—had been ravaged by cockroaches despite Abu Nasser's best efforts. "What about Leila Khaled?"

A murmur ran through the cell. Wissam Abu Nimr's face flashed across Hafez's mind.

"Leila, ya Leila!" Sadeeq suddenly crooned.

"Quiet, you!" Nijmy hissed as he headed toward the toilet. Sadeeq went back to shuffling his cards on the floor.

"And what about the operation you pulled off?" Nasser stood beside Hafez's cot. "Was it not a woman who masterminded the attack, ya Hafez?"

"And killed in a half-assed explosion," Nijmy returned. "A soldier's leg their only plunder." It had become a customary joke.

The other men chuckled and turned to Hafez, eager for more of the story. While he avoided the subject of his daughter, he'd answer their direct questions as best as he could. And when he did, young men like the belligerent Nijmy sidled close to him, hoping to absorb a glory that Hafez had not felt. Because his responses to the operation were fragmented and told without embellishment or spectacle, Nijmy quickly grew bored and soon regarded Hafez as just another prisoner like him.

He never admitted how his time in the Zinzana had splintered his memory, that he could no longer discern what had actually happened and what he'd fabricated to halt the torture. And yet his comrade Wissam Abu Nimr—swiftly killed and expunged from history—remained the most vibrant recollection. Wissam hadn't done it for infamy. She'd embodied a kind of courage Hafez had never known—even when he joined her mission.

In the beginning, he'd volunteered at the hospital in Ramallah where his parents had met, driving an ambulance and fetching supplies before curfews were imposed. He'd steer past his father's shuttered furniture store, which had joined the other businesses on strike. Its security bars were like a steel curtain shielding the large display window.

But that sense of impotence shadowed his heart, and a voice demanded: *Have you sacrificed enough, ya Hafez? Do you think you deserve to stand idly by while your countrymen are struck down?*

When he was thrown into Gahana, the men had quickly admonished him: *How could you give up your life America, ya Hafez?*

They imagined him living a life of ease, enjoying a freedom they'd fantasized each night as they lay their heads on their stiff cots. Indeed, he'd tasted such freedom. But his secret open wound thrummed, and there was no salve to heal it, not even the love of a wife or the miracle of a child.

Nadira had become pregnant two months after they married. Intisar arrived in the fall of 1981. His circumstances had abruptly changed. His student visa didn't provide for a family allowance, and a part-time job on the weekends could barely cover the rent in a studio apartment a mile off campus. To make matters more difficult, Nadira was homesick for her mother and sisters. Without argument or debate, Hafez quietly agreed to return to Chicago.

There's always night school, his new wife had assured him as they drove upstate at the end of the spring term. *It's just until we can get on our feet. We'll be fine.*

At first, he'd convinced himself that Nadira was right. This was America, after all. His trajectory didn't have to be a straight line. And when his darling Intisar arrived, she redefined his happiness. He took the late shift at a gas station so Nadira could work on her cosmetology license during the day.

Despite his exhaustion, his beautiful daughter seemed to replenish his energy. He continuously spoke to her as if she could understand every Arabic word. He fastened her into a stroller and took long walks around the neighborhood, where cars lined the curbs and kids rode their bicycles in the street. He'd stop and lift a fallen leaf on the sidewalk and show Intisar, tracing the intersecting veins. Or when a ladybug landed on his sleeve, he'd gently cup the magical insect for his daughter to see. Wonderfully delighted, Intisar's eyes widened and she attempted to pinch it before it flew away.

On warm days, he'd drive them to the lakefront and they'd sit near the embankment wall, counting sailboats. He'd hoist her on his shoulders and point to the skyline, naming every landmark building in sight. And they were the best days of Hafez's life. Intisar had seemed to soothe the wounds of failure and disappointment. She'd given him a real sense of purpose.

Until the uprising began in Falasteen. And a question gnawed at him: what was service without sacrifice?

At the hospital in Ramallah, he met a janitor named Saad—an alias Hafez would later discover—who'd hinted that more than mopping floors and driving an ambulance needed to be done. *If you're interested, meet me at the old Druze bookshop after your shift,* he'd quietly invited Hafez.

They gathered in the back room of the old bookstore where

his mother had once acquired work by her favorite poets. Um Hafez had taken him along a few times a year when the owner, an old man by then, had restocked.

The store had the same odor of books, a pleasant musk of paper and dust, and his childhood came wafting to the present. Hafez was overcome by a complicated nostalgia. It seemed with every joyful memory, tragedy was attached to it like a parasite. It was here that Um Hafez had browsed while his grandfather, Siddo Yousef, searched for the lost titles of books he'd left behind in Haifa when they'd fled.

Hafez followed Saad—like the man, Hafez would later be assigned a number for tracking and sending messages. They moved between narrow bookshelves surging from floor to ceiling. Hafez had never seen so many books in such a pocket-sized space. Pendant lamps hung from the ceiling, no longer functional but adding a touch of the arabesque. A dark curtain separated the storefront from the back room, and a tall man with frosty blue eyes stood guard, his blondish hair a dense poof.

Saad gave him a nod and the man pulled the curtain aside, letting them pass.

It was a stockroom containing several boxes, some sealed and some opened. In one corner of the room was a small, round table with two chairs and a sink and small portable stove, where a copper ibrik sat. Hemp-rope stools and mismatched chairs were brought in, shrinking the space even more.

Light came from a few single bulbs suspended from the low ceiling, their pull-chains dangling above them. The scene was surreal to Hafez—this secret meeting straight out of a spy movie. Except their mission wasn't espionage. It was, according to Saad's cryptic missive, "to escalate the uprising that had been forged by the will of the people and not the squabbling political factions." How fitting, Hafez had thought, to be devising an armed resistance among poets from the ages.

A woman began to speak. She was young and beautiful in a natural, unkempt way. Her disheveled hair pulled into a loose ponytail, brown wisps framing her face. She wore a shapeless dress that reached her ankles and sandals similar to a pair of babooj—the leather kind Hafez's father wore around the villa. This only amplified her slender body, her long elegant neck and slight shoulders. She was taller than a few of the other men, and eye-level with Hafez when he later stood before her to be briefed on his role. Around her neck was a golden pendant: an engraved miniature scroll of Surah al-Baqarra.

Her name was Wissam Abu Nimr.

Saad pointed to a pair of stools and Hafez settled down, taking in the company who'd gathered one by one in the early morning. A curfew had been lifted and there was a bustle in the market, folks gathering what they could before they were shut back into their homes.

Across the circle was a middle-aged man who appeared to be the eldest among them. Every few minutes, he took a handkerchief from his coat pocket and wiped his perspiration. Beside him was a short, diminutive man with a shaven head called Nu'man. He looked like a teenager, his baritone voice startling Hafez when he greeted him with a simple *Salaam*. Among the known operatives, Nu'man would be the only one to escape until a report confirmed that he'd been located in Cyprus and shot point-blank in the head as he slept in a dingy motel room.

A pair of shabab, clean-cut and articulate, sat together beside Hafez, leaning into each other, one man turning his head to offer his ear while the other spoke softly into it. And there were two women who appeared to be mother and daughter. They nodded at him with the same gap-toothed smile. He later learned that the two of them had been captured and tortured in a covert location. The younger one was raped as her mother was made to watch.

Saad had explained that the unit, as he called it, was greater than the number attending the meeting. For security purposes, they never met at the same time in the same place. This meeting was devoted to preliminary planning of the mission: they would target and destroy a prime military outpost near Jenin.

No one ever disclosed the name of the town or village they came from. He suspected that university affiliations had brought several of them together, including Wissam Abu Nimr—a first-year pharmacology student at the University of Jordan, before she dropped out and returned home.

When she spoke, her hands darted in the air like birds flitting from tree to tree. She possessed a special power that drew others toward her like the waves of a sea. It was clear to Hafez that she was the brains of the operation—or at least the one commanding this particular group.

Why would this amarkani want to join us? she'd wanted to know. She'd been instantly suspicious of Hafez.

Because I will always be Falasteeni, Hafez had returned. *I belong here, with my people.* Had he sounded convincing?

She'd seemed skeptical, taking him in with fierce brown eyes.

He's an engineer, Saad had told her.

An architect, Hafez instinctively corrected him, his face flushing. He was glad the room was dimly lit. He'd exchanged his degree for love.

Wissam Abu Nimr regarded him closely. *Ah, but you must*

know we don't plan to build something here, she had scoffed, eliciting a few chuckles around the circle. *We're interested in dismantling.*

Saad gave Hafez's thigh an emphatic pat. *He can help us. We need as many educated fighters as possible.*

His role was decided: reconnaissance. He would join a small team tasked with scoping and mapping the target location. After a month in hiding, an army of jeeps surrounded him and two of his comrades. Both were shot dead in a round of gunfire before a special forces unit stormed the hovel. They needed at least one alive to lead them to the others.

His lawyer, May Boustany, would later inform him that Wissam Abu Nimr had been among the operatives directly involved in the attack, her body blown from a car that had launched the explosives. Not much was left of her except for a charred pendant and a severed hand.

Later, in his cell, he allowed himself to wonder about her. Who might a young woman that fierce and enigmatic become if she had been born in another country, or on another continent? And what of his own Intisar—had her fate been reversed?

From below the floor, Rasheeda's shrieking once again broke the din of the men. "God smite you all! God smite you all!" she hurled at her jailers.

The men resumed their part, slapping the steel-barred window of their cells with their rubber slippers. "With soul, with blood, we'll liberate you, ya Falasteen! With soul, with blood, we'll liberate you, ya Falasteen!"

The flushing of the toilet, its fetid odor instantly rising in the cell, drowned out the last of Rasheeda's words as she was muzzled and dragged away.

BAYT AL-HAWA: SEPTEMBER 2007

CHAPTER 13

"Hajja Um Hafez."

Sundus stirs from her slumber and finds the young lawyer Nabeel Abu Shareef standing before her under the fig tree. Beside him is a boy drumming his fingers on the bottom of an empty cardboard box.

"Aywa, aywa," she mumbles. "Who's come?" She wipes her mouth with the back of her hand.

"Hajja, my mother wants one kilo of the red," the boy declares. He holds out his box with one hand, fishes for a few shekels in his jeans pocket with the other.

"All this way for a kilo?" Sundus peers up at the boy. She pulls a bunch of the red bulbs from a crate and sets them on an old-fashioned scale. She drops a one-kilo disc on one tray then adds another smaller bunch of grapes until the scale evens out.

"How's your mother? Has her foot healed?" Sundus asks the little boy. She knows every child, woman, and man in the village and nearly everyone in the mokhayam—though less of this new generation.

He shakes his head. "She can't walk yet. Or cook for us."

"Don't despair—I doubt any of you will go hungry," Sundus says, handing him the box of grapes. Nabeel Abu Shareef chuckles. The boy scampers out of the vineyard.

"Mashallah," the young lawyer says. "Another abundant harvest, Hajja Um Hafez." He's a handsome one in a gray suit and crisp white shirt, the top unbuttoned to reveal a white undershirt.

"Alhamdullilah," Sundus responds. "The Lord has been generous."

She gestures for Nabeel to sit on a stool beside her and offers him a water bottle.

Two women come to purchase three kilos each and ask after her granddaughter. "Inshallah it won't be long before bint Hafez finds her mate." Then, eyeing Nabeel Abu Shareef, they add, "A tall one to suit her." Everyone in Bayt al-Hawa knows the young lawyer. The great-grandson of the mukhtar, an honorable mayor who expanded municipal resources including irrigation of crops. Now this young man has become the protégé of May Boustany, her son's longtime lawyer.

"Go in peace," Sundus says to the women, rebuffing their desire for gossip. When they exit through the side entrance, she turns to Nabeel Abu Shareef. "The girl will be back later this afternoon inshallah." Sundus tucks her coin pouch into the chest compartment of her thobe. "You have news?"

"I've spoken with the court magistrate about a possible hearing for our case and—"

But before he can finish his sentence, her cousin Majida interrupts, descending the stone stairs with a tray of steaming tea glasses in her hands. "Ahlan, ahlan!" she coos at the young lawyer.

"Bless your hands," Sundus tells her. Majida always seems to be a step ahead of her. Soon, her cousin will cross the bridge and return to her own family.

And Sundus will be alone in a new kind of way. She's lived without Jalal for eight years, and yet the fact that Hafez was alive—in prison, yes, but still alive—had made her own existence less solitary. She'd waited for her son's release, praying for a new chapter for both of them. Subhan Allah—the Lord had other plans. At least he died at home. At least she could bury his body and visit his grave. How many other mothers still beg for the bodies of their slain children?

Once Majida departs, a new silence will drape the villa, darkening each room.

Unless her granddaughter Intisar disrupts everything.

"Ahlan, ya Nabeel! How are your parents?" On a tattered blanket, her cousin carefully lowers the tray onto a floor-level table. She is beaming like a schoolgirl at the lawyer.

"Alhamdullilah, they send their regards, Khalti," Nabeel Abu Shareef tells her, taking a glass.

"And when will you settle down, my son?" Her cousin is worse than the village busybodies. She flashes the young man a brilliant smile. But Sundus can't blame her solicitous demeanor. Nabeel Abu Shareef cuts a striking figure—he's one of the most eligible bachelors in Bayt al-Hawa. It might prove difficult for Majida to part with any of her unwed granddaughters, but Sundus wagers a marriage to this young man might soften the blow.

"Inshallah khair," he tells her prudently. "I'll leave it to the good Lord, Khalti."

Before Majida can press the subject, Lubna pulls up on her motorbike and Intisar climbs off. Mu'tassim's daughter doesn't offer her customary beep before driving away.

The call for the noon prayer has not yet sounded. "You're back early," Sundus tells the girl.

"Yes. We had a change of plans," her granddaughter says curtly, shifting her bag on her shoulder. There's something more in the girl's morose expression. Has she been crying?

"What happened?" Sundus asks.

"Nothing." Intisar avoids her eyes. "Something came up. We'll do Nablus another time."

Nabeel stands up. "Ah, Nablus? It's one of the best cities in the West Bank." He switches to English, sounding like a professor. "The Romans called it Neopolis—the New City. Its urban architecture is celebrated in world heritage records."

Sundus scrutinizes her granddaughter's face. Something happened on the excursion this morning. She wants to extract it from her but allows the young lawyer to prattle on instead.

"My granddaughter Aisha loves history," Majida, who's been hanging on his every word, interjects.

The young lawyer offers his hand to Intisar. "I am Nabeel Abu Shareef."

Her granddaughter, tentative, shakes it. "Intisar."

"I know," the young lawyer smiles. "I had the honor of meeting your father. He was a very dear member of our community. He sacrificed much for his country. I am very sorry for your loss."

Intisar nods and turns toward the villa.

"Wait, ya sitti," Sundus tells her, gesturing toward the young man. "Nabeel is the family's lawyer."

Her granddaughter looks him over and shifts the weight of her bag again.

"Yes," Nabeel says. "Though it is a great pleasure to meet you, I have come on the matter of the land. I work with my mentor, May Boustany. She's handled your father's case since the beginning of his detainment. May's in London for part of the year. We're representing your family in the lawsuit against Abdul Waheed. Will you speak with me?" He gestures to another stool. Intisar hesitates before sitting down. "Thank you." She fidgets with the strap of her bag and shakes off Majida's offer of a glass of tea.

"Can you follow in Arabic?" the young lawyer asks.

Intisar nods again, her eyes flitting everywhere as if she's expecting to be pounced upon.

"This is a very precarious situation. The more time passes that we do not act, the more Abdul Waheed's fraudulent acquisition will stick. At present, we have two things working against us. The fact that your grandfather was not a legal resident. And the—" he searches for a delicate word—"absence of your father." He leans forward, elbows propped on his knees. "I will answer any questions you have as best as I can."

"Abdul Waheed claims my grandfather sold him this property," the girl says, her tone tired, as if each word is a heavy stone she has to lift and put down again. "He has an official document which you are now contesting. It sounds like he's offered some compensation."

"A payoff," Nabeel interjects. Then, smiling, he gestures for Intisar to continue.

"Whatever," her granddaughter sighs. "I don't know the laws here, but it sounds like nothing can be done."

Disappointment and fear jab Sundus's stomach. Why can't the girl see the land as she does, as her father did, who gave up everything to fight for it? *Tell her where she comes from,* her son's weak voice echoes in her ear. How can she when his daughter is unwilling to listen? Or hasn't she tried hard enough?

Nabeel Abu Shareef leans forward on the stool. "Actually, we can do something. But we'll need your help."

Intisar's eyes dart between Sundus and the young man. She clutches her bag to her chest as if something is going to be snatched from her.

Nabeel leans forward on his stool. "You are the legal heir of this land. You can contest Abdul Waheed's claims."

"How do I do that? Sign something?"

"To start. I'll establish what we call hisil irth. It is a document demonstrating you are the legitimate next of kin of your father, God bless his soul."

"Okay. When can I sign it?" her granddaughter hastily replies.

"I have already filed, but these things take time. We are not as efficient as what you are accustomed to in the States." He gives Intisar a sad smile. "We have quite the bureaucracy here and if Abdul Waheed has influence with the sulta, it might take longer. The Palestinian Authority can slow things down—and sometimes make matters disappear—if they intervene."

"What are you trying to say? I'm supposed to be leaving in a few days," Intisar exclaims, her voice suddenly rising. "You can't expect me to stay and deal with this. I have to get back home."

Home. Sundus closes her eyes at this word. Bayt al-Hawa where she'd moved with her dearest Jalal became a second, viable home for herself, one she'd never dreamed possible after the sea vanished behind her all those years ago. She thought of her parents and how their bodies still carried that first home on their shoulders, how they never stopped seeing themselves as ghurub—outsiders—in Ramallah, unpacking the few items they'd brought with them and arranging them in new spaces that didn't quite fit.

"Do you know how lucky your family is?" Nabeel Abu Shareef is saying. "Some houses of prisoners have been demolished. It's a miracle your father's land had not been confiscated."

Sundus catches a shudder in the girl's shoulders before her face hardens.

"And what do you expect me to do?" Intisar demands, tightly clasping the straps of her bag.

"It will help our case if you appear in person and establish residency—"

Sundus watches her granddaughter's face morph from confusion to shock. "Live here? That's out of the question."

Nabeel smiles sympathetically. "Not immediately. It will be a process. Residing here for three to six months—at least for a few years—will prove legal occupancy of the land. We must start filing as soon as possible. Your permit has been issued for ninety days, yes? Consider it a vacation."

Intisar smirks. "A vacation? And what about my job in the States?"

The young lawyer slowly nods. "Yes. This is a complication. What is it you do?"

"She is a nurse, mashallah," Majida beams.

"An honorable occupation," Nabeel Abu Shareef says. "You know what it means to help others—sometimes to save them."

"This is not the same," Intisar snaps. "This is crazy. I can't upend my life to save this property. To go up against that man. My father—" she halts. "I never knew him." She glances at Sundus. "Or anyone here. I don't belong in this place."

"Pray to the Prophet, my love," Majida says, taking hold of the girl's hand. Sundus, too, wants to reach out and clasp her granddaughter's hand and squeeze out all of the doubt and fear and confusion she imagines coursing through her body. But Intisar stands up, shaking off any attempt to touch her.

"I understand how difficult all this must be for you," Nabeel says, rising to his feet.

"Habibti, take some time to think about it," Majida adds. "Surely something can be arranged."

Sundus hasn't said a word and her granddaughter looks to her now, searching for some kind of answer. Should she do it? Or will Sundus absolve her of this duty? "No need to worry about me," Sundus finally tells her, bile swimming up her throat. "I've been uprooted before." Her bitterness is difficult to disguise—how can she help it? And how can the girl be cured of her selfish blindness? What stake does her granddaughter have in this land? To Sundus? How can her granddaughter ever see the land and its future beyond her present grief? Did Hafez imagine her predicament, leaving Sundus to fight this battle?

Nabeel Abu Shareef tactfully changes the subject for the moment. "How's your visit been, ya Intisar?"

"Fine, thank you," her granddaughter responds in clipped words that barely escape her tight lips. Her face clouds over.

Sundus continues to watch her closely. Something else has happened today, something she refuses to divulge. She feels a new pang of guilt. It hasn't been easy for the child.

"What have you seen?" the lawyer goes on. Sundus can't help but admire the steadiness in his tone, the ability to be unruffled despite his age and passion.

Her granddaughter shrugs her shoulders like a reluctant child.

"Let me be your guide then," Nabeel Abu Shareef says. "A day trip to the Dead Sea." He looks to Sundus. "With your permission, of course, Hajja."

She jerks her chin up at Intisar. "It is not up to me, my son."

Her granddaughter shakes her head again. "Please don't trouble—"

"Tomorrow. I'll make arrangements." He shakes Intisar's hand again, holds it a moment longer. "I will not take no for an answer," he tells her in English. "How can I ask you to consider staying longer if you don't have a chance to really see this beautiful bilad of ours?"

Her granddaughter looks as if she's about to protest, but she finally nods.

Majida gathers their glasses onto the tray and accompanies the young lawyer to the side entrance. Sundus sits in silence with Intisar, who's staring at her feet. "Yalla," she says. "Come walk with me. It's good for my circulation. A woman my age." Sundus holds her hand out. She must try harder.

Her granddaughter looks at her for a moment, then helps her stand and they stroll into the orchard. The day is warm. The joyful noise of children playing at recess echoes from the mokhayam, reaching them from the boundary walls. They walk in silence for some time before Sundus stops at a loquat tree.

The girl has missed the spring harvest of the delicious, apricot-like fruit. She's in time for the last of the figs and grapes. "I didn't want your father to come back here," Sundus declares, pulling a stem from a low branch. The leaves have dulled from their previously waxy sheen.

"What?"

"It's true. I was very sad when he left for America." Sundus shrugs. "But it was his wish. I wanted him to be happy, to be unconditionally free. From our oppressors, from his father's aspirations, God bless his soul. He didn't want your Siddo Jalal's business. They fought for a long time about it."

Her granddaughter fishes out her pack of cigarettes from her bag and shakily lights one. She turns away from Sundus each time she inhales, careful not to douse her in smoke. When she looks at Sundus, her eyes are shining, her lower lip trembling between puffs.

"Your grandfather was a refugee before he returned to Falasteen. And then 1967 shattered our people again. Abu Hafez lost his chance for a haweeya, for residency status." Sundus gives a bitter laugh. "He held a legal deed to this property, but no country to claim him." She hooks her thumbs on the belt of her thobe, looks in the direction of the well. "When your father was born, Jalal could claim an heir. It was one of the proudest moments of his life. A window into posterity. The land would be passed from father to son. And the son would pass it down to his son. Unless, of course, there was a daughter." She gives Intisar a rueful look. "We hadn't expected Hafez to start a life in another country."

Her granddaughter flicks her ashes on the ground and looks past the loquat tree. "Baba wanted to be an architect."

"Yes," Sundus says. "He traveled to America, met your mother and she gave birth to you. It was the happiest day of his life—I could hear it in his voice. I wished I could be there, too."

Sundus motions for Intisar to follow her as they continue through the orchard. She watches for fallen branches and jagged rocks on the ground. Her granddaughter seems to sense this; she stubs out her cigarette and reaches for Sundus's arm.

"Careful, Sitti," the girl cautions her. Is it a nurse's instinct or something more natural than that?

Sundus's heart softens and she loops her arm through Intisar's.

"And your grandfather Jalal, too," she goes on. "How much he'd already loved you before knowing you. The way a grandfather can only cherish his grandchild. Like my own father cherished your father. Your great-grandfather Yousef was a generous man. He used to take Hafez to the famous Rukab." Sundus's eyes glitter with the memory. "It had a line all the way down the Manara when it first opened." She gestures ahead of her, as if seeing the ice-cream shop for the first time.

"I remember this," Intisar says quietly. "He told me his favorite flavor was pistachio."

"Yes." Sundus smiles, patting the girl's hand. "It was mine, too." She sighs and shakes her head. "But that relative peace we'd known would be shattered when Jerusalem fell."

They walk on through the orchard and Sundus tells Intisar about that day, how they were glued to the transistor radio at her parents' flat. It normally played ballads her mother hummed while she cleaned the flat. That day, the potent voice of the Egyptian president poured from the speaker: *"Oh Arabs, this is the day for Holy War. This is the day for vengeance."*

Sundus had sat beside her father. "What does this mean, Yabba?"

"They destroyed his entire fleet." Her father's tone was grim, the same one he'd used all those years ago when he'd accused the fleeing British of cowardice after they'd sold out the Palestinians. "It's not good," he said.

And Sundus knew to leave it alone for the time being, to be still and listen and not worry about her husband. Jalal had traveled to the Port of Aqaba for a delivery of imported tables from Italy. Hafez, eight years old, had begged to go with his father. *I can help you, Yabba.*

I need you to look after your mother, Jalal had said to their son.

Though disappointed, Hafez could bask in the boundless affection of his grandparents in the absence of his father. As soon as he could walk, he'd stroll everywhere in Ramallah with her father. To the produce market and the butcher's, past the Quaker school for boys. They circled Al-Manara and her father explained to Hafez how it got its name—the Lighthouse—when electricity was first municipally sourced.

"This is the end of the Palestinians as we know it," her father had declared, as the radio crackled. For first time, she was glad her parents didn't own a television set like other homes. *What for*, her father had argued. *I read the news and listen to music all the same.* And now Sundus was spared the images of an embroiling war.

"God help us all," her mother said, nervously pinching her chin.

The old hollow fear returned. Sundus handing objects to her mother who folded them into white sheets. But where would they go this time? Flee across the river and end up in an encampment—the same fate as Amjad and his family? How many times would they be uprooted? And what about Sundus's home in Bayt al-Hawa?

I'll be back before you know it, Jalal had assured her. He'd hired a guard, Abu Bakir, to keep watch over the villa, to ensure children didn't sneak into the orchard or vandalize the boundary walls.

Jalal insisted Sundus stay with her parents until his return. Her father had refused to come to stay with Sundus and her son at the villa, for even though her parents' flat was small, it was familiar and her father had all of his newspapers and books within reach.

What would become of their property? She recalls how long her mother had wept after Israel's implementation of the Absentees' Property Law in 1950 that permanently dashed their hopes for reclaiming their house in Haifa. Would Jalal even be permitted to return Falasteen? Sundus tried hard not to appear worried or scared, for Hafez seemed to sense her every emotion, as if he were still tethered to her body, absorbing her inner world. Only when he was drawing did he seem to forget they were shut inside her parents' apartment. He loved to build houses from a deck of cards with his grandfather. But each time a news report on the escalation droned from the radio, her father leaped from the floor, sweeping past Hafez and toppling the house of cards in his wake.

"Will there be war?" Hafez asked innocently.

The question crushed Sundus's heart. How could the word be a part of his language already? And yet wasn't she close to his age when her family was forced out of their home? Her own father had assured her everything would return to the way it was. They'd be back in their bayt near the sea, she and Amjad playing under the loquat tree. How could she explain to her son that nothing was certain, that the brass key her mother had long tucked away no longer had a door?

Her old schoolmate friend Asma had come to say goodbye. "My father is a diplomat. He'll be thrown in prison. We must leave before it is too late."

Sundus discovered that it was a different thing to lose friends during war. Though she hadn't seen Asma since her wedding—she'd lost touch with several schoolmates—this parting was tinged with a distinct kind of sadness, foreshadowing a permanent absence. The face of her old childhood friend Amjad flashed in her mind while she hugged Asma goodbye.

Ultimately, it was a swift takeover. Somehow this felt more insidious, their freedom disappearing without much clamor. Still, they were more fortunate than others across the region. News traveled quickly from the Moroccan Quarter of the Old City about the expulsion of entire clans, all of their homes demolished. They'd later hear about the charred bodies along the road from Jericho to Al-Karameh Bridge, flooded with fleeing families waiting to cross the Jordan River. But Sundus's parents decided to stay put.

"I won't die in exile," her father said, tears brimming his tired, spectacled eyes.

From the street below her parents' flat, a voice on a loudspeaker commanded them: "Remain indoors and you will not be harmed." The accent was thick and foreign. "Surrender your weapons if you have any. If you are caught concealing them..."

When her mother finally flung a window open, Sundus looked down into the street. Hafez squeezed in beside her. "Can we go outside now, Yamma?" he'd pleaded, his round face full of eagerness and hope. He'd been shut in the flat for days, hungering to frolic outdoors, to resume his daily jaunts with Siddo Yusuf to the market, or to play with his friends in front of their flat, shooting marbles.

He pointed to an open-roof shuttle moving at a leisurely pace. It was carrying fair-skinned passengers who poked their heads out of windows. Hebrew reverberated from a loudspeaker and a man pointed to the hillside in the distance.

"Who are they, Yamma?"

Sundus didn't know. Were they tourists? Had Ramallah become a destination for these strangers? Would they venture into Bayt al-Hawa next? To what kind of country would Jalal be returning for a second time—if he could enter at all? She squeezed her eyes shut, imagining the orchard, its vineyard lush with fruit. Would it be harvested by strangers who trampled her land, sat at her kitchen table, slept in her bed? Her green velvet dress swayed in her vision, like a ghost returning to haunt.

Following closely behind the shuttle was a military jeep. The King's army had worn dark-blue uniforms, polished and dignified. But these new soldiers wore ugly green uniforms and heavy mesh helmets, machine guns secured across their chests—as if poised for combat, though there was no one to fight. King Hussein had surrendered and Palestine was no longer Palestine.

"Come away, my love." Sundus pulled her son from the window, praying he couldn't hear the fear in her voice.

When they finally opened their doors, a new occupation was upon them. Every man and woman who'd been a subject of the Hashemite Dynasty had to register with a new census agency under the State of Israel. They'd be issued a haweeya—an identification card to be carried at all times.

Her mother helped Sundus gather their documents, birth certificates stamped by the Mandate, her wedding certificate carrying the seal of the Kingdom of Jordan. Sundus laid out a pair of short pants and a shirt for Hafez before slipping into a shift dress.

Her mother wrapped a white mandeela around her head. Her father wore his customary pressed slacks and a button-down shirt, his neck unfettered by the tie he wore to the hospital. Her parents looked old, with harsh wrinkles carved across their foreheads, like the war had lasted sixty years and not six days. Her son clung to his grandfather's hand, setting aside his burgeoning masculine pride. He kept in step with his siddo, and it seemed her father held Hafez's hand just as tightly, as if searching for some kind of reassurance from the boy.

Other residents on their street had begun to venture outdoors as well. Everyone seemed to move cautiously. Military jeeps passed them in every direction, packed with soldiers throwing cursory glances. Public images depicting King Hussein, the last warden of Falasteen, had disappeared. Municipal facilities were cordoned off with barbed wire.

"What will happen to Jalal?" Sundus wondered out loud.

"You have proof of marriage—it shouldn't be a problem," her father assured her. It was as if she was seven years old again, her father having an answer for any question Sundus posed. When he hadn't known the answer, he offered a possibility. And this had anchored her. But now she felt unmoored, bobbing on a sea of uncertainty, like a ship thrown off its course.

Still, if they could walk freely on the street, perhaps it wouldn't be so terrible. Military occupations were temporary. A peaceful international resolution had to be in the works—a people could not live long under the rule of military occupation. History had always proven that.

By the time they arrived at the town square, the lines were already stretched down to the hisbah, which was empty of any fruit and vegetable vendors. It was an eerie sight, a void where the clamor of daily trade should be.

"They'll return soon enough," her father said, as if reading Sundus's thoughts. "People have to eat."

Sundus thought of her neighbors in Bayt al-Hawa. The widow Um Khaleel, whom Jalal checked on and brought weekly sundries. Or Abu Mu'tassim's family, with a son the same age as Hafez. Were they safe?

The lines were long as men, women, and children waited to be included in the new census. Word spread that anyone older than sixteen would receive a new identification card. Tucked under her mother's arm was a brown accordion folder containing their documents. The three of them looked on in amazement. Hafez didn't complain about standing for so long, as if appreciating the magnitude of the circumstances around him. With wonder, he beheld the soldiers' machine guns and military fatigues. Sundus desperately wanted to shield his innocent eyes.

The people in the queue slowly moved, all with the same bewildered expression on their faces. When it was their turn, Sundus's father spoke first. "I am Doctor Yousef Kareem. This is my wife Wajeeha and my daughter Sundus and her son Hafez." He announced their names with dignity, as if they held some high political position demanding deference. But the hard-faced female officer commanded Sundus to step back into the line.

"Because you're an adult," her father quickly encouraged Sundus, handing all of her documents back to her. She'd have to speak for herself. When had she ever had to do that? She'd gone from her parents' home to her husband's and now she was in some kind of limbo.

The three of them would be issued the haweeya. They would become permanent residents of their own country—no longer rightful citizens. Her parents tried hard to disguise their bleak expressions. Any remaining roots had been severed.

Fighting tears, Sundus hoisted Hafez on her hip and stepped forward. "My husband—he's in Aqaba," she said to the officer.

"Must be present for haweeya," the officer said, her Arabic thick and rehearsed.

After Sundus registered herself, her father took hold of her hand and led her away. "Don't worry, habibti. They'll issue one for Jalal as soon as he returns."

"You'll be together again soon inshallah," her mother added, wrapping an arm around Sundus's shoulder. But their words were half-hearted and a panic began to seize her.

Hafez tugged at her arm. "Yamma, what about me? Will I get one?"

"Bas!" Sundus snapped at him, flustered and worried about Jalal.

Her son's face was crestfallen. She could see how hard he was fighting his tears, his lower lip trembling. They streamed down his cheeks, slicing her heart in two. Her father quickly guided Hafez away from her, stroking his head from his forehead to his nape, instantly soothing her son. All Sundus wanted to do was lash out. She hated these awful invaders. And, in this moment, she hated Jalal for going away and leaving her alone. She might never see him again. How could she raise a child without his father?

Sundus wiped her futile tears on the sleeve of her sweater as they steered away from the lines.

"Doktor Kareem! Doktor Kareem! Alhamdullilah! Allah give us strength!"

Sundus's father stopped to greet patients who called out to him, and she saw the palpable excitement at seeing him alive, an emblem of their normal lives. Men kissed both of his cheeks and fiercely hugged him, grown men who looked as stunned as her father. They'd been too old to fight for their land. Sundus could see the guilt etched in their faces, as if they were complicit in losing to this old enemy. Had any of them imagined it happening again? They'd fooled themselves into believing that 1948 had been a terrible dream, one from which they'd all wake. Thousands and thousands had still not returned, never to set foot again on their native land. Why would the rest of them be spared now?

Her father's reunion was interrupted by a scuffle at the end of the line. A soldier was shouting in Hebrew at someone. It was Basim Al-Majnoon—Mad Basim—who'd recite verses from the Quran on demand. He wore slacks one size too large, kept up by a faded leather belt looped through the last notch. He'd frightened Sundus when she was a little girl, peddling pots and pans at Manara Square. *Maskeen Basim,* her father had told her. *He's not right in the head.* No one knew his origins, or whether he'd been separated from his family during the Catastrophe. The community claimed him, though he belonged to no one.

Her father gestured for Hafez to stay with Sundus before approaching the crowd that had started to form. She pulled her son to her body. Could he hear her heart beating faster? She kissed the crown of his head, assuring him he was her good boy. Then she grabbed her mother's hand and followed her father. Ahead of them, soldiers were attempting to disarm Basim of his long stick, an olive branch she'd seen him carry everywhere he walked since she was a child. The branch was more of a hefty bough Basim had smoothed down into a cane. He'd wave it like a conductor as he recited:

> *When the earth is shaken with its final earthquake*
> *And the earth discharges its burdens...*

Sometimes he used his olive branch cane to chase away cruel children who gathered pebbles to pelt him. Once she'd spied from the window of her parents' flat Hafez and his friends pestering the man. She called her son inside, and he was punished for the rest of the day so as not to ever forget to be kind to others, especially his elders.

The soldiers were both young—no older than Sundus—one with scrappy confidence, repeating his command to Basim, waving a hand downward in a gesture for him to relinquish the cane. The other soldier was red-faced, frightened, his hands clasped tightly around the butt of his rifle, a sheathed knife in his utility belt. His eyes darted from one face to another in the small crowd he was holding back.

Basim was coming unhinged. "It's mine," he shouted. "You cannot take it. It belongs to me."

Sundus's father stepped forward and tried to pacify Basim. "He is not well," he informed the first soldier. He said it in English as their exchange of Arabic and Hebrew had been futile. "He is not right in the head." He pointed at his temple and reached out to touch the soldier's arm.

It was instinct. The way her father did with his patients at the hospital, calming them before a procedure, or when he was forced to deliver a dismal prognosis.

The next thing Sundus saw was blood. Terror clutched her heart. She dropped Hafez's hand and ran toward her father. Her pulse beat in her eardrums as she watched blood pour like a powerful current from a puncture in her father's neck. He was pressing his palm against the wound, red gushing between his fingers. The soldier's eyes had turned wild, her father's blood dripping from the blade of his army knife. He held it up, his hand violently shaking, looking at it incredulously then at her father. The first soldier shot a warning in the air, and everyone ducked to the ground, old and young lying on their stomachs. Soon a dozen soldiers appeared, dispersing the crowd.

A shrill lamentation went up: "They killed the doctor! They killed the doctor!"

Her mother and Sundus knelt on the ground beside her father, Hafez still standing at a distance, paralyzed by fear. The blood flowed and flowed. As her father tried to speak, an awful gurgle rose from his throat. His eyes rolled back into his skull and then he was still.

Someone hooked her under her armpits and dragged Sundus away from her father. She kicked at the ground. "Let me go! Let me go!" She wanted to be free so she could kiss her father's cheek one last time as her mother cradled his head, a crimson flower blooming across her lap.

"I didn't speak for weeks afterwards," Sundus tells her granddaughter, the screams still echoing in her ears. "I couldn't cry. I was numb."

The girl is shaking her head. "My mother told me Baba's father died in the war. Baba—he never told me he'd seen it."

"What war?" Sundus says bitterly. "What is a war against

unarmed people? Against a man who only sought to protect the vulnerable? Who spent his life healing others?"

Intisar's eyes glistened. "Your husband. Siddi Jalal. When did he come back?"

Siddi Jalal. Hearing this term of endearment gives Sundus gooseflesh. How he'd dreamed of many grandchildren to break up the quiet of the villa. Subhan Allah, he would live to meet one child, a granddaughter who'd later become only a thin voice on a long-distance line, a face framed in portrait on a wall.

"Abu Hafez returned two years later, alhamdullilah, after lodging with my cousin Majida's family. Until he arranged a permit to cross the bridge. But he could never register for a haweeya." Sundus shreds the loquat leaf between her fingers and scatters it on the ground. Jalal was forced to leave them—sometimes for weeks at a time—to get his permit renewed at the border. Like an unwanted visitor in his own country. It was during his first absence that her mother came to live with her until her death.

"Your father was almost eleven years old by then," she tells Intisar. "Getting to know his father all over again."

Bayt al-Hawa was mostly unscathed. There were no reported deaths, though the mukhtar Abu Shareef was arrested, along with several young men hiding in sheds and chicken coops. Others had folded their bodies behind wall panels built to store valuables in case of war. Some were released with bruised faces, while the rest—mostly young men—had been deemed a danger to the new State of Israel. They were thrown in prison for the rest of their lives. Those who were eventually freed returned to their families as middle-aged men.

Days after they buried her father, Sundus returned to the villa. Soldiers had stomped through each room, leaving a trail of destruction. She and Hafez carefully maneuvered around shards of glass. Every window had been shattered. Wardrobes were flung open and clothes tossed all over the floor. Even Hafez's room had been raided, his model cars and sketchbooks scattered to every corner. His mattress was knifed to shreds as if it might conceal weapons. Flour and sugar coated the kitchen counters, colonies of ants feasting.

Sundus rushed through the back door, Hafez on her heels. They reached the stone steps and halted.

"Alhamdullilah," Sundus breathed. Her trees were unharmed. The dawali vines had not been stripped of their delicate, flowering buds ahead of another harvest. She fell on her knees, the rocky field digging into her skin. Her sobs were long, releasing all of her dread and anger.

Hafez stood beside her, his hand on her shoulder, waiting for to finish.

"In the end, my father got his wish," Sundus says bitterly. "He didn't die in exile. We laid him to rest in his own country." She gestures ahead. "Your grandfather Jalal walked through this orchard every morning with your father, pointing to every tree, explaining its fruit." Sundus smiles. "Hafez could identify every species of flora by the time he was five years old. It was important to my husband that his son know the land."

Her granddaughter digs the toe of her sneaker into the rocky field, eyes downcast. Is it sinking in?

"We were lucky," Sundus continues. "Our bayt was not taken from us. But not everyone was lucky." She nods her head in the direction beyond the valley. "We watched the mokhayam appear overnight. Tents that turned into permanent cinderblock homes.

Some folks lost their homes for a second time. I'd escaped the encampments twice."

She studies her granddaughter, trying to gauge her reaction. But it's hard to tell how much Intisar has registered. She seems distracted, like something else is gnawing at her.

Sundus reaches out to cup Intisar's chin and gently lifts it. "What is it?"

Tears stream down the girl's face and run over Sundus's hand. "They destroyed all the trees. Burned them. And they were laughing." Her words tumble out and Sundus tries to capture and make sense of them. "Soldiers arrested kids—innocent boys." Her lower lip quivers. "They stepped on his neck—a teenager. He—he—"

Intisar begins to sob and Sundus pulls her in, her face burrowing in the chest pocket of her thobe.

It's a familiar scene to Sundus. But this time she's seeing it through the eyes of a newcomer. Over the decades, her skin has hardened like scar tissue against the oppressors. How else does she—and thousands of her countrymen and women—survive?

She holds her granddaughter close and recites supplication. The verse calms her as well, each word lifting the wretchedness from her heart:

> *In the name of God, the Most Gracious, the Most Merciful*
> *Say, 'I seek refuge in the Lord of mankind, the sovereign of mankind, from the evil of the lurking whisperer, who whispers into the hearts of men…*

By the last line of the verse, her cousin calls to them from the saha.

"Intisar! Ya Intisar!"

Majida comes waddling down the stone steps, waving a dishtowel. "Habibti! Your mother is calling from America."

BAYT AL-HAWA: SEPTEMBER 2007

CHAPTER 14

She doesn't tell Mama about the trees and wailing woman, or about the boys who are arrested and hauled away. She doesn't say a word about the defiant teenager among them who finally submits when a boot bears down on his neck.

None of it gels with her mother's ramblings—complaints from her clients, the plans for her cousin Reema's engagement—"You should be back in plenty of time for that"—how her stepfather Ali misses her. "More than me," her mother jokes.

But Intisar is barely listening; her mind keeps drifting back to everything her grandmother had revealed to her, fragments of a larger story of Baba's life that he'd left out. The one familiar to Intisar—the joyful one—is full of holes, like a moth-eaten blanket. Did her mother get to hear the longer, truer one? Had Baba kept those fragments from her, too?

Had he ever told Mama how he'd watched his father bleed to death? Had that terrified her mother into staying away?

And was her great-grandfather's murder the reason Baba had, at long last, wanted to come back to this country? For revenge masked as duty?

Intisar curls the telephone cord between her fingers. It's early morning in Chicago. She pictures Mama in her two-piece pajama set with tiny lipstick tubes all over, her pedicured feet tucked into fluffy black slippers. She's in the family room, sipping her coffee. From the television, Intisar hears a weather forecast: *We'll be seeing a slight dip in temperatures across the northern states over the next forty-eight hours.*

"You should see Reema's dress," her mother is gushing. "It needs to be taken in, but the color is stunning—"

"Did you know about the land?" Intisar blurts.

There's a beat on the other end of the line, confirming Intisar's suspicion. "Know what?"

"Stop pretending," Intisar says firmly, like an adult reprimanding a child who's been caught in a lie.

She hears the TV volume being lowered. "It was a few years ago," her mother finally confesses. "Before your father was released. A lawyer called—May something. She said they needed you to sign a document."

"Hisil irth," Intisar says, surprised she's remembered the term. "Why didn't you tell me before I came here?"

"I was afraid you'd want to go there," her mother says bluntly. Intisar can hear the righteous indignation in Mama's next words. "What kind of a mother would allow her daughter—her only child—to travel to a war-torn country?" Mama gives a scoffing laugh, as if to punctuate the fact that she's won the argument.

"It's an occupation," Intisar says weakly. The soldier's bulky, unyielding boot flashes again when she closes her eyes.

"I know what it is," her mother snipes. "You think you know more than I do."

"I don't know anything at all because you've kept me in the dark." Intisar's retort is sharp and swift. "You kept me away from Baba's family. From Sitti Sundus." There's an unexpected silence on the other end and Intisar continues to jab. "I'm her only connection to her son. Did that ever occur to you?" She bites her lower lip, refusing to give in to tears.

"Listen, Tee-Tee." Her mother's voice softens. "I know it's been an emotional time for you. I didn't choose this for you." The accusation Intisar has grown up with—*This was Baba's doing. The choice was his.* As if he'd deliberately drove their lives into a tree, totaling the car, but had himself emerged from the wreckage without a single scratch. This was how Mama always saw it; this would be the story she told herself and Intisar.

But Baba had paid price. He'd sacrificed his freedom, his health, and ultimately his own life for his country. "He left us, Tee-Tee," her mother says.

Intisar's anger softens into pity. She sometimes forgets that her mother lost a husband—the love of her life—and had settled for Ali. *There is no right one. It's the one who shows up and stays,* her mother had once told her. Does Mama know their wedding portrait still hangs in the salon here?

"I don't want to fight," her mother is saying. "You can sign their paper and come home."

"It's not that easy, Ma," Intisar says, sinking into the chair. From where she's sitting in the hallway, she has a partial view of the portrait of her great-grandparents. Had they ever predicted the course of their lives? Their stories would have been unfathomable to Intisar if Baba had ever told them in America. Fleeing their home, losing a child, then a murder in a public square in broad daylight—one her father had witnessed. She'd have stayed away, never looked back. Intisar doesn't deny she's a coward, but why couldn't her father see the futility of his decision after all he and his parents had endured?

And now his mother—her grandmother—stands to be evicted from a home she'd built for her only son. Was it worth it? Losing everything, including her?

"What do you mean?" Mama is asking her.

"They need me to stay while all of this goes to court," Intisar says quietly.

"Oh, no!" her mother snaps. "That's not possible."

That was never a possibility, Hafez. Mama's words knock against the same words now.

Outside, someone calls to her grandmother. "Hajja! A kilo, by your permission!" Inside, running water in the kitchen sink, the clinking of tea glasses.

"I know it's not." Intisar sighs. She's exhausted, wants to crawl into her bed and pull the covers over her head.

"Good, good," Mama says, perking up and quickly putting an end to the matter. "So where have you gone? What have you seen?"

Intisar thinks of the road to Nablus on Lubna's motorbike, the stone houses built into rolling hills. The basket weaver. The razed olive grove. The boy on the ground, a boot coming down on his neck. "I'm going to the Dead Sea tomorrow," she manages. She doesn't want to go, but she's accepted the invitation. According to her mother's instructions, she must be a polite guest.

"Wonderful! You know we never got to see it because you came down with a horrible case of diarrhea. You were a mess! Dehydrated! And you lost a pound." Mama sucks her teeth. "Your grandmother tried to talk me into leaving you with her so that your father and I could sightsee. As if I'd abandon my kid. Maybe this time you can sneak back some of that miracle mud..."

She jolts awake then falls back on her pillow, her limbs aching. Intisar feels as if she's been pounded with a bat. Bright sunlight pours onto her bed—someone—Majida?—has already opened the steel shutters—making it difficult to find some dark space and cower. She dreamed of the teenage boy, his body splayed on the ground, dirt kicked in his face, the soldier's ugly, hefty boot disappearing into his neck. The acrid odor of gasoline and smoke, as if she's there again. But when the teenager turns to look up at Intisar, it's her father, blood gushing from his neck.

Majida is at her door, telling her it's time for breakfast.

In the kitchen, they've packed some fruit and water bottles in a small cooler along with foil- wrapped fatayer. "It will be good for you, habibti," Majida tells her. "Go enjoy yourself!"

Sitti Sundus huffily adds, "There are folks around here who are barred from traveling outside of this village."

"You'll have a great time, my love," Majida says, then laughs. "Hajja, do you remember the trip we took in '61? My sister Fatima was pregnant with her third child. Her nausea was so awful, her poor husband had to stop our caravan every kilometer so she could vomit on the side of the road."

Her grandmother nods, a smile tugging at the tiny corners of her wrinkled mouth. Intisar can see that day surging in the old woman's shiny eyes. "We had a good time," she admits. The memory lingers a moment longer before dissolving from her face. "We always traveled together. Before checkpoints."

Intisar nods. Before her stepfather Ali entered the picture, Intisar and her mother had taken road trips with her aunts and their families, station wagons pulling into cheap motels in Ohio and Florida. The children splashed each other in chlorinated pools way past sunset, when the moon reflected on the water. She'd poked her head through the surface of the pool and watched the adults—husbands and wives—sitting on plastic chairs, smoking and playing cards. Next to Mama was an empty seat.

A car honks outside. Nabeel Abu Shareef stands outside the passenger door of the taxicab; he waves at Intisar's grandmother and her cousin. There's a little boy in the front seat. It's Friday and school is out. No doubt he's been brought along to prevent the appearance of any impropriety. Intisar wanted Lubna to join them, but she needs a permit, and that takes weeks apparently.

"Do you know Michael Jordan?" the little boy asks her as soon as she climbs into the back seat of the cab.

Nabeel chuckles. "My nephew Yazeed."

Intisar smiles. "Not personally, but I watched him play at a stadium a long time ago."

Unlike Emad, this driver is stone-faced and quiet. He plays Fairuz on a cassette tape and something flutters in Intisar's stomach. She recognizes the ballad, remembers Baba singing off-key on a Sunday ride to the lakefront, coaxing Mama until she broke in, her harmonious voice filling the car. Intisar could sense her mother's smile from the back seat where she sat, soaking up her parents' love. She hadn't minded when they forgot about her back there. She'd understood she was an extension of their love and that had made her feel safe. Until Baba was gone and a part of her had permanently detached, like in an earthquake, floating away into the ocean. Had Mama suspected it would happen one day? Was that the reason they'd never had more kids?

"Have you been sleeping well at the villa?" Nabeel is asking her.

She glances at him. "Mostly," she responds.

She's somewhat of an insomniac back home, falling asleep then waking up at two or three o'clock in the morning. It had started after her father left. Her bedtime was strictly enforced by Mama—eight o'clock on school days, nine-thirty on the weekends. The first month he was gone, she couldn't sleep at all and just stared at the ceiling, watching the blades of a fan spin like the propellers of a helicopter. She stroked the beak of a pink flamingo Baba had won her at a carnival and calculated the eight-hour time difference. She imagined him still asleep, the dawn about to break. After Mama revealed the news that he had been captured—and no other details—she'd simply informed Intisar that they wouldn't hear from him for a long time. Intisar tried to imagine his cell, the other prisoners who inhabited it. One toilet, no privacy. Like on TV. But those were the bad guys. What crime had Baba committed? And what did *a long time* mean?

"It's much quieter at night here," she tells Nabeel.

They're soon on a narrow road, stratified hills on one side. The legendary Route 90. She knows a little bit about the Dead Sea. It is the lowest point on Earth. Ancient scrolls were discovered in a surrounding cave. And it's actually a lake—not a sea. Its mud contains healing powers that have been packaged into skin care products she's seen on the late-night infomercials her mother watches until she falls asleep. They claim to miraculously stop psoriasis, once and for all. And she knows about the boycott campaign against a particular Israeli skin care line accused of appropriating its natural minerals.

Yazeed is a gleeful boy, chattering about a creek full of tadpoles behind his grandfather's house. When he finally pauses, the driver ejects the tape and turns up the volume on the radio. A raspy voice—an older woman's voice—fills the cab.

"*Greetings to Malik Izzideen Khairallah, from the town of Lod, son of Abdulrahman Izzideen Khairallah. May the Lord keep you safe and healthy, my son. We pray to the Prophet for your speedy return to us. Count on Allah's reckoning. Malik, your brother passed his tawjeehi exam, alhamdullilah…*"

Intisar tilts her head toward the voice. "What is this?" she asks Nabeel in a low voice.

"It's a program for families," the young lawyer explains. "They send messages to their imprisoned sons and daughters—"

"God strike down the occupier-dogs," the quiet driver interjects, startling Intisar.

"They call the radio station and it's broadcast live. The prisoners can hear the messages, but they can't return them." Nabeel smiles sadly. "It only goes one way." He draws a line in the air.

A lump rises in Intisar's throat. "How do they know if they're received?"

Nabeel flicks his fingers in the air. "They don't."

Intisar sinks back in the passenger seat. The next message is from a sister to her brother: "*Greetings to Abdullah Ibn Sabir, from Qalqilya, detained without trial for six-hundred thirty-three days…*"

What message might she have sent to Baba if she'd had the chance? The first year he was gone, she'd kept a diary. A game prize from a birthday party. It had white kittens on it and a lock and key. It was mostly an accounting of what she'd done that day, things that happened at school, who was her friend and who wasn't anymore. When he called once a month, she'd wanted to read them to him, but there was never enough time. Sometimes the line disconnected or he couldn't stay on too long. *We will talk again soon, my heart,* he'd say. But the calls became less frequent until they'd stopped altogether. One day, she stuffed that diary deep down in the garbage bin, beneath her mother's coffee filters and soiled paper towels.

Then Mama finally decided to let him go. By state law, her mother could annul her marriage due to special circumstances. Intisar had overheard Mama talking to her aunts, her voice stricken. *I'll never see him again. I have no choice.*

Intisar had sobbed. She was turning fourteen and still hadn't gotten her first period yet. She was a little girl, too soon for her and Mama to let Baba go.

He'll understand, her mother had said. *I have to move on.* Her eyes were glassy with tears. *We'll be fine, Tee-Tee.*

And just like that, Intisar was expected to let him go, too.

A few years later, Ali entered their lives. He was also divorced and twelve years older than her mother. His ex-wife had custody of their children in Florida. He traveled to see them a few times a year, usually coordinated with their school breaks. They never came to Illinois. Intisar only knew them by their names and ages. When Ali spoke to his kids on the phone, her mother raised the volume on the TV as if to drown out their existence as she had Baba's.

A year after the divorce, her mother received a document from the US State Department. Baba's citizenship had been revoked.

On the radio, the voice of a young woman is sending love to her husband. *To Hamid Shaheen, Abu Lu'ay. Your son is waiting for you…*

Everyone in the cab is silent—even Yazeed—as the transmissions continue.

Moments later, the driver slows down. "Your passport, my sister," he tells Intisar, making eye contact through the rearview mirror. "Just in case."

She peers over the passenger seat. There's a checkpoint ahead. She sits upright. Her stomach knots and her palms begin to sweat. Is this what PTSD feels like? She thinks of old Mr. Coleman's son who came each Sunday morning to visit his father at Pine Woods. Mark, the youngest of four children, had served a tour of Afghanistan and one in Iraq. He couldn't hold a job and his young wife had filed for divorce. She woke up one night and found him sitting on the edge of their bed with a loaded shotgun in his lap. Their toddler was in her crib across the hallway.

Scared the hell out of her, Mr. Coleman had confided to Intisar during his weekly checkup. *Can't blame the poor girl. And can't blame my kid. Damn war.*

She takes a deep breath as they near the checkpoint. Nabeel touches her hand. "Don't worry," he reassures her in English. He pulls out his own green identification card and holds it ready for a soldier who's approaching the driver's side. Yazeed chews his shirt collar, eyes wide.

"They arrested children yesterday," Intisar says in a low voice. "Boys. One no older than him." She jerks her chin at Yazeed. She shakes her head, still in disbelief. And before she can stop herself: "I can't live in a place like this." These awful words fly out of her mouth like bats. Her face burns with shame. She sounds like her mother. Did Nabeel actually believe a trip to the sea would change anything?

Nabeel says nothing for a moment. "Children are not treated as children. But they are resilient."

They both turn their gaze back to the checkpoint. A small caravan of cars lines one side of the road, engines off. Intisar watches Palestinian families flanking their vehicles, mothers on their haunches. They peel oranges and feed them to their children as they wait for permission to proceed to the beach. Fathers stand in a small group, smoking cigarettes and gesturing with nearly empty water bottles. Sweat beads their foreheads. It looks like they've been waiting for some time. "What are they doing?" Intisar asks.

"They won't let them through," the driver says, glancing at her in the rearview mirror. "But the families don't give up."

One little boy—he looks to be about the same age as Yazeed—has caught her staring and he waves and flashes her a toothy grin. He's holding a beach ball until another child swipes it from his hands and they chase each other. A soldier cranes his neck from the security booth and shouts at them. Their mother gestures with a scooped hand. The children return and sit solemnly on blankets intended to be spread across the sand, not on a hot and dusty strip of asphalt.

The soldier takes his time examining Intisar's passport, glancing from the blue booklet to her face as if searching for a discrepancy to prove she wasn't really the pensive-looking girl in the photograph. At the Walgreen's where she'd sat for the picture, the young white man had instructed her not to smile, to keep her face relaxed. She ended up looking mean. She'd applied for one last year for a trip to Puerta Vallarta—a girls' trip with her cousins. They drank virgin pina coladas on the side of the laguna-style pool. And now there's a second stamp, in Hebrew, on a new page of her passport, the letters bold and harsh, permanent and unwelcoming.

The soldier, who is older than most of the ones she's encountered thus far, finally returns her passport to her. When she reaches for it, he glides a finger across the back of her hand before releasing the booklet. He winks at her before moving to the car behind them. Intisar shudders inside, hoping Nabeel hadn't seen it. She looks away from him, cheeks blazing, and fixes her gaze on the families waiting on the side of the road. The boy stares back, clutching his knees to his chest, until the taxicab is permitted to pass.

They arrive at an oasis on the western shore. They park and climb out of the cab. The beach is unlike anything Intisar has ever seen. A strip of sand narrows into a salt-rock shore and a surreal foamy tide. The tranquility overwhelms her. How can this place exist only kilometers away from such chilling violence?

Sunbathing chairs and adirondacks are strewn along the beach. In the few feet of water, some visitors are tanning or floating on their backs while others gather globs of mud and slap them onto limbs and faces. They pose for the camera, absurdly gaping smiles and gleaming teeth.

Intisar rolls up her T-shirt sleeves and gathers the folds of her long skirt. She ties a bulky knot off one leg. The sun hangs hazily above her. "I wish I'd brought a hat," she says.

"Don't worry," Nabeel tells her. "You're not likely to get a sunburn here. There's three layers of atmosphere above us. Remember—we're on the lowest point of the earth." He turns to his nephew who's already wading in the water. "Take it easy, ya Yazeed!"

The boy stoops on skinny legs and scoops silky mud in his palms. He merrily applies it to his arms and face. Intisar can't help but laugh, can't remember the last time something was quite so funny.

She glances back at the driver. He's leaning against the hood of his car, smoking a cigarette. She lights one of her own. "Won't he join us?"

Nabeel wearily shakes his head. "Doesn't like to associate with yahood. Or foreigners."

The sunbathers are a few fair-skinned men, tufts of hair sprouting from their chests, and women who look Mediterranean, toned with no visible tan lines, their dark hair pulled back in slick ponytails.

"You know," Nabeel says. "Cleopatra ordered supplies of the mud for her beauty regimen." He points to lounge chairs. "Please. Let us sit." He carries the cooler Sitti Sundus prepared.

"You know a lot history," Intisar says, flicking ash onto the sand.

"It's our land's history," he responds. "We must know it as readily as we do a popular song."

"Americans barely know geography," she says.

"When you're not in danger of losing something, you pay it little attention." Nabeel hands her a water bottle and settles down next to her. He's wearing a polo shirt that shows off his bronzed biceps.

"So what's your story?" Intisar asks, trying to sound casual. He's a handsome man, well-mannered and interesting. Back home, she'd entertained coffee dates that never grew into anything more. If her mother suspected someone was a romantic possibility, she was instantly thrilled. *Don't let him get away! There's plenty who'll snatch him up!*

Nabeel is smiling. "My story?"

"I mean—your English is really good. Where'd you learn it?"

"I went to Friends Boys School in Ramallah. Originally founded by Quakers. English was mandatory." He flicks sand off the arm of his chair. "I met my sweetheart at the sister-school. We both attended Bir Zeit before graduate school. I studied in Syria, earned my law degree, and then we got engaged." He shrugs as if he's reached the end of the story.

Intisar glances sidelong at him. "So you're married?" She takes another puff, hoping to disguise her surprise.

Nabeel shakes his head. Gazing straight ahead at the water, he says, "She earned a marketing degree and got an offer from an agency in Dubai. I could never leave Falasteen. Even for love."

The skin on Intisar's neck tightens. Love had not kept Baba in the States either. What is it about this land, its magnetic attraction that pulls you away from everything you cherish? "No regrets?" Intisar says in a low voice.

"No regrets." Nabeel grins. "Love is naseeb, as they say. It is meant to be or not. The rest of our lives are made up of choices."

Intisar considers her next question. "So you knew my father? I mean—what was he like?"

Nabeel squints at her as if the overcast sky is suddenly too bright. The question has obviously stumped him. How could she not know her own father? But then his face relaxes into a sad expression. He remembers Intisar hasn't spoken or seen Baba since she was a little girl. She watches Nabeel's face, can see he's working out what to reveal, what might be uplifting and hopeful to his American daughter. "He was quiet," Nabeel finally says.

Intisar nods, deflated. What exactly does she want to hear?

Nabeel continues, "The only time he seemed to listen closely was when he heard your name. It was easy to see how much he loved you."

Shielded behind her sunglasses, her eyes well with tears. Before they fall, Intisar clumsily kicks off her sandals. "I'm going in," she declares, abruptly ending their conversation.

She wades close to Yazeed, who waves at her. Her feet sink into the warm layer of mud. She's tempted to float on her back, but doesn't have a change of clothes. She can feel Nabeel's eyes on her. Her skin is warm, but it's not uncomfortable. She saunters across the lake, pinching the folds of her skirt. The kingdom of Jordan is a hazy mass across the water. It's where Majida's family fled after '48, and that old neighbor-boy Sitti Sundus had told her about? What was his name? Amjad?

Baba had wanted to bring her and Mama here, but never had the chance. She blinks her tears back, careful not to dab her eyes with salt-tinged fingertips.

On their monthly call before he was captured, Baba had sung a catalogue of places he wanted Intisar to see. The city of Tiberias on the western shore of the Sea of Galilee. The architectural wonders of cities like Bethlehem. Places they hadn't made it to on their very first visit because of her horrible case of diarrhea.

As soon as things settle down, he'd promised her, *we'll come back as a family.* Had her father actually believed it then? Or had he been pretending for the benefit of his distraught nine-year-old daughter?

The laughter of children pulls Intisar back, their legs dangling from their father's shoulders.

Yazeed plops more mud on his skin and dips into water to rinse it away, then does it all over again. This simple ritual keeps him and the other children wading nearby amused. She wonders if that boy on the side of the road will make it through the checkpoint one day and have a chance to toss his beach ball. And what about the teenager near Nablus? Was he released to his family and home now?

When it's time to leave, Intisar heads toward the public showers to rinse her legs. She waits patiently as a middle-aged, blotchy-skinned woman takes her turn. She's holding a broad-brimmed straw hat and says to her in a thick European accent, "Nicer before. Too many Arabs now." She gives Intisar a furtive nod before stepping out of the jet stream and padding away.

GAHANA PRISON: NOVEMBER 2000

CHAPTER 15

Two days before the start of Ramadan, Sadeeq was dead. The last time he was dragged into the Zinzana he didn't return. Word got around that he'd taken his own life—had wrapped the rope that dropped from the ceiling of that dark box while the guards watched. Nijmy accused their jailers of murder. There was a look of deep shame on his face, as if he was calculating all the times he'd been cruel to Sadeeq. Abu Jadallah only shook his head, reciting Quran.

How many times had Hafez wanted to wrap a noose around his own neck and pass into eternal darkness? He'd sat in the corner of that black dungeon, in and out of consciousness, the rope taunting him. They'd used it to rack him, looping it around his hands before the ground fell away from him. They shocked his torso, like a hot iron burning his insides. Then they dropped him to the dirty ground and spasms seized his seared limbs.

Bee keffi, Hafez, the rope had whispered to him. *Enough is enough.*

He couldn't see it in the darkness, only heard its croaky voice inviting him closer. He'd crawled to it, one hand swatting the air until it grazed his fingers. He hoisted himself up on one knee and reached for the loop. He tugged it, expanding the coil wide enough to slip his head through. But he was too weak to run and snap his neck. He lost consciousness again and lay with the noose around his neck until the next time the steel door opened and light scornfully poured into the Zinzana, confirming he was still alive.

How quickly had Sadeeq slipped into the next world? Had it been painless in that final breath? Or had his whole body been aflame until nothing?

Hafez dashed to the toilet of the cell and vomited, the bile splashing against the shit-stained bowl. He thought miserably of his father. Had he felt any pain in his final moments? Did a natural death usher a tranquil passage from this world? How much had his father's grief expedited his deterioration?

His mother was the messenger, a wretched role, compounding Hafez's sorrow. He should've been by her side when the mourners came.

His procession stretched all the way from our villa to the cemetery, God bless him, his mother had boasted, as if attempting to lighten his desolation. He'd wept, and the fortress he'd built around his heart and body crumbled, exposing his vulnerability. His father had once seemed to him a permanent fixture, like the earth itself, withstanding millennium after millennium of natural and man-made calamity. His death had widened a chasm of faithlessness in Hafez. He'd witnessed the slaughter of men—and been on the brink of death himself. But it was his father's death that forced him to face his own mortality and utter failure, and the devasting likelihood that he would expire inside this cage.

How many would walk in Sadeeq's procession? Would his

family finally behold his body after a quarter of a century had passed?

"They won't give him back," Nijmy had griped. They'd had cousins and schoolmates whose bodies remained captive to the oppressors—even in death.

A young man soon took Sadeeq's place. His name was Abbas and he had the strangely plump lips of a woman attached to a round face, which made it difficult to concentrate on his words. He was like a man-baby, a comical addition among the prisoners.

In the mess hall, Abbas bragged about all that awaited him on the outside. A fiancée. A new flat. "As soon as my lawyer fixes this," he said as if his detainment was like a broken light bulb or a rusty window hinge. "I'm not meant to be in here."

"None of us are," someone snickered at a long table behind them.

"You'll see," Abbas persisted, pointing a corpulent finger in the air. "I'm not meant to be in here."

"Why don't you shut up with that talk?" Nijmy hissed, dunking a piece of stale bread into a tasteless bowl of broth.

"Bas," Abu Nasser chided his younger son. "Leave him be."

"You really think you're getting out of here anytime soon?" Nijmy persisted.

"I have to," Abbas said, smelling the broth and crinkling his nose. "I'm getting married next month." He turned toward Hafez, who hadn't scorned him. "Her muhr was the highest among her sisters. She'd had suitors day and night at her father's door."

"And they'll be back now that you're here," Nijmy sneered.

"Inshallah khair," Abu Jadallah offered, patting the young man's shoulder.

"My lawyer will fix this," he said again, louder this time, as if trying to convince himself. "And I'll be home again."

Outside the walls of Gahana, a group of contemptuous settlers cooked lambs on open fire pits, taunting the prisoners as they fasted. Hafez and the other men were forced into the courtyard, the early winter cold biting their faces and fingers. Hafez couldn't see the faces of the mustawtaneen, only heard their snickering and excited shouts:

"Achbarosh! You rats!"

"Come and eat with us!"

"You don't know what you're missing, boys!"

The older men gathered around Abu Jadallah, who led them in supplications. Their praying voices grew louder and louder, their words their swords, attempting to vanquish the wicked forces on the other side. The aroma from the roasting meats made some of the younger men screw their eyes shut and sink their heads in their laps on the dusty ground. Hafez suspected it wasn't the labor of fasting that agonized them—they'd all done it since they were children. It was the fact that they might never enjoy a meal of lamb again. Its succulent juices, its fatty tenderness. The gray sky mirrored the melancholy of the prisoners.

On sunny, warmer days, Hafez would sit on his haunches, his back against a wall, without his sketchbook, which he was not allowed to take with him outdoors. He'd lost the very first notepad he acquired in a raid last month. He watched a guard lick his thumb and turn each page before tearing it to pieces while another guard stomped on the midnight blue-and-gold-embossed copy of Abu Jadallah's Quran. Neither Hafez nor the old man could do a thing except watch the awful desecration of each of their sacred texts. The spine of the Holy Book was broken, but his cellmate was able to salvage it; later on he would cradle it his hands to prevent the pages from detaching. Hafez, on the other hand, would start over in a new notepad. And each new day he regenerated the images of his original sketchbook, penciling in a brand-new date in the bottom corner of the 3-x-5 page.

He watched a recurring football game that took place during the one hour of outdoor time the prisoners were allowed. A ball had found its way inside the courtyard shortly before Hafez had arrived. Some believed it had been tossed over the wall—perhaps on a generous whim—though Gahana was far from civilian life. The younger ones hadn't questioned it and triumphantly bumped and straddled it between their feet before kicking it through makeshift goals made from stacks of empty cigarette cartons, one on each side. For an hour, they were Zizou and Ronaldo.

Nijmy was quite serious about the sport. Hafez watched the younger man confront the goalie, shoving him backward when Nijmy's strike didn't land. From a tower, a guard called out a half-hearted order to break it up, his hands resting on the butt of the rifle slung over one shoulder. Nasser always intervened, pulling his brother away by the sleeve of his uniform while their father, like Hafez, watched from the sidelines. Abu Nasser shook his head, amused.

On this cold day, a football game would have warmed up the young men. But they were distracted by their tormentors outside the concrete wall, singing and cursing them, the aroma of lamb cutting through the chill of their bones.

During the next day's visitation, families would endure the brutal castigation of the sneering settlers. As they descended their buses, they were greeted with a shower of rotten fruit and spittle.

Hafez didn't have any visitors. He'd instructed his mother to stay away for the winter, particularly this Ramadan. He remained in his cell, emptied of the other men. The absence of poor Sadeeq, who was never permitted visitors over the span of his imprisonment, filled the space like noxious fumes. It was hard to concentrate on drawing. He sat cross-legged on his cot, a pack of cards in his hand—the same one Sadeeq always held so dearly to him, as Hafez did his notebooks. Now he carefully slipped the deck from its cardboard case and he listlessly began to shuffle. Sadeeq's eager and pained face filled the empty cell. Hafez flung the cards, and they floated noiselessly to the dirty floor.

When the other men returned, they studied the scattered cards then looked up at Hafez.

"Pick them up, boys," Abu Nasser softly ordered his sons.

Abu Jadallah shuffled to the edge of Hafez's bunk, his hand on the corner of his mattress. "Khair inshallah," he said.

"Losing to yourself, ya Hafez," Abbas joked, his voice cheerfully loud. He was holding a plastic container of palm dates, securely taped and with his name on it in black marker. It had made it through security for iftar. Abu Jadallah also held a package of dates—fresh golden-brown tamir, tender and sweet. "Inshallah khair," the old man said again, patting Hafez's leg.

A period of silence followed each man's visitation with a loved one who'd made the whole-day trip to Gahana to remind him that he still existed—in some small place, beyond the concrete cage. In nostalgic musings during the holidays. In portraits his mother hung on cracked cinderblock walls. In the physical features of his children.

But Abbas, their new cellmate, was garrulous, his fat lips babbling on about his wedding plans, how well his khateeb had said he looked.

"I might lose a few kilos in here," Abbas joked, patting his belly.

"Shut the hell up!"

Hafez glanced down from his bunk. It had come from Nasser. The man clutched his jaw, eyes feral with pain. A lower molar was infected and the infirmary refused to extract it.

Hafez remembered the love story of his parents. It had started with a toothache. His father had not only found relief at the hospital in Ramallah, but a lovely wife.

Poor Nasser had been suffering for weeks. The aspirin from the commissary was useless. A few men on their floor had begged for a tablet to quell their own ailments—a flared ulcer, pounding migraines. Hafez had overheard a man offer to suck Nasser's penis for just one pill.

Abu Jadallah had heard it, too. *The Lord keep the shaytan far from our midst,* the old man prayed.

"What's his problem?" Abbas was saying to Hafez, as if they were close mates.

Hafez rolled over on his bunk, ignoring the young man's question.

It would be eid the next time families arrived, the fasting month drawing to an end. Hafez pictured the radiant expressions on the faces of parents and wives. Though he'd asked his mother to stay away, Hafez wished she might surprise him, but his name was not called when the guards commanded a formation along the walkway outside his cell.

The men were gone for only a brief time when Hafez heard a scuffle. He sat upright on his cot. Two guards shoved Abbas through the metal door and he fell to the floor. He was sobbing, his man-baby body convulsing.

In spite of himself, Hafez climbed down his bunk and knelt down beside Abbas. "What happened?"

"I don't understand!" the young man wailed. "She loves me!" He balled himself up in the middle of the floor, his weeping muffled inside his folded arms.

Hafez stepped away. Let the man have his cry without being bothered.

Soon enough, the others returned. Nijmy couldn't disguise his smugness. His brother Nasser shook his head ruefully. He sunk down next to Abbas and patted his back. Abu Jadallah stood beside Hafez's bunk and said in a low voice, "His khateeb ended the engagement." He patted his hands in a gesture of finality. "It's over. She wouldn't wait for him."

Nijmy smirked up at Hafez. "And she sent her brother and father to deliver the news."

"He started punching the security window," Nasser added. "Maskeen. They sent us all back."

His younger brother hovered over the crumpled body on the floor. "I told him it wouldn't last," Nijmy jeered. "He thought she'd wait for him—"

"Shut up!" Abbas suddenly shouted, pulling himself up to face Nijmy. "Shut your mouth, ya haywan!"

Hafez felt pity for Abbas. The loss of his own wife had

been difficult to swallow, sharp and acidic like bile rising up his throat. It had made him sick for days after his mother broke the news to him. He wanted to tell Abbas that the permanence of loss was unbearable at first, but soon it would turn hollow, like a hole once full of earth.

"I'm just saying," Nijmy persisted, holding his hands up, feigning innocence. "Everything changes when you're in here. You can't expect—"

The rest of his sentence was knocked out of his mouth, along with a single tooth. Abbas's fist was poised to deliver another blow, but Nasser intervened, tackling him to the floor. Hafez stared at the bloody tooth, which had ricocheted across the cell and landed near the foot of a bunkbed.

Four guards swiftly entered the cell and one jabbed his rifle into Abbas's flabby abdomen and the young man folded over again. Ignoring Nijmy's pleas that he wasn't responsible, a second stone-faced guard cuffed his hands behind his back and hauled Nijmy away. Blood trickled from his mouth. The remaining guards held Abu Nasser and his older son at bay with rifles aimed at their chests.

The cell was silent again except for Abu Jadallah sucking his teeth in disappointment. "Tst, tst, tst! Pray to the Prophet!" he admonished to no one in particular.

Nasser wore a wondrous expression, as if he was contemplating the irony of his brother losing a tooth.

Hafez watched Abu Nasser walk over to the bunk and bent down to pick up the bloody canine that had detached from his younger son's mouth. He held it in his palm and examined it for a few moments before closing his fist.

BAYT AL-HAWA: SEPTEMBER 2007

CHAPTER 16

Before long, a small mound of mlookhiyah forms in the center of the kitchen table. Her cousin spreads newspapers to capture debris as the two women separate a large bundle of jute mallow stalks. Sundus's granddaughter walks in, her face flushed with a radiance she hasn't seen since bint Hafez arrived.

"How was your trip?" Majida grins. "You're sun-kissed."

She tucks a strand of her dark hair behind her ear. "It was good. The sea is beautiful."

Sundus wonders if Nabeel has made headway with her granddaughter—has at least opened her up to another conversation. Her eyes follow Intisar as she washes her hands at the sink and takes a seat at the table.

"Can I help?"

Sundus hands her a small bundle. "Like this," she instructs her granddaughter, expertly pinching each leaf from its long, slender stem. "Do you like mlookhiyah?"

Intisar hesitates before shaking her head. "I mean—I haven't had it fresh like this before."

Sundus chuckles. "Your father didn't like it, either." The slimy-green consistency had repelled her son. He'd loved almost everything else she made. Her chicken musakhan with chopped onions dredged in olive oil and peppered in sumac. Her savory fava bean and lamb stew. Her spicy kufta balls broiled in a pan of sliced potatoes. And even her simple cumin-flavored addas soup over which he squeezed a lemon wedge and slurped without bread.

"Mlookhiyah is good for your digestive health," Majida says, cheerfully plucking away.

"Maybe you'll give mine a try," Sundus says, peering at the girl. She pauses to scrutinize her granddaughter's progress. Satisfied, she turns back to her own pile. "Your mother called again."

Sundus had picked up this time while Majida was hanging washed bed sheets on the roof. The first seconds were awkward for Nadira, who was expecting—or hoping—someone else would pick up.

How are you, Khalti? her son's ex-wife dutifully asked.

Alhamdullillah, she returned. And they exchanged a few more inquiries on family members.

I was protecting my daughter, Nadira finally admitted. But there was an accusation in her tone—the same one she'd always had concerning Hafez. As if Sundus was responsible for her son leaving his wife.

Against what? Sundus shot back. *The land is hers now. What's left of her father.*

We don't want it, the other woman snaps. Then quickly, *Intisar doesn't need it.*

This dismissive retort slashed her heart. How easy to relinquish the whole of Jalal's legacy.

Sundus pushed back. *She'll have to make up her own mind,* she says, a cold sweat breaking across her back. She pulled a handkerchief from her chest pocket and mopped perspiration from her forehead. Her confidence was threadbare like a stitch coming loose on the flower pattern of her thobe. She kept from tugging at it while she listened to the voice on the other end of the line.

Yes. It's hers, but I know my own daughter, Nadira pressed, her tone dripping with arrogance. *She won't stay, Hajja. You're better off accepting whatever that man's offering you.*

These words burned Sundus's ears. Nadira was partly right. Sundus knows very little of her granddaughter, only what Sundus observes. And from her own elastic memories that stretched to the present, some gradually losing their original form.

I've heard all about the corruption that goes on there, the woman on the other end declared. *And you want to get my daughter mixed up in all of it?*

My daughter. Just as swiftly as Nadira had dissociated her granddaughter of her inheritance, she'd excised Hafez, too.

"I'll phone her tomorrow," Intisar is saying as she concentrates on her stalks. She snaps a leaf, then glides her thumb along the stem to the next one until the process becomes automatic, taking care not to compromise the leaf.

Sundus nods in approval. "You learn fast." She grabs a large wooden cutting board and a knife and begins siphoning off portions from the plucked pile.

"Can I try that?" the girl asks as if hoping she's earned it.

Sundus jerks her head toward the cabinet. "Grab another board and a knife."

Majida gives Sundus a triumphant look as soon as Intisar's

back is turned, her eyebrows cocked, as if to say: *I told you to give her some time.*

The three of them work as a team, Sundus and Intisar chopping the heaps Majida contributes into a large bowl. "I'd be grateful if my granddaughters were so efficient—God bless them! Their mother—my daughter Ahlam—has spoiled them," her cousin half-heartedly scowls. "'Wait until they get married,' I told her. 'Their husbands will send them home before the week is out.'" Majida chuckles. "God gift them every virtue. Girls are a true blessing. Now my eldest granddaughter, Nahla. She is—"

"After Baba was—after he was captured—why didn't you send for me, Sitti?" Intisar suddenly interrupts. The tip of her chopping knife hovers above the coarse mound.

The girl's tone is a sharp whip of accusation. Majida is flummoxed, her eyes darting between Sundus and the girl.

"Now I'm just a—" Intisar searches for the word in Arabic—"ghareeba. A stranger in this place."

Regret swells in Sundus's heart—spikier than grief. "I did, ya Sitti!" She reaches across the table and takes hold of Intisar's hand. Their fingertips are the same green. "Every summer until you were sixteen or seventeen, I asked for you. There was always an excuse. You were taking extra classes, you were away at some—" she switches to English—"camp. Or you have a job. There is always something."

The last phone call Sundus had made to America was after they'd discovered the cancer. Hafez's lawyer was fighting for treatment, but prisoners were denied care, even tolerable pain medication, until it was too late. Sundus's fingers had trembled as she dialed the number overseas.

I want to see my granddaughter. A new kind of terror had pressed against her heart. Worse than losing your first home, or losing your parents, or even your husband. Intisar was her sole connection to her son, one that had frayed over the years. Sundus had to carefully and quickly restore it before it slipped completely from her grasp.

It's too dangerous there, Nadira had simply replied.

Sundus had felt both sorry for the woman her son had loved and incensed at her. How could she quell Nadira's fears when the news was all she saw and read? *The girl must know her roots,* Sundus had weakly argued. *The land is for Hafez. His daughter will be next.*

I'm sorry, Hajja. I won't allow her to travel there. Goodbye.

That was the last time Sundus had spoken to her. Until earlier that day.

"Your mother was protecting you," she tells her granddaughter. "We didn't know if your father would ever be released."

"And now it's too late." She lays down her knife, pushes her chair back. "I can't do this," she says in English, looking down at the bowl of mlookhiyah as if the labor of chopping the edible leaves is too great. But Sundus understands what Intisar actually means. "I'm sorry," her granddaughter continues. "I'm sorry for everything your family has been through, but I can't stay. It's too hard here." She turns to leave.

Sundus stands up and shouts at her, "Wakfi! Stop right there!" She points to the chair. "Sit down." Her granddaughter is stunned by her command. She looks to Majida, who's also frozen, her half-plucked stem raised in the air. Intisar obediently takes her place again at the table.

"Pray to the Prophet," her cousin interjects.

"No!" Sundus pounds her fist on the kitchen table, rattling the bowl and knives. Holding up green-tinged fingers, she says, "I lost your father three times. First when he left to America. The second time was when they took him away. And finally when he—" She takes a deep breath and sinks back down in her chair. "Listen, ya Sitti," Sundus says, lowering her volume. "You have a greater stake than you think—than you want to accept responsibility for. You are your father's daughter. You cannot disrupt the past. You cannot undo it. You must carry it forward now."

It's more than she's said directly about the matter. All this time Sundus has been telling stories of the past. Yet how else can she make her granddaughter understand all that has been lost and reclaimed over several lifetimes? How else can her beloved parents become real to Intisar, their deep love suspending them above an abyss of death and exile like thousands of other Falasteeniya? Or her husband Jalal, who'd found his way back to his homeland as his own son had one day?

"I don't want to hear anymore." The girl's voice is barely above a whisper. She holds up her hand and fans her fingers, which have darkened into a deeper shade than the virgin leaves.

"You will hear me," Sundus demands, her voice rising again. "And then to hell with you."

"Hajja!" her cousin admonishes.

"She will hear me," Sundus says to Majida, though her eyes are fixed on her granddaughter. "You have no idea what it means to sacrifice. This land is being handed to you. Just like this." She grabs a stalk of mlookhiyah and tosses it at Intisar. "You didn't work for it. Or bleed for it." She shuts her eyes and the blood from her father's wound blooms in her mother's lap. "But your father—he couldn't leave Falasteen even when he tried. And of all of us, he'd made the greatest sacrifice. Giving you up."

He'd lied to them, claimed he'd returned to help organize humanitarian aid for families in need, the wives and children of martyrs who'd fallen during the Intifada. He drove an ambulance for the hospital in Ramallah where her father had tended to patients until he was killed. And now here was his grandson, in service of others. Sundus had been at once proud and afraid.

On a particularly incendiary day of demonstrations in the fall of 1989, Hafez didn't return home. Young men and women dodged rubber bullets, masking their mouths and eyes from tear gas as they ran between the streets of Bayt al-Hawa and Ramallah. Jalal called the hospital and spoke with a member of the paramedic team.

No one had seen Hafez for some time.

How long had their son been lying to them?

Next, they hurried across the way to Abu Mu'tassim's house. His best friend had nothing tangible to offer—or perhaps he was sworn to secrecy. But Mu'tassem's worried expression confirmed that, like Sundus and Jalal, he knew little about Hafez's covert affiliation.

"He can't be out there during curfew!" Sundus cried. "They'll arrest him."

The azzan announced the late afternoon prayer. In a few hours, the streets would turn even more dangerous.

"I'll check the detention center," Jalal said. He'd heard other demonstrators had been rounded up earlier that day and deposited there.

"I'm going with you," Sundus had insisted. They drove as far as they could before parking their car ahead of barricades of burning tires and makeshift walls of rocks. They continued on foot, huddled close to one another, fearful of snipers they'd heard were perched on rooftops of raided buildings. Sundus repeated supplications, squeezing Jalal's arm as he led her along. The acrid odor of tear gas penetrated the handkerchief she held to face, prickling her throat, but she continued her prayer:

Say, O Prophet, 'He is Allah—One and Indivisible
Allah—the Sustainer needed by all.
He has never had offspring, nor was He born.
And there is none comparable to Him.'

In the first year of the Intifada, a ledger of the martyrs was started on a cement wall in the village square. The likeness of each fallen man of Bayt al-Hawa was painted in black, his name beneath it in red. A dozen who'd once been boys riding their bicycles or chasing a ball across the valley. Now every one of them had been reduced to a name and a pensive, eerie face, void of color, of life.

Hafez was their only son. Jalal had always envisioned their villa with many children running and laughing through its hallways. And Sundus had tried to honor that desperate wish he carried from the refugee encampment. She'd become pregnant quickly the first time and was secretly pleased. But after Hafez, her periods became erratic and deceiving. When her underwear remained clean of blood, she gave silent du'aa. And then a dark stain would appear and she cried on her mother's shoulder.

Khair inshallah, her mother had soothed, rubbing Sundus's back. *You are young, my love. Have patience.*

She could never bring herself to ask her mother why she'd never had other siblings. The dead figure of her infant brother had gradually receded into the darkness of her consciousness like the sea at night, sometimes a tremor breaking the surface. And when Sundus still couldn't conceive, she believed a curse had been cast after the last of the red dirt was tossed over the roadside grave.

The detention center was a grim building of turnstiles and steel bars. There were no windows, and the main entrance was a heavy clanking door with only a small slot to check visitors. They were admitted into a waiting area with a dozen families. Sundus felt both relief and trepidation at the sight of other parents. They looked like they'd been standing for hours; some had taken to the floor, their backs against a wall they'd already claimed. They glanced at Sundus and Jalal with weary expressions.

They were swiftly turned away at the processing window. The soldiers wouldn't tell them a thing about Hafez, whether he was there or not. Sundus prayed against a highly probable scenario: her son had been hauled away to prison. She didn't allow the other possibility to enter her mind.

"Inshallah khair," Jalal said over and over again, leading her to an empty corner beside a woman in a black thobe, sitting cross-legged. Her upper body rocked back and forth as her lips moved silently in prayer. Jalal clutched Sundus's hand and she could feel his trembling fingers.

If Hafez was still at this detention center, there was hope. And if he was dead she would have known by now—a mother knows, a kind of numbness creeping through her body, signaling a sacred part of her had expired.

She kept one hand tucked inside her large purse, her fingers pressing against a photograph her mother had given her. How dearly her mother had loved her grandson, how it was Hafez who had lifted her from utter despair when they killed her husband, robbing a young Hafez of his grandfather.

Take this, her mother said, pressing the photograph of Hafez standing on the saha, the orchard behind him. It was snapped during his homecoming that summer of 1987. He stood alone, without a wife or child, wearing a serious expression, as if contemplating a grave matter.

If they were forced to identify his body, then she'd hand over the photograph to a news reporter to be featured along with other martyrs in the latest death toll. Her mother had it ready, peeled from an album of family portraits and tucked it inside a blank envelope.

As Sundus waited with Jalal on the hard bench, she thought about how they had arrived at this awful moment.

It had begun in Gaza. Four migrant workers were struck and killed in a collision with an Israeli truck driver. Some called it retaliation for the stabbing of a Jewish man a few days earlier. But there was no time to debate the overlapping incidents. Young people flooded the streets, vehemently demanding an end to oppression.

A tide was turning, folks said.

Occupation was no longer sustainable—a second and third generation demanded, in no uncertain terms, liberation. A fervor ignited them beyond any other recorded movement, obliterating any possibility of turning back. The status quo was as insidious as the Nakba.

But Sundus had thought only of those four men. Their wives and children waiting for them to come home. How in a flash of shattered glass and mangled metal, everything changed. And what about their mothers?

Sundus had already survived displacement, the murder of her father, and a second invasion of her country. And now Hafez would be swept into this turbulent new wave of resistance.

How foolish they'd been! How deliberately blind as Hafez grew sullen, spending hours in his room when he wasn't volunteering at the hospital. When he emerged, he appeared stricken, as if he knew something awful was going to happen. At supper, his eyes flitted anxiously between Sundus and his father.

What is it, yabba? Jalal had implored him.

But Hafez disclosed nothing beyond. *I'm fine, Yabba. Alhamdullilah.*

He's missing his family in America, Sundus had said, lying under the covers beside Jalal. A soft slant of moonlight outlined his silhouette as he faced away from her. She caressed his hair and he clasped her fingers and held them tightly.

Sundus had overheard Hafez on the telephone, his long-distance conversations with his wife and daughter. It was always a brief exchange with Nadira before she handed the phone to Intisar. After her granddaughter hung up, Hafez lingered on the chair, still cradling the receiver against his forehead until a beeping dial tone jarred him to movement again.

She'd selfishly worn blinders. In spite of the dangers, she was glad to have her son here. And it was his choice, she reasoned. His country had called him home. When this uprising was over, would he fly back to America? Sundus found herself perversely torn between panic and resentment. If he stayed, like any man, young or old, Hafez could be killed. But, if the situation hadn't escalated, he might have never returned to her.

A steel door buzzed open. Sundus sat up straight. A pair of soldiers led a line of young, puffy-eyed women to the waiting area. A few were defiant, refusing to surrender to the intimidation, chins jutting out. One of the soldiers signaled the women to stop a few feet away from their anxious families, who had begun to stir from their seats, until he waved his rifle at them, halting their movement. He tapped the butt of his rifle and wagged his finger in the women's faces. "Next time we arrest you, we'll make you unfit to be brides. Maf-hoom?" His Arabic was crude, but his meaning was as clear as glass. "Understood?"

A few of the young women began sobbing.

"Animals," Jalal hissed.

They were released to their relieved parents, who hugged them and kissed their faces. "Alhamdullilah! Alhamdullilah!" rose up in a chorus. Sundus's own heart twisted for them, a mixture of relief and envy. They were free to go, but where was her Hafez?

She adjusted the white mandeela around her head and approached the desk again. Jalal tried to hold her back and she shook off his hand. A female soldier didn't look up from her paperwork. Her long hair was parted evenly down the middle and pulled into a low ponytail. Tiny specks of dandruff flaked her brown strands. Her short-sleeved fatigues revealed a tattoo on her right bicep. It was an exotic tropical bird Sundus didn't recognize. She followed its vibrant plumage up the arm before the head disappeared beneath the soldier's shirt cuff. "I'm begging you," Sundus began. "Please tell me if my son is here. His name is—"

The soldier barely glanced up. "Sit down," she commanded, scrawling words on a file. "If you ask me again, you'll be removed."

Without another word, Sundus returned to the corner, humiliation beating against her forehead. She bit her lower lip and sat back down next to Jalal. He wrapped his arm around her shoulders and she sank against him. All she wanted was her son.

In their ugly green uniforms, the soldiers were unyielding. They spoke to each other in Hebrew and laughed. It was as if she and the other parents were invisible. None of them seemed capable of puncturing the soldiers' steely veneers. The parents' desperate pleas for information went disdainfully unanswered. How could Sundus convince these soldiers, sway them to see her and Jalal—exhausted and without sleep—as a mother and father and not as the enemy?

She glanced around the detention center. They were mostly women like her, cradling their heads in their hands, waiting. How far did the patience of a mother stretch?

"Inshallah khair, my sister," the woman in the black thobe whispered beside Sundus. She patted her thigh. "They want to torture us. Teach us a lesson for raising mutinous children. I'm sure your son is here. Patience." She offered a palmful of pistachios.

But Sundus only wanted to scream at the stone-faced soldier across from her, grab ahold of her hair and yank it hard, demanding to know if she, too, had a child—a son. How could she treat another mother like this? Or had she been forced to fold away that existence each morning she fastened the laces of her stiff combat boots and looped her weapon over her shoulder? Was her machine gun heavier than a newborn baby?

A row of men and women assembled to pray and Jalal joined them. If not for the muezzin's recorded voice—live calls to salat were suspended under curfew—Sundus had lost track of time.

She sat frozen in her spot, her heart closed off to anything except for worry.

When the final summons to prayer reverberated outside, Jalal tugged at Sundus's arm. "It's time to go."

Their dread stretched into the long night as they waited on the barranda, the wind of the valley chilling Sundus beneath her blanket. She glided back and forth, wishing the rhythm could muffle the fear beating at her chest. Jalal sat beside her, worrying his prayer beads. Her mother uttered du'aa from her spot on the dais. They said nothing to each other until Jalal urged them to sleep.

"Tomorrow is a new day," he said. "Inshallah khair."

But sleep eluded Sundus as Jalal softly snored. She would be the first to hear the tires crunching down the path to their villa before the military jeep screeched to a halt outside the stone wall. They had come for her son.

"Jalal! Wake up!" Sundus cried, throwing the blanket off her. She ran to her mother's room. "Yamma! An army is here! Wake up! Get dressed!" Ya rubbi! What had Hafez done? Her heart beat in her throat.

"Khair!" her mother exclaimed, fumbling for her glasses on the nightstand and the mandeela she draped over a chair.

The pounding at the door thundered through their bayt and echoed in the valley. Sundus imagined their neighbors jolted awake, peering through windows in darkened rooms, not daring to turn on any lights.

"Stay back!" Jalal warned, flicking his hand behind him as he descended the stairwell to the main entrance. The soldiers pounded the door with multiple fists until her husband could reach it. In a flash, they were inside, pointing rifles at Jalal. Sundus and her mother watched from the landing.

"Where is Hafez Jaber?" one shouted in Arabic. "We know he resides here. Tell me quickly! Where is he?"

"He's not here," Jalal answered, his hands in the air.

The blow was so swift Sundus thought she'd imagined it until Jalal was level with the floor, clutching his stomach. She flew down the stairs and was met with the mouth of a rifle aimed at her head.

"Do not move!" another soldier yelled. Sundus held up her hands.

"Have mercy in the name of God!" her mother called down.

They yanked Jalal to his feet and commanded all three of them to the salon. Sundus shielded her mother with her body.

"Sit down!" the first soldier bellowed at them. He stood opposite of them. Jalal, his shoulders balled in pain, sat between Sundus and her mother. In a whirlwind, furniture was kicked and turned over, closet doors slammed open and shut, boots clomping across the marble floor. It was as if Sundus was watching a film reel of the first time the villa had been raided twenty years before. Except this time she was observing the destruction in real time, not in the aftermath.

But tonight, they didn't find who they were looking for.

The soldier pretended to examine the salon, knocking a candy dish over with his rifle and toppling an oversized vase holding ostrich feathers with a kick. Most everything in the villa had been imported to Jalal's store and could be replaced—just like the first time. Anything broken could be replaced. Unmarred photographs could be reframed, broken plates and cups exchanged for shiny new sets.

But what would happen if Hafez was captured? How could they replace their only son?

The soldier swept everything off the lacquered coffee table—a copy of the Holy Quran, a gold embossed replica of an olive tree, a heavy crystal ashtray—before seating himself on top of it, hands on his knees, and leaning forward as if about to reprimand them. His rifle was slung over his shoulder, and its butt tapped the surface of the table whenever he moved. It was an eerily delicate sound.

"Make this easy on yourselves. Where is your son?" His thick Arabic was unnatural, menacing.

"Wallahi, we do not know," Jalal protested again, holding up his hands. It was true, after all—they had no idea where their son might be. Hafez had been keeping secrets, trying to spare them. But the secrets had followed him home.

"Yalla, woman," the soldier said, his patronizing tone betraying the sheer hatred Sundus saw in his eyes. "Where is he?"

There was nothing Sundus could offer him. She shook her head.

The soldier turned to Sundus's mother. "And you, hajja? Do you know? You can tell me."

"We know nothing," her mother said emphatically, folding her arms across her chest. "Haram! This is a sin! Terrorizing us!"

"You stupid people," the soldier said, leaning back. "You make this difficult on yourselves." He pulled a pistol from a holster on his side and tapped the space on the sofa between Jalal's legs.

Sundus felt her husband's body stiffen, his voice fighting to remain steady. "We don't know where he is, I swear."

In a flash, Sundus caught the glint of the pistol before its butt crashed down on Jalal's face. He slunk down on the sofa, clutching his left eye. Sundus instinctively shielded him as she had done for her mother, but the soldier pulled her off the sofa, twisting her arm behind her back. She cried out.

"Leave us be, you animals!" her mother shouted, grasping for Sundus's leg.

The soldier held Sundus so long she anticipated the sound of her arm breaking. But he finally released her and pushed her back down on the sofa. Blood ran from a small gash down the side of Jalal's face. The rest of the soldiers had returned, shaking their heads. Her shoulder throbbed and she massaged it, wincing at the pain.

"Dead or alive, we will find him," the soldier declared, before spitting on the ground. He raised his pistol again and Sundus clenched her eyes shut, squeezed her husband's hand.

I testify there is no god but Allah and Muhammad is His prophet, she prayed. Her final testimony before bullets riddled her brain. She clutched the hands of her husband and mother and waited.

The discharge was incredibly close, like someone's breath in her face. She opened her eyes. They were alive. The soldiers were gone but they'd left their grisly promise: a half-dozen bullet holes scarring the wall above their heads.

Sundus rises again from the table. The chopped mlookhiyah fills the kitchen with an air of freshness, like a meadow of wildflowers. "We were not the only ones to suffer," she tells Intisar. "Alhamdullilah, God has been merciful. To surrender the land—to let that crook Abdul Waheed steal it from us—is a more grievous crime."

Her granddaughter avoids her eyes and stares into the pile of green leaves, as if searching for something she'll never find.

BAYT AL-HAWA: SEPTEMBER 2007

CHAPTER 17

As she unlocks the door, Lubna tells Intisar the gallery building was once a poultry market. A ghostly, putrid odor of butchered chickens still lingers—or is it only Intisar's imagination? The studio is empty except for them, sunlight pouring into the space from a large picture window.

"Good natural light to work in," Lubna says, giving her a friendly wink.

Najoom Gallery is located in Ramallah. Lubna was offered a fellowship, sponsored by private donors and a small, but very public, endowment from the Cultural Affairs branch of the Palestinian Authority. In return, she explains to Intisar, she performs the duties of an artist-in-residence and is paid a monthly stipend for giving tours and lectures to visitors of the gallery. She runs workshops for children in the encampment whose classrooms are devoid of supplies, let alone books. Like the one she'd taken Intisar to visit.

"That is my favorite duty," she beams, for she adores the children, as Intisar had observed firsthand.

Lubna doesn't mention the teenage boy, a boot pressed into

his neck, or the charred olive grove. It's like a dirty secret Intisar waits for her friend to bring up first, implicating someone else so she doesn't feel so alone. But the young woman doesn't, instead she prattles on about the owner of the gallery, a chain-smoking widow. "Inshallah you'll get to meet her," Lubna says. Her friend continues to speak as if Intisar will be staying here longer, as if Lubna can change her mind. But her own grandmother can't. How can a stranger convince Intisar?

"That boy," she begins, clearing her throat. "What do you think happened to him?"

Lubna gives her a sad smile. "He'll likely be detained for a few weeks. To teach him a lesson." Her hazel eyes fix on Intisar's face. In this light, they are honey-brown. "It is difficult, no?" she switches to English. "American children. They have better lives, yes?"

Intisar isn't sure how to answer her. It's true—she's been raised in a bubble. Even her work at Pine Woods has shielded her from stab and gunshot wounds, rapes and drunk-driving crashes.

Lubna cups her shoulder. "Come. I want to show you my portraits. After I develop some film, we'll go to the cultural center in town."

Intisar follows her into a dark room, past a small wiry, light installation in the middle of the floor. Hanging on one wall is a series centering an abstract rendition of a bullet. The same painted bullet appears to penetrate several body parts on each subsequent canvas. It starts with an open hand. By the time the bullet reaches a heart, it's transformed into a dove.

In the darkroom, Lubna flicks the safelight above two rows of black-and-white photographs. Intisar immediately recognizes the subject: Abu Fahmy, the old birdkeeper from the mokhayam. Against the backdrop of his cinderblock shanty, he sits on a hemp-rope stool, thumbing his musbaha, a chain of onyx prayer beads. In another, only his craggly finger appears inside an enormous steel cage, inviting the goldfinch to perch, its shiny left eye—a smooth onyx like Abu Fahmy's beads—nestled in a hundred tiny reeds of feathers.

"Wow," Intisar says. "These are good." She moves slowly down the drying line, peering at each photograph, discovering something new. Lubna has an excellent eye, as they say. Intisar doesn't know much about art, but she hopes her immediate reaction—a mix of awe and deference—will be taken as a positive assessment. Lubna beams at her.

The second row of photographs on the drying line introduces the stork, Abu Fahmy's unexpected visitor. Lubna has captured its contemplative gaze, and Intisar recalls its shivering feathers, how it had seemed in need of reassurance from someone to let it know it was safe.

As she approaches the end of the row, Intisar halts, her breath catching in her throat. The subject of several photographs is a young woman standing in an orchard with her back to the camera, a cigarette dangling from her fingers, a hand shielding the sun from her eyes. She wears a black tunic. It's Intisar.

"When did you—" she stammers. "Are these the day I arrived?"

Lubna grins and nods, her eyes shining in the dimmed light.

An emotion she can't quite name floods Intisar's chest. She peers more closely. In the photographs, the young woman's body appears light and relaxed, as if she belongs there, as if she's always walked in that orchard. Intisar turns to Lubna, fighting back tears. "I can't believe—they're so…Thank you," she finally manages.

Lubna cups her shoulder again and squeezes. "I'm calling it *The Return of bint Hafez.*" She carefully pinches the corner of one photograph. "This is my favorite. See how the shadow of the branches—" Her phone interrupts her and she holds up a finger to Intisar as she answers it. "Allo? Yes. I'm at the gallery. Now?" Lubna rolls her eyes. "Tayib, tayib. I'm on my way." She slides her phone into her back pocket. "I need to take you home. That was my sister. She needs an extra hand at the clinic. Wafa—her nurse can't make it today. Amal can help her but they need a receptionist." She leads Intisar out of the darkroom. "I'm sorry. Inshallah we'll catch up—"

Without thinking, Intisar interrupts, "I can do it. I can fill in. I mean—I can assist your sister."

Lubna waves her finger in the air. "Laa, laa, laa! You're my guest. I can't make you work!"

"Please, I want to help," Intisar implores. She grasps Lubna's hand. "I'm a nurse, remember? I can be of—" She struggles with the Arabic word for *use.* "I want to help," she says again.

Lubna narrows her eyes and studies Intisar as if she's examining a portrait, mining its details. "Akeed? Are you sure?"

"Yes!" Intisar insists. She gestures toward the darkroom. "You can work on your project and I can help your sister." The last words beat against her throat. Would Elham welcome her assistance? From a tourist?

"Okay!" Lubna is saying, smiling brightly at Intisar. "You would be of better service than me. I'll drop you off and pick you up later. There's a great café in town…"

Intisar nods, hot anticipation rising in her chest.

Every chair is occupied in the clinic's waiting area. Several women are standing or sitting on the floor, backs against one wall. A portable television plays a local satellite news station in Arabic. An attractive broadcaster with a stylish dark bob framing her face reports on the latest road closures, including the village where the nurse Wafa lives. A young man was killed in a raid overnight, and protests have broken out across the West Bank. As the broadcaster speaks, footage cuts to a crowd carrying his shrouded body through a street. Some of the men have swaddled their heads in the kufiyah, concealing everything but their eyes. The women in the waiting area hold their chins and suck their teeth at the unfolding events. Intisar can't help thinking again of the teenager the soldiers beat up.

She finds that Amal the volunteer is completely unperturbed. Intisar observes how graciously the woman greets everyone, her voice soft, her tone kind and patient like a first-grade teacher. Amal appears to know most of these women from the mokhayam. Her presence lifts their worried expressions—her sympathetic smile and nod reassuring them before they're even examined.

"This is our friend from America," she says, introducing Intisar. Some throw suspicious glances up at her, jutting their chins in perfunctory greeting. Others declare how beautiful she is. She's given a set of gray-blue scrubs that fit loosely on top, but the pants are too tight, so she's allowed to work in her jeans. She pulls on the hem of her top, feeling self-conscious, as Amal leads her around the clinic.

"And smart, mashallah," Amal adds. "She's a nurse. She's here to volunteer with us today."

A young woman exits the examining room, zipping up her long abaya.

"Next," Elham calls from behind the curtain. She didn't say much when Intisar showed up, only raising an eyebrow before showing her around the basic equipment and where medical implements were stocked.

"We've been overwhelmed since this morning," Amal tells Intisar. "Alhamdullilah you can assist our doktorra today. Inshallah Wafa will make it tomorrow." She checks her clipboard then calls the next patient, a thirteen-year-old girl accompanied by her mother, an overbearing woman with a few short whiskers on her upper lip.

"She can barely move when she gets her period," her mother loudly declares, looking at the other patients for affirmation. Doleful nods and "Inshallah khair" go around the waiting area like a sparked fuse.

Intisar feels sorry for the girl, whose face turns a shade of crimson, her eyes trained on the floor. Her chin disappears into the tuft of her hijab. Intisar remembers her first period. She was at a volleyball game and, panicked, stuffed three layers of coarse paper towels into her panties and went on to play with her team. She knew it was coming, but it was a new level of pubescent dread. She'd cried when she divulged it to her mother.

Welcome to the club, Mama had announced, not unkindly, and promptly showed her how to apply a pad—tampons were absolutely forbidden—and how to dispose of it—*never, ever flush it down the toilet!* It was an efficient response, but Intisar was looking for something more. A sense of compassion, a hug to let Intisar know she was still herself, despite the absurdity of her body. Her mother had immediately washed her hands and left Intisar to deal with it.

Now she gestures for the girl to follow her to the examining room.

"Laa, laa, laa!" the mother intervenes, her meaty arm blocking her daughter. "She's still a binit—I don't want you prodding inside her." The woman ushers her daughter through the door, a hand clamped on the girl's shoulder. "I'm going with her."

"How old are you?" Elham asks, patting the examining table for the girl to lie down.

"She's twelve," the mother states.

"Have you had your first period?" The girl nods. "Lay down for me, habibti." Elham rolls the girl's long-sleeved blouse up, revealing a cotton training bra.

Intisar watches the girl's eyes, fearful and wide, as they flit from the doctor to her mother's stern face then back to Elham. Intisar reaches for her hand and squeezes it.

"What is it, ya doktorra?" the mother demands. "What's wrong with her?"

Elham rolls the girl's shirt back down, asks her to sit up again. "Go on and wait out there. I need to speak with your mother." She smiles at her, cups her shoulder. "You're fine, habibti."

As soon as they are out of earshot, Elham tells the girl's mother, "Khalti, she'll need an ultrasound. It might be early endometriosis, but I can't confirm until she's screened at the hospital. An oral contraceptive can help her pain, but—"

"Laa, laa, laa!" the mother blasts. "She's only twelve years old. She's a virgin."

"It's only a screening, Khalti."

But the mother balks.

"Okay. Let's give her turmeric and ginger vitamins," Elham

advises, holding her hands up as if in surrender. "Until she's tested."

After the mother is handed a referral and leaves, Intisar jokes, "Are they all that difficult?" They remind her of the senior citizens whose trust she had to forge over months before they'd follow her recommendations.

"Only every Arab mother," Elham says cynically, sliding away on her swivel chair.

On her first and only break, Intisar sneaks a cigarette behind the clinic. When she returns, the women smell it on her and casually mention it will reduce her chances of fertility. In between patients, she eats half of a labaneh sandwich Amal shares with her and sips from a lukewarm water bottle. A few patients hand Intisar fruit and roasted nuts they've brought along as they wait, insisting she's never tasted anything so fresh and tasty. They won't take no for an answer.

Between bites of her half, Amal tells Intisar that her husband is a prisoner at Gahana for more than two years without a trial. Amal was pregnant at the time they raided her home. They dragged her husband out in the middle of the night. One of the soldiers had pushed her so hard she'd fallen against the corner of a table and blacked out.

"Alhamdullilah," she tells Intisar, "the baby was unharmed." She sets her pita bread down in her lap and pulls back her headscarf to show Intisar a scar behind her ear, a gash that required five stitches. Her husband hasn't seen their firstborn, has missed his daughter's aqiqah, when the imam blesses the baby and the extended family eats from platters of broiled lamb and yogurt-soaked rice.

Intisar doesn't mention Baba. Is it the same prison? She

can't remember the name. She thinks of all that's still to come in Amal's daughter's life that her husband will miss. Out loud, she says, "God help you"—the quick and easy response you give to acknowledge someone else's hardship—and looks down at her sandwich.

By late afternoon, Intisar has prepped a dozen women. One refuses an exam and claims, "It's only a headache. Just give me something for the pain."

Elham recommends a mild prescription that the woman dismisses with the flick of her hand. "I need something stronger."

Intisar finds Elham is efficient and quick, summoning the next patient before Intisar has finished dictating her documentation to Amal in Arabic. Amal, too, moves like a sprite. She sanitizes the examination room between checking in patients, halting only to join a small congregation in a narrow space of the waiting area to pray, their backs to Intisar.

A few of the women are not here for themselves but have come as proxies for family members. A middle-aged woman allows Intisar to check her blood pressure and tells her, "My heart will give out soon, worrying over my son. The yahood revoked his license. Those bastards prefer foreign labor over us. He can't work in Tel Aviv. He's been unemployed for a year. His spirit is low." She looks up at Intisar, beseechingly. "Can you talk to him, ya binti? A young woman like you might perk him up, God bless you."

Another woman wants to know what to give her husband for a coughing fit.

"I can't prescribe anything without an examination, Khalti," Elham tells the frustrated woman.

"He refuses doctors," the woman complains. "Keeps us up half the night."

The other waiting patients swiftly offer their remedies. And it goes on like this. The women are cheerful and forthcoming, so unlike the patients Intisar is used to back home. At Pine Woods, privacy is iron-clad; the senior citizens rarely disclose their ailments. Sickness is not public. Here the women willingly offer up their problems and welcome the feedback of their peers.

By late afternoon, the tidal wave of patients trickles down to a few when two figures appear in the security camera. Amal buzzes them in.

"Khair inshallah!" she cries, running to the young woman, who limps with each step. Blood streaks her nostrils. Intisar gently guides her to an examining room as the last of the patients gawk. They turn to each other, begin speculating.

"She must have fallen!"

"Was she hit by a car? They never slow down—not even for ladies!"

Amal summons Elham who grabs the young woman's hand. She recognizes her. "What happened, ya Muna?"

The older woman—her mother, Intisar surmises—is sniffling into a crumpled tissue. She shakes her head as Elham tries to piece the details of the injury together. But neither mother nor daughter is talking.

"Did someone hit you, ya Muna?" Elham demands more firmly. "Tell me, habibti. You're safe here." She nods to Amal, who pulls the curtain closed behind her. Intisar hears a rise in the chorus of voices of the women waiting outside. Amal swiftly stymies their questions with du'aa.

Tears stream down the young woman's dirt-streaked face, her lips flecked with dried blood. There's a spattering of freckles both she and her mother possess and eyebrows the color of autumn leaves. Intisar tracks Muna's clothes: a long-sleeved, forest green blouse over a pair of jeans and sandals. The young woman clutches the fabric at her throat, and it's clear to Intisar that she's lost a few buttons between the collar and mid-torso.

She'd been attacked.

A chill runs down Intisar's spine. How could soldiers attack an innocent girl? Her hand prickles at the memory of the soldier's finger grazing her. Have they no bounds?

"Please, Doktorra! Treat her so we can go home," the mother is pleading. Her body is shaped like a ripened fig, narrow at the waist, hips straining against her brown thobe.

Muna's eyes dart around the examination room until they settle on Intisar for a moment. She smiles encouragingly at the young woman.

"Icepack," Elham instructs Intisar. She removes Muna's headscarf, revealing brick-red hair. With her thumbs, the doctor applies pressure to Muna's nose and though she winces, it's not broken.

Her back turned to them, Intisar listens as she reaches into a small refrigerator in the corner of the room.

"Um Hakim, tell me what happened." Elham's volume has dropped, but her tone remains firm. "Who did this?" She holds Muna's chin as she carefully dabs at her nostrils with cotton balls.

"May the Lord smite him!" the older woman curses.

"Who, Um Hakim?"

"I don't know how far he's gone! She won't tell me!"

"We'll check her—don't fret. But I need to know what happened, Khalti." Elham turns to Intisar. "Prep her for a full exam."

The doctor guides the mother by the elbow to the second examination room and speaks to her in a hushed voice.

Intisar smiles again at Muna as she finishes treating her nose. There are a few lacerations but nothing serious. The young woman's freckles are like tiny palm dates. Aside from her early practicum, Intisar hasn't tended to any patients younger than fifty-five. The daily emergencies at Pine Woods are a part of natural aging—falling in the shower, missing a step. She's not prepared for someone like Muna, but she focuses hard and responds to the doctor's commands.

"Are you hurt anywhere else?" Intisar asks.

Muna slowly shakes her head.

"Can you please undress? Doktorra Elham is going to exam you."

She peels off her blouse, clutches her torso. Intisar gently lifts her arms up over her head. She finds no visible bruises on Muna's body.

"You can tell us anything," Intisar squeezes Muna's clammy hand. "Who's responsible, Muna?"

It's a whisper and Intisar leans in.

"Abu Sinsal."

"Abu Sinsal?" Intisar repeats.

Muna nods.

Intisar places a hand on her shoulder. "We're going to make sure you stay safe."

The exam reveals no penetration, just a few scratches across her small breasts. Elham provides the mother with a few small oval-shaped tablets. "Valium," she tells Intisar when they are gone.

"She told me his name," Intisar says in a low voice.

Elham settles on her swivel chair and folds her arms across her medical jacket. There's a glint of something in her eyes—skepticism? Why would one of her patients confide in a stranger?

"Abu Sinsal," Intisar announces.

Elham's eyebrows knit together. "Abu Sinsal? I don't know anyone of that name around here. Are you sure that's what Muna said?"

Intisar's certainty begins to fade. "Yes—I mean that's what I heard. She said 'Abu Sinsal.'"

"I have a friend with the police in Ramallah. I'll ask around." Elham kneads her forehead, takes a deep breath. "The family won't be much help. They're going to cover it up as much as possible."

Intisar's stomach sinks. "They won't hurt her—I mean, will they—"

"Perform an honor killing?" Elham sits upright on her chair. "Oh, dear, we're far more civilized, I assure you," the doctor says before swiveling to her computer.

Intisar's face flushes. "I didn't mean—"

"Thanks for your help today," Elham says brusquely, her back to Intisar. Then, "Come back tomorrow. If you wish."

Outside the clinic, Lubna waits on her motorbike. She hands Intisar a helmet. "Let's go have some fun," she announces. "I'll have you home before it's too late."

Intisar, feeling exhausted, smooths the sleeves of her blouse, which she's changed back into. She's had a long day but nods without a word and climbs on behind Lubna.

Lubna rides out of the mokhayam and honks her horn at the old birdkeeper, Abu Fahmy, who sits on his hemp-rope stool, smoking a pipe. He waves at them.

Before long they enter Ramallah and circle the Manara. Minutes later Lubna pulls up to a quaint stone house with a sign hanging from an almond tree in its front yard: Café Zakee. "Let's go," Lubna says, shaking her curly hair free from her helmet.

Intisar follows her onto a terrace bordered by a garden of bougainvillea. Lemon and jacaranda trees form a canopy over pairs and small groups of patrons seated at small wrought iron tables. There's a pretty, animated woman wearing a loose hijab chatting with a man. The smoke from their argeela drifts toward Intisar, bringing hints of cherry-flavored tobacco. A middle-aged man plays the oud in a corner of the garden. Mama and her sisters would have loved this place.

"This is my favorite spot in Ramallah," Lubna declares, leading her to a small table under the shade of a lemon tree. Intisar smiles. Lubna has professed many favorites during her visit.

The scent of gardenias hangs in the air. Intisar's shoulders begin to loosen; the muscles in her neck unwind.

Out of nowhere, a man appears and pulls Lubna to her feet and embraces her. "Lubna, my sister! Happy to see you again!" He has thick curly black hair that hangs below his ears.

Lubna gestures at her. "Mazen, this is my friend Intisar."

"Ahlan, ahlan! 'Triumphant One.' My grandmother's called Intisar, too." He leans down and cups her hand with both of his, his biceps bulging beneath the cuffs of his T-shirt. "Welcome to Zakee, Sister."

"She's come all the way from America," Lubna proudly announces, winking at Intisar.

"So you've escaped the beast?"

Lubna nudges his arm. "Help me persuade her to stay, ya Mazen."

"That shouldn't be too difficult," Mazen says, holding his hands up in the air as if to capture the clouds overhead. "There's no place like Falasteen." His brilliant white teeth are capped with gold fillings.

"What's the special this week?" Lubna turns to her. "They brew their own beer here."

Mazen pulls a small pencil from behind his ear and a pad from his back pocket. "Dusk Delight. A bit of fig and cherry. Hints of nutmeg and chocolate."

"That sounds delicious. What do you think, Intisar?"

Intisar shakes her head. "No thank you. I don't drink."

"I thought all Americans drank beer," Lubna teases. "Well, don't tell on me!"

Intisar looks up at Mazen. "May I have tea, please? With mint leaves?"

"And a combo platter, if you please, Mazen," Lubna adds.

"A'la rassi!" he salutes them. "At your service, my sisters!"

From the terrace, Intisar sees a young woman in the kitchen, preparing plates of appetizers. Her raven hair is streaked with blonde, chunky highlights. A diamond glints from her right nostril.

"So how did it go at the clinic?" Lubna asks, drumming the edge of the table in time to the oud.

"Good," Intisar says. "Everyone works really hard." She wonders about the report Elham will give Lubna later on. Her sister did invite her back, but it might have been out of desperation, until her regular nurse returns. "You think Wafa will be back tomorrow?"

Lubna shakes her head, still drumming her fingers. "There's a curfew in Wafa's village. It's getting worse. I doubt she'll be back any time soon."

"Your sister asked me to fill in again. Can you give me a ride tomorrow?"

"You'll have no time for me!" Lubna pouts in mock exaggeration, but her approving smile shows that she's pleased by this development.

For the first time Intisar feels less like a tourist. "I'm here for a few more days," she smiles back. She can't deny that it felt good to help. Muna's blood-crusted nose flashes across her mind. "You know? A girl came into the clinic. She was attacked." Intisar hates to broach the incident and violate confidentiality, but she wonders if Lubna can help her identify the man.

Lubna stops drumming. "Another one?"

"Another one?" Intisar echoes. "What are you talking about? There's been another attack on a girl?"

"Not officially reported," Lubna says. She makes room for two glasses of water a server brings to the table and waits until he leaves. "Families refuse to go to the police."

"How can they stay quiet?" Intisar demands.

Lubna sips her water, shakes her head. "Threats that he'll ruin them. In different ways."

"And he keeps getting away with it?" Intisar is incredulous.

"It is very hard to hear," Lubna says in English. "My sister is working with the police."

Abu Sinsal. The name Muna whispered to Intisar. She grabs a paper napkin and tears at one corner. "You know the girl? She told me his name."

Lubna leans in. "She did?"

Intisar glances around the terrace. There's a young man with a tidy goatee who looks her way; his eyes appear to be lined with kohl. Another man is seated next to the oud player, his moist forehead glistening under the lights strung from the trees. "Abu Sinsal," she says quietly.

Lubna's eyebrows knit together. "Abu Sinsal. What kind of a name is that?"

Intisar shrugs. "That's what she said."

"He deserves castration," Lubna mutters. Intisar gives her a quizzical look and Lubna makes a snipping gesture with her fingers. "Cut them off!" she declares in English.

Their orders arrive, but Intisar isn't hungry. That familiar thudding begins in her right temple. She'd almost forgotten about her migraines since arriving. She digs inside her bag, her fingers grazing her pack of cigarettes, wallet, lip balm—everything except for her bottle of Excedrin. *Shit.* It's still sitting on the bathroom sink at the villa. Distractedly, she spoons her glass of tea, watches Lubna sip her beer between dips of baba ghanouj.

"Listen, ya Intisar," Lubna says, patting her hand across the table. "They'll catch him sooner or later."

How many girls must be harmed before that happens, Intisar wants to ask. The thudding intensifies like an incessant pounding at a door.

"Lubna! Ya Lubna!" someone calls.

Two people approach their table. The young woman wears masculine trousers, tan and pleated with a black belt, and a white T-shirt tucked in. Her short curly hair is cut asymmetrically, bangs falling over one side of her face. "You made it!" she says, bending to kiss Lubna on both cheeks. She extends her hand to Intisar. "I'm Faiza."

The young man introduces himself as Ehab. He has a stubbled face, deliberately unshaven. His crown of hair is thick and wavy. He runs his fingers through it as he speaks. "Welcome, ya Intisar!"

"We were at university together," Lubna explains. "I told them about your father."

"A hero!" Ehab exclaims in English.

Intisar smiles tightly; the thudding has become a steady beat in her temples, pressure building inside the walls of her skull. "I'm not feeling well—" she cups her forehead— "a headache."

Lubna reaches across the table and clasps her wrist. "Salaamtik!"

Intisar stands. "It's been a long day. I'm just tired. Enjoy your friends. I'll catch a cab."

Lubna stands, too. "I can't let you go alone."

"Lubna," Intisar says firmly before embracing her. "I mean it. Stay. I'll go straight home."

Her friends smile politely, though their eyes wait eagerly for Lubna to let her go.

"You're sure?" Lubna asks, holding onto Intisar's arms.

"Positive." She hooks her bag over one shoulder and hands Lubna the extra helmet. "Inshallah I'll see you tomorrow."

Outside the café, the curb is empty of taxicabs. "Shit," Intisar mutters, lighting a cigarette, ignoring the fact that it speeds up her nausea when a migraine is coming on. But she's too jittery to care and inhales deeply.

Lubna's motorbike is parked on the sidewalk. She glances back at the café; several more groups have arrived and are now waiting for a table to free up.

Intisar bites her lower lip and flicks ashes onto the

pavement. She's traveled to other places where she doesn't speak the language. Surely she can manage a ride home. She turns toward the small paved hill leading to the main drag. At least she's been spared the bright sunlight as evening slowly engulfs the street.

"So we meet again," a voice says behind Intisar, startling her.

It's Abdul Waheed. He wears a sports coat, a white T-shirt, and dark-wash jeans, looking much younger than the first time she met him. The headdress and prayer beads are nowhere in sight. He's a chameleon adapting to his surroundings.

"Are you following me?" Intisar snaps, stubbing out her cigarette.

"It is naseeb, dear sister," he smiles. "What do you call it in English? Fate?" He signals to his Mercedes parked down the street. "Permission to drive you home?" His golden necklace winks in the café's flickering sign. Behind him, the street is dim. Scattered light filters from the windows of residential flats and the headlights of an occasional car.

"No, thank you," Intisar says and begins walking up the hill.

"There will not be a taxi for a while," Abdul Waheed calls after her.

"Then I'll catch a bus," she throws over her shoulder, though she has no idea where a bus depot might be and has no currency on her—only American bills she hasn't exchanged, though taxicab drivers are more than willing to take them over shekels.

"Do not be foolish. I know your family," Abdul Waheed persists, waving her back. "Please, Sister. Give me a chance to explain the—" he searches for the word—"circumstances."

The first time they'd met he'd said something about her being an American, that she'd be practical and smart. His impression is accurate. It would be easier to cut her losses.

"Fine," Intisar mutters through clenched teeth. Talking hurts. She's desperate for a cool compress on her forehead. And desperate to lay down on cool sheets. She walks behind him, casting one last glance at the café as they pass it. The laughter of patrons mingles with the oud.

He opens the passenger door and she climbs in. The interior smells of spicy aftershave. His black prayer beads hang from the rearview mirror. As soon as he turns the ignition, loud music booms from the stereo. He quickly lowers it. "Pardon me." He grins. "You must be missing America, yes?"

"I'm alright," she says. She does miss Mama and Ali, her own car, her easy life.

"You must return with something in your hand," Abdul Waheed urges her. "The land is no longer for you. But there is still a way to take care of yourself and your grandmother. A hundred thousand dollars is not nothing, Sister."

Intisar's eyes widen at this amount, realizing she's never even asked what the buy-off would be. *Foolish girl*, her mother would have admonished. Intisar's cheeks heat up. Abdul Waheed shoots sidelong glances at her. She catches his eyes roving down her body and settling on her breasts. She shifts in her seat, regret clamping her stomach like a vice.

He gives her a salacious wink. "Very nice," he says, then after a beat he adds, "The money. It is nice, yes?"

She doesn't answer. Her tongue tastes bitter, a combination of tobacco and the black tea and the sandwich she ate earlier that day.

"Listen, ya Intisar," he continues, his eyes flitting between the mirror and the road ahead. "I am a businessman. Falasteen is going fast." He waves at the windshield. "It will not be Falasteen anymore." He pats her thigh. "But you have a chance to gain something for your future in America. But your—what do you call it?" He switches between Arabic and English. "Window! Your window to profit is narrow, my sister."

"What are you talking about?" Intisar asks, the place where he touched her thigh burning. She folds her arms across her chest.

Abdul Waheed shakes his head as if she's been denied all of the important facts. "For the last decade the settlements have accelerated in the West Bank. You have seen the one next to your father's villa? Bayt al-Hawa is a prime location. In five to eight years, a power grid will be installed, expanding the settlement at least twice its size now." He pauses, glancing at her, checking her understanding. "You can check any news outlet to know the dire situation here."

At this veiled insult, Intisar digs her fingers into her arms. He is trying to expose her ignorance—a manipulative tack. She is amrikeeya after all. "Nabeel Abu Shareef—the family lawyer—said you worked for them. For the yahood," she says.

Abdul Waheed flicks his wrist above the steering wheel. "Lawyers do nothing but meddle for their own benefit. How could I be working for the mustawtaneen if I am trying to help you sell before they get their hands on it? It is true—they are ruthless and relentless. But, alas, I now own your father's land and I must be smart, too." He pats her thigh again and she flinches this time, but he ignores it. "Sister, it is an impossible dream, holding onto your land. Palestine no longer belongs to the Palestinians. It never will again. Foreign powers—mainly your own country, America, I am afraid—have made certain of that." He honks at children on bicycles. They holler obscenities about his sister back at him. "Do not fuss with lawyers. You will not win against me, ya Intisar."

The sound of her name from his lips makes her skin crawl, an oily, obsequious tone coating his real motives. Why had she accepted his ride? She wants to quickly get as far away from him as possible. But she doesn't want to hint at her discomfort, show him she's vulnerable. "I need more time to think," she finally says, massaging her temples.

This seems to please him. "Azeem," he says.

He drives up the hill to her grandmother's villa and brakes. Relieved, she nearly jumps out the car door. But Abdul Waheed grabs her arm.

"Listen, Sister," he says slowly, as if carefully crafting his next words. "My father was killed." He gestures between them. "We have both lost our fathers. And for what? For a hopeless cause. For a nation of people that has no future." She snatches her arm away. He hands her his card. "Call me before it is too late. If I hear nothing, you get nothing. I know you will do the right thing."

And yet, the right thing eludes Intisar. Had Baba done the right thing in the end? Does it depend on who is hurt the least? And can a hundred thousand dollars make it better for her? For Sitti Sundus?

Feeling dejected and nauseous, Intisar takes the card, slides it into her bag, and climbs out without a word.

Sitting on the stone stairs outside the villa entrance is Nabeel. He's holding a large yellow envelope and is about to wave but stops. Intisar can make out the look of disgust on Nabeel's face as he recognizes the driver of the car. This ugly expression is incongruous with the amicable disposition he's demonstrated since he'd first introduced himself beneath her grandmother's fig tree. Abdul Waheed wickedly honks his horn and reverses his car into the darkness.

"What are you doing here?" she asks him.

"What are *you* doing with *him*?" he counters, pointing the envelope at her.

His angry tone catches her off guard. "He drove me home."

"Stay away from him, Intisar," he tells her in English. "He is a dangerous man."

"Dangerous? Because he's telling me the facts?" Her face heats up despite a breeze. "He's willing to pay us a hundred thousand dollars. He says if we don't sell, the land will be taken anyway. There's an expansion underway." She hates her own accusatory words, but can't back down. "Did you know that?"

"There is always expansion, Intisar. They mean to make us feel hopeless, do you not see? We must continue to resist."

"Resist?" she says bitterly. "And end up with nothing? That doesn't seem practical coming from a lawyer."

"I speak as a Palestinian first," he responds.

She's glad to be in the shadows, concealing the shame she feels spreading across her face. Her head is on the verge of exploding.

His tone turns quieter, kinder. "We must resist. Take every risk. That's all we have."

"Sure," Intisar snaps back. Defiance is the only way to counter her disgrace. "It won't cost you anything."

Nabeel looks injured and is silent for a moment.

"Listen," she says, cupping her forehead. "I don't mean to be rude. I know you're trying to help."

"Then let me help you," he pleads. "Let's get hisil irth drawn up and begin to fight back." He steps forward and raises his free hand, as if wanting to reach out and touch her. But he drops it and throws his head back, searching the night sky. "Intisar, I am here as your friend. I hope you can believe this."

Instead of looking at him, she kicks a pebble on the ground. "If I don't sue, it's a lot of money. My grandmother can still survive here."

He shakes his head, his expression rueful. "She doesn't want the money."

She gives a weary shrug. "I can't stay here to fight for a losing cause." Before she turns away, he steps forward and touches her arm.

"Wait. This is for you." She can see the deep disappointment in his eyes as he hands her the insulated envelope. "May Boustany mailed it to me from London. Your father's prison file."

GAHANA PRISON: JANUARY 2006

CHAPTER 18

It began as a quiet pain in his abdomen that lasted a few moments. Then it stretched for hours, an interminable cramp that pulled him awake on his cot. He kept it to himself and didn't complain, unlike the other middle-aged men at Gahana who announced every pinch and swelling of their limbs. Was it a proclamation of fear that they would die here, that the possibility of release had started to deteriorate like their bodies? Hafez had long resigned himself to that fact. He was fifty years old. All he could wish for at this point was for his own body to be released to his mother so he could lie near his father in Bayt al-Hawa.

His fatigue grew worse, and his cellmates became alarmed that he was losing weight. He dismissed their concerns until one morning he looked down and saw that his blood had turned the toilet water pink. His stomach iced over. A few days later, a stabbing pain in his abdomen collapsed him in the mess hall and he was sent to the infirmary. Following months of torment in the Zinzana when he'd first arrived, he'd spent two days in a white-walled room after he'd broken out in a fever. There had been a young man on a cot to the right of Hafez, who kept an arm draped over his face for hours and never spoke. On his left was an old man who moaned incessantly, begging God to take him.

This time he sat on a worn examination table in a windowless room. The Israeli physician made him open his mouth and he probed with a tongue depressor. He pressed his thumbs against his lymph nodes. He didn't ask Hafez any questions about the precise location of his pain or details about his bowel movements.

"It's not contagious," the physician announced in coarse Arabic. He quickly turned away from Hafez and stepped on the foot pedal of a steel bin. He peeled off his latex gloves and tossed them inside. At a sink, he vigorously scrubbed his hands with his back to Hafez.

Hafez understood his prognosis at once. Before he could restrain the natural question that gurgled in his throat, Hafez blurted, "No treatment?"

The physician glanced over his shoulder, but Hafez couldn't see the man's eyes behind the reflection of his glasses. "Not contagious," the physician said again, then waved at a guard who marched over and cuffed Hafez before leading him back to his cell.

"We're going to fight it," May Boustany told him.

There was that *we* again. Hafez wanted to say it was his body that had betrayed him, that he was the one dying here. But he remained silent, let the lawyer talk. She'd begun to age, tiny crow's feet stamping the corners of her eyes. A few gray wisps sprung from the crown of her head and she'd put on weight that strained the hips of the pant suits she still wore. She never spoke about marriage or family. She was an idealist still as devoted to his case as when she first shook his hand and set her yellow notepad on the table between them. Was this her sacrifice to Falasteen—singlehood? Were her most important relationships with her clients? Hafez never asked her personal questions—more to shield his own emotional reactions. Over the years, they'd exchange brief pleasantries in which she might offer a casual update on her family. She'd become an aunt to her brother's son. Her sister had passed her tawjeehi exams. Her mother had successfully recovered from surgery. But she rarely disclosed anything personal about herself, and Hafez wasn't sure if this was deliberate or it meant nothing meaningful existed beyond her professional life.

Today there was another person with her. A young man named Nabeel Abu Shareef.

Without ceremony, May Boustany introduced him as her intern.

Hafez remembered the young man's grandfather, the honorable mukhtar of Bayt al-Hawa. He'd been beaten during the occupation of 1967, according to his mother, that had left him with a permanent limp. Nabeel gave him an expansive smile with white, straight teeth, as if he'd been waiting for this moment. He half-stood across the square table and extended his hand, and before a voice commanded them to refrain from touching, Hafez grasped it, forgetting his mangled fingertips. Something dormant shifted in his chest.

When was the last time he'd exchanged such a basic greeting with another man? His cellmates lived in tight quarters;

they were always touching. The close proximity of their bodies necessitated brushing shoulders when you crossed the room or grazing thighs when you sat in the mess hall. And yet a handshake from another man was a novel gesture, a signal of civility and humanity. Hafez quickly dropped his hands to his lap again.

"It is an honor, Uncle," the younger lawyer said. "My father knows you..."

As he gushed, Hafez thought of Intisar and how close in age she must be to this young man. She was a nurse, and for a moment he allowed himself to imagine her at his side at an American hospital, hearing the same diagnosis—for would it not have still been cancer erupting in his colon there, the same as here? He pictured her leaning in, taking meticulous notes like May Boustany, nodding at the doctor's assessment. Then she'd turn to him, smiling her encouragement. She would see him through the ordeal.

Hafez choked back a sudden burst of emotion. He didn't know anything about his daughter—she was as much a stranger as the young man seated across from him. He didn't even know the sound of her voice. Had it become deeper, as her mother's had? Did she sing like Nadira? How had her child features stretched into her adult face? Did she look like him? The last picture he'd seen of her was from an eighth-grade graduation. His mother had pulled it from her purse and held it up to the shield for him to view. Her face had begun to shed its baby fat, and her eyes had a serious expression, as if contemplating her entire future at such a tender age.

"They cannot deny you medical treatment," May Boustany declared. "I'm filing an urgent appeal."

But Hafez only nodded. It would be useless to fight for treatment against an insidious bureaucracy. A man on his floor named Abu Sajee had suffered from diabetes. After waiting weeks for his medication, his kidneys failed him.

On some occasions, they'd released men who'd become incapacitated, transferring medical responsibility to the family. In these cases, it was determined that they no longer posed a threat to the State of Israel.

"And a campaign has started by a human rights watch group," Nabeel Abu Shareef added. "They are protesting outside Israeli embassies in America and Europe."

Who were these strangers who'd claimed Hafez as their cause? Had any of them spent time inside a prison? It was hard to be grateful when he resented their good intentions.

"We're here on another serious matter," May Boustany said. "Nabeel has been my eyes and ears in Bayt al-Hawa." She signaled to the young lawyer to speak.

Nabeel Abu Shareef opened his leather backpack and withdrew a file. Neatly typed on a white tab was Hafez's full name. "There's a land hunter," the young lawyer began. "An outsider who's been buying up property and selling at a profit. I've been trying to investigate his links to the settlers. And, we think he's got some connections to the sulta. He's set his eyes on Bayt al-Hawa for some time." He reached into his backpack then handed Hafez a short stack of photographs. "The settlement has been expanding exponentially in the last eight years."

The first image was taken from one corner of his family's lot. The stone border wall and overhanging trees from the orchard made his pulse race. Only in his dreams did he behold the land. He flipped to another, the blurred image of the derelict well where he'd once fallen and collided into its mucky floor. Could he have ever imagined a more menacing darkness than a well? At eight years old, he'd feared he'd never see the light again. He'd whimpered while Mu'tassem descended each iron bar of the ladder bolted inside one wall of the well. It seemed an eternity before Hafez felt his friend's hand on his shoulder and guided him upward, bracing Hafez's back. With Mu'tassim's encouragement, Hafez steadied himself and climbed with his good hand. As soon as sunlight hit his face, the pain of his sprained wrist disappeared. He was never so relieved.

May Boustany wished to draw his attention to the hill beyond that point. A compound lined the summit, a watchtower standing guard over it. It was like an alien ship had landed a few kilometers from his parents' villa.

"A soomsar who's called Abdul Waheed," Nabeel Abu Shareef was saying, jabbing the air. "He's already brokered deals with a few families, intimidating them with the threat of a power grid uprooting their community."

"Is it true?" Hafez quietly asked, his tongue stinging with the possibility of his mother losing her home.

The young man nodded, his bright smile turning downward. "But how can we predict the future, Uncle? No matter what, we must fight."

May Boustany nodded her affirmation.

But what had resistance accomplished for Hafez? He'd lost everything. His return in 1989 had started as a noble cause, albeit one laced with guilt and shame for first leaving Falasteen.

"There are at least two cases in other villages where Abdul Waheed has claimed parcels of land for himself," the young man continued. "One belongs to an American expat. The other one belongs to a prisoner who died in detainment." Nabeel Abu Shareef cleared his throat. "In both, Abdul Waheed produced forged bills of sale in the absence of the original owners."

"And?" Hafez asked, terror thudding in his ears.

The young lawyer's eyes flickered between him and May Boustany. "I'm afraid that Abdul Waheed has made another such claim." He paused.

"Abdul Waheed has registered a deed for your land in his name," May Boustany firmly interjected. "He is insisting your father sold it to him while you were serving time in here."

The thudding became a crashing noise. "He's already stolen it?" Hafez manages to utter. How had his mother kept this from him? She'd sat behind that security window twice in the last few months.

"We've begun filing an injunction ," Nabeel Abu Shareef said. "We've hired an investigator and a surveyor—"

"We need your daughter," May Boustany interrupts again. "It is imperative that your daughter be established as next of kin. Your father was a nonresident. We need Intisar." And then as kindly as she could muster, "I will speak directly to her."

Hafez felt a sharp twinge of jealousy. This stranger would hear his daughter's voice. "Will she need to travel here?" The question tingled his teeth. He might be able to see her again. The idea of her coming to Gahana disturbed him, but their reunion would be worth it. Hafez cleared his throat, clenched his balled hands more tightly in his lap. He'd have a chance to ask for her forgiveness.

"It would help our case," May Boustany said. "Strengthen your mother's position for the court magistrate to see a living person. They have a general disdain for expats." She tapped her pen against her notepad. "I'm leaving for London for several months, but I'll still be working this case with Nabeel. We're doing all we can, Hafez."

He nodded at both of them. Nabeel Abu Shareef smiled back, his unadulterated optimism too bright for the gray walls of the prison.

Back in his cell, the younger men stayed away from Hafez—as if his cancer was contagious, contrary to the impassive physician's singular determination. The older ones looked at him with a combination of pity and fear—would they, too, be forced to live with an agonizing disease and then die alone? Still they offered kind du'aa, gathering around Hafez on the floor and reading Quran.

His cellmates had changed over the years. The jilted Abbas served five years before he was finally released, but the memory of him lingered every time Nijmy opened his mouth and a gap stared back at the other prisoners. Abu Jadallah was transferred to another prison where he died soon after, according to the visitation rumors.

Abu Nasser's boys were eventually separated from their father, and one another, each transferred to a different prison. Abu Nasser would never see his sons again. For days afterward, he refused to eat until he was sent to the infirmary and a tube was forced down his throat. *The bastards couldn't even let a man die with dignity,* the other men grumbled.

The cell was now occupied by two middle-aged men called Abu Hamza and Abu Marwan, and two glum shabab who smoked and cursed incessantly.

Today they were arguing about something—a petty grievance from their former lives.

"Pray to the Prophet," Abu Hamza chided them. But they ignored him, their arguing growing louder and more intense. They'd reached the level of foul cursing, dragging the names of their mothers and sisters through the muck.

Before Hafez or the older men could stop him, one of the shabab lifted the hotplate and hit the other young man over the head. As he raised his arms to deliver another blow, the man was swiftly brought to his knees by the baton of a guard who'd stormed into the cell. Hafez quickly slipped his notepad into the waistband of his uniform pants, the small pencil tucked into the spiral spine. As they'd been conditioned to do, he and the other men held their hands up in submission. The bloodied shab was dragged away, along with his friend-turned-assailant. Hafez watched as several other guards raided their cell for other weapons, seizing every personal item and effect as collective punishment. His notepads—a half dozen he'd stored through a slit in his mattress—were confiscated. He almost cried out, but Abu Hamza nudged his shoulder as if to remind him of the rifles trained on them by two other guards.

Awake on his cot, Hafez felt a terrible ache burning inside his chest. He wondered where his sketches had landed. Were they destroyed, burned in an incinerator, or shredded in a machine? Or perhaps they'd been simply tossed into a dark, dirty bin, a Zinzana of their own.

Hafez was glad to be rid of the pugnacious shabab who were thrown into the Zinzana. The perpetual revolving cell had become a more indelible marker of time. Each new man entered their midst—young, wide-eyed, and frightened, or sometimes scrappy and ready to assert his manhood—until it had been stripped by the Dungeon. And all of the years encasing Hafez and men like Abu Jadallah and Abu Nasser suddenly expanded in the confined space. Suffocating and inescapable.

But there was hope for the first time, if Intisar set foot in Falasteen again. Hafez sank down on the lower bunk—Sadeeq's bunk that he'd claimed some time ago. Something precious glimmered inside his heart like an heirloom ring once imagined forever lost.

BAYT AL-HAWA: SEPTEMBER 2007

CHAPTER 19

The cemetery is quiet this morning, except for a few small birds, perching on a headstone before darting to the next. Sundus stands in front of her husband's grave and reads al-Fatiha, her palms loosely clasped in front of her. When she's done, she runs her hands over her face. She does the same at her son's grave before positioning herself beside it, on the stool she's carried all the way down the valley. She recalls the hadith the imam shared at the azza for Jalal, and again for Hafez: *When a man dies, his good deeds come to an end, except three: his enduring charity, bequeathed knowledge, and a righteous son who will pray for him.*

Her husband had never completely recovered from the raid that night. They watched on live television as their son was dragged from a hovel in a village a few kilometers east of Bayt al-Hawa. He'd been hiding along with two other men who'd been shot and killed. Hafez was marched outside, wrists cuffed behind his back, a black hood thrown over his head. Sundus knew it was him before his name and photograph were released to the press. They'd used Hafez's tawjeehi picture published in the local newspaper, his lips half-parted as if to smile or speak.

And then they showed the photograph of a twenty-five-year-old man with a yarmulke, standing in front of a military jeep. And one of him at his bar mitzvah. He'd survived, but his right leg was severed in the blast from three pipe bombs strategically planted near a military outpost. The wheels of his jeep had denotated the explosives.

Jalal had clutched his chest. *My son! What have you done? You've ruined our bayt!* He was having trouble breathing, and Sundus ran to Abu Mu'tassim's house for help. Jalal was taken to the hospital in Ramallah. His wife, Um Mu'tassem, stayed back with Sundus and her mother. Mu'tassem's eldest daughter Elham tended to them, confirming that Sundus's mother was taking her medications and that Sundus stayed hydrated. She was a lovely young woman, brilliant and confident. She was going to be a doctor one day. Little Lubna, Mu'tassem's other daughter, wriggled on her mother's hip, demanding to know where her father had gone without her.

The hospital gave Jalal sedatives with instructions to take it easy. But her husband had stopped sleeping and eating. He was glued to the television, watching a continuous loop of broadcast news. *A terrorist attack* is what the government called what Hafez had committed. An Israeli defense official denounced it as another example of the violence Palestinians have chosen over peace as the Intifada surged.

They're going to come for us, Jalal moaned. *They'll knock down this house, confiscate the land. Our son has ruined us.*

Pray to the Prophet, Sundus's mother urged in a shaky voice. *We don't know anything yet.*

And this was true. They'd known little concerning Hafez's involvement, what lay beneath the blanket of lies he used to cover over his actions.

A young lawyer contacted them and they met with her in her small, stuffy office in Ramallah. May Boustany looked like a schoolgirl. Could such a diminutive woman help them? But as soon as she began presenting Hafez's case, Sundus felt assured that someone competent was on their side. No matter how grim the outlook.

I'm sorry to say that it's an open-and-shut case, as we call it, she bluntly told them. *He'll be tried and likely confined to solitary.*

Solitary? Sundus asked, deflating again.

May Boustany nodded, her lips in a straight line. *Any kind of physical attack on soldiers or Israeli civilians incurs extreme punitive consequences. Prepare yourselves.* Her eyes flitted between Sundus and Jalal. *You might not have any access to him for a long time. It could be months or years.*

Jalal remained silent, shaking his head as he thumbed his musbaha. Horror drummed in Sundus's ears. She remembered Um Sliman's son, who'd endured several months of solitary confinement. He'd been released after serving a year in prison, but he'd never been the same. His brothers had all married and worked hard. He lay sprawled on his parents' sofa, jobless and listless. What would become of her own dear son?

He won't ever be released, May Boustany told them—another thrust of the knife in Sundus's heart.

That fact had slowly eaten away at Jalal's spirit. Six years would pass before they saw their son again. For Jalal, it would be the one and only time. He couldn't endure the long bus journey to Gahana Prison along with other fathers and mothers, clutching bags of homemade bread and pastries double-wrapped in foil, everyone praying the food would not be smashed to crumbs during inspection. Seeing the utter dejection in Jalal's eyes, Sundus never pressed him to go.

Ignoring her arthritis, her mother insisted on accompanying Sundus. She dressed strictly in black since the murder of Sundus's father, but her bright smile and supplications would assure not only Hafez but Sundus as well that the Lord would return him to Bayt al-Hawa. They stood in line to be searched before being directed to a long metal bench in the receiving area. A siren went off, loud and wailing, and a steel door opened. The men marched through it, trying not to appear eager, catching the eyes of their loved ones lighting up when they spotted them. Hafez always waved before climbing over a bench on his side, parallel to the one Sundus and her mother sat on. The bulletproof shield with tiny holes separated them. Most of the time, Sundus had to lean in to catch Hafez's words as an eager, collective chatter rose to a lively din around them. Wives pressed their hands against the shield, meeting the fanned-out fingers of their husbands; aging mothers like Sundus murmured supplications of gratitude that their sons were alive.

Sometimes it was hard to concentrate as conversations spilled over each other. Most of it was a mundane line of inquiry:

Has so-and-so's heart condition improved? Yes—alhamdullilah.

Did so-and-so fix his engine? No—it's too expensive.

When will so-and-so be married? It's been called off? Oh, well, such is fate.

So-and-so didn't survive their surgery in Amman? To Allah we are come, to Him we…

The jailers walked back and forth behind the men, their dull gray uniforms the color of dirty water. Down the line, a mother held up a batch of hilba, its fenugreek releasing a mouth-watering aroma despite layers of plastic wrap. Whether her son would be granted permission to enjoy it was another matter. Sundus had heard about the cruel acts committed as if the families also deserved the guards' revenge. They snatched wrapped packages of baklawa and hareesa and stomped them on the dirty concrete floor.

And there were things Hafez would never disclose to her, not wanting any part of the prison to inhabit her life once she climbed back on the bus again and rode back to Bayt al-Hawa without him.

During one visit to the prison, Sundus sat beside a beautiful woman with a milky complexion and hazel eyes. She'd spotted her on the bus a few rows ahead, clutching a sack. When her beloved sat across from her, the woman poked her finger through one of the holes in the shield, grazing his fingertip. Sundus tried not to stare, her heart squeezed with sorrow. One of the guards yelled a warning at the man and laughed at what Sundus suspected was a lewd joke told by another guard at this tender display of love.

Hafez fixed his eyes on her and his grandmother, an unflinching gaze hungrily devouring them. She could see the effort it took to sustain normal conversation, his fingers interlocked in his lap, his sentences clipped. He revealed nothing about his caged existence. A gaunt, aged man sat across from them. Sundus would have struggled to recognize Hafez if he'd passed her on the street.

On their return trip, Sundus clasped her mother's hand and they rode in silence. The other families did the same, as if they had left behind all of their words at the prison, extracted from them like the confiscated contents of their pockets.

Her reports to Jalal were upbeat and always the same: Hafez looked well, mashallah. Though she'd spared him the truth, her husband nodded, a cloud of desolation passing over his face. She didn't tell him their son's body had become like a clothes hanger from which his uniform hung. That his once-bright eyes were bloodshot and melancholic. Sundus kept all of this to herself.

The evening Jalal passed away, he'd complained about indigestion.

Marameeya will remedy that, Sundus told him and swiftly brewed a cup for her husband.

Hours later, she tidied up, moving from room to room, turning off the lamps in the villa. She finally crawled into bed next to him and sighed. She gripped his hand, but Jalal's fingers didn't curl themselves around hers as they'd always done since their wedding night. Sundus propped herself up on her elbow and leaned over.

You are the love of my heart, ya Jalal. She murmured these words into his ear already knowing he was gone. She didn't rise up from their bed, race to her mother's room, or stumble to call upon Abu Mu'tassem. Sundus held Jalal's hand as it gradually grew cold and caressed his hair as she quietly wept. One more night was all she wanted before relinquishing his body to the masjid, where the faithful would cleanse and shroud him. She wanted only one more night to smell his skin, trace her fingers over his lips, cradle his head against her chest.

A few months later she took the longest bus ride of her

life. She was carrying news heavier than any package she'd brought Hafez.

One look at her face and he knew. He collapsed on the bench across from her, buried his head in his arms. He sobbed until a guard poked him in the shoulder with the butt of his rifle.

Sundus was surprised and scared by this raw display of emotion. His expression had grown stony during the years of his confinement. But his grief had inevitably breached the walls of defense he'd built up.

I should have been there, Hafez whimpered, wiping his nose with the back of his hand.

Pray for him, my dear, Sundus soothed, though her heart prickled with bitterness. She, too, wished her son had been at her side during that miserable time.

Mu'tassem had stepped in, her surrogate son, making arrangements with the masjid, ordering platters of mensaf from Abu Basel's. With the help of his companions, he assembled folding chairs on the saha for the mourners and poured unsweetened coffee in tiny paper cups. The elders, in turn, poured their blessings on him and his family. When she thanked him for his dutiful attention, Mu'tassem kissed the back of her hand and brought it to his forehead as Hafez might have done. Her heart shattered all over again.

Even the old birdkeeper, Abu Fahmy, trekked across Bayt al-Hawa from the mokhayam to pay his respects.

Hafez is a good boy, he told Sundus, as if her son was still the adolescent boy who helped Abu Fahmy tend his pigeon coop. The old man clasped her hand and she felt the wrinkles and calluses forged by a long life.

In those first weeks, her neighbors had rallied around her,

keeping the chill of grief from her bones. They warmed her with their constant chittering and pots of maklooba and pans of kufta, though it was always too much food.

A year later, her mother died and the villa suddenly shrank, its new silence stifling Sundus. She'd stand in doorways, staring at empty beds in empty rooms, and sit at a dining table intended for six people. She gave away all of her mother's clothes except for a white thobe with purple peacocks embroidered on its panels. And her faithful sewing machine. From Jalal's wardrobe, she kept his favorite navy blue sweater that he wore over a button-down shirt in the winter. She wore it around the villa in the colder seasons and when she sat on the barranda with her book of poetry, flipping the pages of her worn copy of Al Khansa that she hadn't read for some time.

And then she'd rock alone on her glider, staring at the barren dais where her mother once sat, knitting or peeling the skin of a prickly pear, leaning toward Sundus, offering her slivers of the sweet, luscious fruit.

Have you told Intisar? Does she know? Hafez had asked her after each death, his eyes red-rimmed.

She desperately wanted to tear down the security shield between them and gather her son in her arms. For it was as if she was imprisoned, too. Loneliness shackled her heart. It had felt like they were the only ones left in the world, the remaining survivors.

And there was her granddaughter—a stranger whose bloodline was hers and Jalal's.

Both times she made the long-distance call to deliver the news, an answering device picked up. She left the same brief, awkward message: *Salaam a'lakyum. May the Lord grant you life.*

Allah yarhamo Abu Hafez, Intisar's grandfather... Salaam a'lakyum. Allah yarhama Hafez's grandmother, my mother Wajeeha...

What more could she say to a machine?

Nadira's mother Rehab had kindly called back with sincere condolences. When Sundus asked to speak to Intisar, the woman apologized. *My sister, she's not here.* Sundus could hear muffled voices in the background.

To Hafez she'd said, *Aywa, yamma. I spoke with her. The family sends their regards.*

And he accepted her word, for what choice did he have?

Sundus lowers herself on the stool and then plucks a red anemone, its variety blooming untended between the graves. Sunlight falls unobstructed on every resting soul here. Several graves are adorned with flowers, particularly for the martyrs lain to rest. She's only come to the cemetery for eid, along with other families gathering around their deceased. They bring trays of ma'mool and fresh palm dates, which they shyly offer her. Children gleefully pour water on the graves, quenching the thirst of the departed. The air is not quite so somber. Except when there is a new addition and the red earth is broken open for another body, cradling it until human flesh mingles with soil and rock, and bones are the only evidence of a life that had once been.

On the day Hafez was finally released from Gahana, the villagers of Bayt al-Hawa stood off the dusty road outside their homes as Emad's taxicab passed. Hafez sat in the passenger seat, timidly waving. Women ululated, and their celebratory calls rang beneath Sundus's skin. Children carried bouquets of carnations that seemed to swallow Hafez's gaunt frame as he held them in his thin arms. Men formed a line to embrace him, kissing his hollowed cheeks, tears in their eyes when they turned away. They were beholding the ghost of a clansman, once vibrant and upright. Hafez's stooped shoulders made him seem even smaller. Between smiles, his lips tightened into a straight line of pain, and Sundus soon broke up the reception in order to get her son into bed.

He was finally home and yet he didn't seem to fit into the villa. Sundus had naturally aged inside these walls, the groaning doors and creaking floors echoing her own bones. Hafez was like a jarring piece of furniture that clashed with the villa's more settled pieces. But he was home and this was all that mattered to Sundus.

"I'm failing, my love," she says out loud now, half-expecting an answer from the grave. She yearns to hear her son's voice again. And the voice of her beloved Jalal. Then anger creeps through her breast, singeing her throat: Why have they left her alone to fight?

"Time is running out, ya Hafez. What am I to do?"

Perhaps it's hopeless. Her tears muddle the engraving on her son's headstone. "I'm too old to keep fighting." All the years pile up on her shoulders and she feels herself sinking into the ground among her beloved, among the martyred. And will it not be a relief?

She glances in the direction of Amer Abdullah, a shab from the mokhayam, seventeen years old. Felled by a sniper's bullet as he made his way home from a football game. From her barranda, she'd heard the shrieks of his womenfolk as his body—unwashed as was granted martyrs—was carried to the cemetery by a half dozen men. He was cloaked in the flag, his head swaddled in a kufiyah, his face exposed. Only later on the local news did she see a close-up of his half-closed lids, as if the young man was dreaming.

After it was washed at the masjid, Hafez's body was shrouded in white. No longer was it hers to care for. Sundus had bathed him while he was still alive, during his final homecoming. She stood behind him, her arms hooked under his as he carefully lowered himself in the tub, his underwear soaking up the water. His half-nakedness didn't discomfit her. His nakedness was not a man's in her view. He was her son and she saw him as a young boy, full of vigor and mischief and joy—not the sagging body beneath her washcloth. His dearest mate Mu'tassem had been among the faithful, washing and tending to her son's body. Sundus imagined his grief-stricken face. Despite the absence of fingers, he'd lovingly draped Hafez, preparing him for their Maker. Right up to the very end, their friendship endured across continents and prison. Mu'tassem, who had been prohibited from visiting, could only send his regards.

And give him this. He'd handed her a pack of cards, a token of their childhood. *You tell him, Khalti, I'm ready to beat him once he's freed,* he'd joked, his eyes glistening with hope.

And a few nights ago, with that same hope alighting his words like birds falling into a welcoming tree, he'd declared, *She will do the right thing. She is bint Hafez after all.*

BAYT AL-HAWA: SEPTEMBER 2007

CHAPTER 20

Her migraine is gone. A thin layer of vomit coats her tongue. She sits up in her bed and gulps water. The yellow envelope sits on her nightstand. With her fingertip, Intisar traces the myriad postage stamps from London to Israel. The mailing label is addressed to her—care of Nabeel Abu Shareef—handwritten in English. The return address is May Boustany's. Why would she send it to Intisar? What use is a legal file to her now?

She hasn't broken the taped seal yet. She's tempted to slip it into her suitcase until she gets back to Chicago, then file it away between auto insurance policies and medical bills.

From her balcony, Intisar stares out at the dilapidated old well where her father had once smoked cigarettes and fallen into. She snuffs out her own cigarette into an ashtray she's certain Majida has left for her on the balcony. It is meant to replace the half-empty water bottle she's been using, which has turned swampy-brown from cigarette butts floating on the surface.

She'll miss this balcony. Here, she wakes without an alarm clock, and she's seen more sunrises from this spot than in her whole life. Today the horizon is a spectacular burst of red and orange. The world is alight again, as if a lamp has been slowly turned on, illuminating everything that had once been dark and shapeless.

"Intisar, my love!" Majida calls outside her door. "Coffee's ready!"

She leaves the envelope on the nightstand and throws on a long T-shirt over a pair of yoga pants. In the kitchen, Majida greets her with a cup of Nescafe—as close to American coffee as she'll have here—and she carries it to the barranda overlooking the valley. Intisar sits on the dais, her mind drifting between here and home until a movement in the cemetery pulls her attention. She stands up, cradling her cup of coffee, and drapes an arm along the railing.

There's something familiar about the woman in the thobe and she realizes it's Sitti Sundus. Intisar watches her grandmother lower her body onto a stool—has she carried it all the way down there? Her solitary figure strikes a lonely chord in Intisar's chest. She can't make out the old woman's expression, can't tell if she's weeping. Sitti Sundus holds her hands up to her face—a familiar gesture of prayer. Then she becomes very still, like a statue, before lowering herself on her stool. Tears well in Intisar's eyes. It's hard to remember this woman is—was—a mother. Sitti Sundus lost Baba, too. Does her grief cut the same way as a daughter's? They haven't sat down to fully compare how Baba imbued their lives. Would it have helped her grandmother understand her better? And, perhaps, the other way around?

As she studies Sitti Sundus plucking a flower, she suddenly feels like an interloper, an intruder who's stumbled into a private room. Quickly, she mops her tears and heads back inside the villa.

She won't wait for Lubna to pick her up. She'll head to the women's clinic on foot before her grandmother returns from the cemetery. Much easier than facing the old woman. Like Mama, she is good at avoidance. In the kitchen she consults with Majida about directions.

Majida wipes her hands on a dishrag. "Go toward the villa with the green-painted door and shutters," she instructs, holding out a heaping plastic lunch bag. "Then take a right. You'll come to the main road where you'll turn south. God be with you."

Intisar follows the narrow road down the hill. She reaches the bottom and hesitates.

"South," she remembers and her confidence lifts.

There's the town square. Bayt al-Hawa seemed much smaller on a motorbike. She walks along the sidewalk bordered by storefronts where merchants raise their steel gates. She sidesteps a short man hosing down his shop door and windows.

She pauses in front of a furniture store whose sign—LUX—is painted gold in English and Arabic. Through the display windows she sees gaudy lacquered pieces. This was her grandfather Jalal's business. Baba had once told her how he was made to work there during the summers, dusting and polishing bed posts and coffee tables. Despite her long absence, a strange nostalgia grips her chest. Does it signal something meaningful, or is it merely sentimental, like an old song crooning on the radio?

Across the street there's a wall displaying the images of men painted in black, their names scrawled in red. Some of the letters have flaked off and the outline of their heads and noses have faded. It's a martyr's wall, Intisar realizes, her stomach sinking. People move past it without glancing up.

"Do you need help, ya khalti?" A middle-aged woman carrying an enormous round pan on her head smiles at her, one hand gripping an edge. "Are you bint Hafez?"

Intisar nods. "Hello, Khalti." She extends her hand, and the other woman shakes it with her free hand, the stem of her fingers are rough and callused.

"Welcome home," she beams, her neck erect under the weight of her pan. "Where are you going?"

"The mokhayam," Intisar tells her. "The women's clinic. I'm helping out today."

"Ah really? May Allah gift you every blessing. I'm on my way to the khabaz. There's talk of a curfew." She gestures toward the wall. "The mokhayam is that way. If you like, I can walk you after I hand these off to the baker." Her steel pan is covered with a white linen cloth, protecting mounds of raw dough.

"I don't want to trouble you," she says. "I can find my way, Khalti. Thank you."

"I'm Um Munzir. On the other side of the valley from your grandmother's villa. You are welcome anytime, dear. God be with you."

Intisar watches the woman's retreating figure as she expertly crosses the street, the pan firmly positioned on her head. At the edge of Bayt al-Hawa, Intisar stops again. There's a main drag with a white sign that reads "Jerusalem Road," pointing south, and one beneath it that reads "Nablus Road," pointing north. Intisar hesitates. Um Munzir had pointed east. She walks again, hoping she's going the right way. A few minutes later, the entrance of the encampment appears. She hurries through it then halts again when a voice calls to her.

"Over here! Bint Hafez! Over here!"

It's Abu Fahmy, the old birdkeeper. He's standing in front of his shack, waving his cane at her, holding a pipe in the other. "Ahlan! Ahlan!"

She hurries toward him, grateful for a familiar face. "Sabah al khair, Hajj!" she calls back.

"Where are you going so early, my daughter?"

"The clinic. To help Doktorra Elham."

"Mashallah! You're a gift to us!" he gushes, lowering himself on his stool. "And like my own guest, you'll be leaving us." He sucks on his pipe.

"The stork's flown away?"

The old man nods, smoke streaming from his nostrils. "The prince has returned home." He points to the sky with his pipe.

Intisar wonders how far the stork must travel to find its flock. Or does it join a new one?

"We can be of two worlds," Abu Fahmy says, as if reading her thoughts. The folds of his wrinkles stretch into a smile, brown eyes twinkling at her. "That way, bint Hafez. You'll see the clinic." He gestures with his pipe. "May you always be protected."

There are no women waiting patiently outside the clinic. Could it be they're worried about a curfew Um Munzir had mentioned? What does a curfew mean? She recalls an electrical outage during a tornado warning in Chicago, her mother and step-father lighting candles, ordering a young Intisar not to open the fridge and to stay away from the windows. She remembers the sheer isolation, the feeling of being shut in, waiting for power to be restored so she could be free again to play in her room with her dolls.

Perspiration trickles down her back. She buzzes once and Amal lets her in. Today she's wearing a red and white polka-dot hijab, a cheerful contrast to the tension mounting inside Intisar's chest.

"It's a good thing you're here," Amal says. "Wafa called me. She can't get through. It's getting worse. More protests are happening today." She pulls a piece of paper from her white coat and shows Intisar a hand-drawn map—a flyer marking all the locations of planned demonstrations. Amal's voice drops. "They killed another shab last night. May the Lord smite them."

Cold dread prickles Intisar's sweaty neck. "Someone mentioned a curfew," she says.

Amal hands Intisar a pair of scrubs. "Inshallah khair," she smiles sadly. "Let's get to work."

Nearly two-dozen women are packed tightly inside the clinic. Each occupied chair comforts Intisar, and she can forget what's happening outside. One young mother holds out her crying toddler and Intisar takes him, awkwardly balancing him on her hip. "He's been constipated for days," the woman moans.

"Maskeen!" Amal coos, patting his chubby cheek.

Intisar palms his forehead. He doesn't have a temperature. "Sister, if he doesn't have a bowel movement in thirty-six hours, you'll need to take him to the hospital," she says, handing him back to the mother. Intisar is surprised by her own firm tone. Amal grins at her, impressed.

The first half of the day is a blur of women and children, whose ailments Intisar screens before Elham attends to them. Amal follows up with the doctor's written prescriptions.

Unlike the tensions rising across the region, Intisar's

shift is uneventful. Elham remains tight-lipped, nodding her satisfaction, saying little outside of directives. This stringent attitude doesn't bother Intisar today. In here, she feels safe and useful. She knows exactly what to do and each probable clinical outcome.

In the middle of asr prayer, while Amal and the few remaining women prostrate across the mat, there's a terrible pounding at the door, followed by a series of buzzing.

Intisar spots a woman and a man in the security camera. The woman is clutching her swollen belly. "A woman," she announces. "And her husband, I think."

Elham is at her side. "It's Rahma. Let them in."

They stumble through the door, the man supporting the woman until she collapses to her knees. "They've closed the road to the hospital," he pants. "In the name of God, please help my wife. The baby is coming."

Elham rushes to the woman's side. "Rahma! Has your water broken?"

The woman nods, her face glistening with perspiration. "Doktorra, please," she breathes. "It hurts."

"I know, habibti," Elham says. "How close are the contractions?"

"We can't get to the hospital," the man says again.

"Help me move her to the examination room," Elham instructs him. There's an edge in the doctor's voice Intisar hasn't heard before. "Amal, send them home," she jerks her chin at the open-mouthed women in mid-prayer.

Intisar rushes to assist Elham, the tittering of the other women trailing behind her.

"How close are the contractions?" the doctor demands again

as they prop Rahma on the examination table.

Rahma, sweat soaking the edge of her green hijab, shakes her head. "Two, three minutes." Pain blotches her fair skin, turning her cheeks ruddy.

"Take deep breaths through your nose, Rahma," Elham coaches, unfastening the woman's headscarf. "Exhale through your mouth."

"The roads are blocked to the hospital," her husband repeats. He is standing against the wall, dumbfounded.

Intisar vigorously washes her hands and slips on a new pair of disposable latex gloves and pulls up her surgical mask.

"Akhh! I can't stand it!" Rahma bellows, bolting upright. She wraps her arms around her belly.

"Blood pressure!" Elham instructs Intisar as she, too, washes her hands before thrusting her fingers into another pair of gloves and secures her own mask over her face. She guides Rahma back to a reclining position and pulls down the elastic band of her long skirt. Her belly is taut, a dark line running from her protruding navel to her pubis.

Intisar wraps the band around Rahma's arm and she squeezes the black pump. The needle in the gauge rises then falls with a hiss. "One-thirty-three over ninety." It's higher than normal, but not dangerous.

Elham nods. "Listen to me, ya Rahma," she commands. "I want you to breathe in through your nose and exhale through your mouth. Can you do that for me?" She presses the bell of the fetoscope against the woman's high belly and positions her forehead against a small, curved rest. She listens for a heartbeat. To Intisar, Elham looks like a coalminer, ready to excavate in darkness. "You're doing fine, Rahma," Elham coos, though her voice is tight. "Keep breathing through your nose." She continues to listen. "One twenty-three."

Anything above one hundred and ten is good. Intisar smiles at Rahma as she rolls a clean towel and slips it under the woman's head.

Rahma clasps her hand, startling Intisar. "I can't!" she whimpers. "Please! I can't take it any longer! For the love of God!" She lets out a terrible moan, but she holds still as the doctor examines her.

Elham removes the ear plugs and rolls her swivel chair to the foot of the table. She spreads the woman's legs apart. "Take a deep breath, Rahma. That's it." Intisar watches as one gloved hand disappears inside the woman. "Mashallah! You're doing well, Sister!" Elham locks eyes with Intisar. "It is breech," she grimly announces in English. "Footling."

Intisar is unable to read the doctor's expression behind her mask. Sweat turns icy down her back. At one point in her early training, Intisar thought she might be interested in obstetrics, but that quickly changed during a round of observations on the labor and delivery floor. You were responsible for not just one, but two lives at once. Intisar couldn't do it. And now here she is, facing a breech presentation without proper equipment and assistance. The sweat streams into the seat of her underwear.

Rahma's husband moves to her side, eager to be useful, but instead he's getting in the way. Amal gently directs him to stand in a small corner of the examining room. This space is intended for only two or three people at a time. "Say surat al kursi, my brother," Amal instructs him. And his lips move quickly and silently while he folds his arms across his chest as if protecting himself from some kind of evil.

Intisar wipes the sweat from her forehead, monitoring the doctor's eyes for a sign of hope. Perhaps there's still time for the baby to turn. Wet strands have escaped Rahma's low bun and they mat her temples. "Breathe in and out," Intisar coaches.

Elham withdraws her hand and stands over the woman again, listening for a heartbeat. "One-nineteen." Her voice is strained. It's too late. "Listen to me, Rahma. The baby is breech."

"Wha-what do you mean?" the husband stammers from the corner.

"The baby has not turned," Elham says. "Feet are coming first."

"La howla walla koowat illah billah," Amal recites, holding her gloved hands up, as if in prayer.

"Ya rubbi!" the husband cries, clutching his head as if bracing his brain for this news. Heartbeat and blood pressure readings don't mean anything to him. Intisar watches this discovery turn his face white.

Her own thoughts race. The mother will need a C-section. They aren't equipped. How will—

"You can deliver this baby, Rahma." Elham says calmly. "Listen to me. You can do this."

Intisar doesn't think she's heard the doctor. "How?"

"Help me position her," Elham orders Intisar, ignoring her question.

"Akhh!" Rahma moans.

"An ambulance," Intisar offers. "Can we call—"

"An ambulance can't get through a roadblock!" Elham shouts at her in English. "Either assist me or get out!" Her eyes blaze, the first sign of emotion Intisar has seen all day.

Stunned, she forces her body to move and she stands on the other side of Rahma, and each of them take an arm and guide her off the examination table.

"Rahma." The doctor's voice is firm. "Listen to me, Rahma. You can do this. I want you to get down on one knee."

"What?" Rahma cries. "I can't. It hurts!"

"Do you want to stop the pain, Rahma? See your baby?" Elham demands. "Then listen to me."

The woman braces against Intisar, who absorbs her weight as she slowly positions herself on one knee. Her face is tight with pain, but this shift seems to offer some relief. "Yalla, please, Doktorra!" Rahma cries.

"Azeem!" Elham praises. She turns to the husband. "Let her hold onto you. Amal, more towels!"

Both the husband and Intisar kneel beside Rahma and she clasps her arms around their waists, as if trying to move two stone pillars with all of her might. Or seizing two massive, falling trees. From this vantage point, Intisar can trace the dip of the woman's belly where it meets her vagina. Elham has a clean towel she holds open between Rahma's legs, and she coaches the woman through each contraction.

A tiny, wrinkled foot appears, bluish-gray, and Intisar's heart pounds in her ears. Then another pokes through the widening slit.

"I can't—" the husband whispers, his eyes clenched shut. His forehead is beaded with sweat and his light-brown complexion has paled. He leans forward as if he's about to vomit.

"Hey! Hey!" Intisar calls to the man. "What's your name? Brother, what's your name?"

His eyes flicker open again and he tries to locate Intisar's face.

"That's right—concentrate on me," she coaches him. "What is your name?"

"Je—Jehad," he stammers.

"Good, good," Intisar praises, as if he's one of Lubna's art pupils who's just finished his part of the mural. "Jehad, listen to me. Concentrate on my face."

"Azeem, ya Rahma!" Elham cries from the floor, her toweled hands poised beneath the protruding limbs. "You're doing great, Sister! Your baby's coming!"

Everything seems to slow down as a tiny buttocks appears, and then a slick shiny back.

Please, God! Intisar prays: *A head. Please give us a head!*

Rahma clenches her teeth and pushes until finally a whole body rests in Elham's towel.

Indignant shrieks break the agonizing tension of the examination room, and it's all Intisar can hear. The doctor carefully cuts the cord—a cumbersome process with scissors intended for removing stitches—and she finally places the newborn into her mother's arms.

Amal, tears streaming down her cheeks, offers new supplications, her voice shaky and jubilant, but these are muffled by the first cries of life.

Elham's eyes crinkle at Intisar, fear and worry draining from them. Intisar returns her smile, each unseen beneath the other's mask. She is both exhausted and utterly awake. There is a fragile, precarious power hovering over them in the space, its palpable force rushing through Intisar's lungs and flooding her heart.

Amal clasps Intisar's hand and holds it to her breast as they stand over mother and newborn.

They call her Bidaya. The beginning.

It's dusk when Elham insists they go home. She will stay overnight with the infant and her parents until an ambulance can reach them. "Tomorrow, inshallah," the doctor grins.

Outside the clinic, Amal embraces Intisar, her hijab still slightly damp with perspiration. "*Surely with hardship comes ease*," the kind woman recites. "Surat ash-sharh," she smiles, eyes still wet with joy.

Intisar carries the words with her in the opposite direction toward her grandmother's villa, along with a mixture of triumph and terror that she's never felt before. A roadblock, a breech birth. There might have been another outcome. She shivers though she's not cold. It's alright now. Bidaya is here, nestled between two grateful, exhausted parents who peer down into her tiny face, loving her in the present. The unknowable future doesn't matter for the time being.

Through tears, Intisar can make out the old well in the distance. She walks toward it, a hundred thoughts running through her mind. She's never been at the start of a life, has only attended the quiet final phase of old age. A deep satisfaction coats her chest. She wipes her eyes. Is this what having a purpose feels like? Is it enough to pluck the thorny pessimism that had grown inside her?

Tires crunch behind her and Intisar turns around. A black car pulls up slowly and her heart leaps. It's Nabeel Abu Shareef. A new wave of joy washes over her. She can't wait to tell him about Bidaya. She takes a step toward the car and then stops.

It's not Nabeel.

She squints at the car as if the sun is obstructing her view, but it's already set, its afterglow turning to dusk.

"Salaam, Sister!" comes a voice from the driver's window. It's Abdul Waheed.

Disappointment only slightly dims her excitement. "It's late," she calls back. "I have to get home." She turns back to the field.

"Can I have a word?" he entreats her in Arabic. There's something desperate in his tone that makes Intisar uneasy.

She waves him off and starts toward the villa again.

"Wait!" He climbs out of the car. "Will you accept my offer and leave this matter alone?" He's already a few feet away from her, his eyes scanning the field.

Yesterday, her response might have been immediate. *Take the money and come home,* her mother would have urged. *There's nothing more you can do for those people, Tee-Tee.*

But everything's changed. She can't unhear the baby's first cries, muting everything important she's ever done. Intisar thinks of her grandmother, a stranger to her all of these years. *Those people.* How long did Sitti Sundus say before the first grape harvest arrived, a young Baba waiting eagerly for budding flowers? Four, five seasons? And now decades of fruit have formed from the same vines that she's tasted for the first time, just as sweet as she imagines the flavor had once delighted Baba's tongue.

The ground beneath her has begun to shift. She says shakily to Abdul Waheed, "I need more time," and walks away again.

In a flash, his hand is on her arm. "Forgive me," he says in Arabic, quickly withdrawing it. "But this matter is done, Sister. Do not risk an embarrassing public display. Take what I offer. It is fair after everything you have been through."

"You don't know what I've been through," Intisar snaps, fighting the fear in her voice. What is he doing here? Has he been tracking her movements since she's arrived, wanting to catch her alone like he did last night outside the café? Her eyes dart around them. No one is around.

Abdul Waheed smiles, following her eyes. His gold necklace softly glints in the dusk. "A woman's reputation is worth a great deal. Come now. I am sure you do not wish to tarnish your father's name." His impenetrable brown eyes roam her face, her lips, then travel down her body. "What is his good girl doing, walking alone at night during a curfew? Ha, bint Hafez?"

Intisar's jaw tightens. Should she scream? Will anyone hear? She clutches her bag more tightly and looks over his shoulder. The windows in her grandmother's villa are glowing. "I have to go home." She tries not to appear frightened and walks around him.

"I am not finished talking with you," he says, blocking her way. "I know you are smart. And very beautiful," he teases in English. "You have many American boyfriends, yes? A man would be so lucky." His fingers, like slinking snakes, reach for her. "You are worth more than a hundred thousand dollars—or perhaps less?"

"Fuck you," she shouts at him and tries to make a run for it.

But he's already clamped his hand over her mouth and twists her arm behind her neck. He spins her around, his breath hot in her ear. "Scream and I'll break your arm."

But it's too late. She hears a dull pop followed by a sharp stab. Her left shoulder is dislocated, and the pain is blinding. Still, she rears up against him, kicking him hard and unsteadying him enough for her to break free. She stumbles to the ground, then lifts herself up again with her good arm. Abdul Waheed tackles her and she falls again on her injured shoulder and screams. He snatches her ankle and pulls her toward him. He's on top of her and Intisar scratches his face as he tries to muzzle her. His weight crushes her shoulder and she cries out between his fingers. She claws and claws until his necklace comes loose.

The broken chain is cool against her palm.

As his weight comes down on her, he jeers at her in Arabic. "You can keep that. It's my favorite sinsal and I want you to have it as a memory of our time together. You could have walked away and now you'll have nothing. Except for this." He tries to kiss her neck.

My favorite sinsal. Those words echo in Intisar's ears. *My favorite necklace.*

Abu Sinsal! Muna's attacker. And all those other girls from the mokhayam. Easy prey because they had nothing. In spite of the searing pain in her shoulder, the truth breaks like storm clouds in her racing mind. Muna had given Abdul Waheed a code name—a villain's name. Too afraid to reveal his identity, she'd marked him by the golden necklace he wore. The one now looped through Intisar's fingers.

"It's you!" Intisar sputters. Then she bites down hard on his hand, soft flesh and bone between her teeth. He yelps before a fist crashes against her cheek and her vision blurs. Her face is heavy, a pressure spreading to the top of her skull, worse than a migraine.

She can't concentrate anymore, not with the weight of the man on top of her, the awful thudding in her head, and the excruciating pain shooting through her shoulder. Her lids grow heavy.

"Get off of her, you dog!" someone is shouting.

And then her body's light again. Her eyes flutter open. With all the strength she can muster, Intisar shuffles backwards on her right elbow, cradling her shoulder. In the distance, she hears a scuffle and her eyes gradually focus on Sitti Sundus who's wielding something. It's the old-fashioned scale for weighing grapes. The base is upside down, her grandmother clutching its cylinder, her shadow elongated across the field. The clanking scales sway back and forth like two small sea-tossed vessels. The next moments are like a dream, seconds like minutes like hours. Propped on her right side, Intisar watches as the base of the scale crashes against the side of Abdul Waheed's head. His body goes limp on the ground.

She hears more voices, then Lubna appears with her father right behind her. Before she runs to Intisar, Lubna kicks Abdul Waheed in his ribs, a swift and precise gesture of contempt. She spits at him. "Ya ibn haram! You son of a whore!"

Intisar tries to sit up but can't. She peers down at her right hand, the golden chain still laced between her fingers. "Abu Sinsal," she whispers.

Lubna is on her knees at Intisar's side. "Intisar, habibti! Are you hurt?"

She moves her head slowly from side to side, the pain thudding against her face. Her skull feels like it's been stuffed with wool. It's a hazy kind of pain until Lubna tries to move her. Her dislocated shoulder makes her howl in protest. Her head droops against her new friend.

"Keep still," Lubna soothes.

Her grandmother appears on her other side, down on one knee. "Alhamdullilah," she breathes, slipping her mandeela off her head. She fashions a sling and gently guides Intisar's arm through it.

"How's bint Hafez?" Mu'tassim's worried voice floats to her on the night's breeze.

"She's conscious," Sitti Sundus calls back, despite a thin veil of darkness falling behind Intisar's lids.

Like that second day she's arrived, the villa is full of people. From her room, Intisar can hear the clinking of glasses against trays, women talking over each other. Majida's the loudest, regaling the visitors with tales of Sitti Sundus's valiant rescue. By late afternoon, there's quiet again when the last of the visitors trickles out. Intisar waits until they've gone. She hates being a spectacle. Still worse than that is speaking with her mother. Luckily, Majida has already briefed Mama on the long-distance line. She grins at Intisar as she hands her the receiver. "Inshallah khair."

"Mama," Intisar croaks into the telephone. "I'm fine." This isn't entirely true. She woke up this morning with anxiety ballooning her chest. She is safe, but still uneasy.

Her mother can barely speak, her tears muffling Ali's words in the background.

"I'm fine, Ma," Intisar repeats. "It's only my shoulder." Another lie.

In the bathroom mirror, she had reluctantly glimpsed herself. Her left eye is slightly closed, the upper lid puffy and stained wine-red and blue. From there a welt spreads across her cheek. Abdul Waheed's right-handed blows had landed perfectly. But that was all. Unlike Muna and those poor girls from the mokhayam. In time, her shoulder will heal, her bruises will fade. Intisar will never know the permanent injury Abdul Waheed had inflicted on the others. Intisar is lucky.

When Elham came to check up on her early this morning, she'd replaced the sling her grandmother had devised with her white mandeela—the same headscarf she wore outdoors when selling her grapes. According to Elham, Rahma and the baby are doing well. *A mild case of jaundice*, the doctor had told Intisar, but she is otherwise perfect. She's home with her two other siblings. The curfew is still in place.

On the line, there's shuffling noises before her stepfather's voice cuts through loud and clear. "Habibti, Intisar! How are you, kid?"

"Hello, Ali. I'm fine, I swear. Tell Mama not to worry." After a few more minutes of Ali's gentle interrogation and her soft promises, Intisar says goodbye and hangs up the rotary phone.

Lubna keeps her company in her room; her nonstop chatter is a welcome distraction from her thoughts. Intisar has only a few more days until Emad is scheduled to drive her to the airport in Tel Aviv. *You'll be home soon,* Ali had told her.

So why doesn't she feel relieved? Why hasn't she begun to pack her things?

"I wish I had the chance to kick him in the balls," Lubna is muttering.

Intisar chuckles, then winces at the pain in her cheek. She cradles her elbow in the palm of her hand.

Lubna leaps from the bed and pantomimes a karate chop and side kick.

Intisar grins and shakes her head. She'll miss this new friend. She won't be here for her first gallery show. The photographs of Abu Fahmy, the old birdkeeper, and his precious birds flicker across her mind, along with the images of Intisar, standing all alone in the orchard yet somehow belonging there.

"What's this?" Lubna says, examining the envelope Nabeel had given her.

"From my father's lawyer," Intisar tells her. "His case file. Go ahead. Open it." There's no time like the present.

Lubna brings it to the bed and sits beside Intisar, who

watches as Lubna carefully breaks the seal. Intisar nods and her friend pulls out a manila folder. Inside is a stack of official documents with a seal stamped in Hebrew. She hands it to Intisar.

On the first page is a photograph slightly bigger than a passport photo. Her father stares back at her. His hair is shaved off and there are faint bruises on his face. His eyes are dull and distant. A bolt of shock goes through her stomach. She wouldn't have recognized him. With her good hand, she thumbs the corner of photograph.

Why would his lawyer send this to her? This isn't how she wants to remember Baba.

"Wait," Lubna is saying, riffling through the envelope once more. "What's this?" She extracts a small, spiral notepad. Bound by a rubber-band is a business card. Lubna slips it off and hands the card to Intisar.

For Intisar Jaber. From your father Hafez Jaber. Always Peace, May Boustany.

Intisar's sets the notepad on her thigh. With her left hand, she gently flips open to its first page with the right.

It's a little girl in a plain dress, her hair pulled up in two ponytails, gazing from atop the Sears Tower, poised between its two antennas. On the next page, the tiny figure is standing inside the atrium of the Chicago Cultural Center, its domed ceiling shaded with stained glass. Intisar flips the page again, her fingers trembling. The little girl is standing on the DuSable Bridge, overlooking the river. In the bottom corner of each penciled sketch is a caption, identifying each place. But there are no dates.

And then the continent shifts and the little girl is here, in Falasteen. The tiny figure at the Dead Sea, ankles engulfed in saltwater. Standing inside the arched entrance at the top of the stone stairs that lead to the Dome of the Rock. The little girl is the same—she doesn't appear to grow taller or age—her cheerful ponytails bobbing high on her head. Intisar flips to another page and then the tiny figure is inside a small dawali field, its leafy vines form a canopy of shade. Beyond it is the orchard where the little girl appears under a tree. This time a man stands beside her, clutching her hand.

Lubna wraps her arm around Intisar as she cries and laughs between sniffles. "It's me," she says softly. "Bint Hafez."

BAYT AL-HAWA: SEPTEMBER 2007

CHAPTER 21

He turned his cards over. Mu'tassem snapped his good fingers and grinned. His friend had assembled a tray table beside his bed.

"Still can't beat you, ya zalama!" Mu'tassem said. He'd just started to show signs of aging, his dark temples lightly salted with gray. His friend's eyes were still bright and joyful.

Across from Mu'tassem, propped on the edge of the bed, Hafez was an old man, no traces of a boy-child's vitality. And yet this proximity to his beloved friend temporarily lifted his spirit and he mustered what he could from his failing body to play a few rounds of their favorite game of hend. Mu'tassem was the only visitor he permitted.

Villagers from Bayt al-Hawa had come and gone to welcome him home the first week. They were enthusiastic until they shook Hafez's hand and he saw their repugnance, undisguised by kind smiles. He saw how they carefully grasped his hand as if the bones were too brittle for their greeting. And how quickly they looked away from his marred fingernails. His face offered no less of a reprieve from the violence he'd endured.

Hafez spared them their embarrassment with a smile, despite his yellowed and crowded teeth. He asked after anyone he could remember in his former life in Bayt al-Hawa. And the villagers rapidly responded, grateful to shift their attention away from his wretched physical state and onto themselves.

Besides Mu'tassem, his beloved Abu Fahmy had not recoiled from him. He kissed Hafez's forehead and gripped his hand, undaunted. How quickly he swept Hafez back to his young days of birdkeeping, helping the old man tend to his cherished gold finch. Until Abu Fahmy's lessons, a young Hafez hadn't respected an array of species as anything more than a slingshot's prize. He'd become a kind of surrogate grandfather to Hafez. *You are a good boy*, Abu Fahmy told him, eyes crinkling at him.

There were moments in which he'd expect others to come through the blue-painted door of the villa as if time had stood still in his absence. His dearest grandmother Wajeeha, whose room still held her sewing machine, the sound of her needle accompanying his sketches. And his father, whose voice Hafez imagined calling to him from the orchard, like the wind of the valley rushing through his window.

Still, Gahana was never far from Hafez. The darkness of the Zinzana would jolt him from his sleep and he'd quietly weep after assuring his mother he was fine and sending her back to her room. Mu'tassem didn't ask him what it was like in prison and he was grateful. The names of all the men he'd known in that place were never invoked, still locked inside that cell in his heart.

Mu'tassem mostly talked as they played. Hafez nodded or shook his head, occasionally offering a response. His friend didn't seem to mind, giving Hafez a kind of peace the other villagers shattered by their strained tidings.

"How's your family?" Hafez asked, the only genuine inquiry he could marshal each day his friend came to visit. His daughter Elham was a doctor at a women's clinic in the mokhayam that had been recently funded by an NGO. "And Lubna? How is she?"

"Alhamdullilah," Mu'tassem smiled at him, pride stretching the tiny lines around the corners of his mouth. "She'll carry on well with Intisar."

"You made the call?" Hafez asked then shook his head, embarrassed. He'd already asked his friend this at the start of their visit, but his short-term memory had begun to cloud. Hafez felt himself floating through space toward a finality looming ahead of him.

Mu'tassem leaned across the folding table between them and patted Hafez's hand. "I did, my brother. She'll be here soon." His friend's eyes shined at him.

May Boustany had not been present for his release. On a phone call from London, Hafez could hear her voice choked with emotion—it was the first time since he'd known the woman. *Alhamdullillah a'salaama*, she said, sniffling. *Welcome home, Hafez.* After gathering her composure, she was right back to business. She'd instructed Hafez to immediately contact his daughter and convince her to come home. May Boustany herself had no luck getting past Nadira. *It might be better coming from you*, the lawyer had suggested.

Do you have my notepad? he'd asked her.

It's in the post, she'd said. *Nabeel will make sure she has it as soon as she arrives.*

When Hafez gathered his courage, his mother dialed the rotary phone and handed him the receiver. Then Intisar said hello and a lump formed in his throat.

Hafez was desperate to talk to Intisar, but the words were too thick with sorrow. He finally managed, *Intisar? Is that you? I thank God to hear you, my love.* He felt a light-headedness and gripped the receiver even tighter.

Baba? The voice on the other end was grown-up and distant.

It's me, my darling. A wave of grief threatened to drown him and he couldn't speak. He handed the receiver back to his mother.

"Lubna's looking forward to showing her around the village," Mu'tassem was saying, shuffling the deck. "And photographing the two of you."

Hafez wanted to tell his dear friend that it would be too late, but he held the words back. His body was winding down, the sharp stabs of pain were quicker now though not as protracted, as if the disease had finished plundering his insides and was now deserting the battlefield. When he closed his eyes, a warm, calming light glowed, pulling him toward it, abolishing his own power or will, like a leaf on the wind.

"What's worrying you, Brother?" Mu'tassem asked. "We'll get the land back, inshallah." He patted Hafez's arm before shuffling his cards again.

Hafez smiled. He wasn't worried. He felt certain Intisar would do the right thing. What he wanted—his wish—was for his mother, or Mu'tassem, or Lubna or any others meeting his daughter for the first time, to refrain from telling her a heroic tale about him. He wanted only to be her father, as undeserved as that was.

It was enough that he was there the moment Intisar first

entered the world when Nadira had woken him up in their bed and he felt a dampness in the sheets.

It's time, his beautiful young wife had said, her eyes shining with fear and excitement.

As he drove through red lights, he'd prayed a police officer wouldn't obstruct his path to the hospital. Nadira clutched the passenger handrail, her other hand protecting her belly. She was laughing and wincing from the pain.

When a girl arrived, Nadira had cried out, *A name! We didn't choose a girl's name!*

She'd created a short list of boy names, everyone around them insisting Nadira was carrying a son. Malik and Hassan were at the top. Neither had wanted to know the sex when the sonogram technician had asked.

Later, Nadira tearfully apologized to the nurse who stood with her clipboard, ready to register the existence of this tiny human being, saying, *I wasn't ready for a girl.*

Intisar, Hafez offered, breathless and elated. She was his greatest triumph.

Nadira nodded, a smile breaking through her exhaustion. *Little Tee-Tee.*

Her first cry had been shrill and long, as if she'd needed to make certain of her arrival, that she was finally here. He had held his wife's hand as she pushed each time the masked doctor commanded her. Afterward, when he'd gone to deliver the news to Nadira's family, a white man in the waiting room handed him a cigar, his own wife about to give birth.

Whadja have? he asked Hafez in a nasally Chicago accent.

A girl, Hafez proudly announced.

He slid in beside Nadira on her hospital bed and she

handed their daughter to him, a tiny cocooned bundle in the crook of his arm. Hafez had kissed the top of her soft skull, silently promising he'd do her no wrong.

A thrust in his abdomen forced Hafez to release his cards, which fell onto the tray table between him and his friend.

Mu'tassem stood. "Khair!"

Hafez lifted his hand, signaling the pain would pass.

His mother poked her head inside the room as if she'd been hovering in the hallway. "What happened?" She was wearing his grandmother's white thobe—the one with the peacocks. Her white mandeela framed her face, her wrinkles pulled taut by worry. "Khair inshallah!"

"I'm fine," Hafez breathed. "Another time?" He waved at the scattered cards.

His friend removed the tray table and helped Hafez lift his legs onto the bed. He fell back against his pillow, exhausted.

"I'll beat you tomorrow," Mu'tassem said, winking at him from the doorway.

Hafez gave him a tired smile and a final wave.

His mother immediately fussed over him, smoothing the beige quilt. He reached for her hand, gazed into her face. "Remember what I said," he whispered, the closeness of their bodies inspiring an intimate solemnity between them.

"She'll be here soon, inshallah, then you can tell her yourself," his mother quickly responded, tears gathering in her eyes.

He smiled, squeezed her hand. "If it's too late," he persisted. "Tell her where she comes from."

His eyelids fluttered as he listened to a wind whistling past the shutters. He followed its path back through the window and down to the valley of his childhood.

BAYT AL-HAWA: SEPTEMBER 2007

CHAPTER 22

Three other girls come forward. They are from the mokhayam, two having escaped Abdul Waheed relatively unscathed. One has not, her innocence poisoned by the snake. Her father and brother testified on her behalf at the police headquarters in Ramallah, sparing the girl any further humiliation. The sulta offered discreet compensation to the families.

This is what Nabeel Abu Shareef tells Sundus when he checks on her granddaughter's condition. The villagers of Bayt al-Hawa congregate in her salon and her cousin Majida offers them her version of events, embellishing a heroic detail here, omitting a far too intimate detail there.

Alhamdullilah Intisar is safe. Elham congratulates Sundus on the sling she devised for her granddaughter's arm. Sundus instinctively reaches beneath her mandeela. After all these decades, the scar on the back of her head has almost faded to her touch. She sees her mother springing to action, stemming the flow of blood with ground coffee. The young doktorra calls Intisar's injury *a dislocation,* the upper arm bone temporarily forced out of its socket. Privately, she assures Sundus that no other harm was done to her granddaughter's body. Nothing more to remedy her black eye and bruised cheek except time. *She will heal,* Elham says. *No scars. Alhamdullilah.*

When it is quiet again, the girl ventures outside, a pair of sunglasses partially masking her bruised eye. Sundus walks alongside her toward the dawali.

"It took several years for the grapes to come," she tells her granddaughter. "Your grandfather—bless him—was expecting immediate results." She chuckles. "Men are never as patient as us. But I knew they'd come."

Sundus can feel Hafez's hand in hers as they walk along the rocky field. It is the middle of June and she is as eager as her six-year-old boy. The year before, the dawali vines had begun to propagate and expand, their arms growing sturdy but still too young to bear fruit. *Inshallah this year will bring grapes,* she prays.

A breeze flutters the blanket of leaves coiled around the wooden trellis.

Are they ready? Hafez asks, hopping up and down. Sometimes she sees her dear father in his profile before it alters again into Jalal's face. *Yamma, are they ready?*

Let's see, habibi, Sundus laughs and hoists him on her hip. Soon, he will be too heavy to lift and as tall as the stalks. Together, they peer closely at the leafy vine.

There, there! Hafez squeals, pointing to the flowering bud. *They're coming!*

Sundus smiles. She snaps off a leaf from the vine and presses it to her nose, inhaling its earthy mustiness. In the coming days, the villagers will knock at her door, carrying baskets and nylon bags. They are sorry to disturb her and let her know they've come to strip the vineyard to prepare that delicious meal for their families. Piles of leaves will be plucked and pressed, later to be rolled with rice and ground lamb, then stacked and cooked in a pot. Nothing is ever wasted here. Sundus snaps off another leaf and examines its veins.

Her granddaughter watches her, then does the same with her good hand as the other rests in its sling. She's more careful when she pinches the leaf from its stem, as if afraid she might damage the whole branch.

"Can you call Nabeel Abu Shareef?" Intisar says, bringing the leaf to her nose. "I'd like to stay a bit longer." She glances at Sundus. "I'm sure Elham can use me at the clinic until our case is called." She lifts her slinged-up arm and grins, her eyes shining. "As soon as I'm better."

Sundus regards her granddaughter as if seeing her for the first time. "Inshallah khair, ya sitti," is all she says, grief and joy gripping her heart all at once.

They walk back to the villa in silence, the memory of a son and a father the same, like the verdant grape leaf they each hold. Its veins branch from a single stem, like tiny rivers—some continuous, some broken—all flowing from their original source.

ACKNOWLEDGEMENTS

The story of Sundus and her granddaughter has undergone multiple iterations over the years. I'm deeply grateful to everyone who was on this journey with me: my editor Michel Moushabeck, Hannah Moushabeck, and the wonderful Interlink family; my agents Robin Straus and Danielle Matta, whose unwavering confidence buoys me; my brilliant writing sisters, Audrey Petty, Marya Spont-Lemus, Nina Dellaria, and Susan Muaddi Darraj, who read early drafts with tender care, keen eyes, and graciousness; my generous friends Safa Suleiman and Paul Zarou, who offered me community and encouragement; and Hala Abuobeid and Yasmeen Bader, two gifted nurses who aided my technical research for portions of the manuscript.

Many thanks to *The Massachusetts Review*, which featured excerpts from this novel in its special issue *The View from Gaza* in 2024; and *The Missouri Review* for publishing an experimental chapter in 2020.

And, finally, with the boundless support and love of my daughters Sabah and Sabrine, and my husband Khalid, and all of my dearest family members and friends, my work continues to enter this ravaged world. And in doing so, I will always have hope. Thank you.

شكرًا جزيلاً.